AMBER AFFAIRS

CRYSTAL MAGIC, BOOK 6

PATRICIA RICE

Book View
Café

Amber Affair
Patricia Rice

Published by Rice Enterprises, Dana Point, CA, an affiliate of Book View Café Publishing Cooperative
Cover design by Kim Killion
Book View Café Publishing Cooperative
P.O. Box 1624, Cedar Crest, NM 87008-1624
http://bookviewcafe.com
ISBN 978-1-61138-784-1

HILLVALE

The following is a purely directional map, not proportional or representative, but just for the sheer fun of it. Enjoy!

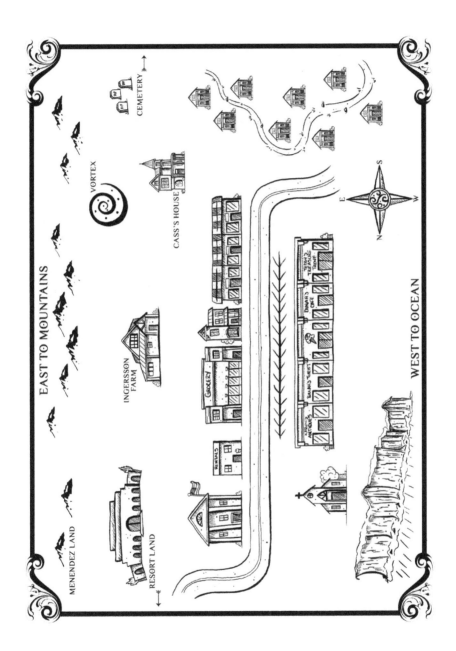

ONE

"YOU WANT TO GET MARRIED IN SLEEPING BEAUTY'S SHRINE?" JOSH GABRIEL asked. He gazed incredulously at the impossible jungle tumbling into one of California's normally arid canyons.

Blonde and willowy beneath her safari shirt and shorts, his fiancée continued snapping photos. "Stand over there so I can show the height of that bougainvillea," Willa ordered.

As a Hollywood fantasy director, Josh appreciated the setting. He almost imagined a blond, spike-haired sprite peering from beneath a rose bush until he realized he was conjuring a face from a past best forgotten. His childhood had been as abnormal as this greenery. He ought to grow up and forget it. Except he had fond memories of chasing dragons and trolls through a Hollywood-landscape, wooden sword in hand. He meant to recreate those days of innocence in this next film. He was damned tired of violent superheroes and exploding buildings.

Which was why he was standing here now with Willa Powell, the queen of coins, who shared his dream—or the financial end of it anyway. He'd been dazzled by her beauty when they first met, terrified by her ambition when she agreed to take on his project. But their goals had clicked, and over the past months working together, they had realized they had more than a film in common.

"Shouldn't there be a glass casket or a few dwarves down there instead of rocks, or at least a bubbling spring of nubile nymphs?" he asked, relishing his fantasy.

"The camellia is still blooming! This is perfect," Willa crowed, snapping more pics.

"A cauldron and witches, maybe," Josh mused, standing where ordered but still studying the famed vortex below that had apparently made this hick town a destination wedding site. "You realize our guests will have to sit on rocks? I can't see your father agreeing to that."

"They have stadium cushions." Willa was a producer, but she had developed directorial tendencies with this wedding business. "Look at the roses! I'll have to use them in my bouquet."

"And of course, *you* won't be sitting in the dirt," Josh said, amused despite himself. His fiancée had a very Germanic need for order she'd inherited from her dictator of a father. Josh was always amazed when she strayed from the beaten path. "I trust you aren't planning on gliding down the aisle wearing heels, or you'll need those walking sticks everyone up here carries." Her heels put her an inch taller than he and were a bit of a sore point.

"Just think of the spread we'll have in *Tinseltown Today*. The publicity alone will *make* your new film."

Well, yeah, there was that. Willa had a good head for publicity. He shoved his hands in his pockets and tried to picture the logistics of a wedding ceremony in a valley of rocks. But this was Willa's production, not his. If he were doing this, he'd build a set and add dinosaurs.

Psychologists had told him that he was living the fantasies he'd been denied by his stressed-out, impoverished childhood. Woo-hoo.

"What about me?" he asked. "Do I drop to the altar by helicopter? Swing in like Tarzan? Or do I parade down the aisle with you?" He rather fancied swinging in like Tarzan, but weddings were supposed to be about the bride, he supposed. His own directorial propensities were showing.

"Hillvale has done this before. I'm sure they have it all worked out. I'll have Brad take photos of you at the jewelry store when you buy the ring. Theodosia Devine Designs are as divine as her name. I don't know why she's hiding up here, but her shop is the first one as you go into town."

They had an entire crew in Hillvale to plan this wedding stunt, including Brad, Willa's favorite contract photographer, a wedding planner, Willa's secretary, assistant, and the vice president of her company. Josh wondered if he should hire his own entourage.

But he had looked at the cost of Devine rings online—only a goddess could afford them. He didn't have wealthy parents and lived on borrowed money. Up until this production, his films had had modest budgets. Entourages were out of the question, but he really wanted to start out on the right foot by giving Willa the romantic ring she deserved. "How much of this wedding will the publicity budget cover?"

"Quit being such a tightwad. The film will earn it all back and then some." Accustomed to wealth, Willa shoved aside a straying strand of flaxen hair and turned her telescopic lens on the rock platform below that resembled an altar. "Your credit is good for it."

"Marrying for my credit line is uncool, my love," he warned with a laugh.

He returned to picturing the amphitheater filled with trolls and elves watching the witches stir their cauldron. How would all the greenery and hedonistic floral arrangements work with witches and elves? A mating ceremony for a virgin and a powerful shape-shifting dragon, maybe. Damn, that aroused him. Could he persuade Willa. . . ?

He eyed his fiancée with interest. Tall, too slender for her enhanced breasts, wearing an expensive tangle of golden curls and weaves, Willa would pass for a movie star, except she had too many brains to become one when she had alternatives.

The sex—well, it was good, even if it was tough fitting two Hollywood egos into one bed. They'd work it out. Since Willa's goal was to run her father's production firm, and his was to get rich, drop out, and write books, he figured she considered him a stepping stone to her future. Maybe he was, but for however long their marriage lasted, it would be a good ride.

Besides, he'd tried romance once and failed beyond abysmally. Since he was making some headway with the business side of life, he'd continue down that pragmatic path.

"You have the wedding planner and PR department to work out details," he told her, bored with the photo shoot. He preferred being behind the camera these days, not in front. "I want to go into town and take a look at the ring selection so we're not dithering, then check into entertainment for our guests. I'm guessing we'll do the bachelor parties in the city?"

"Definitely." She gingerly took a few steps down the rocky trail in her five-inch heels. "But the restaurant here has an excellent reputation. We can do the rehearsal dinner there."

"Rehearsal? If It's just you and me, babe, what is there to rehearse? We walk down with our nearest and dearest, get hitched, and an eagle carries us to Narnia."

Okay, that one earned him a gorgon glare *and* a blast of silence. She continued down the trail. Laughing at Bridezilla, Josh headed the other way in hopes the town with three hundred souls and countless ghosts had a bar.

"AUNT AMBER, PLEASE, YOU HAVE TO TAKE ME IN!" THE BREAKING VOICE OF her adolescent nephew pleaded through the phone. "Granny is a monster!"

Holding the receiver on her landline, Amber Abercrombie studied the glittering amber rings on her fingers. Each one represented a battle won in her determination to be healthy and whole again. The smallest one represented the years it had taken her to lose the pounds to cross the invisible line from obese to just *hefty*.

She'd bought the biggest piece the day she'd moved to Hillvale and hundreds of miles out of her mother's life—her mother, the monster to whom Zeke referred.

Amber and her sister had repeated the epithet often enough for the kid to use the term—which made Zeke's plea all the more poignant. Amethyst had never named his father, so with his mother's death, he had no one but a monster and an impoverished aunt for family.

"When is school out?" she asked, deliberately not reacting to his emotional entreaty. Abercrombies were known for their emoting abilities, and her nephew wasn't exempt from the family drama.

"Next week," he whispered into the phone, as if his grandmother were in the next room, which she probably wasn't. Crystal Abercrombie liked crowds, wealthy ones, in expensive venues where kids didn't belong.

The crappy house Crystal actually lived in had never held her mother's outsized, demanding personality, but good schools were important for Zeke, so it had seemed safe to leave him there.

"I don't know what you're picturing, kid. I live in a tiny cottage. Hillvale has no school." She tried to warn him, hoping he had alternatives he could call on in the larger world of LA.

Even though she had no child-rearing experience, she knew she would be better than her mother, only she was living on rainbows and promises these days. She'd never be able to sell her rings for what they were worth.

"I'll dust and sweep and wash dishes, and you'll never know I'm there," he wheedled. "*Please*. Granny wants to take me to her friend's movie set next week, and you know what that means."

Amber closed her eyes to the iridescent crystals, beautiful colors, and quiet harmony with which she'd feathered her nest. It had been over fourteen years since she'd abandoned Hollywood, and she still recalled vividly and painfully the torment of being forced into a mold that didn't fit. And she'd been a *good* actor. Zeke was not.

"She can't make you. You're underage and don't have a union card," she argued, because that's what she did, looked at all sides of the argument.

"She had a friend forge ID and a card," he whispered. "Mama *warned* me."

And there was the final nail in her coffin. She had promised Amethyst to look after Zeke if anything happened to her. And things *always* happened to her big sister—because Amethyst had put herself out there the way Amber no longer did.

Zeke's mother had died in a tragic fire in an unregulated warehouse rock concert last year.

Amber hated fighting. She had hoped she'd never have to go into battle again. But for Zeke, she'd gear up and wield whatever feeble weapon came to hand.

Zeke was hundreds of miles away, and she didn't drive. Problem Number One.

"Then I'm glad you called, Zeke. That was extremely smart of you. Decide what you want to bring, but it can't take up more than two bags. I'll arrange transportation as soon as the school year ends. We'll figure something out together."

She smiled at Zeke's youthful shriek of joy and gratitude, while her stomach knotted in the old familiar patterns of her youth as she hung up.

How would she feed and clothe a growing teen? He could sleep on the futon in the spare room, but even she knew the kid wouldn't want to spend his summer dusting crystal balls. Recalling her own adolescence, she knew teens were large, demanding babies who required an enormous investment in time and money. She loved Zeke and she would protect him with her life, but. . .

She'd have to leave her comfortable nest in Hillvale, venture into the cruel world she'd left behind. She was stronger now, but returning to her former reality was impossible. She'd thrown away her crown of fame, fortune, and beauty for a life of anonymity, poverty, and health—mental and physical.

She might never overcome the humiliation and shame that had sunk into her marrow and lived in her nightmares. Consequently, she'd never be able to return to the only work she knew unless she lost her multiple chins.

Unfortunately, losing weight was a losing proposition for her. She'd had years of counseling to accept that which could not be changed.

But she rebelled at leaving Zeke unprotected, disillusioned, and all alone—as she had been.

She loved her little shop with its rainbow colors, lush velvets, and delicate laces. She'd created the scented candles with her own hands. Men weren't much prone to consulting psychics, so her shop was as feminine as she was.

Zeke would hate it. He'd been little more than a toddler when he'd been here last. He was probably remembering the lodge's ponies, not the dusty highway and half-empty town.

But now that her sister was gone, Amber couldn't abandon Zeke to the monster who had raised them. She'd hoped, since Zeke was male, that Crystal would let him be. Goes to show how little she grasped her mother's ambition, even after years of counseling.

Maybe she could sue the crazy old bat if she got custody of Zeke.

The bell over her shop door chimed, and she pulled herself from her pillowed nest, just in case it was a customer.

The flash from the past crossing her portal hit her with the force of a physical punch. Despite the years since she'd seen him last, she'd recognize those sharp cheekbones, that square jaw, and ever-curious cobalt eyes anywhere. *Josh.*

Oh filth, damn, crap, and dragon juice. What had she done to deserve a day like this? Why didn't Fate just smite her with a mighty hammer?

While he blinked to accustom his eyes to the dim interior, Amber surreptitiously studied her former colleague. He'd filled out nicely from the eighteen-year-old she last remembered. Despite his years of childish determination, Josh hadn't reached six feet, but he seemed taller than she recalled. His shoulders had developed muscle, and his chest—that was pretty danged spectacular from what she could see under the stylish gray blazer. He'd kept up his workouts, as she hadn't.

"May I help you?" she asked, because an Abercrombie seldom had the sense to flee. Instead, she waited to see if the Jacko she'd once loved had survived and thrived or become another pestilence on the face of the earth.

Josh swung away from snapping a photo of her army of crystal fairies. Of all the men in the universe, creative Josh Gabriel was the only one who might admire her collection.

"Sorry, didn't see you there. Interesting shop." He stepped closer to the counter.

She dropped back into the shadows. "Thank you. Are you looking for a gift?"

"I was actually looking for a psychic. We've scheduled a Hillvale wedding, and I thought some of the guests might enjoy the entertainment."

A wedding—Josh was getting married. Of course he was.

She winced as his comment let her know he didn't recognize her. She didn't know if that was a disappointment or a relief. "I'm not an entertainer," she said as pleasantly as she was able. But knowing how desperately she needed extra cash, she added, "I would be happy to make individual appointments for your guests. My card is on the table with the crystal globes."

He ignored her business cards to examine the globes and take more photos. "I don't suppose anyone makes sand globes. Maybe with little palm trees inside. We could give them as party favors."

"Try Florida," she said, her tongue dry in misery. "You're looking at hand-blown scrying glasses for those whose gift it is to see beyond the immediate. The crystal in the one you're holding was found here in Hillvale and processed by one of the best glassmakers in Austria."

He looked at the price. "Not a party favor," he agreed. "People actually buy this stuff?"

"Obviously, they haven't bought that one yet. I'd hoped I could use it myself, but my gift is with the tarot, not crystal."

Damn. She had to keep flapping her lips, defying fate. Her words must have triggered a memory. He gently put the glass back and turned to face her dark corner. "I knew a girl once. . ." He came closer.

She was an actress. She knew how to don an insouciant mask. She could even call up a smile to make him think she didn't care in the least who he was or if he remembered her. But she couldn't hide her own shattering heart from herself when his long-lashed cobalt eyes widened and his lips pulled tight—in disgust? Hate?

"*Ginger*?" he asked in incredulity. "I spent ten years of my life hunting for you and you've been hiding here in plain sight?"

She read people with cards, not body language. But his balled fists and rough voice had to mean intense emotion of some sort. She shivered and defiantly lifted her chins. "Ginger James was a make-believe construct, concocted by my mother and our producer. She never existed."

TWO

JOSH CONSIDERED HOW MANY WAYS HE COULD EXPLODE. HE MADE A LIVING at detonating objects in films and books—but shattering from a barrage of emotions, that was a new one. He'd have to work out the details later. He still couldn't unclench his fists or he might leak fury.

The girl of his teenage dreams stood there telling him she didn't exist? That his entire adolescence had been a fallacy?

"A *construct*?" he asked, holding back his temper. "Like a robot? I don't think it was a robot I made love to. And robots don't run and hide the instant a friend turns his back. *What the hell happened?*" Damn, he hadn't thought all that pressure was still in there.

Looking like a riotous sunset with surprisingly colorful hair and Gypsy clothes, she stepped back. She'd always been sensitive to his moods.

His anger still simmered. "I came back from the horrible Romania shoot and you were *gone*! I almost called the police to ask them to dig up the lot to see where your body was buried."

He could remember the day he returned to the *Jack and Ginger* set as clearly as if it were yesterday—it had been completely dismantled. The production crew had gone. And Ginger had vanished as if she really had been a fantasy construct. He'd seriously imploded.

She stared at him as if *he* were the AI. Then she blinked, and the Ginger face returned—the mind-melting, dimpled smile of the imp who'd captured the hearts of teen America, not to mention his. Outrageous as Orphan Annie or Pippi Longstocking on screen, she'd been as tragic as Judy Garland off-screen. He'd dreamed of that smile far longer than had been good for him.

"Watching the cops bulldoze the lot might have been interesting," she admitted with that devastating smile. "But I wasn't there and would have missed the fun. I don't have a TV."

Her dismissal of his very real terror raised the horrible rage of his nerdy adolescent years. But Josh had learned confidence since then. An old teenage crush didn't have power over him any longer.

With the half-smile that once slayed his teenage audiences, he returned her indifference. "That's a pity. Cable streams great film these days, anything from fairy tales to superheroes, none of that pathetic crap we did." He waited to see if her eyes might light with recognition of some of his work.

They didn't. "I hope you went on to better things," she said softly, in her real voice, not the fake upbeat Ginger one. "And I'm very sorry I wasn't there when you returned. I thought you'd left for the career you deserved. You really didn't need me holding you back."

Damn, and there was the caring sprite he'd known behind the façade, the good-natured mediator who'd understood him and had prevented him from killing people, or at least, his career. "You were the only thing keeping me sane at that point," Josh admitted, against his will. "But you're right. Dell was a prick, and his show had run its course. Looks like we've both successfully moved on. Did you have to murder your mother to do it?"

She blinked again, not in fake-Ginger mode but in what appeared to be astonishment. Score one for him. This time, a genuine dimpled smile brightened her translucent redhead's complexion. "In effect, almost. I hired a lawyer, got emancipated, took charge of what was left of my money and contracts, and moved on without her."

"And I couldn't find you as Ginger James because you changed your name?" He'd spent nearly all his Romanian pay trying to prove Dell, their producer, or Crystal, her mother, hadn't killed her and buried her on the set. The show's bigwig lawyers must have really suppressed the scandal of genial Ginger suing her voracious mother.

His teenage dream offered a soft, plump hand. "Amber Abercrombie, my ridiculously real name."

He shook hands without thinking these days, but her soft hand. . . wiped away years.

"If my mother had an ounce of compassion in her dragon bones, she would have told you what happened. I *should* find it hard to believe she and Dell told you nothing, but I'm afraid it's not difficult to imagine them chuckling up their sleeves and letting you rage. I'm really sorry I put you through that. But I was only sixteen and just didn't think it would matter."

The *Jack and Ginger Show* had started when they'd been in grade school, an homage to old comedy-drama shows like *Lassie* or *Andy Grif-fith*. It had lasted well into their adolescence and probably should have ended sooner if everyone concerned hadn't needed the money.

He wasn't ready to forgive her desertion, but he was an adult now. Josh beat down the physical thrill her touch had always engendered and released her hand. "Man, suing your mother and walking out on the show took guts. Good to meet you at last, Amber. If we must give your mother any credit at all, she picked a name that suits you."

Now that he'd cleared his addled brain of tempests, he could admire the thick layers of silky copper falling over her shoulders. He remembered how her pale blond hair had naturally waved—until Dell had ordered it cut and spiked, to suit the tomboy Ginger character. "Is the red natural? It's perfect."

From what he could tell in the dim light, her cheeks colored, and she ran a nervous hand through her luxurious mop. "Mama used to bleach it. She said men liked blondes, and that Ginger shouldn't really be a ginger because no one liked redheads."

"Oh yeah, that makes perfect Crystal sense. Damn, I'm glad you escaped the hag. Did you come straight here after you escaped Dell's hell?"

He studied the set she'd built for herself. It was pure Ginger—*Amber*. Colorful, coordinated, feminine, intriguing. . .and that was just the shop. She'd draped herself in amber and gold beads that hung down over a frilly, off-the-shoulder gold blouse that set off the plump breasts he'd drooled over as a kid, sometimes literally. They'd grown up together. Her plumpness had always been a part of her, just as his lack of height had been. Size had never been an issue when they turned to each other for sanity.

Shutting down his lust, Josh noted her skirt was in the autumn colors she'd loved but no one had allowed her to wear. As tomboy Ginger, she'd been forced to wear denim and mud brown all the time, even off camera, in case a photographer caught her. She'd despised jeans. Instinctively, unobtrusively, he tilted his camera and snapped this colorful glory, hoping one of the shots would come out.

Covered in dangling gold and copper bracelets, her creamy bare arm gestured at her rainbow-hued shop. "I'm not hiding from my mother. She knows where I am. I was born in Hillvale. She grew up here but fled when I was just a kid. The town always fascinated me, and the rent was cheap, so I decided to settle here and learn more about my other talent." She waited, almost defiantly.

Josh wanted to drag her from the shadows, into the sunlight of a café where they could drink coffee and talk about dreams as they once had. But he'd been young and stupid back then. He was an adult who knew what he wanted now. Marriage would bring him one step closer to a dream that obviously no longer interested her.

"You've elevated tarot cards and Ouija boards to a career?" he asked, trying to sound upbeat and not incredulous.

"My abilities are not perfect, by any means, but I'm good. I have repeat customers. And this town suits me." Her melting smile and dimples disappeared. She picked up and shuffled a pack of well-worn cards sitting on the counter. "Shall I prove myself to you again? A simple spread, past, present, future." She held the cards for him to shuffle.

"Just like old times?" Warily, he took the deck, shuffled and divided it into three stacks the way she'd taught him all those years ago.

He was oddly eager to see how she did what she did, now that he was no longer a superstitious youth. He'd been older than her, but she'd always pretended to be wiser with her card tricks. Of course, she'd kicked the crap out of him the first time he'd tried to kiss her. The fight for supremacy had been pretty damned fair since he couldn't kick her back. He hid a smile at the memory.

She flipped over the top card on the first stack and nodded. "The Hierophant. You were always a student, always learning new things and eager to know more. Did you go on to college?"

"I did, haphazardly, between acting jobs. Not exactly the normal college experience, but I now have a useless degree to hang on my wall. How about you?"

She shook her head. "They don't give degrees in being a psychic. My degree is in hard knocks." She flipped the top card from the middle stack and frowned. "The Hanged Man, two major arcana cards in a single draw—you're giving off some really powerful vibrations. This is not a good card to draw on the eve of a life-changing event like marriage. From what I'm reading from you, you feel as if you have no other choice. I'm picking up a sense that you're still into negativity, you're entangled in a pattern of negative behaviors, relationships, thought patterns. . . There's no *love* here."

Josh shrugged, hiding his discomfort at her accuracy. She was even better at seeing through him than she'd been when they were kids. "Love is about as reliable as those cards. Willa and I understand each other, and that's what matters."

And they were marrying because they didn't believe they could succeed any other way—negative thinking maybe, but pragmatic.

She shot him a glance from beneath her long lashes but mercifully, didn't argue. He remembered her youthful self arguing passionately about love and life and what was important, but back then, arguing was all they could do because they had no control over what happened to them. As adults, they had the freedom to act on their beliefs instead of talk about them.

She flipped the top card of the last stack. Even Josh recognized the skeletal knight—Death. She paled, and he waited with interest to see how she interpreted it. If he remembered rightly, the death card was a metaphor. Translating the metaphor required considering the other cards —and Amber's own psychic interpretation.

"Don't put a lot of money in this wedding," she said, shuffling the cards together again.

The finality in her voice gave him cold chills. Josh shrugged it off. "Most of it is coming out of the publicity budget for the next film. Why don't you come up to the lodge and have dinner with us? You can meet Willa before she turns the entire town into Wedding Central."

Her smile stayed gone, and Josh felt its absence like a cold north wind.

"I wish you happy, Josh, but no one here knows me as Ginger, and I want to keep it that way. If we appear in public together, someone is likely to add two and two."

After those damned cards, her rejection had him bubbling and foaming, but he'd never been able to yell at Ginger/Amber. She was like a cuddly puppy who did the most awful things and got away with them because she was so damned cute. To him, anyway. To Dell and Crystal. . . They were inhuman monsters who'd never met a puppy they wouldn't crush.

Perversely, he refused to give her up now that he'd found her again. After what she'd put him through, she *owed* him a few hours of company. "Okay, no public reunions, got it. Do you still swim? I can persuade the lodge manager to let us have the pool for a private session. It's enclosed with darkened windows for night use. I need to keep up my exercise schedule and you were always good at challenging me."

They'd had some of their most spectacular fights in the swimming pool—and even better make-up sessions afterward.

Her big turquoise eyes widened, until she lowered her long lashes to hide them. "Don't be ridiculous. Your bride should be the one challenging you." She stepped away, almost into the curtain divider behind her.

"Willa won't go in a pool, says it wrecks her hair. The pool closes at ten and opens at six. It's the only way I can wind down, so I have permission to use it after hours. Ten at night or five in the morning?"

This time, she glared at him. "We are no longer teenagers pretending we can make ourselves acceptable by playing in water. I haven't had a need to swim for fourteen years."

"You should be over the fat shaming thing by now!" He *knew* Ginger. She'd always had to be pushed into revealing attire. What the hell was he doing pretending they could turn back time?

"Don't be absurd. I like exactly who I am—anonymous, amiable Amber, without a bathing suit to my name *because there is no ocean and no pool.*" She yanked the cards away to shuffle them.

Josh relaxed now that he had a familiar reaction. Ginger had always been ambivalent about everything. She just needed nudging to pry her from her comfort zone. "Swim naked. Swim in your nightgown. It will be just us and I won't care. Bring dry clothes to change into and it's all good. Where do you live? I'll send a car for you just before ten."

She looked as if she wanted to hit him, and he was practically dancing in anticipation. No one had ever challenged him the way Amber had. He could almost see her as *Amber* now—much more colorful than spiky-haired blonde Ginger, way more voluptuous, and all grown up—telling him to take a flying leap off the tallest building or daring him to.

"A fancy car on my small-town street would call more attention than dancing naked on the square. Are you not *hearing* me?"

Oh yeah, there was the kid who'd defied him for years. He needed closure, damn it. They'd been peas in the same pod for eight years, and she'd split without telling him where she'd gone, leaving him literally terrified that she'd died. "I hear you. I'm all ears. My car will wait for you out in the parking lot. Blue Prius, boring as hell, no one will notice it. I'll have the driver bring you around to the private entrance. Wear black and tie on a white apron and pretend you're a maid, if that makes you happy. We have a lot of catching up to do."

Josh slapped his hand on her glass counter and glared down at her. "You *owe* me, Amber Abercrombie," he repeated the familiar catch-phrase from their show that had always got the characters into the worst trouble. "We missed out on over a dozen good years because of your cowardice. See you there."

JOSH STALKED OUT. *ARIES*—ANGRY IMPATIENCE AND FRUSTRATION, SHE mentally recited. Easily stressed, hence the need to work out, but so honest and direct that she never had to worry about what he really thought. Some things hadn't changed, including herself. Her reaction to

Josh was still that strong. She *wanted* to swim and talk to him again. Those were some of the best memories of her life.

She collapsed into her chair feeling as if she'd just been run over by a bulldozer and maybe a street sweeper and a train engine.

She was shaking. She hadn't been this out of control since she was a kid. She'd spent these last years piecing herself together, strengthening her backbone, learning to like herself again. She might look pleasant and helpless, but she would *not* be bullied, and certainly not by Jacko, as she'd once called him.

Josh's demands were startling enough—*bathing suit*? Was the man blind? But she could tell him to jump in his own pool without a qualm. No, that particular demand was more ludicrous than terrifying—it was the black aura of death surrounding him that terrified her. His cards were far darker than she'd dared tell him. He was blithely skipping along the brink of hell and utterly unaware of the danger.

Josh had been her one and only friend when her mother and her producer had constantly criticized her looks, the way she dressed, her *acting* ability. Without Josh, she wouldn't have survived the torment. She couldn't abandon him again, not when he was in very real danger.

As if drawn by Amber's turmoil—quite possible given the psychic resonance in Hillvale's energy fields—Cass and Mariah appeared shortly after Josh's departure.

One of the town's oldest residents, self-appointed queen of the Lucys, as they called themselves, Cassandra Tolliver appeared as regal and well-kept as any aging movie star. Tall, slender, her silver hair knotted and held with a silver pick, she strolled in with her skirt barely swaying around her trim ankles.

Mariah, on the other hand, was around Amber's age and everything Amber was not—tall, muscled, black-braided, and swarthy, with the hooked nose of her native ancestors, a mind almost literally like a steel trap—and seven months pregnant. Her talent involved computers, which suited her perfectly. But she also had one foot on the Other Side. She and Cass communicated mentally in ways the rest of the Lucys couldn't duplicate.

"He upset you, why?" Cass demanded.

"I just looked him up," Mariah answered for Amber. "You don't have to tell us anything except whether we need to push him off a cliff."

So, now Mariah knew about *Jack and Ginger* and wasn't giving away her identity. Amber relaxed a smidgeon at this goodwill from her friends. This was the reason she lived up here, where people would never tell her she was a fat airhead with no style.

She shook her head in denial. "Joshua Gabriel won't hurt me. He's the one in danger. He has the death and the devil cards in his present and future, and they're giving off very bad vibes."

Mariah muttered an obscenity. Cass looked concerned. "Could we send him away?" Cass asked. "We don't need any more evil polluting the vortex. We've had enough death. I understand celebrity weddings might help the town, but not if it means another person dying here."

Amber shook her head. "Personally, I wish we could send him away, but how can I ask the town to give up this opportunity if I'm wrong? Josh doesn't live here. I could be picking up on something that will happen in LA."

Mariah nodded agreement. "Willa Powell's family is Hollywood legend. Her wedding will be the event of the year. As a destination wedding site, we can fill the town's coffers, maybe even give us a chance to build a school."

Which was important to Mariah now that she was having a baby. If they wanted young people to move here, a school was a necessity. And now that she might have Zeke. . .

"Besides, from the sounds of it," Amber added in resignation, "the wedding is already a full-scale production in progress. How would I put a stop to that?"

"If you really think we need to, I could remove the ghost-catchers at the lodge," Mariah said. "Once the poltergeists gather force, they'll terrify the princess bride and her staff. Have you met her? Fiona says she's a holy terror, and Dinah is considering closing the restaurant for maintenance to avoid her demands."

"Does Fee say any of them smell fishy?" Amber asked, worrying at her beads, trying to decide what to do.

"No, they just reek of wealth and privilege or some such. She's feeding them beans, I think out of meanness." Mariah twisted her crystal-knobbed walking stick in her hands as she did when she didn't have a keyboard handy. "We should call a meeting."

Fiona ran the lunch counter and café next to Dinah's upscale restaurant. She'd only been living in Hillvale for a few months, but she'd made her reputation by snaring the town's mayor and saving a kidnapped child. Fee had a gift for sensing character by smell and feeding everyone what they needed. Amber could swear she'd lost a few pounds these last months just eating what Fee prepared for her. But admittedly, the little cook had a dangerous tendency toward vengeance.

"Find out more," Cass commanded. "This wedding business is good for the town in more ways than profit. Love, hope, and excitement counter the evil energies from the mountain. I don't want to see Amber's friend hurt, but he's not from here. As Amber says, he'll go home at the end of the day, and whatever darkness is surrounding him may go with him."

Amber didn't want Josh to suffer anywhere, and she didn't want his Hollywood friends laughing at her. That made her a less than objective party to this conversation, so she stayed silent on any decision. Admittedly, her business would thrive with more tourists, but at this point, she doubted it would be enough to raise a teenager and hire a lawyer to sue the crap out of her mother.

"I'm supposed to see Josh this evening," she told them. "But I need the cards to read him, and he's not likely to ask for them again. Could you look into the bride some more? She's part of the picture, but I don't know in what way."

"Don't let him talk you into leaving Hillvale," Mariah warned, her expression showing she understood what Josh was to her. "You belong here as much as I do."

"I know that," Amber said softly, but the other two women were already making plans and heading out the door.

If life had taught her nothing else, it had taught her that every battle had its price. The last battle had cost everything she held dear. Could she afford another?

THREE

"IT'S JOSH," AMBER TOLD HER ENEMY, THE MIRROR. "I CAN'T ABANDON HIM if he needs me."

She waited for the image to angrily toss her hair and walk away—as she'd done all those years ago. Walked, anyway. She hadn't had long hair to toss back then.

Unfortunately, the unhelpful glass revealed the fifty-pound-heavier version of her real self, not the sturdy teenager who'd been too hefty already. Once upon a time, she'd starved and worked herself to death in an attempt to keep off the pounds. She'd quit torturing herself after she'd left Hollywood.

She'd had enough counseling over the years to know that wasn't the whole truth.

"Josh doesn't need you," the teenager behind the mirror said with scorn. "He has money, a filthy rich bride, tons of friends, probably lawyers out the wazoo. He never needed you."

That had been the argument that had allowed her to run away without telling her best friend where she'd gone. She'd been a bit misleading when she'd told Josh that her mother knew where she was. All those years ago, Amber hadn't told Crystal or anyone her location until she was settled and comfortable. That had taken years. By then, everyone had forgotten her, which was exactly what she'd wanted.

The rebellious, careless teenager had died fourteen years ago and did not need to be resurrected.

So, the adult needed to take responsibility for her actions. She'd obviously hurt Josh more than she'd realized. His cards indicated danger and a tragic life decision. She had to let him know she was there for him. And he'd offered a way to do it privately, so the public didn't know who she was—who she had been.

But a swimming pool? She sighed and turned to her limited wardrobe. She liked lace and frills. The Gypsy look suited her. Spandex did not. But like every woman who occasionally wanted to wear something sexy, she owned garments that held her in and up. They were probably as substantial as any flimsy bathing suit. She'd look like one of those old-time ladies in their thigh-length bathing outfits, maybe, but she'd had Josh's admiration long ago and had thrown it away. This was for her, because she needed his friendship. And he just might need hers, although that was probably reaching into daydream country.

So, for Josh, she tugged on black fat-crushers, then dug out her prettiest gauzy caftan, one that floated like a turquoise cloud when she walked. She'd spent her youth in front of mirrors, and counseling had taught her not to be afraid of them now. Since she didn't have a chance to wear her pretty clothes often, she admired the result in the mirror, sticking her tongue out at the unhappy teenager. And because her cleavage looked damned good in the low-cut gown, she pinned her naturally orange hair up, leaving only a few dangling curls.

She turned to her wall of beaded jewelry, but this was a casual pool date, not an evening out. If she had to actually get in the water—and if Josh hadn't changed much, that was a certainty—she didn't want to be taking jewelry on and off.

"This is how an adult behaves," she told her image.

"You'll never see him again once he sees you looking like that," the teenager griped.

"You sound just like my mother. Go away, little girl." Shoulders back Amber floated from her tiny bedroom into her only slightly larger main room. She could still do heels, if she didn't have to walk far. But just in case, she grabbed the crystal-headed walking stick that declared her as one of Hillvale's Lucys.

The teenager inside her wept and wailed with fear and shame, but Amber ruthlessly crushed the little brat. She'd never been weepy Snow White or Cinderella. In the stories she and Josh had acted out, she'd been the powerful witch who saved the knight who slayed the dragon and saved the day.

JOSH ATE HIS DINNER ALONE, NOT FOR THE FIRST TIME. WILLA HAD CALLED saying she had an emergency and was heading back to the city, taking her crew with her. As a busy producer, she had a lot of demands on her time. Until filming started, he didn't, so he kicked back and made notes on his script while he waited for Amber.

Damn, he couldn't believe he'd found her after all these years.

He remembered the first time he'd seen Ginger, looking like a golden-haired princess in a fluffy pink gown at the audition he'd been dragged to. He'd been ten and just becoming aware that his father was a drunken loser, and that his little sister cried all the time because she was hungry and couldn't keep down beans and rice. He'd seen the desperation on his mother's lined face when he'd balked at going on a stage.

And then the eight-year-old princess had grinned, pulled up the froufrou dress, and offered him a chocolate bar from a pouch she'd tied around her bare waist. It had been the start of a not-always glorious friendship.

The *Jack and Ginger Show* had been a financial success that had pulled both their families out of poverty, but it had stolen their childhoods, robbed them of self-respect, and shattered dreams. He'd have thrown a champagne party for thousands when Ginger had walked—if he'd been there when she'd done it.

Returning from that miserable experience on the snowy, isolated set in Romania to find she'd vanished had nearly broken him. Josh slashed at the script he was working on and rewrote rather than contemplate what had driven a sixteen-year-old girl to the extreme of divorcing her mother and running. At the time, he'd had plenty of reason to think her mother or Dell or the two in cahoots had killed her—probably with diet pills and ruinous exercise.

He was kind of proud that she had escaped—and royally pissed that she hadn't told him where or why.

So he waited to see if she'd rise to the challenge and show up tonight. If she didn't, he'd have to hunt her down again. He wasn't particularly superstitious, but it seemed like Fate had a plan when it had thrown his childhood fantasy on his doorstep at this juncture in his life.

A few minutes before ten, he wandered out to the private entrance where the valet was supposed to drop Amber.

The Prius rolled up, and Josh breathed a sigh of relief. He had lots of acquaintances—everyone wanted to know an up-and-coming director. But true friends. . .didn't happen often.

Amber had ripped a huge hole in his life. He didn't trust easily these days.

She climbed out wearing some kind of flowing caftan thing and carrying one of the crystal-knobbed walking sticks he'd seen around town. She hadn't lost that imposing princess impression she'd possessed even at age eight. Tonight, in the light from the security lamp, she looked like a regal goddess with her scepter, striding toward her worshippers. Amber was short even in heels, but her graceful carriage had always given the illusion of height. With all that gorgeous hair piled high, she reached past his chin.

He belatedly discovered that she still had a slight hitch in her stride, but he was too focused on tracing the changes in her face to notice more. He'd always wanted to lick her as if she were vanilla ice cream, her complexion was that delicious—and still devoid of cosmetics. She'd despised the crap the studio had painted her with.

"I have guards at ze doors," he said in his best sinister voice. "No one vill disturb us."

"I might," she said serenely, taking the arm he offered. "What does your fiancée think of your secret hideaway?"

"Willa?" Relieved that she was still a voice of reason, he returned to his normal tone. "She's at her own secret hideaway this evening, apparently. I got stood up for dinner. You could have joined me, and I could have trounced you at Monster Pavilion."

He understood the glance she sent his way. He had always been the more idealistic of the two. She wouldn't understand why he'd settled for this relationship with Willa. Pragmatist that she was, she didn't question.

"I haven't played video games in over a decade," she said as they traversed the hedge-lined path. "You would have to give me a handicap. You don't really want me to swim, do you? I haven't been in a pool since I left La-La Land. I can't believe I used to worry about my weight when I was young and toned."

They'd had late night discussions like this when they were teenagers, griping about their flaws. He'd wanted to stretch his height on a rack. She'd wanted to lose five pounds. Then ten. But the sessions had always ended in parody and laughter.

"*You* didn't worry," he reminded her. "Your mother and Dell-the-Damned Producer did. You grew up and filled out, and they didn't like it. The show needed Shirley Temple, and you were turning into Marilyn Monroe." Josh opened the door to the pool room and locked it behind him. "But since it meant that they allowed you in the pool with me, I didn't complain."

"I'm lazy. I hated exercising, but you made it fun." Dismissing his flattery, she glanced around at the pool enclosure. "Can we turn down the lights?"

"Ah, secret moonlight rhapsody. Got it." He switched off the mains and dimmed the rest. "Shall I turn on romantic music to set the mood?"

"You wish," she said.

He almost smiled at the memories her defiance stirred. By the time he turned from the switches, she'd left her caftan gracing a poolside chair and was already in the water. Without thinking, he grabbed the small camera that was practically a part of him and took a few snaps.

"I'll give you a fifty-yard handicap on this first lap." He stripped down to his bathing suit. Recreating his youth was probably a stupid move, but he needed this break after the pressure of the past week.

"I'll be lucky to stay afloat," she grumbled, striking out.

He'd been a ninety-pound weakling, but Amber had always been a strong swimmer, despite her grumbling. Tonight, she wasn't up to her youthful form, he noted, but this was all about the company, and Josh didn't care. He jumped in when she was halfway across the pool.

They stroked in silence, as they always had, not really competing but encouraging each other to keep going. Of course, back then, Josh realized, a certain level of sexuality crept in as they aged and developed hormones. Amber had developed a voluptuous figure, and the cool pool water was the only way to hide his horniness.

Some things hadn't changed a hell of a lot.

Obviously gasping for air, she quit after only two laps and let him continue until he had his full workout. She sat on the pool steps, with the water concealing much of her entertaining underwear.

Once he was done, he climbed out and rummaged for towels, throwing her several and draping himself before collapsing in a lounge chair. "Pity we don't have anyone serving mai tais. Think I can persuade room service to deliver out here?"

"You'd be drinking as many calories as you just worked off." Tucking a large towel around her waist and draping another around her neck, she took the chair beside him and pulled a bottle of water from her bag. "I'll share."

"Sensible," he grumbled, taking a swallow and handing it back. "I hope you aren't still doing that diet thing. It made you grumpy."

She gave him a loud raspberry, just as she used to do, and he had to drop a towel over his lap.

"I'm not you," she said. "You burn calories like a steam engine. I don't. And we don't have fancy gyms up here, so exercise doesn't come easily. I just eat in moderation these days."

"Want me to ask management to let you use the pool?" he asked, because that was easier than all the other questions he wanted answered. Influence, he could do.

"No. I am nobody here, and I want it that way. I'm not asking the Kennedys to treat me special. This isn't a community pool. It's for paying guests. Tell me what you've been doing since I saw you last. How did you meet your fiancée?"

Josh wished the water was a beer, but he had never been anything less than honest with Amber. "You don't keep up with the weeklies anymore? It's all there."

She blew another raspberry. "No, I don't read that sensational trash. I know you're a romantic at heart, so tell me you love her more than life itself."

Josh laughed at the notion that he could still be that naïve. Amber had pretty much ground those fantasies to dust. "That's not how the world works, Blue Eyes, and you know it. Willa and I are like the couples in those romances you used to read, the ones where the noble aristocrats marry because of power and wealth. I'm good with that."

"A marriage of convenience?" she asked, incredulity coloring her voice. "I'm not believing you've changed that much. Tell me she's your rebound after a disastrous love affair, and I'll accept that you're currently feeling jaded and mean."

He snorted. "Okay, then you were my disastrous love affair, because I *am* jaded and mean. I couldn't get where I am any other way."

"That's sad." She took the bottle and sipped it while staring over the shadowy waters of the pool. "We were babies then. We never would have lasted. You should have had a glorious love affair in college and married and had your own babies by now."

"That's your fantasy, not mine. I grew up watching my mother work her fingers to the bone to keep a roof over our heads. I wanted enough money to keep my family safe, but I didn't want to be in the power of pricks like Dell for the rest of my life. So I worked my tail off while taking classes when I could—no fancy college experience there. And by the time I got that degree, I was easing into production. I'm too short and too bad an actor for anything but the side-kick role, and that got old fast."

"Bull hockey," she said with a snort. "Tom Cruise is no giant, and you have more to offer than he will ever have. Go back to telling me you didn't want more Dell-the-Damned Producers running the show. That, I'll believe."

Since he was marrying a damned producer, he had to bite his tongue. "Enough about me. Tell me why you ran away. I thought you told me once that your family never had the sense to flee."

He'd counted on her being there when he got back. He'd spun fantasies of how he'd rescue her once he had the film money. Instead of buying an engagement ring as he'd planned, he'd spent those earnings trying to find her, caught up in that rescue fantasy. He'd obviously hired the wrong people because, dammit, it looked as if she'd saved herself.

"I told you, once your career took off, I didn't want to hold you back," she said without a hint of regret. "It was time for me to look after myself. I was pretty mature for a sixteen-year-old, just handicapped by too many laws. Did you know I couldn't even open a bank account on my own? So I found ways of earning cash my mother didn't know about, hired a lawyer, slapped her with a big, fat lawsuit, threatened criminal action, and escaped."

"What the hell did you do to earn cash?" he asked in suspicion.

She snapped him with one of her towels. Josh grabbed it and whipped it away, leaving more of her cleavage for his perusal. The straight-as-a-stick teenager had developed a glorious prow. If Dell hadn't been into little boys, he'd have seen he had a budding sex goddess he could have exploited far easier than tomboy Ginger.

"Voice-overs, mostly," she said in what almost sounded like anger. "And I had a pretty good side gig making others pay me to read lines with them. I persuaded the scriptwriters to slip me cash every time I caught a loophole or anachronism. I'd been on the show longer than any of them, so I knew what Ginger and Jack would do and had done. I even got my mother to give me an allowance by telling her I was bribing the costumers."

"Damn," he muttered. "But that would barely earn enough to pay for a single hour of a decent lawyer's time."

He turned in time to catch her smile of satisfaction.

"But once the lawyer heard me out, she took the job on the basis of how much she could screw out of my mother and the show. My case was so solid, we never even went to court. I settled for almost nothing after paying the lawyer, but I was free."

"Nothing? You got *nothing*? You were on that show since you were eight! You earned every damned penny and then some. Your mother should have invested a fortune in your name." He thought his brain exploded at the loss of all that money.

"Freedom was worth it," she said with a wave of dismissal. "Besides, my sister was still at home, and I made keeping her out of the business part of the deal. With all her problems, Amethyst would have been crushed by our mother's wheeling and dealing. And I never earned what you did. I think Crystal and Dell had some side deal happening that never went on the books. I couldn't hire accountants to get into that. Now tell me about Willa."

He was still fuming about selling her childhood for crap-diddley. He hated to admit that he'd sold out his dreams too. "Her father's a big shot producer. He's given Willa what he considers one of the less important branches of his kingdom, a branch that's currently financing my next film. Willa and I decided we'd bump the production up to the next level. She's ambitious, and my name should help her take her company another step higher."

He waited for her disapproval. She just sounded sad when she finally spoke.

"You never wanted to stay in the business. You hated the pressure. Whatever happened to the farm you wanted to buy? The books you were going to write?"

"I grew up," he said with a shrug. "It happens. Did you think you'd make a living at tarot reading when you were a kid?"

She laughed. "Actually, I did, although I thought I'd have money to do it in style while I went to acting school. Psychic to the Stars has a nice ring, doesn't it?"

"I can probably make that happen," he suggested tentatively. "I don't believe in a lot of that stuff the way you do, but a hell of a lot of people do."

"I like it here," she said softly. "I don't want to leave."

And then she added sadly, "But I may have to."

Without explaining, she stood and pulled on her caftan and announced it was time for her to go.

Their trip down memory lane had relaxed some of his tension—until she'd cut him off again. He got it. She didn't want him prying. He didn't want her to leave, but even he knew spending the night wouldn't happen.

"I'm going home tomorrow," Josh told her as he walked her to his car. "Give me your email and phone number. Let's talk again."

She handed him a business card from her over-sized bag but shook her head sadly. Her face was almost heart-shaped with her wide cheeks and narrow chin, but it was the long-lashed pools of turquoise he fell into every time. They were dark with shadows now. The low sidewalk lights provided little illumination.

"Different worlds, Jacko. I'm here if you need your cards read, but you and I both know the distance is too much for your busy career. I'll always cherish our friendship, and maybe I'll even try to keep up with your work now that I know you haven't forgotten me."

When they reached the drive, he kissed her creamy cheek and tried not to remember a time when he'd had the right to hold her in his arms. "I'll always love you, even if you don't need my swords and dragons."

She laughed, touched his bristled jaw, and slid into the car without saying more.

Josh felt as if he were cutting an invisible bond when he let her go. He wasn't much on sentimentality anymore, but Amber . . . had been his entire childhood and adolescence. She'd been the brat who'd kicked his shin with her cowboy boot when he'd teased her, crippling him for nearly a week. At age twelve, she'd beaten him with a magazine when he'd kissed her. Then she'd become the pest who had demanded that he teach her to dance. They'd been pretty damned good too, although they'd used old movies to learn the routines. They'd never make it on a modern dance floor.

He'd never sleep tonight. He might as well get some work done.

FOUR

I WILL ALWAYS LOVE YOU.

Had she dreamed last night? She'd gone swimming in her underwear with her teenage heartthrob, and he'd said those words she'd always hoped to hear someday.

Except he'd said it on the eve of his marriage, damn him. Life was cruel. And Josh had probably meant it in that film star way that was as meaningless as air kisses.

A knock hit her front door. The bell hadn't worked in years. Amber finished fastening an earring and ambled out to her front room. She might wish that was Josh on her porch, but he'd be on his way back to the big world.

"Hold your horses," she muttered, then winced, realizing she sounded like her mother. That's what happened when transported back in time for an evening.

Sam and Mariah usually just waltzed in since Amber didn't bother locking her door. Hillvale wasn't exactly a hotbed of crime. Crazy Daisy, may she rest in peace, had lined her porch with protective stone guardians, and that was good enough for Amber. Besides, she had nothing worth stealing.

She needed to consider what Zeke would need to feel at home here—

starting with a television, she suspected. But first, she had to twist her mother's arm to let him visit. She needed a few cups of tea before she was ready for that battle. She opened the door.

Hillvale's chief of police, Sam's husband, Chen Ling Walker, stood outside. Tall, with an intimidatingly blank expression in his flat eyes, Walker was impressive even without uniform. When he was wearing his gun and gear, he was downright scary. Her heart thumped harder, not in a good way.

"What's wrong?" she demanded.

"Where were you from the time you left the shop last night to midnight?"

"That doesn't answer my question," she retorted, unhappy that Walker obviously knew she hadn't been home. "Quit behaving like an asshole from a bad cop show, come in, and let me drink my tea. What happened?"

She thought he snorted, but she knew Walker preferred his enigmatic face when on a case. And if he was on a case. . . she really needed her tea before facing it. She offered him a cup, but he shook his head. She poured hers and drank it black.

Did she verify that she had been with Josh? What if Josh's fiancée found out? Or word spread and everyone figured out she was part of Ginger and Jack? She really didn't want to be Ginger anymore.

"Do I have to tell you where I was?" she asked, leaning against her counter. She liked to examine all possibilities before deciding. Impulsive, she was not.

Walker didn't do relaxed. Crossing his short-sleeved, muscled arms, he filled her tiny kitchen. "No, but you might help out a friend if you did."

Her rather large stomach fell to her feet. "Josh? Did something happen to Josh?"

"He's fine, for the moment. Answer the question, Amber. You know I don't gossip."

"You'll tell me what's wrong if I answer?" she demanded.

"You'll hear anyway. I just want honest confirmation first."

"I came home after work, all alone. I walked down to town a little before ten. Josh's driver picked me up and took me to the lodge right about ten. It was sometime around midnight when he returned me to town. I was with Josh in the pool in between those times. Does that help?" She crossed her fingers and prayed, covering all bases.

He nodded. "Partially, for now. A hiker found your Josh's fiancée in a canyon outside of town this morning, in an area where someone in high heels isn't likely to have walked on her own. We don't have the time of death yet. I just wanted you to confirm what he told me."

"Willa? Willa Powell is dead?" she asked, horror washing over her. The death card, he'd pulled the death card. It usually wasn't literal, but Josh's vibrations had been really bad. She couldn't corral all the ramifications to even start asking questions. "There's been another death in Hillvale?"

"It might not have happened here," Walker reminded her. "Looks to me as if she'd been dumped. But she was found near here, so it looks bad."

"Oh, hell. Josh thought she'd gone back to LA. Take me over to the lodge, please." Tears filled her eyes. To fight them, she slammed down her cup and marched out.

She needed to talk to her friends, go to the café and hear the gossip, but she couldn't leave Josh bereft and alone, not again. He had to be devastated.

"This is what happens when I marry friends, right? I don't get to be chief anymore?" Walker asked, helping her into his official SUV.

"Exactly. You're just Sam's husband, and you know Sam would want you to take me to Josh." Although now that she said it, she wanted to smack herself silly. Being seen in public with Jack/Josh was the last thing she wanted.

But this wasn't about her anymore. Besides, despite Walker's protestations that he didn't gossip, the news would be all over town by midmorning that she'd been with the famed Joshua Gabriel in the middle of the night for a pool rendezvous. People weren't dumb and lodge staff talked.

Maybe she should read her own cards more often, but that required reading herself, and that was a game of Russian roulette.

Walker drove her to the lodge and politely walked her back to Josh's suite. He knocked, and Kurt Kennedy, the resort's owner, answered. Seeing Walker, he looked relieved. "Any news?"

"I brought your local psychic to read the stars," Walker said grimly. "I have to go back and use more mundane methods." He stalked away, abandoning Amber to her fate.

Tall and handsome in a very mundane Null way, Kurt grimaced and ran his hand through his hair. Amber patted his shoulder in sympathy. Recently married, attempting to establish his own architectural firm while dealing with the multiple difficulties of owning half the resort and town, he had his hands full. At least, now that he was married to Teddy, he was learning to accept Lucy eccentricity.

"How is he?" she asked, because that mattered first.

"Manic. I have to go back to town. How well do you know him? Are you okay staying here? I think he has staff on the way up, but it's a long drive from LA." Kurt cast a glance over his shoulder at a shout of fury from inside the suite.

"His temper goes down as fast as it goes up," she said reassuringly. "Send food, orange juice, no coffee. Coffee will drive him ballistic."

Kurt raised his eyebrows in surprise but nodded. "Got it. Thanks, Amber. I didn't want to leave him alone."

"He needs friends. Just be available if he needs help. He has some bad things happening in his cards, which may reflect some bad things in his life. Tell Teddy. She'll know what to do." Amber set down her bag and walking stick on the foyer table and entered the main room of the suite, letting Kurt escape.

"Tell the scurrilous knaves whatever the hell you want, just keep them away from me," Josh was shouting into the landline. "Tell them I crawled into my dragon cave and pulled a mountain over me. Let the grave robbers haunt the coroner's office. It's not as if I can tell them anything."

Oh yeah, she remembered those days of publicity pressure. She didn't miss them in the least.

Josh didn't even seem to notice as she continued on to the kitchen and emptied the coffee pot. He'd had enough caffeine from the sounds of it. She found a tomato juice bottle in the mini-fridge, poured some in a glass, and carried that out to where he paced up and down the carpet, still shouting at his minions.

When he inevitably flung the receiver across the room, she handed him a glass of nutrition.

Josh looked awful. He hadn't shaved. His thick brown locks fell over his broad forehead, giving him a hobbit look. The emptiness in his beautiful cobalt eyes almost broke her heart all over again.

He took a sip of juice and returned to pacing. "I'm sorry, kid. I don't know how I'll keep you out of this. I can send you far, far away, if that will help. Want to visit Paris?"

"I'd love to visit Paris, but my nephew is here next week, so I'll have to decline. Thank you for the thought. I can see how you're holding up, so I won't ask. What about Willa's parents?" She took a seat on the luxurious sofa. The Kennedys didn't stint on comfort for their wealthy guests.

She glanced around, seeing papers strewn across the tables and half the chairs, and a laptop running on the long, elegant dining table. A video game bounced on the TV screen.

"Willa's mother has been on an African safari or European tour for years. Her father is unavailable. I have no idea if anyone has reached either of them yet. I've left voice mail on every number I have. They're not a close family," he said with acerbic dryness.

"Well, I know how that goes. Tell me about Willa. I heard she was really pretty."

"Taller than I am when she wore heels," he said with a half laugh, reaching for the juice again. "Whip-smart, ambitious. I think she wanted to prove to her father that she was better than him. She would have too. Ivan is too set in his ways to understand the new media culture." He flung papers off a lounge chair and slid into it. "I wish I'd asked her which friend she was driving back with, but she had her car with her, so I figured it was Ernest, the assistant she'd brought up with her."

He slumped and buried his face in his hands. "Willa was a force of nature. I can't believe she's gone. I'm waiting for her to walk out of the closet and yell at me for not milking this for publicity."

"You'll get more publicity by playing the part of grieving lover and hiding out for a while. Speculation will explode the headlines."

Reporters would be all over the town by dusk, Amber knew. She almost wished she could take him up on Paris.

"Maybe *you* should go to Paris," she suggested hopefully.

He lifted his head. "I'm not leaving until I know what happened. I owe Willa that much."

Amber sighed and wondered if she could order mimosas. "Yeah, I figured."

"Shit, the reporters will be all over town, won't they? They'll hear about the pool. Let me call my PR person back," he said, wearily rubbing his face.

Amber waved her rings in dismissal. "No one has a reason to put an overweight tarot reader together with teenage Ginger. Just find some way of keeping the jackals from making it sound like last night was some kind of love triangle."

Josh nodded and hunted down the cordless phone he'd flung. "Then I'll arrange someone to shoot her father and give them something new to gnaw on. Piece of cake."

Room service knocked while he was on the phone. Amber answered it. Instead of the usual rolling cart and uniformed staff, Fiona from the café winked at her and held up a tray. "I haven't met Josh yet," she whispered. "I'll know what he needs better once I have. So this is mostly for you."

Amber almost expired in gratitude that her friends had her back. "If you tell me he smells of fish, I'll smack you with one," she whispered.

"You're too sensitive to hang with fish," Fee said, carrying her tray toward the table while studying Josh striding over strewn papers, yelling into his phone. "Oh yeah, Jackie outgrew the nerd role. He rocks that cowboy look now, doesn't he? I purely loved that show when I was a kid. Jack and Ginger were the family I didn't have."

Fiona had grown up in the foster system. With her peculiar sense of smell, the little cook had always been an outcast, until she'd arrived in Hillvale. Fee had kept her mouth shut when she recognized Amber, so she could be trusted.

And Fee was right. With his unbuttoned shirt revealing washboard abs, Josh had definitely grown out of the skinny nerd stage.

"You are part of a family now," Amber reminded her. "Although I suppose the Lucys are a little less normal than Jack and Ginger. Thank you for coming here. The café must be going insane."

"Dinah stepped up. She was the one who said I had to help." Fee discreetly sniffed the air. "He smells of honesty, generosity, and impatience. I don't recognize emotion as well as Teddy does, so saying I think he also smells of sorrow and anger simply means that's my interpretation, based on what he ought to be feeling. But there doesn't seem to be an evil scent on him. I'll send up some herbal snacks that may help a little. The orange juice is fresh squeezed and should be better for him than the sugary stuff."

Josh didn't even appear to notice when she let Fee out again. Amber examined the tray of goodies, found avocado toast that he could munch as he paced, and carried it over to him. Absent-mindedly, he accepted a piece and ate while waiting for someone on the other end of the phone line.

Damn, this felt too much like the old days when they'd helped each other over childhood anxieties and through homework. She needed to be working on her nephew's problem. Although—once the news broke—this could become part of Zeke's problem. Willa's death would bring all Hollywood news down on them, just when she needed to convince a court that she could take care of Zeke better than Crystal.

If anyone discovered she was really Ginger—it wouldn't take a minute for the press to put Jack and Ginger together in a love triangle with the dead woman and there would go any chance of getting custody.

In a semi-panic, she sat down at Josh's neglected computer and sent off an email to her lawyer with a quick summary of Zeke's situation. Alicia knew Amber's mother. She'd be all over Crystal like fleas on cats. Now, if only they could hold off the press. . .

That done, Amber took a deep breath and opened up the Hollywood websites to see how the gossip was rolling. The news had just hit, so there wasn't a lot of speculation yet.

She and Josh, as teenage geeks, had learned to manipulate internet publicity better than their PR department back in the day. She didn't know if the basics still applied, but she'd have to sink into those depths of depravity again if she wanted to keep a handle on their reputations. She could almost feel the muddy ooze between her toes already.

But if she brought Zeke up here, she'd have to support him somehow. All she knew how to do was act, although she wasn't much good for anything but voice-overs these days. Would Josh help her find jobs?

He hung up and rummaged on the table for more food. That had to be a good sign. Amber abandoned the computer and joined him.

"Did they persuade you to be sensible and head back to LA to handle this?" she asked point blank.

He snarled mean enough for a feral wolf. "No way. Willa was here. What happened to her was here. I'm staying until I know who did this."

Which meant that Hillvale would again be inundated with reporters covering a murder story and not the upbeat wedding one the town needed.

As Jacko might have said, farkin' pig swivers.

FIVE

"I NEED TO GET OUT OF HERE BEFORE I GO STARK RAVING BONKERS," JOSH shouted at the room. The food had restored some of his brain power, and he glanced at the mess he'd made in his emotional break-down. Well, half the chaos had probably been caused by his working all night.

"Are you planning on going incognito as Wolfman or would you prefer to shave and dress first?" a familiar sultry voice asked from the shadows of the kitchen. How many years had he spent carrying on conversations in his head with that seductive voice?

Ginger. Maddening, refreshing Ginger had crossed time portals into his life again, except she wasn't Ginger anymore. She was Amber, and he hadn't really known her at all. He glanced down at himself—he hadn't buttoned his shirt and yesterday's jeans still had ink on them from where he'd snapped his pen.

Her hips swayed in her ruffled skirt as she entered the main room, and it was as if the sun had broken through the clouds. She glittered in amber beads and gold bangles, frilly blouse and Gypsy skirt. Her bright coppery hair could easily rival the sun. And then there were those high, *real* breasts. . .

Okay, he was on full alert now. Back down, boy. "Right, on it. Do I wear black and feed the crows?" He started for the bedroom, which looked even worse than the trashed front room, with clothes strewn everywhere—including some of Willa's. That was why he wasn't dressed. She must have packed hastily.

"I believe sackcloth, ashes, and whips are the appropriate attire," she called after him. "But we're not fussy. Clean is good."

"I didn't bring much. I may have to special order sackcloth, although Willa probably has a collection of whips in her closet." Trying not to look at a lacy bra and a pair of sandals half under the dresser, he slammed into the bathroom and let the shower wash away some of the aches.

Willa had been friend and lover these past months. They'd conspired together, made plans, had laughs. He recognized her for the controlling bitch she was, but he was a director. He handled crap like that for breakfast. The wedding had never been more than a publicity stunt. They may never have made it as a couple after this film was over, but he liked to think they would have remained friends.

Now he would never know.

He scrubbed at his hair and hoped to wash some sense into his head. He could see Willa's dream crashing while her company struggled to replace her. He needed to call Tessa, her VP. He'd sunk a lot of cash into the project. So had Willa. If Tessa pulled the plug. . . Both their dreams would go down the drain with the film. And if Willa's father reeled in his shares. . . He was doomed.

He needed to find new backers, but his heart simply wasn't in it. Willa had understood his vision. She'd known his script would be a difficult sale. That's why they'd conjured up the wedding scheme. Try explaining that to reporters and her father.

Why would anyone kill Willa?

That's what he could focus on. He, of all people, was in the best position to determine motivation.

Unless, of course, she'd been kidnapped, raped, and murdered by some random stranger. Josh had a feeling that Willa would have blasted a few holes in any stranger who dared approach. She carried a Glock.

Vengeance wasn't his shtick, but justice. . . he could get behind that full steam.

He dragged on a white linen shirt and clean jeans and padded back to the front room, drying his hair. "I need to know what the cops know. I don't suppose your psychic powers can help me there?"

He used to ask her stupid questions like that. And she'd pat him on his stupid head and give him the common sense answers he needed.

"Sam's husband is the chief of police. I'll know when she knows," she said, proving she hadn't changed, and then she spoiled it by adding, "It's too soon to see if Cass can contact Willa's spirit, but the Lucys will be out looking for her. Spirits tend to cling to Hillvale. It's something to do with the vortex and the crystal energy, but we don't have specifics." She waited expectantly.

"You could have stopped with the chief of police," he growled, giving her the reaction she expected, he presumed. They used to read each other like books, but they'd both added a few pages over the years. "Tell me the chief tells this Sam everything, and I'm with the program. After that, I need the script."

Her wide red lips curved approvingly. "This isn't Hobbiton. We'll never be picturesque. We use terms like Nulls and Lucys instead of trolls and elves. But Hillvale is where magic happens. If you're willing to accept that, welcome to my world. Come along, and I'll introduce you."

She took his arm and steered him toward the door.

"Why do I have the feeling the train just left Harry Potter's platform?" He lifted her heavy bag, remembering it from last night. "What do you carry in here, crystal balls?"

"Cards, mostly. They're pretty heavy stock. I considered Fiona's trick of carrying rocks to bash muggers, but the cards ought to do the trick." She dragged him into the corridor, checked both ways, and headed for the rear exit. "You have a car handy?"

"I'm processing on no sleep, kid. Give me time to catch up." Josh pulled out his phone, then remembered it didn't work here and cursed. "I haven't set this up with the lodge's wi-fi. I'll have to go back in to phone a valet to bring the car around."

"You've forgotten how to drive?" she asked, not turning back. "And in case you haven't noticed, I'm not a kid anymore."

"You were never a kid. I just called you that to remind you I was older." He fumbled in his pockets, found his wallet, but the key fob wasn't there. "We could walk. It's only what, about a mile? That will give us time to prepare for the circling orcs."

She shot him a look as if he'd just taken off his head and batted it down the hall.

"What? You can't walk? You have your hiking stick. You must use it." Josh shoved open the rear door and checked to be certain no reporters lurked. "I want a Gandalf hood and cloak. I could grow a long beard and see if it turns white. It's not as if my face is all that familiar anymore."

"Delusional," she concluded, stopping in the lot and obviously waiting for him to choose a car. "Unless you think I'm equally unrecognizable. I am, actually. I've been invisible for years. But put us together. . . brains start clicking."

He mock cuffed her ear. "Don't start sounding like your mother. Let's walk. It's a gorgeous day."

She emitted a long-suffering sigh. "I might make it down the hill without breaking my neck and two limbs, but if you ask me to walk back later, I will have to kill you to prevent spreading the madness."

"Lazy. You were always lazy."

"My metabolism is slower than yours," she asserted.

They'd once argued like this all the time. It made him feel youthful. He took off at a brisk trot, then stopped when she hadn't made it past the first cars. He was still remembering teenage Ginger, who brightened the day with laughter and wisdom. Adult Amber moved slower and actually seemed to need the funky stick. "You're injured?" he asked in concern. "I'll get the car. I'm sorry for being such a selfish bastard."

"It's just that old injury to my knee from that stupid stunt. My weight makes it worse. I suppose it's good for me to move, but I'm stiff. I'll walk, just not at a rabbit hop."

"Don't give me the obese crap again," he warned. "That's the Harpy talking." He used the nickname they'd once given Amber's nagging mother. "You're just out of shape. We'll walk as far as you're comfortable, then I'll jog down and call a valet to pick you up. You always needed a shove to get moving." He slowed his pace to walk beside her.

Maybe there was something to this more leisurely pace. Amber's laidback style had a way of calming his fuming boil. "You're better than a toke," he decided. "You let me bliss out, when everyone else rags on my last nerve."

Her laughter broke like crystalline notes over the crisp morning air. "Put that in a review on my website, please."

"Okay, if you tell me the story of Lucys and Nulls." He shoved his hands in his jean pockets and admired the lush greenery. Willa had been right. A place like this would film better than New Zealand. He didn't know how Hillvale produced greenery in desert, but the photo shoot would have been spectacular.

He needed to make the film happen in Willa's memory. That gave him something solid he could put his hands around.

"The Lucent Ladies were spiritualists who occupied the town back in the 1800s," Amber said as they walked. "Do you recall Lily Dale? It was pretty famous in its day, back when the Victorians believed in psychics and speaking to the dead."

Josh dragged his thoughts back to the fairy tale princess at his side. "People are sheep," he said cynically. "Yell *burn the witches*, and they do, without rhyme or reason. Then some wit comes along and calls them psychics and all of a sudden, the very same women are worshipped."

"Worship is going too far. Laughed at instead of feared, maybe. Anyway, the legend says the spiritualists heard about Hillvale's little ghost problem and began gathering here. Most of us with aberrant talents probably descended from those Victorian spiritualists."

"Aberrant," he scoffed. "I can see it now, the League of Aberrant Powers. Okay, I've got it. The Lucys are the local eccentrics and the Nulls are the mundanes. And you think the Lucys can summon spirits who know what happened to Willa?"

She was silent as they navigated a particularly steep portion of the road. A few cars drove past, and Josh began to understand the difficulty of walking this narrow drive. He offered his arm, and she accepted it until they rounded the curve. She wasn't breathing heavily, but she'd started to limp.

"Do we need to stop here?" he asked in concern, looking for a rock or bench to sit on.

She shook her sunset hair. "No, not for the little distance left. The incline is the worst. I can't explain what the Lucys do. We're like anyone else. We mull around, doing our own things, and stuff happens."

"Examples," he demanded, wanting to believe.

"Do you remember a toddler kidnapped a few months back?"

"Unless it was in the Hollywood news, nope. I've been pretty heavy into pulling together the new project." And Willa had been a slave driver, but he refrained from speaking ill of the dead, even if it was truth.

"It's a complicated story. But we drew all the suspects up here with Fiona's food. Mariah used ectoplasm to make them tell the truth. Harvey's walking sticks—" She brandished the one she'd been leaning on. "—added energy when the bad guys kidnapped Fee and Keegan, and. . .well, things happened. Of course, it helped that Mayor Monty got mad and knocked off one of the jerks with a football, but that could have been crystal energy too."

"Crystal energy?" he asked, fascinated despite himself. He'd look up the story later, ascertain the facts.

"Talk to Keegan and Teddy about crystals. Energy vibrations aren't my specialty. But the theory is that the crystals mined in this area react in some way to the spiritual vortex by the cemetery, making it easier for some of us to reach beyond the veil between life and death." She was starting to breathe harder, but they'd reached the bottom of the hill.

"You mentioned ectoplasm. How does that work into this energy theory?" His mind spun possibilities for a new script.

She released his arm to lean on her staff, and he missed the bit of closeness.

"Mariah says that the energy in our physical bodies after we die transmutes into metaphysical energy in the form of ectoplasm that she can feel."

"Energy cannot be destroyed, only transformed, basic physics. I like it, pseudo-science at its very best. I'll take results any way I can. What do we do next?" He gazed over the sleepy town. Too early for the shops to open. It would be hours before reporters arrived. The only activity appeared to be at the café.

Although he heard music carrying on the clear mountain air. The sound grew louder as they approached a church-sized building that he'd been told housed an art gallery.

"Depends on how much you want to reveal to complete strangers and how much you trust me." She halted when he did, outside the gallery's double doors. "That's Val and Harvey, practicing their wedding repertoire. Willa probably wasn't on Val's spiritual radar. She's our resident Death Goddess and usually makes the death announcements, so she must not have heard. I don't know what her death will do to the rest of the wedding schedule. June was booked solid yesterday, but murder has a dampening effect on festivities."

The music was so haunting, Josh was certain the acoustics in the gallery had to be amazing. "Is it okay if we go in?"

She looked uncertain. "They're both Lucys. Like me, they're here for a reason. Every time reporters show up, they strip away a little more of our privacy. Can you just accept them as they are?"

"You do realize that just made me more curious, don't you?" he asked, opening one large door.

She didn't answer, rightfully so. The voice pouring from inside filled the nearly-empty building, rolling off the walls and lifting any listener into the realms of the sublime. And just as the music threatened to carry him away, the piano wove into the harmony as if it were one with the singer, and Josh simply collapsed into the nearest chair. He didn't even recognize the song until the haunting final refrains of *Ave Maria* echoed like a choir of angels.

"Wow," he muttered, imagining how that would fill a cathedral. A bride would be an afterthought.

Amber sank into a chair beside him. "The one in the black veil is Val. Her real name is Valerie Ingersson."

"The musical sensation of San Francisco a few decades ago—Willa pointed out her bio online when she told me who she'd hired for the wedding." Josh recognized the death goddess allusion from a video game. Willa hadn't explained that one—and probably hadn't been interested. "I guess I don't get to know everyone's story."

"Not unless they're willing to tell you. We've only recently persuaded Val to sing for something other than the dead. Once she hears about Willa, she'll be out looking for her spirit."

He nodded as if he understood that weirdness, but he was fixated on the present in the form of the pianist. Slender, in black t-shirt and jeans, with long black hair tied at the nape, the musician once wore a tux on the concert circuit, if Josh was any judge. "And this is where Isaac Berkovich holes up? Why?"

"Isaac?" she asked in amusement. "That's Harvey Menendez, although he doesn't claim the last name. I don't know his story either, but he carved our walking sticks and can choose crystals that suit our personalities and enhance our energies."

She showed him the amber-studded dragon's head on hers.

"That's Isaac," Josh said in confidence, studying the stick, then the man flipping pages of music. "He was an international sensation until he disappeared a few years back. How long has your Harvey lived here?"

"He came and went for years before he moved in a few years back. We knew he was a concert pianist. But here, he plays guitar, writes music, and carves sticks."

"Walking sticks with magical energies, presumably. There's a hell of a lot of talent hiding up here," Josh concluded.

"We're not all creative. It's just that creative minds are more open to possibility. We notice when we're different and experiment with exercising those differences instead of hiding them. Nulls prefer to be—"

"Sheep," Josh finished for her. "Although I'm guessing there's a lot more to it than that. I am officially fascinated."

"Shall I start here then? Once I tell Val about Willa, she'll connect with Cass, and before noon, the Lucys will be traversing the countryside. They'll want to see that Willa finds her way across the veil. We don't need any more lost souls stuck in Hillvale."

That made just enough sense to resonate with the hole in his heart. Josh nodded. "Do it."

SIX

VAL AND HARVEY WERE TWO OF THE LESS SOCIAL LUCYS. THEY SHIED FROM strangers, not because they were timid, but because they didn't wish to be recognized. They acknowledged Amber's introduction to Josh, offered condolences when told of Willa, and performed their amazing vanishing act soon after.

But they were Hillvale's communication system. Harvey would tell Aaron, who would connect with Monty the mayor and the other men. Val would head straight for Cass, the closest thing Lucys had to a leader.

"We can stop here at the central nervous system or head straight into the heart of town," Amber said once they were back outside in the sunshine. "How are you feeling?"

Josh tilted his head and snapped photos of a colorfully beaded ghost-catcher net hanging from the boardwalk roof. "Overwhelmed, exhausted, frustrated, worried beyond measure, and weirdly expectant. Is that how one describes grief?"

"Shouldn't you be *writing* the scripts for these films you make?" she asked, almost irritated with his reply. "You still have a way with words."

"Scripts are written by committee these days, and books sell like crap, so there's no money in writing. People want flash and bang. I can do that with film." He examined the nearly empty parking lot. "Tarot reading and weddings can't produce a lot of income either. How does anyone survive up here?"

"We help each other. As long as there are no reporters here yet, you might as well see what I mean." She started down the boardwalk toward Dinah's café. Fee ran it now, but she hadn't changed the name.

"You need to video your local talent," Josh said, scuffling along at her side, apparently inhabiting his own little world. "There's money to be made online. It wouldn't take long to find an audience for talent like we saw back there. Throw in the scenery, a few ghost stories, a wedding or two, and you have a storyline happening. The more followers you have, the more money you can make in sponsorships."

"I'll let someone else fill you in on the rise and fall of the artists who built a commune up the hill back in the seventies. Wealth, fame, they had it all. But the mountain corrupts. We don't know how or why. It all went bad and destroyed entire families. We're just coming back from that. We don't seek fame and fortune these days." Steeling herself, Amber directed him into the café.

"*Power* corrupts," he said. "And greed. Not mountains." He shut up when the café went silent at their entrance.

Fiona emerged from the kitchen, waving menus. "Have a booth. Juice, right?" Once she had them seated, she leaned over and whispered, "Stranger on far end. Doesn't smell quite fishy, but he's not an honest person."

"I thought you decided fishy went with drug dealers. You don't have a comparison for killers." Amber handed back the menu, knowing Fee would bring her what she needed.

Fee grimaced. "You're right. Our last killer smelled fishy, but he associated with drug dealers. Still, our crooked county attorney also had an off odor like this guy. I'm calling it *dishonest* until I know better." She hurried back to her kitchen.

"She smells honesty? Isn't that a little far-fetched?" Josh glanced over his shoulder in the direction indicated. "That's just Brad Jones, Willa's cameraman. He works hard, probably hung around for more shots, and he's waiting for orders. I don't know him well enough to know if he's honest, but how many people are these days?"

"Define honesty," she countered. "Is acting honest? Fiction? If Harvey is really Isaac, is he being honest? But the crooked attorney Fee mentioned was a killer, so I'm going with her version of dishonesty as being bad."

"You can't call a man a killer because you think he smells bad," Josh protested.

"No, and that's why what we do can't be explained. I couldn't tell from reading your cards yesterday what would happen. I could just tell you it would be bad. We can only use our instincts to steer clear of dangerous people or keep an eye on them while evidence directs us one way or the other. And then it gets weirder." Amber scooted over as Mariah approached.

"Sam will have already told Mariah what little Walker knows," Amber told him.

Mariah was tall and carried her muscular weight with more grace than Amber. She was also seven months pregnant and took up more than her fair share of space. She held out a broad brown hand to Josh. "I'm called Mariah these days."

Josh took her hand and shook. "And I gather I would probably recognize your other name but you'd rather not go into that. I'm really liking this town."

Amber snickered. "You like Hillvale because it's just like Hollywood. No one is who they say they are."

"It's like a mystery book, where I get to guess who everyone is." Josh accepted the juice Fee delivered to the table and swallowed half of it in one gulp. "I'm just not liking being one of the characters in the story. I'd rather be the author and go after the killer with a hatchet."

"That's where Mariah comes in. She can research the characters and tell us who they really are." Amber nodded her head at the back of the room. "We need to know more about Brad Jones, the cameraman at the counter."

"I'm only doing normal searches these days," Mariah warned, rubbing her belly. "We don't know the effect on the princess here."

"Do you have a name for her yet?" Josh asked.

A man who asked after an unborn baby instead of following the logical question about *normal* was a dangerous charmer. Amber narrowed her eyes at him, but he seemed genuinely interested.

"Cassandra already has the best name," Mariah said with a laugh. "So we're researching Keegan's genealogy for a powerful one. His family tree is littered with gifted women. Amber explained about Lucys, didn't she?"

"She did. So you think there's a genetic connection to Lucy gifts?" Totally focused on the conversation, Josh didn't notice the gorgeous waitress placing a plate of burritos in front of him.

"Beware, he will put us all into a film," the waitress warned as she released the plate.

Knowing the burrito deliverer didn't care if Josh noticed her, Amber grinned at Sam, the police chief's wife. Tall, slim, a natural platinum blond, the environmental scientist/waitress regarded Josh with sympathy. "We are devastated by your loss and will do everything in our power to find out what happened."

"Walker will be delighted to hear that," Amber said wryly. "He can just sit back and wait for us to mumble magic spells."

"Feed her." Sam pointed at the fruit and granola she'd set in front of Amber, then returned to working behind the counter.

Mariah slid awkwardly from the booth. "Walker can provide the forensics we can't. It all works out. I'll take a little peek into the police files once I think there's anything there to find. That's a basic hack and doesn't need any energy."

"This is Narnia, isn't it?" Josh asked, picking at his burrito. "Pretty soon, the animals will be arriving to tell us their tales."

"Do you think C.S. Lewis visited Hillvale? Or maybe there are other towns like us elsewhere? Or maybe he just met some of Keegan's relations. Keegan is from Scotland and has family all over the UK." Amber popped a sweet strawberry in her mouth and savored it. Fruit was filled with sugar, and she shouldn't indulge, but Fee kept reminding her that it was all about balance and some sugars were better than others. She needed the reassurance occasionally.

Josh rubbed his head. "I'm still waiting for Willa to pop out of a closet. This is a nightmare, and I'm afraid it's just beginning."

"Real life isn't as much fun as make-believe, is it?" Amber said, understanding. "Are you sure you wouldn't rather go home, where your friends are? What about your family? Are they still in Nevada?"

"Mom is happy in her retirement cottage. She only met Willa once and wasn't impressed, so I've kept them apart. My brothers graduated college and took off on their own careers. There's nothing they can do to help. I feel better if I stay here. You've always been able to keep me stable. I need that right now."

She waved her spoon cynically. "I'll be your teddy bear. I'm too big to fling across the room the way you do phones."

He chuckled and snapped her picture. "Not necessarily. I took up martial arts when I made my first film. But I never lose my temper with you, so you're safe. I think I've calmed down enough to get a little rest. Thank you for holding my hand."

That sounded like a dismissal to her. She should be relieved. Once strangers started pouring into town, she'd rather hide in the shadows of her shop. "I'm here to hold your hand anytime you like. I'm sorry if you felt I abandoned you earlier. I had no idea that my mother or Dell wouldn't tell you at once what I'd done."

"They tried, in their own limited way. I just didn't believe them. That's on me. You had a right to escape in any way you could, and I'm proud that you did." Josh pushed away his half-eaten burrito. "And you're probably right. You gave me the freedom to walk out on my own. So I'm guessing I owe you. Have dinner with me tonight? We can have it in my suite, out of sight of strangers. We can go swimming again."

"In my underwear? You liked that, did you?" Amber didn't know whether to be appalled or thrilled at the idea.

"I'll have a suit delivered. Black? One piece? Lots of frills?" He grinned at her.

"Can it come down to my knees?" She shifted along the bench in an effort to escape the boyish grin that had tugged so hard on her heart all those years ago.

"I'll see what I can do." He stood up and kissed her on the cheek.

Damn, but she almost fell weeping into his arms thinking of all the lost years of friendship and the reason he needed her now.

A NONDESCRIPT BURLY MAN WEARING A BALL CAP, BRAD JONES, WILLA'S cameraman, was paying his bill just as Josh stepped up to the register. Even after talking to Harvey and Val, he was having difficulty forming the words to say Willa was no more. It was a surreal experience having her vividly in mind from yesterday and gone from this earth today. He couldn't wrap his head around it.

"Do you know who Willa left with yesterday?" Josh asked as a conversation starter.

Brad shrugged and shoved his wallet back in his pocket. "Probably the wedding planner or Ernest. They just told me to finish up the shoot and take the truck back. Why?"

They'd all arrived in different vehicles at different times, so that made sense with what Josh knew so far. He struggled for words as they left the café together. "Willa died last night. Send me yesterday's photos and your invoice, and I'll take care of it. I don't know what else to tell you right now."

He couldn't read the photographer's eyes under the ball cap, but Josh thought he heard shock and sympathy as he accepted condolences. Becoming a hermit until this was over sounded better than ever, but he had a purpose now. He simply had to grit his teeth and keep moving forward.

Rather than rest, he tracked down the police chief's office. The imposing Chen Ling Walker occupied half the second floor of Hillvale's antiquated City Hall. The chief's office held one battered wooden desk, an old metal filing cabinet, and two sagging chairs that might once have adorned the lodge's lobby—not exactly reassuring.

"Park a horse outside, and this place might graduate to a one-horse town," Josh said as he entered.

"The horses are at the resort and have been known to come in handy. What can I do for you?" Hanging up his landline and punching his computer keyboard, the chief barely looked up to acknowledge him.

A quick Google search had shown the chief was far more than a rural patrol officer. Walker owned one of the best detective agencies in the state and had resources at his disposal even the CHP didn't possess—for a price.

"Unless you tell me Willa was killed by a random stranger, I want to help." Josh took one of the aging chairs. "I can provide a list of staff Willa brought with her and their contact numbers. They arrived separately, so I'm not certain which cars they brought, but I can make discreet inquiries."

"The sheriff is in charge of this case, since the initial report was made to them and not me." Walker leaned back and folded his hands on his chest. "And anything you produce will be considered tainted until time of death is established and you clear your name with an alibi."

"Which isn't happening since I was working by myself. But I have no motive. Willa's death kills my project. I'm not so self-centered as to believe anyone would kill Willa to stop my film, but there might be other reasons someone didn't want Willa to succeed." Josh was flying by the seat of his pants here, but that produced some of his best plots.

Walker picked up a pen and held it over a pad on his desk. "Spill."

"Does that mean she probably wasn't killed by a stranger?" He wanted a fair trade of information. The Lucys could talk to spirits, but the real world required facts.

Walker tapped his pen on the desk and eyed Josh warily. "She wasn't raped. She was still wearing her diamond watch. Did you give her a ring?"

"We hadn't reached that stage of the production yet. She would have been wearing a gold chain with a weird iridescent pendant and half a dozen gold bracelets. No silver, she liked gold. I can describe the bracelets I gave her but she wasn't necessarily wearing them." He didn't add that Willa had a closet full of jewelry and his contribution was chump change in comparison.

Walker called up an image on his computer and turned the monitor so Josh could see. "This pendant?"

"Yes. She always wore it unless she had an evening event requiring jewels. I think her father gave it to her. A thief would have taken the chain even if he didn't know the pendant was an expensive antique."

"Would she have been carrying anything of less obvious value—film, documents?"

"Everything of importance was accessible from Willa's phone. I think her office scanned everything into the cloud so she could access it any time, any place, except here," Josh added, frowning. "Maybe she left town early because she needed something private on her cell phone? She didn't like connecting to public wi-fi."

"They didn't find the phone with her," Walker admitted, reading a file.

"Then someone could be walking around with Willa's entire life in their hands." Josh rubbed his face, realizing the stupidity of what he'd just said. But Willa's life was in that phone. "I doubt that her PIN number is unhackable or if the apps on her phone were adequately protected. So yeah, the phone might be more valuable than jewelry."

"We're not picking up any signal from it, though. It's either dead or turned off. Was she in any financial trouble?"

"Good Lord, no. If anything, she plunged others into financial trouble." Josh wasn't any financial genius, but he thought about the power Willa wielded. He just couldn't see a motive. "The woman owned substantial stock in half the film corporations in LA. For all I know, she owned Saudi Arabia. She didn't touch her personal wealth for individual projects though. She leveraged other people's debt."

"Including yours?"

"Including mine, yes. If the project dies with her, I'll have to sell my house. But it makes no sense to kill her because she borrowed money. All her investors were gambling she'd make their fortunes and provide them tickets to the premier and red carpet treatment for the awards. They'll get bupkis without her."

"Did she have a will?"

Josh grimaced. "I'm sure Daddy Dearest would have insisted. The company lawyer would know. He was drawing up our prenups." He scrolled up the contact on his phone and handed it to Walker to write down.

"You don't like her father?"

Josh had the feeling Walker's flat expression concealed a sharp perceptiveness that could skewer him if he lied. He had no reason to lie. "Ivan the Terrible and I did not have a happy relationship, no. He makes Big Pictures, in all caps, the kind with huge, expensive talent. I make childish fantasies with cartoon characters and unknowns. I'm not serious enough for Ivan's one and only child."

If Ivan thought Josh had anything to do with Willa's death, he'd bring the power of an atomic bomb down on Josh's head. It would all be over except the radiation poisoning.

"You've filled a few holes," Walker said without inflection. "Can you give me anyone with motivation? Did she have any enemies?"

"Do you have a list of Hollywood luminaries? Starting with the stars, working down through producers and directors to the lowest food cart worker?" Josh shoved his hair off his forehead. "Willa did not consider it her mission in life to make friends. The people who worked with her respected her vision and obeyed her orders. She paid well and always succeeded. Mostly, she did not recognize their existence as more than tools."

"And if the tools didn't adequately perform their function, she fired them?"

Josh nodded. "Or just didn't hire them again. She used a lot of contract workers. Employees are expensive. All the people up here yesterday were contract workers, except the VP of her corporation, Tessa English."

"Contract workers aren't loyal." Walker tapped the keyboard a few more times, then looked up with what almost seemed to be sympathy. "She was lucky to have found someone like you to put up with her."

Josh slumped in his chair. "I'm not sure I'm any better, which is why we understood each other."

SEVEN

Amber knew it was a waste of time to lay out a tarot for herself. Her psychic abilities weren't needed to read her own mind. All she could hope was that the Other Side had a hand in which cards she turned up. She might do a simple diamond spread if she could determine what her conflict was, but she seemed to be inundated with ambivalence at the moment.

The landline rang. She recognized her lawyer's number and answered rather than tackle the impossible.

"Zeke's what now? Ten, eleven?" Alicia asked without preamble. At her cost per hour, she kept calls quick, knowing Amber couldn't pay much.

"Twelve. I want guardianship. Can we go after the rest of the money if I get it?" Amber sent prayers to the Universe.

"You think there is any money left?" Alicia asked cynically. "Wouldn't your mother have bought a mansion if she had cash?"

"I'd hoped you could squeeze your fees out of her like last time," Amber said, collapsing into her nest chair. "Tell me it will be an easy job, and I'll borrow the money." That was optimistic. Banks didn't loan money to tarot shops, she was pretty sure.

"Guardianship is never easy if the other party fights it. Let me see what I can turn up on her, and we'll go from there. I'd advise getting him in your house before she learns your plans though. She could take him and run."

"Shoot sugar, I hadn't thought of that. I wanted him to finish school. Can we keep quiet another week?"

"She'll not hear a peep from me. But pin down an exit and swoop him out of there. If she's running out of money, things could turn ugly. If I remember, he's a pretty kid. Dell is involved in some pretty raunchy stuff these days."

That's what Amber had feared. Their former producer and director was a voyeur partial to pretty boys. He'd been walking a fine line when she'd left. She didn't know if he'd crossed it since. Other kids had parents to protect them. Zeke didn't, which made him even more vulnerable than she had been. She'd thought being a girl had made her safe. It hadn't.

Amber nodded, even though Alicia couldn't see her. "I'll make some calls. Zeke is smart, but a kid that age doesn't have many choices."

She started making to-do lists in her head while saying farewell to Alicia. Call the school, pretend she was Crystal, ask about finals. Call the neighbors to verify Crystal wasn't home when Zeke was there so she could talk to him without her mother knowing. Who could she find to pick him up? She didn't have a car, and LA to Hillvale was a long trek.

Walker was from LA. Maybe he could make a trip to visit his office and pick up Zeke on the way home. Zeke would get a thrill out of a ride in an official police vehicle, and it would scare Crystal into temporary paralysis.

Picturing her mother's horror, Amber was almost smiling when Tullah burst into her shop.

Amber had cast Tullah in her mind as an African Voodoo Queen. Tall and stately, normally composed and non-talkative, she ran a thrift shop that mysteriously provided anything anyone in town needed—when they needed it. She was one of Cass's closest companions and presided over Lucy séances, but she seldom spoke of her gifts.

"The spirit has Cass and won't let go," Tullah declared, her dark eyes wide with fear. "Bring your ball. We need to remove the spirit and store her somewhere safe before she takes over."

Amber trusted Tullah, but she didn't do anything without questioning. "What ball? And where is Cass?"

"Down by the vortex." Tullah lifted the Austrian crystal and headed for the door. "That's one angry ghost."

"The vortex?" In horror at the possibility of how the energies there could magnify power, Amber grabbed her walking stick and locked the door behind her. "There shouldn't be any strong spirit in the vortex. We cleared them out."

But Tullah's long legs had carried her half way down the boardwalk. Amber couldn't possibly catch up.

Aaron loped up from his antique store at the far end of town. He offered his arm to aid her down the step into the road. "I didn't see the golf cart in the lot and thought you were already up there. Should I run back and get the ATV?"

"I'm not riding on that menace. I'll be fine. Tullah has the crystal ball. If she can't handle this, I'm sure I can't. Go on and see what you can do."

"Not much except carry bodies out," Aaron said fatalistically, before breaking into a run up the hill to the amphitheater—the wedding chapel to the tourists.

She'd never been athletic, but she was embarrassed that she walked slower than an old lady. She should have had the knee surgery back when she'd hurt it, but escaping Dell and Crystal had been of more importance at the time. And now—it was too late.

She hoped Teddy and Mariah were there. They had strong spirit talents. Teddy had once encountered a particularly violent apparition in her attic—a vengeful murder victim who'd been dead a decade and still had the power to shove men down stairs. Did spirits build up energy over time? Cass inhabited by an angry ghost could do a lot of damage, she suspected.

Harvey lingered in the shadows of the beautiful greenery-lined path Sam had created for brides to use for descending into the amphitheater. Roses spilled over camellias and hawthorns. Floral scents perfumed the air. In his preferred post as guard, Harvey lifted his walking stick in acknowledgment as she limped past.

Val was singing her dirge with unusual urgency. Amber picked up her pace. It was all downhill from here, but the rocky footing was tricky.

Past the shrubbery, she could see the basin spread out below. The Lucys had trapped a shouting Cass in a circle on a rock platform above the vortex. They dodged her fists, swinging in rage.

Amber had never seen the normally serene elder lash out with more than her sharp tongue. Aaron was using his greater size as a shield for whichever person Cass turned on. Cass wheeled to go after pregnant Mariah, who couldn't move fast enough to escape. Aaron dashed past Cass to place himself between them.

This could not be good.

Fee ran down the path carrying bags of heavenly aromas. Small and new to Hillvale, she looked uncertain as she hesitated beside Amber. "I have no idea what she needs, so I brought everything I could think of."

Amber didn't think Cass was in the mood for eating, but maybe the aromas would calm her. She took one of the bags and they headed down the rocky stairs together.

"I'll kill them," Cass shouted as they approached. "They can't do this me! Just let me get my hands on the bastards."

"Who will you kill?" Samantha asked, frowning with worry. Cass was her great-aunt.

Tullah gestured for Fee and Amber to set down the bags and join the circle. She held the crystal ball in one hand and her stick in the other. Amber tried not to cringe. The ball was fragile and hideously expensive.

"I'll kill the scheming lying bastards who did this to me," Cass cried, swinging around to face Amber and Fee. "You!" she shouted, pointing at Amber. "Are you behind this too? Did you wish me dead?"

Amber cringed at the accusation. Instinctively, she sought a hole in the rock to fit her stick, as the others were doing. The earth energy rocked her grip, but she hung on. "I don't know who you are to wish you dead."

"Don't play Miss Innocent with me, Fatty," Cass cried.

The cruel insult from the lips of someone she respected cut through Amber's thick carapace. It squarely struck the shame lurking beneath layers of flesh. The old taunts she'd suffered as a teen returned—and then adult Amber's fury rose up to beat back the old pain. She clenched her fingers.

"The bastard told me he *saw* you."

An icy wind blew through Amber's insides at the accusation—there was only one *him* she might have seen recently. *This wasn't Cass speaking.* She'd attended enough of Cass's séances to recognize that a spirit possessed her. The horror of who that spirit might be overrode shame and anger.

Almost afraid to discover the spirit's identity, Amber attempted a different tactic, addressing the spirit as if she recognized her. "Why would anyone wish you dead? Aren't you worth more alive?"

Cass returned to swinging in restless circles. Spirits didn't always respond logically.

If this one was as new as Amber feared, she was amazed she could respond at all.

"Now," Sam called softly. "Sticks ready, focus on the crystal ball. Val, do your thing."

The energy buzzed up the carved wood of the stick in Amber's hand, harmonized with the crystal in the handle, vibrated with the funeral notes of the Death Goddess's song.

The perfume of roses mixed with the heavenly aromas wafting from Fiona's food. A breeze whirled the dust and leaves inside the circle, grounding the circle in earthly sensation to call Cass's human self. They chanted along with Val. Aaron circled with Cass, staying between her and any target. Tullah held the crystal ball high, letting it catch the sun and shoot rainbows through the clearing, calling the spirit to higher levels.

Amber could see the struggle in Cass's face. Usually unlined and serene, her skin seemed to fall in on itself, wrinkling with effort, hollowing her cheeks.

The fight was hard to watch. Cass had years of experience in dealing with the spirit world. If Amber's surmise was correct, this spirit was new and lost—but strong-willed and furious. The battle had to be painful. Along with the others, she raised her voice so the natural basin filled with the energy of their chant.

Cass leaped for Tullah as if to strangle her. Aaron ducked. The light exploded inside the crystal ball. Rainbows shattered, but the glass held. Tullah staggered. Mariah grabbed her and held her up.

Aaron caught Cass before she collapsed.

~

FINALLY GIVING IN TO EXHAUSTION, JOSH FELL ASLEEP IN THE RECLINER IN HIS suite, with the computer on his lap.

He jarred awake at a racket at his door and the phone on the desk shrieking.

"Mr. Gabriel, Mr. Gabriel, I'm here, tell them to let me in!" High-pitched and frantic, the voice could only belong to one person.

Josh sighed and set aside his laptop. He didn't know if he was ready for this. But Ernest had been Willa's closest companion for years. The guy had every reason to be frantic.

Josh opened the door to find the flashily-dressed assistant surrounded by security guards.

The lodge's business-suited manager was apologetic. "I'm so sorry, Mr. Gabriel. I don't know how he escaped security. We take our guests' privacy very seriously. Reporters have arrived, so we're keeping everyone from this corridor."

"That's why I'm here," Ernest said dramatically, flinging skinny arms clothed in a hideous blue-and-red checked jacket.

Josh didn't have time to dodge when Willa's assistant flung those arms around his shoulders and began to weep. With a sigh, he patted the back of the atrocious jacket and acknowledged the manager and guards. "It's all right. Ernest has been using my suite as an office. He probably has a key and lost it."

Or Willa had taken it away for some reason—to lend to someone else? Despite his tendency toward drama, Ernest was an extremely organized assistant.

"Shall I provide another key?" the manager asked stiffly, eyeing a weeping Ernest with displeasure.

"If you would, please. He'll be useful in handling the reporters. Call and talk to him anytime you have a question." Josh nudged the door closed and pried Ernest off him, dropping him in the nearest chair.

Ernest continued to weep. A flamboyantly gay man of forty-some years with a receding hairline, invisible chin, and sloping shoulders, Ernest had no presence beyond his outrageous clothes. But his mind was a sticky web any spider would take pride in.

With another sigh, Josh found a tissue box and dropped it on the table beside Willa's assistant. "I'm sorry I couldn't break the news personally. I left a message on your voice mail to call me."

Ernest nodded and blew his nose. "I know. I appreciate it. But Willa had told me to go back to LA with Sarah to straighten out some matters with her father. It was too late to do much when we arrived, and then I got the news this morning. . ." He started weeping again.

A dozen questions danced through Josh's mind. He started with the easiest. "Have you talked with the police yet?"

"That's who woke me up!" he said in indignation, grabbing another tissue. "They called and asked me where I was and demanded I give them my entire itinerary. Can they do that?"

"Yes, they can, and you should tell them the truth if we want to find out who did this. I couldn't tell them anything. Willa just told me she had to leave. She didn't say who she was with. I thought she was with you." Josh paced, trying to figure out who else among the party she might have traveled with, but as far as he was aware, everyone had their own cars except Ernest.

"I thought she was staying with you! That's what I told the police. She sent *me* back to LA to deal with her father. She didn't need to go herself!"

"She also sent Sarah, you said," Josh pointed out. "Willa never goes anywhere without one of you. Went," he corrected, still grappling with Willa's absence. "She must have been planning on following you. Who was she with?"

"She and Tessa were talking with Brad and the wedding planner when we left. We thought one of them would take her back to the lodge." Ernest sent a peeved look at the ringing telephone. "I told the desk to forward all calls to the other room."

Josh ignored the phone. "Brad was still here this morning. Did you give the planner's number to the cops? And Tessa's? I don't have them in my contact list."

Instead of answering, Ernest leaped from his seat to grab the shrieking phone. "Yes?" he answered in a drawl of disdain.

Ernest could be anyone he wished—as long as no one saw him.

After disposing of whoever was on the other end of the line, Ernest returned to the question at hand. "I gave them a list of everyone who accompanied us. If I may use the fold-out sofa in the office, I'll stay here and handle the reporters You can deal with officialdom. The cops make me vaporish."

Everything made Ernest vaporish, except Willa. Josh had never understood their symbiotic relationship, but he appreciated her assistant's organizational skills. "The reporters are all yours. You'll have to know that Ginger lives up here. Once they realize that, they'll be out of their minds in search of a scandal that doesn't exist."

"Ginger?" Ernest lit up like a chandelier. "I adored Ginger! Can I meet her?"

"You were too old to have watched Ginger and Jack. And the Ginger on the show is not the real person, whose name is Amber. If she calls, put her straight through to me. I've invited her here for dinner, so you can meet her then."

"Oops," Ernest said, covering his mouth.

Josh spun on his heel to glare at the man. "What?"

"That was Amber on the phone. I told her you were too busy and asked for a message. Her reply was not sensible."

Josh closed his eyes and tried to imagine how Amber would respond, but he didn't know her well enough these days. "What did she say?"

"It was just mumbo-jumbo about spirits and crystal balls and talking to Willa. I thought she was selling something." Ernest looked anxious. "That was *Ginger*?"

"That was Amber. And if she thinks she's talking to Willa, we need to listen. Call her back, *now*."

EIGHT

Amber put down the receiver and tried to determine who she'd just talked to. It hadn't been Josh. Had he brought in help to keep her away? That didn't seem likely. But she didn't know how to bypass the gatekeeper to reach him—just like the bad old days when Dell and Crystal had tried to keep them apart. They'd resorted to using sign language on the set and laundry carts in hotels.

Amber glared at the black velvet concealing the crystal ball on its pedestal. Uncovered, the crystal swirled with angry colors, and Amber was afraid to touch it, but Tullah had insisted that the ball be kept away from Cass. After covering the crystal, all Amber had known to do with it was tuck it on a shelf in her back room.

Her phone rang and the lodge's number appeared. Preparing herself to speak with the officious jerk who'd taken her message, she was relieved to hear Josh instead.

"Sorry about that," he said almost breathlessly. "Ernest is Willa's assistant. He didn't recognize you. That won't happen again. Are you coming up for dinner? The bathing suit won't be delivered until tomorrow, but you're beautiful in anything."

"You haven't forgotten your acting skills," she said dryly, trying not to imagine a busy Josh hunting for a bathing suit for *her*. What size had he chosen? She had more important things on her mind though, and she hesitated, looking for words that wouldn't sound insane. "Maybe you should come here for dinner. I have something I want to show you, and I don't know if it travels well. We've never dealt with anything quite like this before."

"Show me? Okay," he sounded doubtful. "Reporters are roaming. Any suggestions for avoiding them?"

She carried her cordless receiver to the big front window and studied the parking lot. "I'm not seeing a lot of cars here yet. It's hard to tell a reporter from a tourist though. I could entertain you with suggestions about laundry vans, but no matter what you ride in, you'll be visible as you enter the shop. You need a disguise."

"Hiding in laundry, just like old times!" He sounded pleased. "I can do laundry, but a delivery truck might make more sense. I'll wear a uniform and hat and no one will notice."

"Except the driver, who will presumably be wearing your clothes, but that works. I'll ask Dinah for take-out, and I'll shut the shop after you arrive. We might need to call on Tullah or Mariah after dinner. I think that has to be up to you."

"And then it will be late, and we can have someone drive us back here and we can swim," he said in satisfaction. "We can both use the workout after today. We can compare notes over dinner and plan our next steps for tomorrow."

Next steps? But he'd hung up, leaving Amber to wonder what he meant.

Although—if that was Willa's spirit they'd captured in the crystal ball—planning their next steps could take some interesting paths. She shivered and returned to the front room rather than imagine an angry Willa whirling in her crystal.

A flurry of customers—one of whom was probably a reporter—prevented her from closing early to go home and change. Apparently the wrong age to have watched Jack and Ginger, the reporter left without recognizing her. The actual customers purchased tarot cards and walking sticks and left chattering happily, unaware of the tragedy hanging over the town.

Dinah was the chef at the restaurant next to the café. Amber called and asked if it was possible to have something delivered. She had never imposed on the cook before. Dinah simply accepted that it was of importance and agreed to send one of the staff across the street with muffulettas and gumbo. Creole cooking in California was such a rarity, that Dinah had a strong customer base only six months after she'd opened Delphines.

On her own, Amber would just have had salad, but dinner with Josh was a special occasion deserving indulgence.

She only kept a few plates and utensils in the shop for her lunches. They'd have to do. She wasn't carrying that crystal ball up to her house. Refusing to fuss over her looks, she just brushed out her hair, donned a pale lipstick, set the table, and watched the delivery truck pull up outside.

Dressed in a brown uniform, Josh strode in carrying a familiar brown box—one of her normal deliveries. He was wearing shorts and sandals, and she realized she'd not really seen much of him last night in the dark pool. He was tanned and muscular, and she even adored his masculine toes. Damn, she really didn't need this.

The delivery truck pulled off without him. She locked the door and put up the CLOSED sign, then gasped when Josh grabbed her by the waist and hauled her into his arms.

She almost fainted in shock. *Men did not touch her. . .* She instinctively shoved at him.

Instead of letting go, he squeezed her in a hug that left her breathless and almost terrified. He was so damned strong. . .

"Damn, I needed you around today!" he declared, releasing her to prowl her shop.

Heart pounding faster than it should, Amber retreated to the counter. "Sorry I couldn't be there," she replied, drifting to that safe place in her head that slowed her pulse.

He looked so damned good. . . Josh's sharp cheekbones weren't classically handsome, but his features were mobile and expressive and so full of life that it was impossible not to be drawn to him. And watching him wasn't conducive to finding her mellow.

"What did you want to show me?" he asked, stopping his prowling.

Deep breaths, Amber, you can do this. "I don't know how to explain. It's in back." She pulled aside the beads and gauzy curtain to her private tea room where she'd set up a table for their use.

He stepped into the room she'd lit with candles. He filled her feminine hideaway with raw testosterone that increased her nervousness, but this was Josh. She was safe with him. *Breathe deeply, count to one hundred. . .*

He glanced around at the candles and shadowy ambiance. His wide shoulders brushed the beaded drapery. "Nice. Is this where you hit me over the head and stuff my body under the floorboards?"

That was so much the Josh she remembered, poking fun at her with his movie references, that she instantly calmed down. "I'm not Sweeney Todd. It's either candles or that swinging bulb up there." She pointed at the bare bulb hanging over the table. "My customers prefer candles."

With the polished ease of a professional performer, he leaned his shoulder against the wall, crossed his muscled arms, and exuded movie star sexuality. The boy was all grown up. He raised his eyebrows and waited.

Swallowing hard, keeping her hands steady, Amber uncovered the crystal ball. It seethed with gray mists instead of the color of earlier. Mariah had thought the mists might solidify into ectoplasm, but she refused to touch it and endanger her unborn child.

"That's the pricey crystal that was sitting out front yesterday?" he asked in surprise. "What's got into it?"

"This. . ." Amber gestured, unable to come up with the right word. "Whatever you see in this ball. . . was driving Cass insane earlier today. She ranted and raved and wanted to kill whoever had done this to her."

Josh drew his expressive brow down in a frown. "More explanation, please."

Amber gestured at the table. "Sit. Dinah sent a nice wine. I think we'll both need it. Maybe we should eat first. Tell me about your assistant."

He glared suspiciously at the swirling crystal ball. Apparently willing to be distracted, he took a seat and began opening food boxes. "Ernest is a drama queen, rather literally. But he's smart and efficient and he's dealing with reporters and Willa's staff and whatever other matters are piling up. I apologize again. He's a fan of yours, but he didn't recognize your name."

"He knows about me?" she asked anxiously.

"He can keep a confidence. I'm fairly certain that he'll go to his grave carrying any secrets Willa entrusted to him. That's not necessarily convenient if he knew who she was with yesterday and promised not to tell."

"Even if that person may have murdered her?" Amber asked, appalled.

"He would need proof because Willa could do no wrong in his eyes. He doted on her." Josh stirred his gumbo and glanced at the crystal ball again.

"Awkward. Do you think she may have been seeing someone else?" Amber savored the gumbo.

Josh contemplated that as if it were a math equation and not an emotional grenade. "I don't know how she'd find time, to be honest. I won't claim Willa meant to be faithful, but we were in business meetings night and day. We barely had time to see each other privately. Our communication was mostly unending texts. Unless she was screwing someone while texting, I'm guessing she didn't have anyone else on the side."

"Interesting relationship."

He shrugged. "We'd known each other for years, worked together, understood each other. I guess that made us friends. That's the most anyone can ask in the hothouse atmosphere of Hollywood."

Amber peeled some meat off her muffuletta but didn't feel like indulging enough to eat bread. "Did you tell Willa you met me up here?"

"Of course. She was thrilled and meant to use it in publicity. Why?"

She winced and was almost glad Willa was no longer in charge of his publicity. She did not want to be anyone's puff piece. It was her turn to glance at the whirling mist. "Because whatever inhabited Cass today spoke directly to me. It said *He told me he saw you.* I don't know who else but Willa might say that. Then the voice asked if I wanted her dead and called me Fatty. Did Willa by any chance speak like that?"

Setting down the camera he'd been using to catch a few photos, Josh stared at her through the candle flame. "Whatever *inhabited* Cass?"

Here was where she threw away any chance of resuming their friendship.

JOSH KNEW AMBER HAD ALWAYS HAD A FLAIR FOR THE DRAMATIC. SHE'D SET a mood with the candles, wine, and Creole dishes that had him relaxed enough to admire her fairy queen looks and forget the outside world. He loved the red-gold of her long wavy hair far better than the spiky blonde she'd sported as a kid. He'd had to capture the image on film, hoping he could replicate it in his production.

She wore a gauzy scarf over her generous breasts tonight, but that didn't prevent him from remembering how they'd once felt in his hands, or how her swim-muscled legs had felt around his hips. She'd been his first sexual experience, and that was permanently engraved on his brain.

It was probably a damned good thing she didn't watch his shows. The love scenes occasionally veered a little too close to that encounter, probably because the films were made for adolescents, and despite the awkwardness, their lovemaking was his only good adolescent memory.

He studied the weird foggy crystal. The swirling mist intrigued his curiosity. Even as he watched, reds and purples began to pulsate, almost appearing angry, which was ridiculous. He was simply having difficulty translating what Amber was telling him.

"Cass is a medium," she patiently explained. "Among other things, not all of which I understand. But she connects with spirits from beyond the veil."

"Like the spiritualists you told me about. The dead come to her and tell her their secrets and everyone sits around holding hands and lighting candles." He glanced at the candles, then back to the crystal ball. "Aren't crystal balls for Gypsies?"

"Crystal has many purposes, as you'll learn if you stay here for long. Fake psychics pretend to read the future in crystal balls, but foreseeing is fraught with complications. Like holding hands, though, crystal can channel energy. Candles allow us to focus too. Speaking to the dead is not magic. The vortex is like a hole between the living and the spirit world. There are limitations." She pushed her spoon around in her gumbo, looking troubled.

Josh wanted to reassure her, but he wasn't sure of what. "What kind of limitations?" He snapped a photo of his food to send to Instagram.

She gestured with a soft white hand bedecked in rings. "Our perception, of course. Not everyone who dies is interested in returning to this plane and dumping their grief on their loved ones. They happily move on to the next plane without a trace. The spirits most accessible to our mediums seem to have earthly connections with Hillvale. Cass has a chatty miner willing to hunt around in the afterlife for spirits who might answer our questions, for instance. But like everything else Lucys do, nothing is cut and dried. We have no routine."

"You almost make it sound feasible," he said, biting into his spicy sandwich to keep from saying anything he shouldn't.

"Not really. The newly dead generally aren't available. We guess that they're too confused by the transition. The ones who have been dead a long time tend to fade out. A séance is an interesting experience but seldom practical. We sort of talked to Walker's father once, but he'd been gone for a long time and couldn't tell us who murdered him."

"You honestly believe you talked to Walker's dead father?" Josh used his wine to wash down the sandwich, pondering that. "You are occasionally spookily correct with the cards, but I always thought that was good guessing. Talking to the dead. . . I'm having difficulty with that one."

She sighed. "Then maybe I shouldn't tell you more. I just thought you should be warned in case that really is Willa's spirit in there."

"*Willa's* spirit?" Josh stared at the whirling glass, appalled. He scrambled to recollect what Amber had been telling him. *Whatever inhabited Cass today said he told me he saw you, then asked if I wanted her dead, and called me Fatty.*

Not computing. But Willa's voice echoed in those words. He shoved away from the table, feeling a little sick.

"It's okay, Josh. I guess sometimes we *should* keep secrets from each other. I won't bother you with this again." She pushed away from the table too.

Rebelling against that notion, he grabbed the bottle of wine and refilled their glasses. "No, don't keep secrets. Let me process. You've had years to deal with this place. I've only had a few days. You're telling me this Cass—she's the one who was supposed to conduct the marriage ceremony, right?"

Amber nodded, watching him warily. Josh mentally built up the script. "Cass got something in her head and started speaking like Willa?"

Amber wrinkled her nose and thought about it. "Close, except we don't really know how Willa speaks. That's why I asked you."

He took a deep gulp of a very palatable red. "Willa was not a politically correct person. She said whatever it took to get what she wanted, and she believed vinegar worked better than honey."

"I don't think I would have liked her very much," Amber admitted sadly, glancing at the crystal ball.

Josh shrugged. "No one did, except her father, and she was at constant war with him too. I *understood* her. That didn't mean I actually *liked* her. I admired her. She was abrasive, but man, she was successful. So I couldn't argue with her tactics—until she was deliberately mean, which she could be. She once fired a stagehand who stumbled over a prop. She called him Fatty and told him if he couldn't see his own feet, he had no business on her set."

Amber glanced down at her toes. So did Josh. She wore sparkly sandals and had painted her toenails to match—with sparkly gold polish. He had a ridiculous urge to kiss them, especially after he noticed her ankle bracelet. Even her legs were curvaceous. She was essentially telling him she believed in craziness, and he still lusted after her. His head was in a strange place.

"Willa was probably right," Amber said, interrupting his distraction. "I'm prone to tripping over anything that hides beneath my skirts. It's a liability issue for an employer. Rude to mention it, of course, but from the way you've described her, practical."

"And this spirit thing called you *Fatty*?" He eyed the whirling colors, trying to imagine it talking.

"Cass was talking to me in a voice not her own when she said it, yes. You told Willa that you'd found me?"

Josh nodded absent-mindedly. "I don't know where she was calling from. I told her I'd just met you and wanted her to meet you at dinner. That's when she told me she wouldn't be back, she had to head to LA."

"And that was the last anyone heard from her?" Amber asked, not concealing her horror.

"It's like a time warp, isn't it?" Josh mused. "You leave me, my past ends, and I start anew. You return, and my new life disappears. It's as if a magic genie is toying with us."

"Or a bad screenwriter."

They both stared at the whirling mist.

NINE

AMBER CALLED TULLAH AND ASKED IF SHE'D BE INTERESTED IN TRYING TO contact the spirit trapped in the crystal ball. The thrift store owner flat out refused.

"Cass is practically comatose," Tullah declared. "I'm not letting that evil *vodun* inside my head. And you'd best not let Mariah near it either."

"We can't leave a spirit *trapped*," Amber protested. "We need to talk with her if it's Willa. We *owe* her that."

"We don't owe her no such thing. That was one angry bitch. Find her killer, put him in a cell with her, and then we'll try something." Tullah hung up.

Amber glanced apologetically at Josh, who was staring enrapt at the crystal ball. "I'm sorry. The Lucys are pretty shaken. Cass means a lot to us, and if she can be controlled by whatever's in that crystal, it's pretty risky for everyone else. We'll have to find another way of solving the crime."

She'd wanted to be helpful. She'd fallen flat. She waited for the inevitable dismissal. It wasn't as if she had much to offer anyone, especially not a man who had the world at his fingertips once he recovered from shock.

"Your friends are probably right," Josh said with a shrug. "I'm trying to imagine Willa in the afterlife, raging against her killer, and it's not pretty. There would be a lot of damage. I have a quick temper. Willa's was phenomenal."

Amber blinked, trying to register what had just happened here. She'd told him his fiancée might be trapped in a crystal ball, that Willa was too evil to contact, that Amber couldn't help him after all, and he *shrugged*?

"Like Jacko, you'll just find another ball?" she asked, skeptical enough to reference the character in their old show.

He quirked one eyebrow—a trick he'd practiced to send his teen fans swooning. "I don't think Ginger can fix this one, okay? I'm a big boy now. I'm on my own." He turned back to the table and poked in the dessert carton. "There's only one slice of pie."

She wanted to slap him upside the head and ask where he kept his brains, but it wasn't the pie she was thinking about. What the hell kind of relationship had he and Willa had?

He was telling her it was no longer her business. Great. Swell. "Dinah knows I don't eat sugar. I don't have coffee either. Would you like tea?" She started to get up.

He waved her back down. "The wine is fine. You should have some of this pie, it's incredible."

Her mouth no longer watered when she looked at sweets. It had taken years before she'd admitted she had a problem. It had taken a while to wean herself off sugar and now was no time to relapse, not when she was half way to her next ring. "I'm a sugar addict, and I don't want to be a diabetic. So please do not tempt me."

He grimaced and accepted this without argument. "No messing with diabetes, got it, sorry. I know better. My mom and aunt fight to keep their sugar down too."

Most of his family had been large, what Hollywood had called Midwestern Obese—because they'd scraped by on cheap canned food. Back then, Amber had been skinny in comparison to his family, as he had been. They'd weirdly bonded over body size or lack thereof. So much she had forgotten—or tried to forget.

He closed up his pie rather eat it in front of her. "If we can't get psychic help, where do we go from here?"

Rendered speechless that he not only didn't argue about her eating habits, but hadn't given up on her help, even after she'd displayed her ineffectiveness, Amber simply shook her head. Words like *Where have you been all my life?* were senseless. She had been the one to leave him behind. And he wouldn't have stayed around long anyway. He had a real life, one he needed to return to.

She needed to do all she could to send him there before she hurt herself.

Josh threw the black velvet back over the crystal. "Let's try the old-fashioned way of sorting through clues. I get it that it's bad for us to be seen together. Is there some way you can come up to my room, out of sight? We can have Ernest make notes and do searches while we brainstorm. If I try to do it myself, I'll sink into my work to avoid thinking. I need outside stimulation, if that makes sense."

He'd always been that way—creative but unfocused unless given structure. She desperately wanted to send Josh back where he belonged, so she stupidly nodded. "I'll borrow Val's golf cart and come up later. How were you planning on returning to the lodge without being seen?"

"Do you think anyone will recognize me in this outfit?" he asked, with a gesture of self-deprecation at the unflattering drab brown uniform. "I'll just jog up. After this dinner, I'll need the exercise." He stood and pressed a kiss to her hair. "It's a rough way of finding you again, but I'm glad I did."

Paralyzed by that casual touch, Amber stayed where she was until he left, taking his pie with him. Then she wiped away a tear, collected herself, and cleared away dinner remains. She didn't indulge in what-might-have-been anymore. She'd had a decision forced on her at sixteen that had spun her life around. Leaving had been necessary for her mental and physical well-being. She'd been a mess and hadn't coped as well as she should have, but she'd survived.

Only seeing Josh made her feel as if she'd been in stasis for years. The first years of licking her wounds had been understandable. No matter how mature she'd been, it hadn't been easy for a kid to start life on her own. She'd taken comfort and security where she could—mostly in the food she'd been denied for so long. But once she'd stabilized, she should have tried to shake off her protective cocoon.

So here was her chance. She had to think about her nephew. She had to put herself back out there for Zeke, if nothing else. Josh had useful contacts. He might even get her the voice-overs that would allow her to continue living here. He was offering an opportunity to brush up against his world, maybe reestablish a few connections, even if just the possibility of seeing Dell or his ilk again nauseated her.

She called Mariah, the computer research expert, and verified that she would be available if needed. Mariah might be pregnant and nesting, but she loved puzzles and liked nothing better than bringing down bad men. Amber hadn't doubted her cooperation for a minute.

She loved having friends she could rely on, but this wasn't a problem the Lucys could easily solve. Maybe in a day or two, after Cass had time to recover, she might have a safe solution for speaking with the spirit in the ball—before it broke out and became a poltergeist terrorizing the whole town.

~

"HAVE YOU CALLED EVERY INVESTOR ON WILLA'S LIST?" JOSH ASKED ERNEST. "We still have a blockbuster script and cast and too many people relying on us to let the ball drop now."

Ernest nodded and scrolled through his computer notepad. "I've left messages everywhere. I think they're all waiting to see what Ivan will do. He only gave Willa his smallest production company, the one not worth his time. She was the powerhouse driving it."

Josh knew that. He growled and returned to pacing. He'd discarded the delivery uniform for his preferred one of jeans and t-shirt. "And I make a lousy powerhouse, I know. What about Tessa? Willa wouldn't have made her VP if she didn't expect Tess to hold up her end of the game."

Ernest wrinkled his bony nose. "Willa chose Tess because the spineless wimp did whatever Willa told her to do. I haven't been able to reach her. She left about the same time we did yesterday. Any real corporate officer would be breathing down my neck right now."

Damn. Ernest was a perceptive drip. At least he was honest about Willa's flaws.

The phone rang and Ernest grabbed it, then handed it to Josh. "Brad, about those shots he took of the wedding venue."

Brad worked for Ivan as well as Willa. Josh grabbed the receiver. "Send them to me along with the invoice. Have you talked to Ivan? How's he taking the news?"

Brad's laconic drawl never expressed emotion. "Not heard from him. Hope you'll keep me in mind for your next production." He hung up.

Josh scowled. Brad had the personality of a gorilla but he was a damned good photographer. Not hearing from Ivan couldn't be good.

"Since Willa's company is bound to go back to her father, Tessa is probably hiding out until Ivan tells her what to do. In which case, we'll never get our funding. Shit." Josh stared out the suite's bay window overlooking a mountain that was just returning to life from what must have been a serious fire.

He couldn't even be allowed to grieve the woman he'd intended to marry, not if he was to keep her dream alive.

Whatever inhabited Cass today asked if I wanted her dead and called me Fatty.

That sounded just like Willa. Amber had said the ghost asked if Amber *wanted her dead.* In his over-imaginative mind, that sounded as if Amber's crystal ball spirit didn't know who'd killed her. Was that possible? Of course not.

The phone rang and Ernest grabbed it. From the way he gushed, Josh assumed Amber was on the other end. Before he could cross the room, his new assistant was sporting an expression of ecstasy and had hung up.

"She's leaving her house and will be here in ten minutes. I told her the coast was currently clear and that I'd meet her at the security gate and bring her back." Ernest was already preening in the mirror over the fireplace.

Josh checked his watch. The pool wouldn't close for over an hour. He'd have to share her with Ernest until then. "I can meet her."

"Don't be silly. The risk of a reporter seeing the two of you together isn't worth it. I'll wear a ball cap and no one will look twice at me." He sashayed into his office bedroom, presumably to spruce up.

Since Ernest was wearing checked shorts and a shirt with flamingos on it, Josh was pretty certain it was impossible *not* to notice him. But reporters had no reason to be interested in Ernest—yet.

After his new assistant left, Josh stared into his own mirror and wished he'd taken time to shave. He looked like the monster from the black lagoon. He wet a comb and ran product in his hair to push rebellious strands off his face, but it was too late to do much else.

He could hear them coming down the corridor. Ernest spoke in a hushed, excited tone, and Amber sounded amused. Had anyone been staying in the suite across from them, they probably wouldn't notice, but if voices carried that well—maybe he should rent the other suite too. He'd stick the bill to the production company Ivan would be inheriting.

Josh opened the door. Amber had changed into the floaty caftan she'd worn last night, stacked up her hair, and removed all her glittery jewelry. He hoped that meant she would swim with him later. He needed the exercise to clear his head, but the voluptuous mermaid in black underwear had jump-started his libido. Amber hadn't been small when they'd swum together as teens, but the studio had put her through such vigorous exercise and diet programs that she'd never had much in the way of curves either. That had changed for the better. He snapped more pictures when she entered, capturing the glow of her translucent skin.

"Mariah is ready and waiting to hack whatever we need," she announced, dropping her big bag on the floor. "She sent me the police files, for what little they're worth at this point." She removed her phone and held it up. "What email do you want them sent to?"

"Hack? She *hacked* police files?" Josh asked in astonishment as Ernest took the phone and sent the file to their computers.

"I warned you. We're a little unorthodox up here." She settled into the sofa and began reading the file aloud, as if it were a script they were practicing.

"No autopsy yet," Ernest reported from his device while Josh read on his phone email. "But they're saying the body was carried to that canyon."

"No time of death yet," Amber added, seeing the same report. "Peculiar."

This was larger-than-life *Willa* they were talking about. Josh couldn't keep reading. He paced up and down and tried to imagine her last moments, but he didn't even know where she'd died.

"Bruises, abrasions, possibly from before and after death. She fell, died, and then was hauled elsewhere and thrown down that cliff?" Ernest asked.

Unable to partake in ghoulish speculation, Josh poured drinks from the bar's limited selection.

Amber had grown silent. She looked troubled when he handed her a glass of Prosecco. "Since her spirit is so strong and so easily accessed at the vortex, is there any chance she died there? There are some pretty rough drop-offs if she wandered off the marked paths."

"Why take her elsewhere?" Josh finally asked. In his films, he liked details nailed down. In real life, they weren't that easy to come by.

"You said she had a crew up there taking photographs. Maybe the killer was worried her crew would come back and find her body? And he needed time to get away." Amber set her glass down without drinking from it.

"We'd mostly left by mid-afternoon," Ernest said. "She sent us all away, said she needed to take a few more shots. I thought maybe she meant to practice walking down those steps in heels, and she didn't want anyone watching."

"That sounds exactly like something she would do," Josh agreed, rubbing the cool glass against his forehead. "She was a perfectionist. She wouldn't have missed a chance to rehearse with no one watching."

"Or she could have been meeting someone and didn't want any of you to know," Amber added in a thoughtful tone.

"How did she call me?" Josh asked, brushing aside Willa's potential infidelity. "There's no cell service. I left her before one. She called me here around three-thirty. Ernest, what time did she send you back to LA?"

"Mid-afternoon, three-ish maybe?" He put down his notebook computer and picked up his phone. "She was alive and well when she met us at Brad's van in the parking lot and told Sarah, Tessa, and me to go back to LA. My cell service returned when we were halfway down the mountain. Looks like I started making calls around 3:30."

"Did you resolve her father's problem?" Josh asked, returning to pacing in hopes of keeping his thoughts focused.

"We couldn't reach him. I left messages at his office and home. Sarah called around to his usual hang-outs. We decided he didn't want to talk to us and was forcing Willa to call him, so we gave up."

"If you and Sarah can prove you were in LA, that leaves you out as suspects. Willa was alive after you left when she called me." Not that there was much chance of Ernest or Sarah harming Willa, Josh knew. They both idolized her, and she was their only source of income and housing. They lived in her mansion and would be out on the streets with her death.

Brad, the photographer, had still been here the next morning. Ernest had said Tessa left at the same time as the wedding planner, but either of them could have turned around, except they had no good reason to harm Willa. Again, she was a source of income for all concerned.

Ernest shrugged. "Sarah and I are witnesses for each other, and can't they track our phone calls and see where we were?"

Josh refilled his glass and leaned against the bar, watching Amber slowly punch text into her phone. She must have the hotel's wi-fi already in her system. Since it was the only place in town to meet people, that made sense.

"I sent a group email. Aaron says Willa made a call from his antique store," she finally said. "She was looking for props and asked to use his landline. He didn't pay much attention to the conversation, but it was about three-thirty, when he likes to take a coffee break, and there was no one with her."

"I left Willa at the vortex around one. Ernest saw her around three. And at three-thirty, then, she was still in Hillvale. She must have had her bags packed before we even left to explore the town. I didn't notice they were gone." Josh rubbed his head and looked for a clock. The damned pool wasn't closed yet. He needed that workout to release the tension and keep his head functioning.

Amber was scribbling what appeared to be a timeline on one of the lodge's notepads. "Where was Willa between the time you left her at one, and she talked to Ernest at three? Josh, where did you go after you left my place?"

"I bought a smoothie at the café, cruised the boardwalk looking for entertainment for our guests, wandered in the antique and thrift stores because they looked funky, and returned to the lodge around three. I didn't see Willa in any of those places. I don't have any record of my return, unless the hotel phone system does. I made a few business calls when I got back here." Josh tried to run that day through his overloaded brain. "She drove into town with me after brunch, so her car should have still been at the lodge, but I can't say I noticed. I expected her to return with her crew. I didn't know she'd sent everyone away."

"Ernest, you said you weren't with her between one and three?" Amber diligently noted her timeline.

"No. Willa and Josh had eaten but the staff hadn't. So we left Willa and Josh at the venue after Brad had his photos. We walked down for lunch and to talk to the restaurant about the reception. Did the police find her car?" Ernest stared at his computer and looked bereft.

"Write all this down," Josh told him, feeling sorry for the man. Both their futures were uncertain, but Ernest didn't have a house to sell to prevent starvation.

While Josh scrolled through the police report in search of anything about the car, Amber continued to tick off her timeline. "So Willa could have walked up to the lodge between the time Josh left her and before he returned, got her car and bags, drove to the parking lot, and told everyone to go home. Half an hour later, she called Josh from the antique store. Time gaps there." She began texting again.

"No mention of her car in the police report," Josh reported. "Willa might have returned to the amphitheater for more photos in a different light. She wouldn't need her car for that. It's an easy hike."

"Our police chief installed a security camera on the new parking lot lamppost after it got wrecked a few months back. I'm betting he's checked the video. I'll send him our timeline to see if he'll be nice and tell us anything. It's a public camera and I'm a shop owner. I should be entitled to see what was on it."

Josh dropped his laptop in her lap. "It will be easier to type with this than with a phone. I'm amazed you can even text on that thing. It has to be a thousand years old."

She shot him a scathing look that woke every cell in his body. He loved tangling with Amber. Like the character she'd played, she'd always had the confidence and spunk to shoot him down with a look.

"Why would I need to upgrade a phone in a town with no cell tower?" she asked. But she took the laptop and began typing.

He was a director. He liked organizing and choreographing and getting results. But working without a script meant using both the creative and organizational sides of his brain at once, and he thought it might explode. He punched in a contact on his list and listened to the phone ring on the other end. Willa's father still wasn't answering.

Ivan was healthy as a horse and had a houseful of servants, so it was out of pure maliciousness that he called the cops and asked them to do a welfare check on the old man. Maybe the housekeeper had killed him, who knew?

The minute he set down his receiver, the other landline rang. Ernest grabbed it. He grimaced as the caller spoke. "Tell them Mr. Gabriel is grieving. There will be no press conferences tonight." He rolled his eyes and stared at the ceiling. "No comment. Nope, no comment on anything. Do you seriously expect me to ask Mr. Gabriel about business matters at a time like this?" He slammed down the receiver.

Josh didn't even bother looking up from the wine he was pouring. He couldn't think about business while imagining Willa lying on a flat slab in a coroner's office. His stomach rebelled.

"*Tinseltown Today* asking if your project is still a go," Ernest announced, unnecessarily. "Which probably means they can't reach Ivan either."

He'd wonder if someone had killed Ivan too, except he knew the tactic well. Ivan was hiding from the press, although for what reason could only be surmised.

"Incoming video," Amber announced without inflection, setting the laptop on the long dining table. "Hours of watching cars come and go. Who wants to do the honors?"

TEN

MUSCLES ACHING AFTER THREE LAPS IN THE POOL LAST NIGHT, AMBER dusted her inventory in hopes of working out the kinks.

Josh had kept the pool lights dim again. He'd been so preoccupied that she hadn't even felt out of place in her unorthodox swimwear. There hadn't been any long talks or uncomfortable touching. He'd attacked the water as if it had been Willa's killer. He didn't really need her to keep him going.

She needed to be good with that. He was just using her as a sounding board, as he'd once done. She was using him in hopes of connections that would ease her foot back into the industry for Zeke's sake.

She'd hoped he'd call and let her know what Ernest had found on the security video last night, but she couldn't remember if he had her home phone. So she'd opened up the shop early to wait for his call. She supposed she could sit down and do this week's bookkeeping, but she was too restless.

Fee from the café arrived bearing scrumptious-smelling goodies. The little cook didn't look as if food ever passed her lips, but she smiled a lot more now that she'd hooked up with the town mayor. Her eyes danced as she set the box on Amber's counter. "These are healthier than they smell. Feed some to that movie star. He needs a little spice in his life. And there are at least two reporters sitting at the counter right now. We're all playing ignorant—*Don't know Willa. Never saw her. So sorry and we've booked another wedding in that slot already.*"

"Have we really?" Amber opened the box and studied what appeared to be health food bars.

"We have. Not exactly a celebrity wedding, but Teddy called names on the waiting list and one jumped right on it. June wedding venues are pretty much booked everywhere, and we're informal enough that they don't have to do a lot of planning. How's your movie star doing?"

"He's a director, not an actor anymore. He's coping, but that's all I can say. Thanks for these and the warning. I can play dumb without blinking." Amber broke off a piece of the bar and savored it. "It's not sweet!"

"Just smells good, told you." Fee waved and departed, jogging across the street to her busy café.

Realizing she was avoiding the back room and the crystal ball, Amber steeled herself, picked up the box, and marched it back to her tea table. Finding a paper napkin, she broke off a small bite, set it on the shelf with the ball, and removed the velvet cover. "Spice," she told the whirling gray. "Try it, you'll like it."

And then she lay out a tarot spread for the whirling mist, even knowing it was nuts. No one deserved a violent death or to be trapped in crystal. If that was Willa in there, Amber offered her some respect, even though there was one chance in hell that a spirit could communicate with cards.

The phone rang and she answered it from her desk.

"Aunt Amber?" Zeke's voice sounded scared and weak. "Can you come get me?"

Pulse accelerating, she went on instant alert. "Where are you? What happened?"

"I'm at the bus station in Monterey. That's all I could afford."

He'd been riding a bus all night? Holy crap. "Are you hurt? Are you okay? Where's Granny?" Trembling in over-reaction, Amber made a mental list of locals with cars.

"I don't know where she is. She took me to some guy's house. They were talking money and big deals and it sounded wrong, so I just walked out. I had my ATM card," he said proudly. "So I hiked down to the bank and emptied my account."

"Okay, that was very smart of you to have an account." Equally smart to persuade Crystal to sign for it. "It will take a few hours for me to reach you. Is there someplace nearby where you'll feel safe? A library maybe?"

"There's stores all over. I saw a Costco as we drove up. I can pretend I'm with someone and walk in with them. I've done it before. And maybe I have enough to buy a hot dog. Then I can be sitting at the tables when you get here."

"I don't think they're open yet," she fretted, thinking aloud. "And you may need a card to buy a hot dog, but if there are stores around, that's a start. I'll call you once I'm on the road and cell service kicks in. You may not be able to reach me for the next hour, so make sure you're good and safe, okay? Is your phone charged up?"

He went silent for a moment, giving her time for two heart attacks.

"Not so much," he admitted. "I'll get off now and turn it off for an hour."

Amber swore every curse word she'd ever heard as the line went dead.

She called Walker. He was already down the mountain, talking to the sheriff's office. She called Sam, but no one answered. Tullah didn't have a car. Cass might, but she shouldn't be driving. Mariah probably shouldn't be driving either, and Keegan would be at the mine. *Teddy*.

She called the jewelry shop. "Do you have anyone who can mind your shop for a few hours? I wouldn't ask, but it's a bit of an emergency."

"What's wrong?" Teddy demanded. In the background, voices grew insistent.

"It's my nephew. I think he's run away. He's down in Monterey by himself. He's safe, for now, if my mother hasn't called the cops to look for him." Amber looked at her own empty shop and realized just because she wasn't busy, that didn't mean Teddy wasn't. Jewelry store, June weddings, rings. . .

"Kurt and Monty are on their way into the city. Let me see if they can turn around. I'll call you. . ."

"No, wait, I'll call Aaron. You sound busy."

"It's a bit crazy. And my sister and her kids are on the way up. But we can't leave your nephew stranded. Call me back and let me know what's happening."

Amber had never had a car or learned to drive. When she'd been old enough to buy one, she didn't have enough money left or anyone to teach her. She still didn't have the funds. Josh was right. Tarot reading wasn't much of a business plan. But she'd been happy, until now.

She hadn't thought Dell would return to haunt her. She'd told herself that other kids had real parents who made informed decisions about using their child prodigies—parents who watched over those kids so nothing happened. Most of the time, nothing did happen. But Crystal had never made any attempt to be a real parent. Amber kicked herself ten times over for not realizing her mother might exploit whiz-smart *Zeke*.

She reached Aaron, who said he could drive her, but he'd have to wake Harvey to cover the store. Since Harvey was a night owl who had probably only just gone to bed, Amber took a deep breath and tried to stay calm. "Let me make one more call before you wake him, okay?"

Gathering her courage, she called the lodge, identified herself, and asked for Josh. Ernest answered, but this time, he passed her immediately to his employer.

"Amber? What's happening?" He sounded concerned.

"I don't know if you remember my sister Amethyst, but she had a kid a few years after the show shut down. He's twelve now, and I think my mother is trying to set him up with Dell's studio." With Josh, she didn't have to explain what that meant. "He ran away, and I need to reach him before my mother or the cops do."

"I'll be right there."

She closed her eyes and tried to calm her pounding pulse. She hadn't realized how tense she'd been until he'd said yes.

She didn't see Zeke often, but she'd made it one of her goals to establish a relationship with him. They Skyped regularly. He'd visited a few summers for a week or two. Or she took him to the beach or Disneyland or anywhere away from Crystal. He was built like a block, had a real brain and no interest in acting. She thought he was smart enough to stay safe, but he was so young. . .

She and Josh had had each other back then. They'd needed the studio job and knew better than to complain to outsiders. They whined to the staff like any school kids about the diets, the exercise, the long hours, but they didn't know how to complain about the prickly feelings Dell gave them when he physically manipulated them on the set. So they'd ganged up against him, persuaded the other kids to interfere as well, and he'd backed off—most of the time.

Zeke might be better informed than she'd been, but he'd be all alone —as she had been once Josh left.

Instead of hiding her shame and licking her wounds, she should have gone after Dell. . . But he'd been too powerful, and she'd been only sixteen, and she had to fight one monster at a time.

She wouldn't fail Zeke. She called Teddy and Aaron back to tell them they were off the hook, then gathered up anything she thought she might need, including Fee's food bars.

Not until Josh's little blue Prius pulled up outside the shop did she realize what she'd done. . . put herself in a position to be seen with Josh/Jack. Praying no one noticed, she locked the door and got in as quickly as she could manage.

He took off before she was even buckled in.

"Where?" he said curtly, obviously in a mood. Wearing a collared shirt and linen blazer, he looked as if he'd been born behind the wheel of a pricey sports car instead of in a rural dump in Nevada.

"Bus station in Monterey. He said it's near a Costco and that's where he was headed. Do you have one of those GPS things on your phone? When we're down the mountain, I can call it up." She didn't have to put up with Josh's mood. She was in one of her own.

She handed him a food bar, and he crunched it as if chewing nails.

"How could you leave a kid with Crystal?" he finally snarled, taking the narrow two-lane at terrifying speed.

"I didn't have a choice. Amethyst lived with our mother after Zeke was born. There's no dad in the picture. After Amethyst flamed out, rather literally, my mother got custody of Zeke before I even learned my sister was dead. It's not as if Crystal would call me." Amber squeezed her eyes shut in a futile attempt to block memories of those horrible days when she'd realized how useless she was to help anyone.

Josh relaxed a hair and drove with one hand as he fiddled with buttons. A GPS screen showed up on the dash, and he left her to add directions.

"Now you have a custody fight on your hands. Bloody hell."

"I have a lawyer on it. I'll need to call her, but I think I'll wait until we have Zeke. Maybe if Crystal is forced to call the police, that will aid our case. I have no idea." Amber played with the GPS buttons until she'd figured them out and could add a search for Costco in Monterey and look for bus stations.

"It might be easier on the phone." He swung into the only gas station on the way down the hill and dug around in his pocket until he produced his high-tech device. Then he hit the road again.

Josh's father had been an alcoholic who had left his family homeless. He understood desperation better than anyone, Amber knew. He remained silent while she worked with the devices. Once they were up and running, he followed the route and began talking.

"I told Willa I wanted to put Dell out of business. While the *Jack and Ginger* show was churning out cash, he mostly behaved himself. But now that he's not had another hit, he's branching out. To keep the money machine rolling, he filmed a few kiddy shows for the local stations and for cable. Ugly rumors started flying, and after one of the mothers sued one of his actors for molestation, he lost that programming. I have a suspicion he's filming porn now, but no proof. And lately, he's been pedaling a new version of *Jack and Ginger* and has some serious nibbles. Willa said she'd help me put an end to that."

Amber had a lot of experience in blanking out those long ago days. Her insides rebelled at churning up old memories, but she needed ammunition if she went to court. "He's not even paying the residuals he owes me from the last show, so how can he start another?"

"He's cheating you. The show is running on cable. I get decent checks. You need to lawyer up."

"Lawyers take money," she muttered, mentally cursing her passivity. "How did Willa plan on taking Dell down?"

"She had rights to one of his productions. After I asked her to help me, she had him audited. I don't know if the audit found anything, or if I can legally ask for the results, but the bastard needs to be stopped before he can traumatize more kids."

Or worse. Fighting the gnawing troll in her insides, Amber glared at the road ahead. "Crystal must have heard about the new production and thought she could sell Zeke as the new Jack. That would be hot publicity —Ginger's nephew as you. I refuse to believe she'd stoop so low as to sell him for kiddy porn." But she had reason to believe it of Dell.

"Your mother *encouraged* Dell's abuse. I know she's your mother and you're trying to protect her, but Crystal is an abusive asshat. And Dell is slime from the bottom of a shit bucket." Hitting the highway, Josh picked up speed.

Josh was only talking about the daily verbal abuse and punitive diets and exercise. Dell was even worse than Josh knew, but Zeke was the more important topic.

"I'm not disagreeing. I told Zeke to call me if he ever felt uncomfortable. Even Amethyst warned him to call me if Crystal did something he didn't think right. He's a smart kid. He might be trying to skip finals, but I don't think so." Now that she had cell service, she tried punching in his number but only reached voice mail. "How much does it cost to have Dell audited again if you can't get the results Willa paid for?"

"A lot and I may not have the authority to ask," he admitted. "And I doubt Willa's father will give up those results. All these old guys are in bed with each other."

"Yeah, that's what I thought. I can't gamble my savings on going after the residuals either, not if I'm taking in Zeke. There's no school in Hillvale. I'll have to move." She really didn't want to move, but she supposed if she could find a place in the next town down, if she could learn to drive and commute to her shop. If, if, if. . .

"Hillvale needs to recruit a few teachers, like in an old western, bring the schoolmarm to town." Josh spoke in an upbeat voice, but his expression was still grim as he maneuvered the highway at high speed.

"Once the Kennedys start developing the land above town, that might be feasible, but that all takes time. We've been looking for new kinds of income to support community projects like a school, but everyone is afraid of following the path to destruction that afflicted the commune when the artists became successful." It was easier to talk about local politics than think about Zeke, all alone in a strange city. Or what she'd have to do to keep him.

"Fear and paranoia hold back needed change," Josh said prosaically. "Someone just has to grab the ring and show the way. You have a famous musician and singer living there. You could have a musical dinner theater if your talented cooks joined in."

Amber smiled imagining Val and Harvey performing for a crowd in Dinah's small restaurant. "Just a year ago, those two hid so well that no one ever knew where to find them. Since then, the art gallery has brought in a lot of strangers, and they've learned not to be so wary, but the wedding productions are stretching their limits. And why should they support the town? They don't have kids who need a school."

But Teddy's sister did. She was an interior designer and didn't have much work to occupy her in Hillvale. But if she could be persuaded to stay. . .

"I'm near the Costco," Josh reported. "Have you reached him yet?"

It was after ten. The store should be open. Amber punched again and still got voice mail. She left a message saying they were near and to sit at the benches by the food. She clutched the phone in her fist, willing it to ring.

Josh pulled into the enormous parking lot and cast her a glance. "Do you want me to come with you?"

"No reporters here," she decided. "No reason for anyone to recognize us, right?"

He accepted that and climbed out without waiting for further instructions.

It felt awkward walking at Josh's side in public again. Amber was too aware of her ample frame, her unconventional attire, and Josh's stiff stride. He was still angry—about Dell, she hoped.

He didn't touch her but stayed close, for which she was grateful.

No outside picnic benches, dang. "I don't have a Costco card," she murmured. "Do you think I could sign up for one, and they'll let me in today?"

"I have one." He already had his wallet out and was sorting through it. "Willa might have minions, but I still do my own shopping."

Wordlessly, they entered the warehouse. Josh led her straight to the food area.

"There's Zeke," she cried, recognizing her skinny nephew in shorts and t-shirt. "Who is that with him?"

ELEVEN

ZEKE LOOKED UP AND GRINNED. "I HAVEN'T FINISHED MY HOT DOG! MRS. Garagiola bought me two."

Amber felt Josh stiffen. She normally avoided touching men, but she daringly placed a hand on his arm to keep him from blowing steam. The gray-haired lady looked harmless. People sometimes were as good as they seemed, even if their experiences had been otherwise.

"Bless you, Mrs. Garagiola, that was generous of you. I had no idea Zeke was coming or I'd have been at the station waiting for him."

"I'm just relieved he was telling the truth. Sometimes children stretch it a little further than they should. If you hadn't arrived soon, I would have had to call the police."

Zeke frowned. Amber tapped him on his red head. "That's what any responsible adult would have done, old boy. You should have turned your phone back on. I tried calling." She turned to the stout older lady. "Let us reimburse you. Hungry boys aren't cheap."

"I told her you read tarot," Zeke said proudly. "She wants you to read her cards."

"Here?" Amber glanced around at the bustling crowd. "Awkward."

"Please?" the lady asked, her face a wreath of anxious wrinkles. "I've never had my cards read, and I'm curious."

She was more than curious. The lady looked lonely. She was missing someone was Amber's guess. Her psychic vibes pinged, and she sat down next to Zeke on the picnic bench. "I can do a short read and maybe no one will notice. I don't have much time. I need to take Zeke shopping. I'm gathering he didn't bother packing a suitcase."

Standing to one side, unintroduced, Josh stepped up. "I can take him around and see what we can find." He held out his hand to Zeke. "Hi, I'm an old friend of your aunt's."

Amber bit her tongue on her fear. It was silly to be afraid of saying his name in public. "Zeke, this is Josh. Your mother knew him, so he's good. You'll need a toothbrush and a change of clothes, at least." She glanced up at Josh, who seemed to have let down some of his thorny attitude. "Thank you. I'll pay you back when you're done."

Mrs. Garagiola watched the two walk away with a hint of envy. "You are fortunate to have two such handsome men in your life."

With amusement at such naiveté, Amber removed the deck of cards from her purse—one that was safe even for children. "Never tell a tarot reader or psychic anything that will give them a hint of why you're visiting them. I can practically read you without help of the cards. You're like a beautiful piece of crystal with your warm heart beating inside."

The lady grew somber. "That's sweet of you to say. I'll be quiet now."

"I'll just do a brief reading, past, present, and possible future. It's really not possible to predict a certain future, only a judgment of what might be based on the other cards. If you'll shuffle the deck, please, and divide it into three stacks."

She let the old lady take her time, study the cards, get a feel for them. She didn't expect Josh to return quickly.

Once the cards were admired, shuffled and divided, Amber flipped the card on the first stack—The Sun. In this deck, it took on deeper nuances, and she let her mind drift along the patterns. "You've lost someone you loved, your husband, I'm guessing. It looks like you had many children?" She traced the childish figures on the card.

"None of my own," the lady said with a sigh. "I regret that. John would have loved having children."

"Then you're a schoolteacher? Look at all these happy cherubs surrounding the sun! Did your husband also work with children? I'm picking up lots of warmth and goodwill."

"Bless your heart, yes! I taught school for fifty years. John worked with the Boy Scouts on his weekends. But I'm not supposed to be talking, am I?"

"No, but that's okay. You're just clarifying what I already see." Amber flipped the next card—the Ace of Cups. "This is your present. The children are gone and you're missing them. But you're surrounded by love. You've changed lives for the better. Look, this is you with the shining halo. See how all the people look at you with longing? They want to connect with you again but don't know how. You ought to try Facebook, see if your students are on there. I'm thinking you didn't need your own children because you had the opportunity to be such a positive influence on so many others."

"It's true. I didn't have to work. I might have stayed home if I'd had children. John used to tell me that he didn't mind that we had an empty nest, but. . ." She sniffed and pulled out a Kleenex.

"He doesn't mind," Amber assured her. "Look at him smiling at you here." She tapped the armored knight in the card. "He's watching over you, and I'm betting he wants you to find more children to love. Do you belong to a church?"

"I do." She caressed the card Amber showed her. "Do you really think he's watching?"

"You know it in your heart, don't you? He's with you." She flipped the last card. "And here you are, surrounded by children again. You can make it happen, if not through your church, then other organizations. Your students will have children of their own by now. They'd visit, if they had a way to find you. The cards show that you need to open your heart again, open your doors and windows, let life back in. See how well you helped with my nephew. There are plenty more like me, grateful for your kindness."

Mrs. Garagiola took Amber's hand in her gnarled ones. "This is a truly beautiful gift you have, dear. Don't waste it. I feel so much better. When I came here today, I was so depressed and unhappy, and now I feel as if you've given me rainbows. Thank you!"

Amber blushed and pushed the cards at her. "The cards aren't always as happy as yours. You have earned your sunshine and rainbows. This is an old deck. Why don't you keep it and remember this day anytime you're feeling sad."

By the time she looked up, they had a small crowd around them, listening.

And Josh stood there, too, a bemused look on his face and his ever-present camera in hand.

JOSH HAD KNOWN AMBER HAD A TALENT FOR REASSURING PEOPLE WITH HER Ouija boards and tarot decks and the other charms she once wielded. He'd figured she just used that talent to make him feel better when he'd been angry or depressed. But then she'd turned up that terrible spread for him the day Willa died. . . and he'd thought she was taking out her anger or depression on him.

But no, Amber simply spoke whatever came into her head—and what came into her head could be wickedly on target.

People started to crowd around her, and she looked a little frightened. Josh grabbed her shoulders to gently nudge her toward the exit. She stiffened at his touch, as she had the other night. What the hell was with that? "We need to go now, before Zeke gets hungry again."

Zeke had been waiting, watching with interest as well. All budding teenager, Zeke instantly took this mention of him as permission to chatter. "Josh bought me a suitcase and filled it up!"

Amber hurried toward the door but glanced at the metal rolling suitcase. "Good heavens! We may need a garage to park that thing!"

"We had to buy the whole set," Josh admitted. "I made a deal with a couple who was looking at the same set. They wanted the smaller pieces, so we split the cost, and we took the big one. He can use the thing as a dresser and closet, all in one."

Amber perked up a little at that. "Ingenious! Do I owe you my first-born child for whatever you're carrying in there?"

Josh held the suitcase open for the clerk marking receipts at the door. He ignored Amber's gasp until they were outside again.

"Josh bought me a Nintendo," Zeke cried in excitement. "He said you don't have a TV or cell reception, and I had to keep myself entertained."

"My gift," Josh said hurriedly. "I don't expect you to repay me because I indulged my inner adolescent."

"I was thinking underwear and toothpaste," Amber said, marching for the car.

"We got those too, really cheap," Zeke said happily, trotting along behind. "And socks and some really cool hoodies. Granny would never take me to Costco. She said it was for peasants."

Josh looked around at the BMWs and Mercedes in the lot and chuckled. Amber laughed out loud.

"Granny was born on a dirt farm outside Bakersfield. They don't come any more peasant. There's nothing wrong with working for a living and cutting costs. In Hillvale, I shop at the thrift store so I have enough money for things I enjoy more than clothes."

Josh threw the suitcase into the trunk of his car, then let Zeke slide into the back seat while offering his hand to Amber. As before, she dodged touching him and settled in without his aid.

Josh preferred worrying about why Amber wouldn't touch him than thinking about Willa and the parking-lot video Ernest had shown him. He was grateful Amber had been too worried to ask questions.

"I'd rather have the Nintendo than clothes," Zeke countered. "And we saved enough money to buy pizza and more hot dogs."

"Not your money," Amber corrected, although amusement laced her voice.

Josh was enjoying this slice of mundane life. It kept him from dwelling on what waited for them back in Hillvale. But Zeke's sturdy presence was a reminder of the filth slithering underneath the world the kid inhabited. "Zeke, you want to tell us more about what sent you running to a bus station?"

Uncomfortable silence emanated from the previously chattering back seat.

"You don't have to tell us," Amber reassured him. "But I'll have to call my lawyer and let her know you're with me. If you don't want to be returned to Granny, she'll need good reason to block it."

Josh glanced in the rearview mirror. The football-player-square kid was staring pensively out the window. "Does Dell still have that big swimming pool with the water slides?"

Zeke turned to eye the back of his head. "Yeah. The place had a lot of kids playing in a pool. The guy granny talked to told me I could borrow swim trunks and join them."

"Did you?" Amber asked.

"Nah, I saw the cameras. They were everywhere. I'm not getting naked in front of cameras and swimming with a bunch of models." Zeke sounded worldly-wise and cynical, but Josh heard the doubt behind the bravado.

"Yeah, I never got in either," he told the kid. "I was always skinny, and the other kids looked as if they lived in gyms."

"Were they all actors?" Zeke asked. "My mom told me I shouldn't follow in Aunt Amber's footsteps, I should go into math or science or something. I was lousy in the school play."

"Most of them are would-be actors," Amber acknowledged. "You can be anything you want to be, but you have to be choosy about how you get there. Dell is not a good choice."

"So why did Granny take me there?" he demanded. "I heard them yelling at each other. I don't think they're friends."

"They've known each other for a long time, but I don't think either of them knows how to have friends," Amber explained. "It's all about business for them, and that's how they talk business."

Josh would have said a lot worse, but Granny Crystal wasn't his mother. "So what did they say that sent you running?"

Silence again. Then the kid reluctantly replied. "It was the films he kept in his theater. I thought I'd find something to watch while I was waiting. I popped in one that sounded like a super-hero flick." Silence again.

"And it was nude kids, right?" Josh asked, knowing how hard it was for a kid that age to speak about sex.

"Yeah. So I went to Granny to tell her I wanted to leave, and she was telling him that if he wanted me as his next star, he would have to do better than he did for Ginger. She actually called Aunt Amber *Ginger*. That's when I got to thinking something wasn't right and left." He slumped sullenly in the seat.

"That's exactly what your mother would have wanted you to do," Amber said proudly. "I don't think Granny understands what Dell is. She probably just wanted you to earn enough to go to college."

"That's what she told *you*, wasn't it?" Josh asked, keeping his voice down while the kid pondered that fairy tale.

"I wanted to go to New York and acting school," she said with a shrug. "I thought TV credentials would help me get in. And Dell was fairly legit at the beginning, I think."

"He was always a pervert," Josh said angrily. "He just mostly left us alone because we had voices and knew how to use them. I think our websites and social media following scared him to death."

She went as silent as her nephew, and Josh got a really bad feeling deep down in his gut.

Once he'd left for Europe, she'd had to face Dell on her own.

AMBER HAD JOSH DRIVE HER TO THE PRIVATE STREET WHERE SHE LIVED SO SHE and Zeke could climb out without reporters noticing. Josh insisted on hauling in the suitcase, and nervously, she allowed him inside her safe haven.

"Zeke, I'll need to clean out the back room and fix up the futon for you. You've grown so much, you're almost too big for it." She tousled his carrot-colored curls. "Why don't you go back and see what you need to set it up like your new home?"

Once Zeke was out of sight, she turned to Josh. He was studying the art she'd collected since arriving in Hillvale. The artists who still lived here often bartered for services with their work.

"Eclectic collection," he said with what sounded like admiration. Then he turned around and glared. "If you don't call your lawyer right this instant, I'm calling mine. This time, Dell is going down."

"I have Alicia on speed dial," Amber admitted. "I have to establish guardianship before I can even think about Dell."

"Fair enough. I'll call my guy about Dell, see what he says. We need to get our hands on those films and show them to a few of the mothers of those kids."

Unable to face the horror of confronting the past, Amber shoved at a straying strand of hair. "I think we both have a little much on our plates right now. Don't you have a project to save? What did Ernest find out from the parking lot video?"

"You focus on Zeke, let me handle Willa. I just need you to back me up on Dell, and I'll set wheels in motion. It's like you told that old woman—you have to open your heart and let life in and help others."

Faced with what she should have done long ago, Amber gulped. Going after Dell would destroy her anonymous comfort.

She clenched her fingers with indecision. In a way, he was right. It would take everything she had and then some just to gear up for returning to the real world. But she wanted to help *Josh*. Working together again would have bolstered her confidence. . . *Don't go there, Amber.*

"If they love their kids at all, the mothers won't want to push their Little Johnnies into the slimelight Dell's come-down will produce," she warned. "You'll have difficulty persuading them to testify."

"If I can find just one, the others will come forward. Herd mentality works. Dinner with me tonight? Your swimsuit should have arrived." He opened the door, prepared to take all that restless male energy out of her cozy nest.

"I have Zeke," she reminded him.

"I bought him a suit. Bring him with you." He walked out, closing the door before she could make excuses.

Watching his car pull away, Amber sighed. Josh had always been focused on his goals. She'd forgotten that about him.

Not wanting to be accused of kidnapping on top of all her other troubles, she punched in Alicia's number.

TWELVE

EMOTIONALLY DRAINED AFTER ZEKE'S RESCUE AND CALLING HER LAWYER, physically exhausted from moving furniture to set up a room for Zeke, Amber gazed into her empty kitchen cabinets to plan dinner and gave up.

"We'll have to go the grocery," she told her nephew. "Why don't we snack at the health food bar so we don't shop hungry?"

Zeke dropped his computer game and shot out of the chair. "Do they have hot dogs?"

"Hot dogs are a onetime thing," she said, trying to sound severe and maternal. "They're not good for you. You can have a smoothie. The café kitchen is closed at this hour and all they have open is the health food bar."

"A smoothie is good. Can I have Frosted Flakes for breakfast?" Having showered and put on his new clothes, he looked squeaky clean with his red hair slicked down. His was a brighter, more carroty orange than hers. He would have made a handsome Jack—if it had been anyone but Dell running the production.

"Our grocery store is pretty small. We'll have to see what's available. But you need nutrition more than you need sugar. You don't want to grow up weak, do you?" She didn't like being obsessed with food, but it had become a way of life in her childhood, and a medical necessity now. So she was more or less stuck fretting over every bite.

"I'll work out," he said with enthusiasm as they entered town.

Picking up angry vibrations inside the café, hearing muted, furious voices, Amber halted in the parking lot. "Why don't you run over to the grocery and start picking out your favorite food while I order our smoothies? Sometimes, there's a long line at the juice bar, and Pasquale will be closing the store soon."

"Mango," he told her. "I want a mango smoothie." He trotted across the street, eager to be helpful—or choose sugary cereal.

Amber cautiously pushed open the café door. Mid-afternoon and the crowd was small. Most people took their juices and left. One or two tourists sat on the stools at the counter or in the vinyl booths, snacking on some of Fee's bakery items and surreptitiously eavesdropping on the argument.

The center of the fury emanating from the café was Mayor Monty's mother, Carmel Kennedy. Tall, with a carefully coiffed golden mane, wearing designer clothes that showed off her model-thin figure, Carmel was leaning over the counter in a most unladylike posture, snarling at small, quiet Fiona.

"I will break you, you little slut," Carmel sneered. "I will not allow another of my sons to marry a piece of worthless shit and ruin his career. Monty could be governor of this state, maybe even president. I want you gone, *now!*"

Remembering Monty and his brother were in the city on business today, Amber wrinkled her nose in distaste. She raised her crystal-headed walking stick to salute Fee, who sent her a small smile. Fee wasn't shy. She just didn't talk much.

"Monty left you running his juice bar today, did he?" Amber asked, taking a seat as close to Carmel as she dared.

Carmel was not entirely sane, especially if she thought her jock son with the concussed brain had any intention of running for anything more than mayor.

"Lucky me," Fee said, following Amber's example and ignoring the hurler of insults. "The kale is fresh today. I'm testing a few new ingredients if you'd like to try it."

"Kale for me and mango for my nephew," Amber agreed.

"You're not listening to me!" Carmel slammed her palms on the aging Formica counter.

"Oh, the whole town is listening," Amber said courteously while Fee fixed the smoothies. "You're not very quiet. Have you tried yelling at Teddy yet? She enjoys a good brawl."

Teddy was married to Kurt, Carmel's oldest son, the one who was supposed to be running the family resort and had quit to start his own architectural firm.

Carmel turned her snarl on Amber. "She, at least, has money and contacts. This. . ." She gestured at poor, orphaned Fee. "This slut knows no one but criminals. I'm putting an end to this nonsense now."

At the juice bar, Fee lifted her left hand to flash a diamond. "Monty asked me to marry him. We're still talking dates."

Knowing Fee wasn't fond of hugs, Amber threw up her arms and cheered. Carmel looked as if she would spit. Amber now understood the trigger that had set off this explosion.

"I can take you and that murdering boyfriend of yours down too." Carmel turned her fury on Amber. "Stay out of this."

Murdering boyfriend? Amber wanted to sink under the counter as heads turned in her direction. But she was still an actress. Praying there were no reporters and no one would recognize her, she flashed her famous Ginger insouciant smile. "Oh, it's soap opera you want? Excellent. Offer Fee a fortune to leave town. That's how they do it on TV."

Fee returned with two smoothies, flashing her diamond in the process. "But we all know she doesn't have a fortune anymore, which is the whole problem, isn't it? Monty said they have to cut the corporate budget. The chauffeur has to go and they're selling the condo in Hawaii —or one of them has to marry someone rich."

Looking like a curly-haired elf, taught to be invisible, Fee might never engage in a shouting match, but she got her blows in as needed. Carmel paled beneath her artificial tan.

"You have not heard the last of this," she said in a low threatening voice. "I *will* bring you down." She didn't waste her breath on Amber but merely shot her a withering look before marching out—to her chauffeured car.

"If you had more Lucys in here, we'd give you a standing ovation," Amber murmured, sipping her drink. "I'm trying not to call attention to myself though."

Fee snorted and took the cash Amber slid toward her. "No one paid a bit of attention to me until you walked in. You're like this wonderful warm sun that brightens a room when you enter, shining light on dark corners. You're still riding to the rescue, just like your alter ego." She kept her voice low so others couldn't hear.

"You wasted your childhood watching that show," Amber complained, picking up her order. "That wasn't me riding to the rescue. That was a character in a script. And you don't need rescuing. I've just had a rough day and wanted to needle a public nuisance."

Fee chortled, and Amber left to check on Zeke. She had always felt a bit sorry for Carmel Kennedy. Her husband had died, leaving a legal, political, and community disaster on her hands. Carmel had turned the resort around while raising two boys on her own. She'd never looked less than gracious and elegant while doing so. But over the years, she'd apparently become brittle and cracked. Or if Lucy legend had any meaning—Carmel had absorbed evil. Her sons bore the weight gallantly, but they deserved their own lives. How much longer could the Kennedy brothers deal with the vicious woman determined to control them?

Spotting camera-wearing strangers walking down the lane from the vortex, Amber darted into the grocery store. That crack about the *murdering boyfriend* would circulate. Carmel could easily have discovered that Amber and Josh were using the pool after hours. She owned the lodge, after all. The epithet had just been meanness, but that wouldn't stop gossip.

She located Zeke in the cookie aisle and steered him toward the meat counter in back. "Always avoid the middle aisles," she told him. "That's where all the non-nutritious, chemical-laden junk resides. Fruits, vegetables, and meat are what we need, and they're all on the perimeter of the store."

"I like chemical-laden junk," Zeke told her happily.

Glancing at the basket, Amber rolled her eyes. "You have enough chemicals in there to pollute an ocean. Let's find real food now."

Josh had invited them to dinner, but she didn't want to bring Zeke into the craziness around Willa's death, and she didn't want to take Josh's invitation for granted. She and Zeke needed to develop their own routine.

A familiar blue Prius was waiting for them outside her cottage door when they returned with arms full of shopping bags.

~

JOSH KNEW HE WAS BEING PRESUMPTUOUS BY INTRUDING ON AMBER'S LIFE. At this point, he was too desperate to care. He'd just spent hours in the sheriff's office in Baskerville being grilled on everything from Willa's finances to their sex life. He'd uploaded his camera shots from the day of Willa's death into their computers and felt like slime. And then they'd told him to lawyer up.

He needed Ginger's cheerful brand of defiant optimism. Whether she realized it or not, Amber's true character had crept into the script over the years.

Carrying in her grocery bags, Josh shoved packages in cabinets and refrigerator as directed and let her disapproval wash right over him.

"I'm used to a sounding board, okay? You spoiled me like that. I'm working too many tricky things to go in without thinking them through." He began rearranging her pantry to fit in the extra boxes.

"And you're missing Willa," she said. "I get that, I really do. But Carmel is already spreading nasty rumors about us, and neither of us needs that kind of aggravation."

"I am *not* missing Willa." He slammed a box into a cabinet. "Willa never listened to me. I was a means to an end for her. I knew that. It's okay. I usually have assistants who can help me on the set, but this is real life, not a set. I've called my lawyer about Dell and called Willa's accountants about the film project and the audit. Ernest is working through the parking lot video and the shots Brad sent from the last day and nothing is helping. I swung this even though the cops are all over me. I have too damned many balls in the air. And if this project fails, I'm dead in the water. I need help. Come have dinner with me."

"I don't see how I can help. I have no money, no contacts, and I can barely take care of myself. What do you want me to do?" She sounded almost sad.

"You don't need to do anything except listen or pull out your tarot or Ouija board, if you like. You were always able to help me straighten my head. Zeke will be fine. He can play video games in my bedroom while we talk. Ernest will be in his room and available if Zeke needs anything. We'll do dinner, talk, then swim, and I'll be ready to face tomorrow."

Amber had sent the kid to play games in his room. Josh figured Zeke was listening to every word. That's what kids did. So he tried not to beg too obviously.

"After what Carmel said in the café today, everyone will know where I'm going if I take the cart up to the lodge. Can't we just talk on the phone?" She finished off her nasty green drink and dropped the plastic cup in the trash.

"That was going to be your dinner, wasn't it?" he said, growing angrier. "You're still starving yourself, for what? You don't need anyone's approval anymore."

"*I need my own,*" she shouted back at him.

"Finally, I'm getting to you," he said in satisfaction. "You don't have to play Miss Sunshine for me. I appreciate it when you stop people in their tracks with that breathtaking smile, but I don't appreciate it when you fake it with me."

She rolled her eyes. "I've only ever stopped people in their tracks with my bulk. I need to stay healthy for Zeke. I don't starve myself. I eat the way I should, in the right amounts and with the proper nutrients. The food at the lodge is too packed with fat and carbs and things I don't need. So sue me for preferring an organic health food bar."

Josh crushed his hair with both hands to keep his head from flying off. "Fine. I'll have rabbit food sent up here. Or to my place, where Zeke has a little more room."

"I'm old enough to stay here alone," Zeke shouted through the thin walls. "I rode the bus all by myself!"

Amber stomped down the hall to the kid's room. Josh followed and watched her hug her nephew the way she used to hug him when he was that age. Until they'd developed hormones, she'd taken the place of the annoying little sister he'd never had. He hadn't appreciated hugs then.

Zeke didn't particularly either, but he submitted graciously.

"I know you can take of yourself," she told the kid. "But right now, I'm a nervous mother. Humor me."

"Nervous?" Josh pounced. "What do you have to be nervous about?"

"Crystal finally got around to filing a police report this afternoon. My lawyer called her and the cops. She reported that Zeke is fine with me and that she was filing a custodial suit based on child abuse and neglect. She's also filing a protective order to keep Crystal away. I'm waiting for the sky to fall. So, no, I'm not leaving Zeke alone."

She looked ready to jump out of her skin. Josh smacked his temple to rearrange his thinking. "I've been making this all about me, sorry. This is why it's not good to leave me cooped up by myself. I need someone to whack me occasionally."

"You're Aries," she said with a shrug. "I know you're just throwing your weight around in frustration. I get that. And I know I can argue both sides of any argument you throw at me, which is why you need me as sounding board. I just don't see any way to make that work right now."

"Neutral ground," he suggested. "Neutral ground with wi-fi. I can leave my car at the lodge and no one will know I'm not in my suite. You can walk around with Zeke, and they'll think you're showing him the town. If there's neutral ground out of sight of the public where we can meet, bring along your friends, if you like. Order whatever food makes you happy, I'll cover it. Just let me have you as my friend for a while."

Her ocean-blue eyes moistened, and Josh thought he probably needed to kick himself again. He just didn't know why.

"The gallery," she said with a sigh. "It's a fairly public place, but it's locked up at night. Val and Harvey have keys and practice there. I'll call around and see who can let us in. I don't know how you'll keep from being seen though. I don't think your delivery driver uniform will work at this hour and with no truck."

"I'll handle it," he said with confidence and utterly no idea how. "Let me remove my tell-tale car from your drive. I'll meet you at the gallery at six. Come hungry."

Josh pecked her cheek, felt her flinch, and wanted to crush something —preferably Dell's windpipe. He had known Amber would never have deserted him without a very good reason. That flinch told him he needed to learn that reason.

Ernest met him at the lodge with still another list of to-dos. "If you want to stay on top of this project, you have to start taking calls," he insisted, waving notes in Josh's face. "I can only play phone tag for so long. Tessa is driving me insane with questions. Tell me I can fire her."

Josh had parked behind the lodge, where he'd had a light bulb moment while watching kitchen staff unloading a bread truck. Ignoring the paper waving, he walked past Ernest, stripping off his shirt and reaching for his cell—before realizing the phone wouldn't do him any good.

"No, neither of us can fire the vice-president of Willa's company. Ivan probably will when he takes it back. But in the meantime, we're establishing our own company. Pretend you're me," he told his assistant in frustration. "Call everyone back, say you're Josh Gabriel, and we're starting our own damned production company. You know how it's done. I'm lousy at numbers and schmoozing. I'll talk to my script people and the cast, if needed. But right now, I have a different production in mind."

"Me?" Ernest squeaked. "You want *me* to be you?"

Ernest blessedly hushed while Josh called the lodge manager and made his request. He realized his assistant had been mulling over his command after he hung up.

Before Josh could ring up the kitchen, Ernest shook his head and held up his hand. "If you want me to line up sponsors for your production, I'll have to go after a different list than Willa's. And now that I think of it, that's the reason we're not getting much response."

Focused on Amber, Josh didn't respond but called the kitchen and ordered the menu he wanted delivered to the gallery. But in the back of his brain, he considered Ernest's usually correct assumptions—Willa's sponsors weren't calling back, why?

Once he hung up, he eyed the usually fainthearted Ernest wearing a defiant expression. "Do I want to know why?" he asked warily.

"You *know* why," Ernest declared. "Don't make me spell it out for you. Just think about the list of dirty old men Willa called sponsors and tell me how you want me to proceed."

Josh rubbed his forehead and tried to remember the money-grubbing details. He'd met all the men who wrote the checks. It didn't take an idiot to grasp the dirty old man crack. "Shit. The morons thought her flirting meant she'd follow through with sexual favors, didn't they? We need breasts instead of balls."

He crossed back to the front room to answer the door. A maid handed him a black jacket and tie with the lodge's logo on them. Josh handed her a five, and she nearly dipped him a curtsy.

"Sex greases the wheels," Ernest said, following him around. "Willa knew that. She learned it at the knees of the best."

"Ivan is a prick." Josh yanked a wrinkled white shirt out of his suitcase.

"A prick who oozes charm at bored wives who know how to twist their husband's arms. You could do what Ivan does. I can't tap into that scenario. So if you're refusing to schmooze the wives of Willa's sponsors, you may want to find someone besides me. Maybe you should hire Tessa." Ernest propped his fist on a cocked hip, demonstrating his ineffectiveness at seducing bored wealthy wives.

Buttoning his shirt, Josh didn't really have to think about what Ernest was telling him. He'd been in the business long enough to grasp the ramifications. "Ivan and Willa used sex. That's their shtick, not ours," he said bluntly. "There are plenty of decent people out there. You can call on anyone you like, but this is a kid's film. It's an investment that will make strong returns in money and goodwill. We want sponsors who want to be associated with a kiddie film, not lecherous old men."

Ernest clicked the pen he held in his fist, thought about it, and nodded. "Not easy, but if you mean this, I'm on it. Benefit there is that the clean types don't know you from Adam, so I can be you *and* me without a problem. What the hell are you wearing?"

"I'm a waiter, what do you think?" Josh held out his arms. The jacket was made for a smaller man, but waiters didn't usually have tailors. "And be yourself instead of me unless necessary. You are now the official head of Josh Gabriel Productions. To hell with Ivan."

Ernest's eyes widened. He mock staggered, holding a hand to his heart. Then he straightened and pointed his pen at Josh. "Ivan has money. You don't. This should be right entertaining." He spun around and marched out, a man on a mission.

Even Josh knew he was spinning castles in the air, but he didn't care. Willa might have been a sophisticated slut, but she'd been a brilliant, hard-working woman, and good to him, in her own way. He wouldn't let her death go unavenged. Someone was going down for her murder. It wouldn't be him.

THIRTEEN

AMBER'S REQUEST TO BORROW THE GALLERY KEY HAD INEVITABLY LED TO half a dozen Lucys showing up out of curiosity and support. Fortunately, Josh arrived with the lodge's catering staff and enough food for an army. He'd always been prepared for any event, once he'd worked out what he wanted and how he wanted to do it. Which is what she supposed she was there for—helping him plan a war on a killer.

She just didn't see how she could brainstorm justice, so she prepared herself for an evening of watching parking-lot video.

Mariah had wired the gallery for cable and wi-fi and probably a satellite or two. After Amber pointed out the hidden computer screen, Josh removed the painting concealing it and started setting up his laptop.

Zeke grabbed a plateful of food and wandered around the gallery, studying the artwork while his hands were full. She figured he'd return to his video game once he'd filled his perpetually empty stomach. She just needed to keep him in sight for a while until her nerves settled.

Val and Harvey quit practicing and came over to investigate the table of food. They lingered to watch the video Josh had loaded. With their men still out of town, Fee and Teddy arrived, grabbed plates, and settled down to watch cars come and go on the screen.

Josh halted the video to point out highlights. "Ernest edited this, so you're not seeing it all, just the people we know, basically. There's where Willa and I came down from the lodge in my Prius. The time stamp says before noon."

Amber handed him a sandwich so he could eat while playing with the keyboard. She studied the image of Willa looking as if she'd walked off a page in a fashion magazine. She was snapping pictures of the town, even as Josh held the door open for her. They didn't look like a couple who had just spent the morning in bed.

"The wedding planner was already there when we arrived. I don't know which car is hers. That's Brad Jones, the photographer, pulling up in his van a little later. Willa's personal assistants, Sarah and Ernest, traveled together and were already there talking with the planner. That's Sarah's Chevy. There's Tessa English, Willa's VP of productions, pulling up in the pink Mazda shortly after Brad arrives. She parks it on the far side of the van, so it's not very visible from this perspective. Willa left her Mercedes at the lodge, otherwise, that's all our vehicles."

"Hold it there so we can study the people," Teddy ordered. "I recognize Willa, of course. We had a long discussion on trending jewelry fashion. I don't think I met the others."

"Fee?" Amber asked. "Did any of them come in the café? Did you have any sense of. . . I don't know, whatever it is you sense?"

"The assistants and planner stopped for coffee that morning." With her usual self-deprecation, the little cook gestured at the screen. "They did not strike me as offensive. I do not recognize the one with red hair, Tessa? The photographer was there the other day when you came in, remember? I told you he smelled sort of off. . . as if he might have secrets? It's a burnt toast sort of thing. I can't explain."

"Good assumption," Josh decided. "Brad is a contract employee who works for a lot of other people, including Willa's father. I daresay he has lots of secrets. He stays employed because he keeps them."

Amber assumed one of the Lucys texted Samantha, because the environmental scientist showed up with her police chief husband, Walker before Josh was halfway through the video.

They helped themselves to brownies from the table and settled in to watch.

"After Willa gives her orders, we all go our separate ways, but we're on foot. The camera only catches the parking lot and the road coming into town. At some point, Willa had to return to the lodge to pack her bags, but it's not showing on here. Has anyone found her bags or the car yet?" Josh turned to the police chief.

"Nothing. No phone either. They hid those better than her body, so we're guessing they panicked at first, then had more time to think about car disposal." Walker settled into a chair and finished his brownie.

Amber caught Josh wincing at this callous description. When he glanced at her for support, she gestured from her diaphragm in the "deep breath" gesture they'd perfected all those years ago. He may not have loved Willa, but she'd meant a lot to him.

He sucked in air and returned to the video. "After three, I was in the room and would have seen her. I didn't drive her up to the lodge. My car stays in the lot until three. Willa might hike to the lodge, but she would most definitely not haul suitcases anywhere."

"And the van, the Mazda, and the Chevy stay in the lot," Walker said, after licking chocolate off his fingers. "Willa does not climb into any vehicle there. So what vehicle came into town and picked her up somewhere other than the parking lot?"

"Exactly." Josh ran the video backward to the point where they all parted ways. "All the vehicles in the lot at one o'clock stay there until three."

Amber studied the image of Josh in director mode as he talked to the crew in the parking lot. He gave his instructions with authority and confidence and still managed to keep that youthful ranginess and roguish smile. "After you went to the vortex with Willa, you left her there taking pictures while you returned to town?"

"Yes, and if she meant to practice walking that hillside, that would have been the time I'd say she did it. I had just asked her how she meant to navigate that aisle in heels." Josh bit angrily into his sandwich and began a slow-motion forward. "Here, anyone recognize that car entering town? It doesn't stop in the lot."

"We need Monty," Fee said. "He can identify every car on the road. It just looks like a black sedan to me."

"Porsche Panamera," Walker said. "Not the sporty one."

Amber sensed Josh's shock but not the reason for it. From the bench beside him, she patted his arm. There was muscle under that ridiculous waiter's jacket. "Deep breath," she reminded him again. His temper often got the better of him unless he took time before speaking.

He nodded and inhaled and exhaled before responding. "Willa's father owns one of those. So does a producer I know." He abruptly squeezed her shoulder, almost as if steadying himself.

That gesture was all it took for her to recognize who that producer might be. She stared at the car on the screen in shock. No wonder Josh was giving off bad vibrations. She covered his hard hand with hers and squeezed back.

"It's a fairly popular model," the police chief said, studying the image of the car going past the parking lot and continuing to the right, out of camera range. "Why is it headed to the cemetery?"

"Willa was still up there. That would have been shortly after I walked back to town and everyone else is scattered, doing their jobs." Josh continued forwarding the film with the hand not holding Amber's shoulder.

"We should ask Cass," Samantha suggested. "She's the only person who lives off that dead end. I know she can't see the road, but she might have seen something."

"Or the car might have been one of Cass's visitors or someone who wanted to see the cemetery," Teddy suggested optimistically. "Cass knows a lot of people in the city who drive fancy cars."

Amber's mind whirled at the possibilities. She released Josh's hand, allowing him to better manipulate his keyboard.

"We need to situate a camera better able to read license plates," Walker decided, getting up for another brownie, not even noticing Amber's distress.

Fee did. She slipped from her seat, filled a glass with wine, and handed it to her. Amber nodded but her hand shook.

"Invasion of privacy," Josh countered. "But yeah, that would have been handy. The camera only catches that one piece of the main highway, so we don't see the car returning. When we do see it again a few hours later, it's leaving town on that same stretch. Given the way the road bends there, it's not easy to tell what direction it's coming from. It could as easily be the lodge as the cemetery."

Amber sipped her wine and anxiously wondered if it was possible to track the names of everyone owning a Porsche.

"I'll check with the sheriff, see if he's reached Willa's father yet. Have you given the name of the producer to anyone?" Walker asked, walking up to the screen to study the car image. "Is there any reason to think he'd be involved?"

"Yes. It's not a subject to be discussed in public. I'll explain later. I just want to work this day through my head, get a clear vision of what could have happened and when. Ernest has included the video of every car coming into town after noon. I don't recognize any others. The flashy Porsche stands out, but the other cars all look alike." He clicked through a parade of vehicles. "Cars entering the lot from the lodge aren't as visible. The camera is angled toward the road entering town."

He stopped to show the brief glimpse of his Prius leaving the parking lot just before three. The camera did not cover the highway to the lodge. Then he clicked forward to the crew and Willa gathering between the Chevy and the van after three.

"Ernest claims Willa told him and Sarah to go back to LA to talk to her father at this point, so she must have been somewhere to receive messages—or the Porsche driver told her something. Ernest and Sarah drive off together. The wedding planner and Tessa walk away, presumably tidying up details. Brad stays behind to talk with Willa." Josh moved the video forward a few frames at a time. "After Sarah's Chevy leaves, Brad walks over to the café, and Willa heads down the boardwalk with her camera."

"She wouldn't have sent Ernest and Sarah back to LA to help her father if Ivan was in the Porsche, would she?" Amber finally asked.

"It could be the governor's Porsche for all we know," Teddy said dismissively. "With no license plate, we have nothing."

"Except timing," Josh said with what sounded like finality. "Willa called me at three-thirty from the antique store to say she was going back to LA." He fast-forwarded. "There's the Porsche leaving town."

The time stamp showed ten after four.

"If she left with this person, he had to have been waiting on the street," Walker concluded. "The camera doesn't reach that end of town. The pink car and the van are still in the lot."

"What about Willa's car?" Amber asked. "It's not at the hotel now. Where does it go? And her suitcases?"

Evidently having run this video numerous times, Josh reversed it. "This is all I have, and I'm not sure what to make of it. Willa's car is a sporty red Mercedes. Right before everyone gathers in the parking lot around three, there's a glimpse of a small red car parking in front of Brad's van. We can't tell what direction it comes from with the camera angle. It slips in and parks between SUVs, so the camera doesn't catch a good image. I don't see anyone who might be the driver crossing the lot. That flash of red pulls out again at four-fifteen. But the van blocks our view of who's driving, and the camera isn't good enough to show the drivers as cars enter the road."

Amber felt a lead lump form in her stomach. "So the Porsche driver could have picked her up at the vortex when it arrived at one, driven her back to the lodge for her car and suitcases. Maybe they hung out at the bar for a while. The driver stays until four, but Willa drives back into town at three, parks between SUVs, and avoids being caught by the camera getting out of her car. She meets with her crew, wanders around town, then calls you at three-thirty? Why would she linger if she planned on leaving with the Porsche driver?"

"That's where all of you come in," Josh said wearily. "I've run out of theories."

"I don't know if I'm cut out for this," Amber murmured from her pool chair while they watched Zeke still splashing around.

Josh was pretty certain she wasn't talking about her new swimsuit but their earlier discussion. They'd found no working theories, his brain was tired, and he was into denial. "You were most definitely cut out for that suit. It was made for you."

She rightfully cast him a nasty glance, but she knew him well and didn't deny him his diversion. "Ernest has a good eye. I'll have to thank him."

"How do you know I didn't personally pick that out?" He used the voice of feigned indignation that his Jack character would have used.

She laughed softly. After this past day, that sexy laugh was a *Hallelujah* chorus that picked his trampled spirits off the floor. His talk with the police chief after the video session, about his and Willa's vendetta against Dell and his production company, had been an uncomfortable one.

"It's pink, for one." She admired the gauzy fabric draping her full figure. "I adore pink but *you* always told me I couldn't wear it. And it would never have occurred to you that I'd like a cover-up."

"It's not pink," Josh argued, simply because he enjoyed an excuse for studying her. "It's a whole bunch of colors. You look like a floating rainbow."

"All rainbows float, and this is a pink one. Melon, tangerine, rose. . ." She lifted her arm so the gauze drifted in whatever air currents were stirring. "Give Ernest a kiss from me."

Josh snorted. "Kiss him yourself. He'll faint either way, but my reputation is hanging by a thread as it is. Ginger can get away with kisses easier. And I wouldn't have bought a cover-up because I like looking at you. I didn't know Zeke would be here when we ordered it, though, so I guess that worked out."

She glanced at the kid diving off the board. "He needs rest. Tomorrow could be a long day."

"Are you expecting Crystal to show up?" He'd love a good fight right about now. If he couldn't crush Dell's windpipe, he could take on an old bitch.

She began gathering up her things. "I don't know what to expect. I'm trying not to believe that was Dell's Porsche."

The complications were beyond numerous, now that Josh was forced to face them. If Dell had been in Hillvale, he could have seen Amber. If Dell had talked to Willa, Willa could have told him Amber was here. And now the kid was here too, and Dell and the kid's guardian were in cahoots. It wasn't all about him anymore.

"Maybe it's time you told me what went down between you and Dell," Josh said, hating himself for having to say it.

Amber's pained expression told him she hated him for saying it too.

FOURTEEN

JOSH'S CELL PHONE BEEPED.

Relieved at the narrow escape from an uncomfortable conversation, Amber sent Zeke off to change into street clothes. Now that she was dry, she merely pulled on her caftan. She really loved the way the new bathing suit supported her breasts and nipped in at her waist, making it look as if she had real curves, but she'd spent too many years concealed by fabric to be comfortable half naked.

Josh wrinkled his nose in objection at her covering-up but read his phone without saying anything.

His heated looks this evening had churned memories better laid to rest. He made her feel like the teenager she no longer was, and he looked at her as if she hadn't changed. Admittedly, her teenage-self had never been much to look at—sturdy and straight as a stick, thanks to constant dieting to stay in her boyish adolescent role. Josh's taste had matured since then, if Willa was any example.

Josh cursed at the text message and pressed her shoulder, preventing her from rising. "Wait," he ordered in a low voice.

She froze, not just at his touch but the authority in his voice. She'd accepted his touch earlier, when she'd been paralyzed at the thought of Dell in Hillvale. So she stifled her instinctive reaction and waited.

He released her to answer the text, then turned the phone so she could read it.

CK AND TTT AT DOOR. INVITED IN. HIDE

"From Ernest?" she asked. "Who is CK and TTT?"

"He's in my suite, working. My guess would be Carmel Kennedy and *Tinseltown Today*. It's nearly midnight. No one but the lodge manager knows what room I'm in, but Carmel is an owner. The manager couldn't stop her if she wanted to find me. I can't imagine why they'd be intruding at this hour, though, unless something urgent came up." Josh rose to fling towels in the bin.

She pulled on shoes. "I had a minor confrontation with Carmel earlier. She knows we've been using the pool and may just be getting even. And she called you my *murdering boyfriend*, so I'm guessing in her sick mind, she's trying to show that you are two-timing Willa. Which is pretty ridiculous unless she knows I'm Ginger."

He sent her a sharp look. "Not ridiculous. You're as gorgeous as Willa, if looks are what you're referring to."

Amber gifted him with a glare at the flattery. "Carmel Kennedy is a sick person who apparently derives pleasure in making everyone as miserable as she is."

Which could be pretty darned miserable if reporters discovered Amber's identity. She could see her current fat-self splashed on the front page of the tabloids, side-by-side with images from her younger days. She'd had enough humiliation for a lifetime. She didn't want to encourage more.

Josh produced a card key from his bag. "The lodge manager apparently has some experience in concealing guests. I had him rent the suite across from mine without using my name. There's a private entrance. Wait in the suite, and I'll come get you when the coast is clear. Or better yet, make yourself at home, put Zeke to bed, and I'll come over so we can talk."

Walker had brought her over earlier. Josh had promised to take them home. At this hour, walking was not an option, even if she could manage a couple of miles, which she couldn't. Amber gazed at the dark windows surrounding the pool. Despite the nighttime privacy, she still felt exposed.

"This is beginning to feel like a Jack and Ginger episode, one where we sneak around at night and get caught with our hands in the cookie jar," she complained, hiding her trepidation. "Is Hollywood catching?"

"I'm not into the drama any more than you are." He greeted a damp-haired Zeke as he emerged from the dressing room in shorts and t-shirt. "We're playing hide and seek, kid. Take this key. Use it to take the back exit and hide your aunt in this room number."

It was Amber's turn to wrinkle the Nose of Distaste at him. They'd developed these signals years ago but the habit returned easily. She might disapprove of his means of stifling Zeke's questions, but they worked. Zeke eagerly took the card and raced for the exit.

Josh planted a reassuring kiss on her hair. "I'll do my best aw-shucks Jack act and get rid of them." He aimed for the corridor entrance they'd used earlier.

The damned man made it so damned easy to believe they could go back to who they once were. . . But they were adults now, and it just wasn't happening.

"Is Granny here?" Zeke whispered as they slipped into the cool night air.

Of course, he would think it was all about him. Did she lie? How would she explain about a crazy woman and her own desire to avoid publicity?

"We don't know what it's about," she told him, honestly. "But for right now, we don't want anyone knowing I'm Ginger, got that?"

Zeke uttered an inelegant sound as he looked for room numbers along the back of the lodge. "Ladies don't change their faces with their hair."

Her hair, her size. . . "I got old, okay? People think Ginger is a kid." She waited as Zeke importantly waved the key over the lock and turned the light green.

Unfortunately, he hadn't learned manners and dashed in ahead of her. "Wow, look at this place. It's a palace!" Zeke leaped for the huge screen TV.

Amber thought a string of curse words but merely grabbed the remote. "Josh and I have things to talk about. Let's check out the bed. He said you can sleep here, if you like."

Willing to be distracted, he raced for the nearest door. "There's another TV in here," he called back. "I want this room!"

Rolling her eyes, Amber crossed the living area to check the second bedroom. A sumptuous king bed, desk, TV, mirrors. . . Good grief, the suite was probably larger than her cottage.

She'd stayed in bigger hotel rooms, she supposed. There had been one presidential suite with a grand piano, if she remembered correctly. With a sigh, she crossed back to her nephew's chosen room and took the other TV remote from him.

"Sleep," she told him. "No TV until after breakfast. And if I'm still asleep, you'd better not wake me."

He bounced up and down on one of the two regular-sized beds. "If you're not awake by eight, I get to turn on this TV," he argued. "I don't have my Nintendo."

"You'll have to find the remote," she taunted, holding it over her head.

"Nah, I'll just use the buttons." He found the panel and turned it on manually.

Relieved at this little piece of normality, Amber laughed and swatted him with a pillow. "Smarty. Then just be quiet unless we're being invaded."

Unexpectedly, Zeke hugged her waist. "I want to stay here with you. Granny shouts and never laughs."

Melting, near tears, she knuckled his tousled hair. "We'll make it happen, but we both have to be on our best behavior until the lawyers work it out, okay?"

He nodded against her, then stomped off to wash and prepare for bed.

Her heart ached as she closed the door on him. She'd never really thought about having kids. Marriage had been too much of an impossibility. But having Zeke with her. . . filled an empty place she hadn't known existed.

The landline rang. She couldn't decide if she hoped it was Josh calling off their *meeting* or not. She longed to see him, but she didn't want to tell him what he wanted to know. Clenching her teeth, she lifted the receiver.

Ernest whispered, "Josh is lousy at lying. Give me a distraction that will get them out of here."

Underneath her fretting and fear simmered a cauldron of anger. That made this an easy request—because lying was second nature to her. After what Zeke had told them, Dell deserved whatever she threw at him. "Tell them you just received word that the police and feds are searching Dell's place for child porn. Say Josh needs to call the kids' mothers and warn them the press will be on Dell's doorstep in the morning."

Ernest cackled. "That's evil. I love it. Love you." He hung up.

Evil, yup, the lodge had infected her already. Good thing she hadn't brought her crystal walking stick or it would be bopping her on the head. Sooner or later, her lawyer *would* bring the police down on Dell, so maybe she could say she was psychic.

It was nice to know that Josh was still lousy at lying. He'd never been much of an actor, but he'd been creative with expressions and voices, and the role of Jack had been written for his brash, honest self as the show went on. She'd been the one who had to really dig down and pretend she was the tomboy she most definitely was not. She'd wanted to be frilly and flirty and drive men mad with her smile. She'd wanted heels and prom dresses.

They'd cut her hair even shorter and dressed her in sparkly overalls for award shows. Her counselor had called it psychological abuse, a form of bullying, but as a kid, she hadn't known better.

She turned off the air conditioning and pulled a shawl out of her swim bag. She'd already had wine this evening. Wine was mostly sugar. She shouldn't have more. So she paced, waiting to see if Josh would show up.

She'd swum four laps tonight. Surely that deserved a second glass.

She was headed for the bar when she heard the latch turn.

Josh slipped in and shut the door. When he saw her, he smiled wearily. Everything he felt was in his eyes, and she nearly wept for him. Hesitating, she opened her arms. She'd always been a hugger. It had only been after. . .

She didn't think about it but wrapped her arms around his waist.

"Buzzards," he muttered, encompassing her in his arms. "I despise this business."

"It's not the business," she said, fighting the instinctive urge to push away. "It's the rotten apples. There are always rotten apples."

"And fruit flies and maggots," he said with a laugh. "I needed that." He released her and walked off to find the bar.

Despite her spineless quiver, she missed his hug.

"Ernest told me you were the instigator of that awful rumor, thank you. The jerk from *Tinseltown* ran as if his pants were on fire, cursing all the way when he couldn't reach anyone on his cell."

"That will teach him to follow legit stories instead of going for slime." Amber accepted the wine he handed her, hoping it would settle her nerves. "And Carmel?"

"Is a nasty piece of work, you're right. She had no other reason to be there and had to follow him out. But the rags know where I am now. I'll have to find a new place." Weariness lining his whiskered jaw, he sipped his wine and watched her. "Now tell me why you really left Dell and why you don't like me touching you."

Crap. He was too damned observant. She set the glass down and tugged her shawl around her. "Old news. We need to call Xavier, the rental agent, in the morning, see if any of the cottages are empty for you to hide in."

Emerging from behind the bar carrying his glass, Josh approached her with grim intent. "I'll hold you until you tell me, until you let me hold you without hesitating or quivering again. I've missed you for over a decade. You hacked out my heart. I want to know why."

Tears misted her eyes. "I was tired of being used and manipulated. Isn't that enough?"

"Dell was a voyeur who liked little boys. You were sixteen and definitely not a boy. *What happened?*" He set aside his glass and tugged her into his arms again.

She shuddered. She tried not to, but it was automatic. "I barely weighed a hundred pounds. I was practically *anorexic*. I looked like a kid." The old shame lived too close to the surface. She wanted to shove away, to run again.

He hugged her tighter. "Your *bones* weigh more than a hundred pounds," he said angrily. "You were nearly a skeleton when I left. That's why I left. I wanted enough money to buy out your contract and get you out of there. I was afraid they'd *kill* you."

"So was I," she whispered. "If I couldn't fit into a costume, they'd give me water pills. Crystal showed me this gorgeous gown I wanted with all my heart and soul, then told me I'd have to take diet pills to fit into it. Dell. . ."

Josh's embrace softened, and he kissed her hair. "Dell had pills for everything," he said. "I spit them at him, and he gave up. I was eighteen. My contract was up. Everyone knew he was looking for my replacement."

She nodded against his broad shoulder. "I know. Some of the kids were desperate to take your role. If Dell told them to stand on the roof and crow, they would, sure fame and fortune followed. I get that. But I was trapped. I wasn't old enough to escape. I thought if I could make it two more years, I'd be out of the contract, I'd have money for New York, and everything would be all right."

He ran his hand up and down her back. "So, what happened?"

Fighting an emotional and physical battle at being held, she pushed back, unable to say the words she'd never said. "I don't want to blame the kid. Dell told him it was an audition, that I was acting, that he had to show he could perform as well as I did. You know the power he had over us."

Josh muttered curses. She thought she felt a hot tear fall on her head, but she couldn't look him in the face. They'd been lovers before he left. They'd made promises, even knowing in that crazy business, they'd be impossible to keep. But she'd loved him with all her adolescent heart. And she'd waited for him—until she couldn't any longer.

"Let me guess," he said, his voice rough. "They told you the drinks were a prop. They tasted like soda, and you never got enough sugar, so you drank them. And you had utterly no head for alcohol or drugs."

Amber sighed and closed her eyes, finally accepting Josh's embrace. He understood. He'd always understood, even when she didn't. Her dreams had been pretty fantasies. Not his. He'd always filled his imaginary worlds with monsters.

"I was conscious enough to fight," she whispered. "That made it even worse. Dell got excited, which excited the kid. It hurt. Then I passed out. When I woke up, I was in one of Dell's bedrooms and Crystal was happily planning my career because she had Dell over a barrel. I think she knew what he'd planned and probably arranged to arrive before I woke so she could threaten and blackmail him."

Josh's face was definitely wet when he lifted her and carried her to the couch. He *lifted* her, as if she were some frail sylph. And he set her down on his lap as if she were no more than a feather. Weeping harder, she turned her head into his shoulder and refused to meet his eyes. She'd had years of counseling, but the shame and guilt still haunted her. "I should have done more. I should have stopped him then. But I thought it just about me. That if I escaped. . ."

He rocked her like a baby. "It *was* just about you," he said angrily. "You were sixteen with no allies and you did exactly what you should have—you escaped and survived. Had you done anything else, they would have crushed you flat. Tell me you know I will never hurt you," he demanded. "Tell me you trust me. Give me that much, Amber."

Stifling sobs, she nodded. She couldn't yell and be angry at his selfish view, when she'd been shamefully selfish by running away. This was Josh, and he *understood*. They'd been so close, that he took her violation personally. She'd known he would. And so she'd tried to save him from her anguish. And she should tell him that, too, but he knew. He had to know. They didn't need those words.

She hadn't told him about the next years, when she'd drowned her shame in self-indulgence—self-harm her counselor had called it. Her brain had eventually caught up with her emotions, but she would never be the same again, in more ways than one.

She didn't want to cry anymore, but tears leaked down her face. She'd been terrified of men for too long. Even though she trusted the men she'd come to know in Hillvale, she'd never let them touch her. It felt strange to smell Josh's masculine odors, feel his big arms holding her, but the fear had melted away with her tears and his familiarity. She clung to the good memories.

He fell silent while they both fought to restore their adult selves. "We're no longer helpless kids," he murmured, rubbing her back. "We can stop him now."

He made her feel as if it was possible to finally fight back. It wasn't.

She shook her head. "I'm terrified for Zeke. You said you'd set Willa on Dell—is there any chance he may have *killed* her?"

"Do sexual perverts kill? Sure, sometimes." Still on overload from Amber's tale and ready to commit murder himself, Josh forced his temper into abatement.

He couldn't and wouldn't imagine how his sensitive, mischief-loving Ginger had suffered through that trauma alone. He'd plot throttling Dell and her mother later. Right now, the strong woman called Amber didn't need him losing his cool.

He tried to work his memory of Dell into Willa's murder scenario, as he had been all afternoon. He'd even jotted notes for a script, but something just didn't fit. "But think about it. Dell's a cowardly voyeur. He's what, in his sixties now? Willa could take him out with a punch. If he's accused of fraud or perversion, he's far more likely to empty his coffers into a foreign bank account and settle on the Riviera than kill Willa."

It had been a long day. He was in desperate need of solace, but Amber needed support more. She'd hidden that horror story for fourteen years—recalling the memory had to scald bitterly. He was ready to go up in flames just listening. He had to keep reminding himself that beating the pulp out of Dell wouldn't help.

At least she wasn't flinching from him. The memory of the glory they'd once shared had soured him on anything less. He'd given up having a normal relationship and settled for Willa. And now he had Amber in his arms. . . and knew he could never have her.

"Do you hate me?" he whispered wearily.

"Yeah, a little," she admitted. She pushed away and slid out of his arms, leaving him alone and aching. "But not any more than I hate myself. I ate myself into this state, you know. Once I had freedom, I ate every food I'd ever been denied. I had midnight ice cream orgies. I crashed just like an alcoholic and ended up in the hospital. My starved state screwed up my metabolism so bad, I couldn't eat like a normal person, and I still tried. My counselor said it was a form of suicide. Eventually, I grew up and went back to a nutritional diet, but I refuse to starve myself. I survived, sort of. I will no longer collapse and die if I have a hamburger, but I gain weight if I just look at carbs."

"You look *healthy*," he insisted. "And any normal person would have done the exact same thing you did—eat everything you were denied. Teens are *supposed* to eat crap."

She poured her wine down the sink. "Only if their metabolism is normal—mine never was and probably never will be after what it's been through. I've learned to live with that. I know I need to exercise more, but I spent too many years resenting exercise, so I've resisted. And now I can't. The knee I damaged in one of our stupid stunts can't heal with all this extra weight I'm carrying. Swimming is about all I can do, and swimming pools are out of my budget."

Letting her ramble on, Josh rubbed his whiskers and watched her float around the room like a butterfly. She'd always been pretty and lively and possessed a hip-swaying grace that had held his adolescent attention. The limp didn't seem to be bothering her tonight. Sure, she wasn't skinny, but she wasn't meant to be, no more than he was meant to be tall.

"How the hell do I make you see yourself?" he asked in exasperation. "You're still looking through your mother's eyes. And maybe Dell's. Maybe I should take you through a gallery of Italian art. Anorexia is *not* pretty. I loved you anyway, but your bones scared me to death. I love your new curves. And yes, exercise will firm up your muscles and that's attractive too. But mostly, because healthy is sexy. And right now, you're not healthy enough emotionally and maybe even mentally to go for the gym rat look."

She gave a deprecating laugh. "Don't say that in public. I need to be healthy for Zeke's sake. And if there's any chance that the court will give him back to Crystal, I need to sell everything I own and head for Siberia. I don't think I can afford the Riviera."

Her reminder returned him to the real world with a crash. The blood drained from his prick and returned to his brain, enabling him to stand again. "Dell is going down. That's a promise. Without him, Crystal will lose interest in a kid who will be nothing more than a growing expense."

"You have your hands full already," she reminded him. "You should probably go back to LA and deal with the news rags without me, play the grieving lover, turn up the sympathy factor. That might get you the sponsorship you need for your film. You can dedicate it to Willa, tell the press she'd put her heart into it. You know the routine."

He waved away the knowledge that she was right. "I just can't get into that BS. I'll leave Ernest to play it. Let me stay here tonight. I need a facsimile of normal. Do you have any idea how often I dreamed of us spending the night together when I was a kid?"

Amber was one of those women who were beautiful even after she'd been crying. Without a speck of cosmetics, her lashes glittered, her eyes sparkled, and her color heightened at his request.

"I didn't exactly come prepared for a sleep-over," she said pragmatically, bringing him down to earth. "I'd rather go home, except Zeke needs his sleep."

With a grin, Josh began unbuttoning. "You can wear my shirt."

FIFTEEN

A PERSISTENT RINGING ROUSED AMBER FROM AN EROTIC DREAM OF HARD flesh, steamy waters, and a tropical jungle. She automatically reached for her bedside stand to stop the clamor, then realized nothing was where it should be. Raising one sleepy eyelid, she couldn't even see if there was a phone in that vast expanse.

That's when a slight snore made her want to dive under the covers.

Except Josh was under those covers.

And he wasn't wearing anything except underwear. Lots of hard male flesh. . . Next to her flab.

Tugging his shirt over her bottom, she slid her fat thighs over the side as quietly as she could. What time was it? Would the phone wake Zeke?

She grabbed the receiver from the far side of the stand. It was cordless, so she carried it to the bathroom. Having no idea who would be calling or if they wanted her or Josh, she cautiously answered with a *Hello,* keeping her voice low.

"Amber?" Samantha's voice sounded concerned. "Is that you?"

"Yes, what's happening?" She lived with a sense of alarm these days. She rummaged around for her clothes. "How did you find me?"

"I called Josh's room first and woke poor Ernest. Your front door looks as if it's been jimmied. Walker didn't want to go in without your permission. Thank goodness you're somewhere safe!"

Safe. She was sleeping—emphasis on *sleeping*—with a Hollywood director, and Hillvale considered that *safe*. Amber rolled her eyes and found a brush in her purse while she processed Sam's announcement.

"Jimmied? You mean someone broke into my house?" Fear escalated over lust and embarrassment. Putting the phone on speaker, she hastily shimmied into the underwear she'd stored in her bag.

"That's what it looks like. I'll come over and get you. Give me permission to tell Walker to go in and look around, and he'll make certain it's safe for you to enter."

"I give him permission to shoot anyone he sees inside," Amber said, replacing panic with anger. "I don't own anything, not even a TV! Why would anyone break in?"

"It makes no sense. I'm calling the neighbors to see if they're all right, but I'm guessing they were all home, and yours was the only empty house. You can tell me about that later," she added with a more upbeat note before she hit *off*.

Explain why she was sleeping in Josh's bed. . . probably not happening.

She waited for the shame and fear to catch up with her, but miraculously, the present replaced the past. She had a gorgeous man in her bed and a kid she needed to protect.

Pulling on her caftan, leaving Josh's dress shirt on a hook, Amber tiptoed back to the bedroom. Josh was still out cold. He'd had a really rough day yesterday, and it probably wouldn't be better today.

She jotted him a note, folded it to stand up so he'd see it as soon as he opened his eyes, and slipped through the main room to the other bedroom.

Zeke was already up, dressed, and watching TV. "Breakfast!" he shouted with glee.

"No time," she answered with regret. "There's a problem at home. We'll go to the café after, okay? Fee will fix you anything you like."

It said something about her nephew's life that he instantly sobered and yanked on his shoes, going from kid to miniature adult in the blink of an eye.

She hated leaving Josh alone, but he was a big boy now. He'd be returning to LA and his real life after this mess was over. She ought to do everything in her power to help solve Willa's murder just so he'd leave before he broke her heart.

Samantha was waiting in her aging Subaru by the time Amber and Zeke walked to the front of the lodge. Gorgeous, skinny Sam looked as if she'd been up for hours—grubbing in the dirt.

"What had Walker checking my house?" Amber asked as she slid into the front seat while Zeke climbed in back.

"Cass called with one of her premonitions. Right after that, Mariah called and said hell was about to break loose, and we'd better find you. You know, the usual." Sam gestured dismissively.

Amber snorted, even as she shivered in fear. Mariah had an uncanny way of finding information on computers that no one else knew. "Only in Hillvale. What hell is breaking loose? I really don't need any more excitement."

"According to Mariah, Willa's lawyers have an information leak. I don't know the details, but the online buzz Mariah is picking up is that Josh has inherited everything Willa owned, including her production company plus stock in her father's holdings."

"Cool, he can hire Aunt Amber," Zeke cried from the back.

That wasn't Amber's first thought. "That gives Josh motive for *murder*. Oh crap, he'll have to flee for the Riviera."

Sam quirked her eyebrow as she pulled into Amber's driveway. "What?"

"Bad joke. Sorry. We really need to find some way to speak to Willa's spirit, if that's what's in my crystal ball. Why on earth would she leave everything to Josh? They weren't even married yet." At her cottage, Amber pushed open the car door to greet Sam's husband, the police chief, waiting on her doorstep. She wished she could keep her nephew out of this, but Zeke was right on her heels.

"No one in there," Walker reported. "I'll let you take a look, tell me what you think."

She didn't need to be psychic to know someone had been inside her house. Her place was small, and she had to be neat and orderly to keep everything contained. But now, drawers weren't completely closed.

Closets were left open as if someone had taken a quick look and moved on. The papers on her desk had been rifled through, and the files in her drawer were jumbled.

"I can't tell if anything was taken," she said apologetically. "But if they were after paperwork. . . I don't keep important ones on hand. It's mostly invoices and credit card statements and miscellaneous like that." She flipped through the files, trying to think of anything anyone might take. All her legal documents were in a lockbox at the bank.

"They could have been after credit card and bank account numbers," Walker suggested. "I can dust for prints, but I'll guess half of Hillvale has been through here at one time or another, and you probably don't want to ink all your friends." Walker nudged a drawer closed and took another look around.

"Even I know you don't use ink anymore," she protested. "But they're not going to want their prints in a computer either. And chances are, if anyone really was looking for papers, they'd be smart enough to wear gloves."

"Do you have some reason to believe anyone would want any papers beside account numbers?" Walker asked in his best cautious cop tone.

"I can't imagine what they might do with them, but yeah, there are a few people who don't like me very much. They may have just been looking for trouble." Like her mother and Dell? Reporters? No, she didn't think the news had identified her yet.

"You'd better check your shop then," Walker suggested.

"Oh, sugar crap." Heart plunging, she followed Walker out with a worried Zeke trailing behind. "We'll walk down. I promised Zeke breakfast." She rubbed his head, letting him know she was okay and he wasn't to worry.

"They didn't take my Nintendo," he offered. "That's worth a lot."

Well, no, it wasn't to a thief, just to poor people, but she squeezed his shoulder. "So maybe they weren't thieves," she agreed, reassuring him.

If her shop, and no one else's, had been broken into, then the intruder had definitely been targeting her.

~

A BLAST OF THE *HALLELUJAH* CHORUS BLEW JOSH OUT OF BED.

Fumbling for his alarm or his phone or whatever the hell was making that racket, he hit the floor, his feet sinking into plush carpet he didn't have at home.

Ernest cackled.

Remembering where he was, Josh flung a pillow at his ridiculously dressed assistant waving an iPod and hastily turned to check on Amber. She was gone.

Of course she was.

Rubbing his eyes, Josh told Ernest in explicit terms what he could do with the iPod. He checked the time—almost ten. Amber would have had to open her shop. And he'd slept right through her leaving. That was on him.

He hadn't slept like that in eons. Amber's presence was so. . . familiar. . . that he'd relaxed and let all the stress go.

Catching sight of the propped up note, he refused to read it in front of his nosy assistant.

"You don't have enough to keep you occupied?" he grumbled, pulling on last night's trousers and tucking the note in his pocket.

"Way too much," Ernest said in glee. "Waaaaaayyyy too much, rich boy."

Josh grunted and slammed the bathroom door. Coffee, he decided. He needed a pot of straight caffeine before he was ready to face this day. After he strangled Ernest, he had to kill Dell. He had to save his project. He had to find Willa's killer. And somewhere in there, he had to convince Amber he wasn't the enemy.

That he wasn't entirely sure what he'd do after he'd conquered that last task kept him moving forward. He dragged on the shirt she'd left hanging on a hook. It smelled of her, a faint floral, almost natural fragrance that he couldn't identify but loved. None of that blaring musky scent for Amber. Beauty like hers—the kind that shone from within as well as without—didn't need artificial scent to be noticed.

He wanted clever, amiable, argumentative Amber back in his life again. That was the one certainty he could count on. She let him be himself and relax because she made no demands. Decision made, he stomped back out to find Ernest gone.

He'd been anticipating a leisurely breakfast with Amber, learning more about how she lived now, what she wanted, how she meant to go on. A pot of raw coffee burning his gut wasn't the same. He was almost afraid to read the note in his pocket.

Ernest was on the phone when Josh entered the office suite. His assistant pointed at his open laptop while he made reassuring noises into the receiver.

Josh poured water into the coffeemaker and added the packaged pod before facing whatever had Ernest all excited. Excitement was a good thing, right? Maybe Ivan had got smart and decided to finance the project in his daughter's name. Yeah, and maybe hell had icebergs.

Waiting for the coffee, he woke the laptop. Ernest had it open to an online Hollywood blog. Staring at the headline, Josh rubbed his eyes again. *What the friggin' hell?*

He poured coffee before it was done and continued staring at the screen until Ernest hung up. "Is this what they call fake news? Are they so desperate that they have to make up crap now?"

"Don't think so," Ernest said gleefully. "It's all over the place. Surely some of them checked sources. The queen left you her palace, rich boy. You can finance your own project."

Josh felt nothing but a cold lump of lead in his midsection. "They're going to crucify me. Why in hell would she do that? We were having prenups drawn up, not wills!"

"She told me the lawyers said she was worth too much not to keep hers up to date. I told her to leave it all to me, but she never listened," Ernest said, shrugging. "I thought maybe she meant to leave it to charity. Who else would she leave it to? Daddy dearest?"

"Daddy dearest will be after me with a hatchet. According to Willa, she'd built her holdings to almost a quarter of his worth." Not feeling the joy, Josh headed for the shower with his coffee cup. Maybe hot water would clear his head.

"Which is why Tessa just called. As new owner of the company, you're officially her boss, and she wants to make sure she's still in charge."

Josh's head began to thump. "You're in charge. Tessa is a lump of cheese."

"I'm an assistant, not a vice president. Read Amber's note, sleepy-head," Ernest called as Josh stomped into the bathroom where he could read the note in private.

The bastard never missed a thing.

Josh flipped on the light and pulled out the paper. He needed sense and kindness and Amber's earthy practicality to ground him.

Aries defies authority and loves romance. Libra is a mediator who indulges in excess. Thank you, Aries, for being there when this Libra needed you.

So much for earthy practicality. And he hadn't been there when she really needed him, which ate at his gut.

Loves romance? There wasn't a romantic bone in his body or he'd never have proposed to Willa. Okay, so he'd made it a romantic proposal with candlelight and champagne and the moon shining over the ocean, but he figured the woman he married deserved a little stardust.

And now Willa was gone and had left him her fortune. The police would lock him up shortly.

Shaving, Josh called up every Shakespearean curse he'd ever learned and made up a few of his own. The Riviera was starting to sound good.

Amber had said there might be rental cottages available. Maybe he could hide in the woods.

Ernest had an entire pad of phone messages for him by the time he emerged from the shower wearing the disguise he'd decided on for the day. Josh skimmed through the notes, but none were from the cops or Amber. He flung them back to the table.

"I need to find a cottage in the woods," Josh told him. "You can stay here, man the phones, tell reporters I've left for Europe. I'm not letting this go until I know what happened to Willa."

"That hideosity you're wearing won't hide you. You need to hold a press conference and tell the reporters yourself, or they'll scour the woods looking for you. I'll write something pithy, and you can just read it." Ernest jotted notes on his pad.

"Whatever. I'm borrowing a bike and going into town." He rummaged through his bag, found a ball cap, and called up to the front desk for a bike and helmet.

He was either rich or a dead man. He needed to see that Amber was safe before he succumbed to either. He wasn't losing any more women on his watch.

IN THE CAFÉ, AMBER GLANCED UP FROM POKING AT HER EGGS WHEN JOSH'S shadow fell over her plate. He slid in beside Zeke, who'd consumed more food than she even contemplated in a week. Wearing a biker's tight togs and looking like the movie star he'd been, Josh helped himself to her toast.

Fee was already hurrying over with a coffeepot and order pad.

"Can't keep hired help or the kitchen too boring for you?" Amber teased the cook, suddenly feeling a little better now that Josh had arrived.

"Can't keep enough help. We even have the business reporter from the *LA Times* up here today," Fee muttered. "I thought maybe I could sweeten him up, but he smells of old books."

Dang. Amber glanced at Josh with alarm. In the turmoil following the break-ins, she'd simply accepted Josh as a welcome presence. But if anyone saw them together. . .

Josh held up his hand. "Don't. I'm just a biker having breakfast with a pretty lady and her nephew. Don't make me go away. I'm starving. Give me the works," he told Fee.

"Zeke's finished eating. Fee, make Josh's order to-go. We can take it over to the shop," Amber suggested worriedly. "Someone broke in last night, and I've had to call a locksmith. He should be here shortly."

Already acquainted with that news, Fee signaled she'd heard and hurried back to her kitchen.

"Broke in?" Josh's eyebrows soared. "Did they take anything?"

"Not that I can tell. They seemed to be looking at papers. But I don't keep written records of my clients. My books are online, and they didn't touch the computers that I can tell. They even left my checkbook. Walker is filing a report, and I'm freezing my credit records. I don't know what else to do."

"Would they find any connection that would make them see you as

Ginger?" he asked quietly, glancing at the row of strangers at the counter.

"*Reporters* wouldn't break in, would they?" she whispered back. "I doubt the name Ginger is on anything. She was just a character. Back then, I used the name Ginger James for publicity purposes. My mother signed my contracts in her company name. A little courthouse research might put her name together with mine without resorting to theft!"

"I don't like it," he grumbled as the food bags were delivered. "C'mon, Zeke, take this to the cash register and then let's scout the land." He handed Zeke a large bill to cover their order.

"That's too much," she protested. "This isn't LA."

"Haven't you heard? I'm a rich man now," he said sourly. "I'll hire accountants to handle it all."

She'd not really believed what Sam had told her earlier. She glanced at Josh uneasily. He didn't look happy with his new riches. The death of a loved one wasn't the way anyone wanted to get rich.

They slipped out without any of the strangers even looking in her direction. It was amazing how invisible a fat person could be.

"It's the hair," Josh told her, catching a strand of her hair and rolling it on his finger as they crossed the street. "People don't see faces, they see hair. Ginger's was blond, stick straight, and short."

"Yeah, right." But it was as if he'd read her mind. Maybe she only thought she was psychic because they had some funky two-way path between their brains.

Zeke darted inside the shop to grab the action comics they'd picked up at the thrift store. He settled into a bean bag chair found in the same place. Josh examined her broken door.

"I know you need to work," he said, "but I don't like this. I want to take you somewhere safe. You've made this place too welcoming to be polluted by ugliness."

Pleased that he'd noticed, Amber opened the beaded curtains to the back room and began clearing her paraphernalia off the table so he could sit there to eat his breakfast.

That's when she noticed the gray mist swirling over the shelf holding her card decks. Even as she watched, the colorful cards flew from the edge.

SIXTEEN

AT HER SQUEAL OF SHOCK, THE TWO PROTECTIVE MEN IN HER LIFE DIVED FOR the flying cards. Recovering, Amber waved them down. "Don't. She's trying to speak. I offered her cards yesterday, and she's had time to think about them."

"Bull," Josh muttered.

But there was no wind in this airless room, and the cards were forming a tornado. He shut up as they studied the phenomenon.

"Show me who you are," Amber intoned in the hypnotic voice she'd learned to use with her customers. "Lay the card on the cloth."

A Queen of Wands hesitated, then dropped on the felt. Amber swallowed hard. She'd never attempted to understand how her clients turned over blind cards that seemed to hit the mark. But in this instance, could the ghost *see* the cards? Did it understand tarot? Because if this was Willa, she'd hit the identifying card spot on, from what she knew of the woman.

"That card represents decisiveness," she explained to the non-believers. "She's telling me she's a strong leader who reaps great rewards."

"*Willa?*" Josh asked, instantly grasping the reference.

Amber wasn't prepared to agree to anything yet. "Can you show us who you were with last?" She didn't say *before you died*. Sometimes spirits were confused and didn't recognize their mortality.

The page of swords dropped down. "A spy?" she asked in shock, reacting without thinking, then scrambling for other meanings.

As if agreeing with that assessment, another card dropped, and Amber gasped. The King of Coins. If this was Willa. . .

The devil card fell next to the king. And then all the cards plummeted to the floor, the energy gone out of them.

"Did you do that, Aunt Amber?" Zeke asked in awe. "That was awesome!"

Josh remained silent, watching her. She'd read his cards many times in the past, but he had little grasp of their meaning. She hoped he understood that the cards were related to the person choosing them—and that hadn't been her.

"I didn't consciously do this." She lined up the ones that had been dropped on the table. "But if the spirit in the ball drew them, and that spirit identifies as Willa. . ."

Josh poked the page card. "You asked who she was with last, and this fell. You called it a spy."

"As you well know, every card has numerous meanings that have to be interpreted through the person choosing them, which is where my psychic abilities come in. On its own, this one can mean a messenger, a diplomat, a liaison between two entities. But the page of swords always takes information back to the person paying for it, which is why I called it the spy. I can't read spirit minds, and the card doesn't tell us more, so that's just an educated guess."

She pushed the King of Coins forward. "This dropped down next, however. He's occasionally called Midas. He represents wealth and power. If these gifts are used wisely, he can create great good. But Midas was greedy and thoughtless and accidentally turned his daughter to gold. All cards have two sides."

She didn't have to explain more to Josh. He grew pale beneath his tan.

He pushed the last card forward. "I recognize the devil card. It came up often enough in the past."

"Yeah, that's what scares me. He represents the darker side of ourselves, perversion, primal cravings. He can just mean exploring sexual hungers, gluttonous desires, but he used to come up in your readings in a way that suggested Dell. If this really is Willa. . ." Feeling sick, Amber crouched down to pick up her scattered decks. "Couple the devil with Midas. . . You might want to see how strong the connection is between Ivan and Dell."

Josh and Zeke crouched down to help her. The spirit had succeeded in silencing them.

"I'll clear a place at the table in front to eat," Amber murmured. "And call Mariah and Cass about the crystal ball."

"Not sure I'm hungry," Josh muttered back, handing her a deck.

Yeah, she knew that feeling. Her breakfast was roiling in her stomach. She carried the decks to the front and set them on a bookshelf before clearing a place between the crystals where Josh could sit. He took food boxes out of the bag but didn't look eager to open them. He picked up one of the decks and checked the top card.

"*Eat*. If you really want to hide in Hillvale, have your assistant call the property management office about finding available property. It's prime tourist season. This is Friday, and I don't think there will be much open on weekends, but maybe there will be a cancellation, and we can sort this out. . ." She handed him her cordless landline receiver, then added tentatively, "Or maybe it's better if you returned to LA?"

She knew she should be all behind that idea. She wasn't. She really wanted Josh to stay and. . . what? She'd like to keep him as a friend, but the gap between them was too wide. An associate who could help her find a job, maybe?

"*Hell, no*," he said decisively.

Amber just about collapsed in her chair behind the counter, from relief as much as the aftershock of their ghostly encounter.

Josh finally opened a breakfast box, found bacon, and grabbed the phone. "You think I'm going back to LA after that performance? No way."

Zeke was practically bouncing up and down, examining the back room from top to bottom, searching for secret air vents.

After some phoning back and forth, Josh hung up and nodded at the back room. "The kid needs a bike. I'll rent one for him, and he can go with me to inspect these places. He's great camouflage and it will get him out of your hair a bit."

Amber didn't even have to think twice. "Tullah will have a bike. She knows I'm good for it. That's a truly brilliant idea, thank you. What does Xavier have?"

"Is Xavier the rental agent? Not much, apparently. But there was discussion of a studio over a garage near the cemetery that isn't owned by the property management company that sounds more promising than the rest. Someone is making calls."

"Cass's place," Amber said, frowning. "She claims to have a B&B, but she doesn't often let people stay there. It has a gorgeous view. . . but it's right across from the vortex."

Giving evidence that he'd recovered from his encounter with the afterlife, Josh finished his egg burrito. "The studio might be available long term, whereas the others are only for a few days. Tullah's is the thrift shop?"

Josh stood and peered into the back room. "Interested in a bike, kid? I hear there's one to be had."

Predictably, Zeke burst from the back room and raced for the front door.

Filling her senses with the scent of subtle shaving soap and pure male, Josh bent to kiss her cheek. "I'll be back. Don't think you'll be rid of me yet."

He departed, a man confident that he had the world in his hands.

Amber rubbed her cheek and wanted to curse him for that ease, but she knew he'd been a socially awkward nerd once. He'd just learned to handle life better than she had.

She glanced over her shoulder to be certain no mist was emerging from the back room, then reached for the phone to call Cass.

With Zeke in tow on his new-used bike, Josh cheerfully sailed past a reporter he recognized. He should wear helmets and bike clothes all the time. He could get into being a nobody. Willa had been the one who'd insisted they needed recognition to build the reputation of her company.

The company he now owned, apparently. What the hell would he do with that?

He wrote and directed fantasy. He'd never had much fondness for business. Willa flinging cards from the spirit world fascinated him. Confronting her father and Dell did not. He couldn't even find a motive for Ivan to wish his daughter harm. Believing in flying cards made even less sense. So he biked down to look at a shack to see if he could hide for a few days.

Even Zeke made a face when he saw the tumble-down stone cottage with only one room, no a/c, and a sofa bed for sleeping. "Better than a tent," the kid said in distaste.

So, maybe Josh should return to LA and face the music.

Amber wouldn't go with him.

"One more and we'll go for lunch," he told the kid, knowing the way to a growing boy's heart. "If I'm staying in a spooky town, maybe I should stay in a spooky house near a cemetery."

"Yeah! Then you'll be near Amber's, and I can bike up and watch your TV." Zeke was off and pedaling before Josh could respond.

The heavily pregnant woman called Mariah met him in the pine-lined drive across from the vortex park where Josh had expected to be married —where Willa may have died, if Amber's spooky crystal ball said anything at all.

But admiring the tall pines lining the drive, blocking any view of the house, he loved the privacy already.

"Cass says you have good intentions," the dark-braided woman said as they walked up the drive. "But if you hurt Amber, I can cut you off at the knees without lifting more than a keyboard."

"Nice to know." He studied the white stucco garage. Terra cotta tile lined the stairs up to a small balcony. Bright red geraniums adorned the step and a marmalade cat slept on the balcony wall. He'd seen dozens of houses like it in LA and felt instantly at home.

"And I'm glad Amber has good friends," he added. "Things could get sticky for her shortly."

"Yeah, having your snotty fiancée flinging cards at her isn't the best way to start the day. You go up and look. I'm not supposed to climb stairs." She took a seat on a wooden bench next to the garage door.

Undeterred, Josh let Zeke race up the stairs and followed at a more leisurely pace. As Amber had said, the view of the mountain was excellent. The key fit into a heavy timber front door. Inside was an open studio with tile floors, and windows with a panoramic western view that would be spectacular at sunset. The kitchen was granite and steel, and the luxurious king-size bed was cut off from the spacious living space with a colorful Mexican blanket.

"It has a TV," Zeke shouted. "Take it, take it! Aunt Amber lives just down that lane. I won't even have to bike in the road."

That was how a twelve-year old's life should be, simple. Josh had never had that opportunity. He'd been working since he was eight, courtesy of his cobalt eyes and Hungarian cheekbones. He'd enjoyed the attention once. Not anymore.

"It even has a real refrigerator," he told the boy in amusement. "When you eat your aunt out of hers, you can come up here."

Zeke flashed him a heartbreaking smile that greatly resembled Amber's. "Yeah. You got an Xbox? I'm super good."

"This is just a vacation," he warned the kid. "I don't pack toys on my vacation." At Zeke's disappointment, Josh had to add, "But at home, I have a theater room with consoles, super-huge speakers, and the biggest Xbox collection you've ever seen."

He didn't think he'd ever persuade Amber to see that room or any other room in his house. Willa had called it his toy box. She was pretty much right.

He presumably owned Willa's mansion now. He didn't want it. He'd worked for every penny he'd ever spent, and a life of leisure just wasn't his style.

"Come on, let's go back and tell them we'll take this." Josh dragged Zeke away from the TV, locked the door, and jogged down the stairs two at a time.

Instead of black-haired Mariah, a tall slender woman with silver hair waited for them. Josh supposed if he meant to live here, he needed to meet all the inhabitants, including the spooky ones.

"I am Cassandra Tolliver." The woman spoke in the same tone a professor would use to a student. "Amber will need your aid. In exchange, you may stay here. But I will not go near the crystal ball and the spirit trapped within. You made a narrow escape when you lost that one."

She turned on her heel, prepared to walk away.

Narrow escape, from Willa? Yeah, probably.

Josh shouted after her, "Did you see a black Porsche up here the day Willa died?"

She turned and narrowed her eyes. "I cannot see the road with my eyes. I see with my mind. The spirits were unusually agitated that day. I shut them out. I regret that, but I'm an old woman, and I tire easily. You will have to reach your wicked woman in some other manner."

This time, she walked briskly away, ignoring Josh's attempt to question more.

What did Willa have to do to be wicked in an old lady's mind?

"Spooky," Zeke whispered, bringing him back to earth.

"Cool, huh? Let's get lunch." Troubled but not willing to let the kid know, Josh wheeled toward town, taking the lane that went past the row of cottages where the locals lived.

A white Cadillac was parked outside Amber's place.

In front of Josh, Zeke squealed to a halt and turned his bike around. "Not this way."

The black-braided computer genius stood on her porch, watching. She gestured for them to join her. "I have a new computer game I need tested. Zeke will be good with me. I ran the plates on the Caddie. It belongs to Crystal Abercrombie. Warn Amber."

SEVENTEEN

AMBER SIGHED IN ADMIRATION AS JOSH ENTERED. HE HAD TOO MANY muscles to be a skinny biker, but the disguise worked. Who would look for a busy Hollywood executive in biking attire? Of course, rather than the lean biker look, his thighs strained at the tight spandex shorts. She almost fanned herself.

The worried strain pulling skin taut over his sharp cheekbones slapped her back to reality.

"I left Zeke with your neighbor," were his first words. "Your mother is sitting in a car outside your house. There's a man with her. I couldn't see who through the tinted windows. Can you ride a bike? You could take it up to the suite at the lodge and hide there."

Her phone rang before she could find her tongue. Recognizing Mariah's number, she picked it up. "Josh is here," she said after Mariah explained what was happening. "If you don't mind having Zeke, thank you."

Josh was pacing the front room, anxiously checking the parking lot out the window. "Mariah said she writes computer games?"

"Among other things," Amber replied. "And I'll take the jalopy of a golf cart before I'll ride a bike. But I'm not in the mood for hiding. Crystal knows where to find me. I'm calling Alicia."

She sounded braver than she felt, but sometime last night, she'd shed enough of her childhood fear to realize she wasn't a helpless sixteen anymore.

By the time she got off the phone with her lawyer, she wanted to find a rock and crawl under it. Josh waited expectantly, and her stomach clenched at having to explain the latest news.

"After I told my lawyer why Zeke ran, Alicia started calling the mothers of other kids Dell has been auditioning." She got up and began straightening her inventory. She tried to put herself in her mother's head but couldn't. Coupled with the break-ins. . . Her mind just didn't work that way.

Josh looked like a statue posed by the window, waiting for disaster to strike. "After we distracted the reporter last night with those rumors of pornography, gossip ought to be in a fine state," he acknowledged, showing none of the fear roiling Amber's gut.

"Social media is buzzing. Dell is probably fuming and hiring the nastiest. . ." She stopped and glanced back at the desk a thief had rummaged through. "They have to know it's me behind the rumors. The only explanation of why anyone would break into my place is that they're looking for something to hold against me and shut me up."

"They?" Josh grimaced. "You mean Crystal would work with Dell against you?"

"They're here together, I'm betting. Crystal is the one who knows where I am. I doubt Dell ever cared enough to look. But he wants a new Jack, and she wants Zeke for the part. She needs a famous movie star to support her. She has a few third-rate clients, but no one with any future would choose her as an agent. I was stuck with her because she's my mother. Presumably, Dell wants to keep the Jack and Ginger franchise going, and he sees Zeke as key."

"So they've hired. . . a *spy*?" Josh suggested, quoting her description of the card. "Maybe your spirit isn't Willa but related to your mother and Dell?"

"I'm not seeing any connection between my mother and a ghost." Amber picked up a deck and shuffled it. "Willa is the only one who has died here recently, and we're not even certain of that."

"Walker told me the autopsy shows she was moved after death, so it's possible." Josh ran his hand through his hair, and his cobalt eyes filled with anguish. "I've been trying not to think about it."

Yanked out of her own troubles, Amber rubbed his bare arm and wished she could do more. "I'm sorry, Josh. Willa's death is far more horrible than my annoying mother. Do they know how she died yet?"

He shrugged and returned to watching the street. "Cranial damage on the right temple might have incapacitated but not killed her. She was wearing a silk scarf, so they didn't find obvious bruising, but there were signs of strangulation. The police are operating under the theory that she fell or was pushed and knocked unconscious. While in that state, someone strangled her with her scarf. I don't understand the forensics but apparently they can tell that the body lay where she was murdered for a little while before it was dumped into the canyon. If those hikers hadn't found her, she would have been a skeleton buried in overgrowth, not found for years."

Amber had heard worse. The skeletal remains of bodies ripped apart by animals had been found in the hills and canyons, where bluffs were steep, overgrowth thick, and population sparse. They frequently didn't find all the parts.

"That looks bad, doesn't it? Like you could have strangled her at the vortex, gone back to the lodge, then hired someone to haul her away?" She watched the street with him, mentally preparing herself for an ugly confrontation.

"The time of death is unclear enough to make that a plausible theory, yeah. I'm sure there's evidence of me in the amphitheater, but I doubt they can find evidence of Willa in the back of my Prius. I think they'd have to find the person who hauled her away to get a conviction. If they don't, I'll have to live with that cloud over my head for the rest of my life. Maybe I can find a country with no internet," he said gloomily.

"With Willa's wealth, you could probably buy a small country and ban the internet," she said, trying to lighten the mood.

"I'd have to hire Ernest to run it. I'm not a money person. Forget me. If you really want a faceoff with your mother, you don't want it with your *murdering boyfriend* around. If that's Dell with her, I'm likely to punch him."

"Negativity, Mr. Gabriel, will get you nowhere," she admonished, weighing the pros and cons of insisting that he stay.

Josh cocked his head in that dangerous manner she recognized from their youth. He had never done well as an actor because he didn't take direction lightly. He had his own ideas. She was both terrified and thrilled when he pondered their dilemma.

"We don't know what they intend to throw at you besides the usual insults. You shouldn't be alone when they arrive. Close the shop and head over to the café," he decided with true Jack bravado—the kind that got Ginger into trouble.

They could expose her as Ginger.

She should be terrified out of her mind—but weirdly, she wasn't. She was no longer a helpless child hiding from bullies. If Josh didn't mind having reporters down their backs—she could expose Dell and Crystal as child abusers—

Still, she despised the publicity that would elicit. She vacillated.

"I'll round up your friends." With the confidence she didn't possess, Josh reached over the counter to haul her up. "We'll stage the Bitch Fight at the Hillvale Café for everyone's entertainment."

He was telling her she had friends now. That swayed the decision. Amber considered it for all of two more seconds. Then in relief, she wrapped her fingers around his hard palm and got up. "You make a good director, Murdering Boyfriend. You probably ought to be on hand to watch—*but don't punch anyone.*"

He grinned. Josh had the world's most endearingly crooked grin. She almost stumbled over her own feet as he led her out the door.

JOSH DIDN'T HAVE TO DO MORE THAN STOP BY THE JEWELRY STORE TO TELL the auburn-haired jeweler about the showdown. After that, the Lucys seemed to grasp the situation by osmosis. The shopkeepers began closing their doors. Men carrying crystal-knobbed walking sticks came in off the mountain and out of the woods.

Still in his biking togs, Josh ambled up the street and admired the collective security. The white Cadillac maneuvered into one of the last spaces in the parking lot. Staying in the shadows of the boardwalk, he slipped into the café. As much as he wanted to pummel Dell into dirt, this was Amber's show, as the audience proved. If Dell was here, he'd settle with him later, on his own grounds.

The place was packed. Most of the occupants were watching the parking lot. Several lifted walking sticks in acknowledgment of his entry, but they left him to find a place in a dark back corner of the counter near the juice bar. He could see out the window and keep an eye on Amber at the same time. She had taken a stool center front at the counter, with her back to the door. If she were six inches taller, she'd be a Viking goddess.

He tried to catch a glimpse of the car's occupants, but only Crystal Abercrombie emerged. A broad-featured blond, she stormed toward the tarot shop and glared at the tarot shop's CLOSED sign. She rattled the knob, pounded on the window, then kicked the door for good measure. When that produced no results, she swung around—and marched straight for the café. Good call.

She had not aged well. Once a heavy smoker and addicted to tanning beds, her skin had turned to wrinkled leather. Apparently she'd run out of money for Botox, and crow's feet lined her eyes. She wore fake black lashes that clashed badly with her bleached hair, currently cut short in an apparent effort to achieve a Nordic elf look, maybe. She was built like a thick stump. Amber's soft curves were much more interesting.

The noise level in the café dropped several decibels as Crystal marched in. Amber's bright hair and colorful clothes were an easy target. She winked at him to show she was okay. Josh gratefully accepted the cup of coffee someone shoved at him.

"Where's Zeke?" Crystal demanded loud enough for half the town to hear.

"Hello, Mother." Amber swung around on her stool. "Has there ever been a time when you greeted me with a smile of welcome and a hug?"

"Don't be ridiculous. I had to keep you in line so you didn't ruin your life. And you managed to do so anyway, despite all my efforts." She gestured at the old-fashioned café with its aging mural of hippies and Formica counter. "Look at this dump! You could have had a mansion in Malibu and you settle for the set of Deliverance? I won't allow Zeke to waste his life as a failure like you."

Fiona, who was running this set from Deliverance, offered a crooked smile. "Would you like a menu? We have a nice rack of raccoon or squirrel soup today."

Josh knew he'd enjoy this. He sipped his coffee and held his tongue. Crystal didn't have time to acknowledge the offer of a menu. Before she could start another rant, Amber intervened.

"I hear half Malibu went up in flames and washed into the ocean last year, not exactly safe. I checked Google and our old home seems to still be standing. The Valley doesn't have much to burn, does it? Is that concrete jungle your idea of success?"

"I won't let you do to Zeke what you've done to yourself!" Crystal shouted.

Josh was almost halfway out of his seat, when a firm hand pushed him back down.

"Her mother, her fight," Walker murmured. "Let's try to keep you out of it for now. The Lucys have kept reporters out, but word spreads."

Grimacing and grudgingly acknowledging the correction, Josh sipped his coffee and bit his tongue.

"What, you don't want Zeke to be happy like me?" Amber asked. "Or you think he'll get *fat*?"

Josh winced. "I'll have to fight both of them," he complained to Walker.

The cop chuckled. "Good luck with that. Seems to me your woman has a stubborn streak wider than she is."

"And a spine of pure steel tempered by fire," Josh reluctantly agreed. "Can't they just wave wands and make the witch disappear? After a lifetime of that trash talk, Amber shouldn't have to suffer more."

"We have her back," Fee whispered, refilling his cup. "All Amber has to do is signal. I have a glass of juice ready that will take the woman a week to recover from. She reeks of swamp and sewer, and I'd like her gone."

"Could you give it to her even if Amber doesn't approve?" Josh asked cynically. "The harpy needs a serious attitude adjustment."

Fee winked and returned to her kitchen.

Apparently not caring that she had an audience, Crystal continued, "Just give Zeke back, and I won't take you to court over breaking the settlement."

"*You* broke the settlement when you and Dell kept the residuals you owe me," Amber declared without flinching. "You have my money. I have Zeke."

"They probably split the difference," Josh muttered, realizing that was precisely what must have happened.

He must have spoken louder than he'd thought. Crystal swung on her high heels and turned pale, then red with fury. "You! *You're* the reason she's hiding up here. I should just shoot you now. From what I've been reading, you deserve it. Your poor fiancée! Her father would probably reward me for removing you from the planet."

"An equal opportunity abuser," Walker muttered from behind him.

But Josh had had enough. He didn't bother rising, just winked at Amber, who saluted him in a signal that she'd had all she had to say, and it was okay for him to defend himself.

"I don't punch women who insult me," Josh offered genially, sipping his coffee. "Since I can't punch you for breaking into Amber's place, either, shall I see if that's Dell cowering in your car? Breaking in sounds just like something he'd encourage." He gestured at the window. "I can punch *him*. I've done it before. He might even spill all your secrets if I threaten him."

"We didn't break in anywhere," Crystal said angrily, as if actually capable of being insulted and presumably unworried about Dell being punched.

"Half Hillvale is here," Amber reminded him, sounding amused, to Josh's relief. "We could stand in the parking lot, wave wands and candles, and expel evil spirits like Dell. No punching required."

"I'm liking this town better every day," Josh said in approval. Deciding he'd heard enough, he laid down cash for his coffee, rose, and towered over the pathetic bitch sneering at her more talented daughter. "Would you like to leave now?" he asked courteously. "I've seen Amber's friends in action. They are rather. . . persuasive."

Outnumbered, Crystal glared at Amber. "You haven't heard the last of this. No court in the world will let you have guardianship after I'm through with you."

On that chilling statement, she marched out, not giving Josh a second glance. He watched as she climbed into the Cadillac and backed out, heading for the lodge. He whistled in disbelief. "She's worse than ever. That's hard to believe."

The café returned to normal volume and Amber rose from her seat of triumph. Several of the women hugged her, and she hugged them back, while aiming for the door. Knowing when the realization hit her, she'd go down hard, Josh followed.

At her continued silence, he cursed and dropped an arm over her shoulders. Tears ran down her fine porcelain cheeks as they crossed the street. Thank all that was holy, she'd quit flinching from him. He helped her unlock her door, then closed it behind them. The instant they were alone, Amber wrapped her arms around his waist and just hung on.

He wanted more than hugs, much, much more. And he had utterly no right to ask for more, not while life was a bowl of ugly.

"I'm sorry you never knew a real mother," he whispered into her glorious sunset hair, holding her against him. "I'm sorry I can't wave a magic wand and make her disappear. But I'm not sorry I found you again. Let's go back to the old ways and get through this together. Want to start a website?"

She giggled a little. "Trashy Mothers and Crooked Killers?"

Relieved that the bout of weeping was only temporary, he pulled a tissue from the box on her desk and patted her cheeks. "The SEO would be wicked, but it needs a better acronym. What works with bitch?"

She pulled away to sniff into the tissue. "A Facebook group would be easier these days, but you'd have to avoid obscenities in a group name. Sorry, I'm usually not such a weeper."

"Yeah, you are. That's why you're such a good actress, you emotionally relate to your character. They really stifled you in that stupid Ginger role. How long do you think it will take before Crystal or Dell start sending out press releases about us? Do I need to leave town now so you don't have a murdering boyfriend hanging over your head?"

Because like it or not, he'd just played the part of Jack rushing to Ginger's rescue. If the reporters weren't here yet, they would be by tomorrow.

To his complete and utter surprise, she pulled his head down and kissed him in reply.

EIGHTEEN

AMBER SAVORED JOSH'S COFFEE-FLAVORED MOUTH ON HERS, THE WAY HIS body tightened as he pressed into her, and all the ways they still fit together. She relished even more that he didn't start in surprise and shove her away but kissed her hungrily, as if he'd only been waiting for her to kiss him. This was Josh, she told herself. Josh was safe. And she so desperately needed this physical reassurance that she wasn't a total failure. . .

She was hot, sweaty, and breathless before she pushed away. He reluctantly let her go at her insistence, which gave her breathing room. But once she was steady again, he ran his hand into her hair and tugged her back for a few lingering kisses on her ear and cheek, proving it hadn't just been her.

"I want more," he told her. "But I'm at your mercy. I won't take what you won't give."

She nodded, not knowing if the shiver she felt was thrill or fear. "I can't ask you to wait until the time is right. It may never work for us. But I won't say I'm sorry I did that because it didn't feel wrong. I'm just sorry I can't offer more."

"I'm not making the mistake of giving up this time," he said, almost angrily. "I recognize we've changed. Maybe we won't work out. But I'm not giving up on our friendship. For now, I'll scram before the reporters come knocking. I have to go rent an apartment. I'm *staying*."

Josh had no sooner left to sign the rental contract on Cass's studio when a stranger ambled in and glanced around Amber's shop. Men seldom ventured into her fantasy cave, and she knew instantly that he wasn't hunting for a gift.

Maybe she could sit the crystal ball on the counter and hope Willa would terrorize the nosy intruder into leaving.

Well, she'd insisted on a public showdown. This was on her head.

Hands still shaking from the morning's encounters, she spread a deck on the desk behind the counter and looked for sweetness and light. All she turned up was dark and ugly. Or maybe that was her mood.

"Your mother hasn't changed much over the years," the stranger said, checking out one of the souvenir walking sticks Harvey had left on consignment.

If he knew Crystal, then he had recognized *Ginger*. She studied him from behind the array of objects on her counter.

The reporter was in his fifties, with cropped gray hair probably concealing a receding hairline and bald spot. If this were an old Superman film, Clark Kent would be wearing a fedora and a raincoat. But this was twenty-first century California in late spring. He wore a camera vest with pockets, over a t-shirt and camping shorts. Tall, tanned, and not too out-of-shape, he probably worked the LA TV circuit where appearances counted, and entertainment was news. He could very well know her mother.

Well, Mariah had said all hell was about to break loose.

"The walking sticks are hand-carved, and the crystal embedded comes from the Hillvale crystals that made our artist colony famous," she said, refusing to gossip about her own damned mother.

"You'll need someone on your side when the shit hits the fan," he told her, hanging up the stick and handing her a business card. "I can give you an exclusive, let you tell your side of the story first."

She glanced at the card. "Thank you, Mr. Stone." She tucked the card in a holder. "Shall I read your tarot? I'm quite good."

He shrugged and tipped an imaginary hat. "Call me when you're ready, but not too late. The rats are already sniffing the trash."

"Nice way with words," she muttered as he departed. With her secret unofficially out, she sighed and lifted the receiver. Time to call in a few favors.

~

THE LUCYS GATHERED IN THE UNDERGROUND BOMB SHELTER THE COMMUNE had once used to store their artwork. Since the town had begun cleaning up the site and building a foundation for the Hillvale History Museum, lighting had been added to the bunker and the walls shored up. Most of the artwork had been sold to pay for the museum, but the pieces that had been plastered and etched into the walls remained. Crystals studded the concrete and glimmered in the overhead light.

Amber set her velvet-covered crystal ball on a table made from a tree trunk. Harvey had rolled the wood down after the fire on the mountain, carved, stained, and polished the base, then cut out rough, burned planks for the top—a new piece of art and craftsmanship. Amber threw one of her velvet cloths over the top and set the ball in the center. Natural settings seemed safer for what they needed to do.

"Are you sure you want to be here?" she worriedly asked Josh, who was studying the artwork embedded in the concrete walls. He'd kissed her on the cheek in front of her friends when he entered but not acted any differently than before she assaulted him, so she wasn't certain how to comport herself. She was almost afraid that he'd *meant* his promise to stay as long as it took to know her and hadn't just said it to make her feel good. "I see only darkness in the cards. You might be better off playing in the pool with Zeke."

He waved off her suggestion. "Ernest loves playing guard dog. He has spies all over the lodge already and knows exactly where your mother is at any moment. I think Fee sent up an ipecac potion to feed her if she causes trouble. Zeke is fine. I'm not. I need to be here."

She needed him to be here, although that was ridiculous. She'd fared fine without him for years. Well, maybe not as fine as she would have liked. But she didn't think he was here because *she* needed help. He was alone and unhappy. She couldn't fix that.

"Did you ever find out who is traveling with her?" In the rear of the bunker, Sam whisked the walls with sage and lit candles.

Too pregnant to climb ladders, Mariah took the ghost-catcher her tall Scots husband handed her from the ceiling and cleaned off ectoplasm. She answered Sam's question first. "Whoever it is took his own room and used a corporate name. I did a quick check but don't recognize any of the board of directors. It's an LA firm and seems to be linked to the film industry."

"Send the names to me when you have a chance. Ernest and I will trace the connections." Josh returned to the table to study the Willa-inhabited crystal.

Sadness and uncertainty creased his face. Amber knew she was asking him to believe that the woman he'd intended to marry now occupied a piece of glass, that she essentially held the remains of his future in her palms. He had good reason to be in one of his moods.

If he'd been anyone else, Amber would have told him to go away, it was too dangerous for him to stay. But that would only make Josh dig in.

"We've never done this with a Null in the house," she warned. "It might be best if you joined Walker and the Kennedys in the bar."

"They're not in the bar," Keegan said, lifting another net for his wife to check. "They're toasting marshmallows over a fire inside the new museum."

Sam laughed as she lit the final candle. "They're grilling steaks. You're welcome to join them, Josh."

Harvey clattered down the stairs still chewing on a sandwich he'd probably scavenged from the Nulls at the fire. Amber could smell the grilled meat, and her stomach protested. She hadn't been able to eat much all day. *Tension*—a new diet technique to explore.

Behind him, Val stalked down carrying two food baskets. Tall, dressed in widow's weeds and long veil, she wielded the presence of a Valkyrie. On stage, she must have been impressive. As the town's death goddess, she sent spirits on before they could infect the living—or so everyone hoped.

Amber smelled more food and checked the contents of Val's baskets. "Fee has provided!" She chose a grilled chicken leg and set out a platter of marinated vegetables.

"Nice that your séances come with food," Josh murmured, helping himself to a cherry tomato as he watched the spread forming on the bench.

"They don't usually. But this is also a town meeting, and we need our strength," Tullah said, arriving with a drink keg.

Knowing Lucys would never bring alcohol to a séance, Amber found a cup and tried the spout—lemonade.

"Is Aaron joining us or staying with the Nulls?" Finishing her last net, Mariah cleaned her hands on a wet hand wipe and picked through the baskets.

"He'll be down." Harvey settled on another of the benches. "He was just checking with Walker for any late-breaking news."

Amber shuddered. "How many reporters have we counted so far?"

"Thanks to Crystal and her big mouth, way too many," Josh answered. "Ernest has set up a press conference for the morning in hopes of giving them enough story to send them packing. I plan on getting drunk tonight so I look properly destroyed when I lie to them."

"There's the cynic I know and love." She patted his arm and shared her veggie plate. "I'll just play dumb and hope they give up and go away."

"Have you heard from Willa's lawyer yet?" Aaron took the steps down two at a time. "Or even her father? Walker is frustrated with the lack of communication from the sheriff."

Josh waved his herb roll. "To the lawyer, briefly. I verified Willa made me her heir when she had the prenup drawn up, but I have to go into LA to hear the details." He broke off a piece of his bread and handed it to Amber. "This stuff is amazing. Can I just hide in here and you bring me a basket like this once a day?"

Amber had introduced her friends to Josh earlier in the day. He and Aaron had hit it off discussing props for the fantasy movie Josh was directing. Josh had always been easy-going and personable, but she could tell he was wearing off around the edges under this stress. He'd never handled pressure well. An explosion was imminent—a bomb shelter was fitting.

"If the lawyer hasn't sent the will yet, I can show you a copy when we have wi-fi." Mariah settled on a bench with a sub sandwich. "Willa had a good lawyer. Her father just fired him for not bowing to his demands and handing over her papers."

"That's why I hired him to handle the estate. He knows I'll pay him what he's worth, and he's probably tired of dealing with Ivan. So, telling the arrogant ass to take a flying leap probably made his day. Nice to know Ivan is still alive and just being his usual asshat self." Pouring a cup of lemonade, Josh settled beside Amber on the bench.

"Current gossip says Ivan's alive and so pissed—or grief-stricken, depending on the source—that he's not speaking to anyone," Mariah said. "He tried to fire the cops you sent out to check on him."

"And you know this how?" Josh helped himself to more of Amber's marinated veggies.

"Never ask how Mariah gets her information, and it can't be held against you in a court of law," Keegan said, taking a seat beside his computer-code-wielding wife.

"I think I lit the candles too soon." Sam sat next to Harvey. "I miss Cass telling me the order of things. But if food is what it takes to bring everyone together, this is nice."

"Tell us what our chief of police knows so far about the case, before Mariah incriminates herself more," Amber suggested. "We should know what to ask before we start."

Sam wrinkled her nose. "I don't know what you don't know."

"Have they established a time of death?" Josh asked.

"Apparently that's seldom a precise thing." All scientist, Sam took a moment to arrange her thoughts. "They know Willa was alive when she stopped at Aaron's and called you, which means the sheriff is starting with shortly after three-thirty. If she was knocked unconscious, as they suspect, then she could have been out for hours. The blow was pretty severe. Her body was found around seven the next morning. That's only fifteen hours, so rigor was still in flux. She wasn't wearing a watch or carrying a phone that might have broken when she fell. The state of lividity altered, which is the only strong evidence they have that she was moved within six hours of her death. I should have taken up forensic science instead of environmental." She bit into her sandwich.

"Which leaves me with no alibi." Josh tore his roll apart. "Willa's staff had all departed by then. Amber didn't arrive until ten, and I was in my room alone. I could have killed Willa, carried her off, and dumped her between three-thirty and ten."

"Have they established where all her staff was during those hours?" Amber rested her hand on Josh's thigh and rubbed, distracting him from his impending meltdown. He caught her hand and held it. The familiarity made it easier to slip back to a more innocent time.

"Ernest and Sarah are pretty well clear since their presence in LA was confirmed." Sam sipped her lemonade and apparently ran down a mental list. "Brad Jones, the cameraman, stayed over and slept in his van, but he has no motive at all. With Willa's death, he's out a reliable business contact. The wedding planner and Willa's VP apparently drove in separate cars to San Francisco for late dinner meetings. There's some sketchy timing there since the city is only an hour or so away, depending on traffic. Again, there doesn't seem to be any motive."

"Tessa might have assumed she'd step from VP into Willa's job, but that would have been a wild assumption. Everyone originally thought the company would revert to Ivan, and Ivan has his own people. So, yeah, not much motive there—unless she knew about the will and thought I'd leave her in charge. That's pushing credulity." Josh drank his lemonade as if it were beer. "And Tessa isn't exactly a weight lifter. She couldn't have carried Willa anywhere."

"Which means it all comes back to the driver of the black Porsche?" Amber asked, verifying what she'd heard so far. "Except Ivan has no reason to kill his daughter, which kind of leaves Dell. That's awful convenient."

"Or me," Josh added gloomily. "I've got it all. If Ivan puts enough pressure on the cops, they'll haul me in shortly, with or without evidence."

"Especially if they go for the love triangle nonsense, now that Crystal is making up lies about us," Amber added, removing her hand from his thigh. "I'm not even sure what we can ask Willa tonight, if that's her spirit in the crystal. If she was unconscious, she has no idea who strangled her."

"Ask her why Ivan wanted to talk with her," Josh suggested. "She sent her assistants back to pacify him, so it had to be important."

"And we can ask about Dell. If she ordered an audit of his company, then they probably communicated at some point." Amber didn't feel like eating anymore. She tore apart her roll and crumbled it into her tray. "We can ask who was with her after she left Aaron's."

Tullah finished her meal and set aside her tray. "We have no chairs. We'll have to stand around the table. With this spirit, that might be a stronger position. Our crystals may have over-amplified the vibrations when she took over Cass, so let's set them aside. Our Null can put them in our hands if it looks as if we're in trouble."

Josh frowned and appeared ready to protest. Amber beat him to it.

"Are you sure you're willing to try this?" she asked Tullah in concern. "We don't want you hurt."

"I have my personal crystals and my beads this time. I am prepared. If we do not control this spirit, she will eventually control us, so she must be sent on." Tullah turned to Mariah. "Your nets are strong? If she escapes, she will be caught?"

"I only know what my granny taught me. She never got into crazed murder victims." Mariah rubbed her protruding abdomen and contemplated her tall husband. "Maybe Keegan should stand back with Josh, just in case. He doesn't have experience with spirits, but he can reach the nets and swing them around with his stick."

"You'll remember Harvey and I don't normally participate," Aaron warned. "After what happened to Cass, I think we need to be here, but our experience is limited."

"I am balance." Usually silent, Val spoke up. "We will prevail. As preventive measure, I have set Daisy's guardians around the room."

Her words held an almost hypnotic quality that enthralled. Amber had to shake free of the spell to recognize Val's voice was compelling enough to quell fear—no wonder she seldom spoke. The Death Goddess must have been amazing in live theater. Apparently singing didn't just send spirits on but concealed her Lucy ability. Which left Amber wondering how dangerous Val could be if she deliberately turned on the full force of her compulsion.

Glancing around, Amber saw Daisy's little stone statues blending in with the bunker's walls. The small, rounded gray stones wired together merged with the shadows. Daisy had been one of the original commune artists. She'd protected the artwork in the bunker for decades with the magic of the statues and their crystal eyes. Whether they worked against the spirit world was anyone's guess.

"That's perfect, Val, thank you." Mariah touched one of the stone guardians with reverence. "I feel as if Daisy is with us again."

Mariah had been heartbroken at her mentor's loss, so her approval sealed the deal.

"Then we begin," Tullah intoned. "Samantha, if you will dim the lights."

The bunker went dark except for the flickering candles. Amber leaned over and kissed Josh's stubbled jaw, glad that he had accepted the eccentricities of her friends. He squeezed her hand in return and released her. "Your production, not mine," he murmured.

"Remember that," she whispered back. "Don't speak, don't intrude."

As the others joined hands around the table, Amber removed the velvet cloth from the crystal ball. The gray mist inside glowed with an odd luminescence that shivered her spine. Taking Mariah's hand on her right and Tullah's on her left, she watched as the mist swirled with silver.

They chanted to reach the meditative state the ritual required, while the mist grew brighter and angrier with reds and blacks twining through the silver.

Amber concentrated on the questions she wanted to ask. She didn't expect much. Séances moved in mysterious ways, just as her cards did. But an open mind could find clues.

"We are here," Tullah intoned. "Speak, spirit, tell us who you are."

The ball brightened enough to reveal their faces in the darkness. It pulsed with light that seemed intent on escape. Tullah's palm began to sweat as she controlled the energy flowing through their joined hands.

"She is not in her right mind, dear," Mariah unexpectedly said.

Mariah had always been a strong conduit for Tullah and Cass, but she had never openly spoken before. And this was definitely not Mariah speaking. The voice sounded old, almost amused, and cynical Mariah had never called anyone *dear* in her life, unless she'd meant it as an insult.

"Who?" Amber asked, knowing her place as interpreter in these sessions. "Who is caught between worlds?"

"The poor lady who thought art is found in *things*," the voice emerging from Mariah's lips said. "Art is love and nature, make sure Mariah remembers that. She knows it. She feels it. But she's afraid. The trapped lady was fearless, but she had no empathy."

They'd learned long ago that names tended to be irrelevant in the spirit world. Not knowing Willa well enough to identify her from the medium's vague response, Amber tried another direction. "Does she know who was with her before she passed?"

The mist glowed a dark angry red.

"She's using ugly words," Mariah's spirit complained. "One is for a wicked female, the other may refer to a man. Until she accepts what has happened, she is not worth your time. Tell dear Mariah I am with her always and the child is a blessing."

Which sounded exceedingly strange emerging from Mariah's mouth.

"Can we help her pass?" Sam asked from the other side of the table.

But Mariah was silent.

Val began to sing in low, urgent notes that rose as the mist inside the ball drew in on itself until it almost formed a shape. The high operatic notes soared.

The crystal ball exploded and the candles blew out, casting the bunker into total darkness.

NINETEEN

EXPLODING CRYSTAL COULDN'T BE GOOD. TRYING NOT TO PANIC, JOSH FOUND Amber in the bunker's darkness.

Not wanting to startle her, he pushed her magic stick into her hand, then drew her back to the wall. From the sound of Mariah's protests, Keegan did the same with his wife—before he began distributing the other sticks around the table.

Apparently too stunned for speech, the circle of Lucys watched the weird mist drifting upward—seeking escape?

"Ghost-catcher," Aaron abruptly shouted as the mist floated toward the stairs. "Block the exit."

The rest of the women stepped away from the mist-shrouded table, while touching their sticks to maintain their circle.

Josh hoped if the mist was Willa, she'd come after *him*. Not having any magic powers or stick, he climbed on a bench, snagged one of the nets from the ceiling, then placed himself solidly in the stairwell, waving the circle of silly string adorned with feathers and crystals. He didn't like leaving Amber unprotected, but the mist didn't seem to be interested in her. Yet.

The crystal heads of the walking sticks began to glow the way the ball had earlier, except the colors were more muted and oddly serene in blues and greens and gold. The opera singer continued her funeral dirge. Josh didn't think the ghost cared.

Because now that the mist was loose, he was quite convinced he was seeing his first ever *ghost*. He wrote and directed fantasy. That boiling red and black mist was a little too real, made for a horror film and not a kid flick.

"Willa, if that's you, you need to cool it," he yelled at the ceiling. "These people are trying to help."

The mist coiled tighter. He had the weird sense that it was searching for the person who had spoken. Maybe he'd better shut the hell up.

Val's dirge became a chant that the others picked up. He darted a look in Amber's direction. In the dark, she was a mere shadow against the wall, but her wand was raised like the others. The dragon figure-head gleamed a soft orange-gold sunset, like her hair—like her beautiful nature. In a minute, he'd start imagining this ugly mist as Willa's soul and that Amber had a sunny one. Hillvale had a way of warping brains.

"Blink once for yes, twice for no," he shouted, succumbing to the ludicrous. "Is that you, Willa?"

The chant hummed with interest, and maybe a thin thread of humor, if that was possible. More likely it was his overheated imagination. His reaction to stress often bordered on irrational.

The mist hesitated, then actually seemed to dim, then flare up again. Josh held his breath. . . as did everyone in the room. He damned well had the attention of all the Lucys.

The luminescence remained steady and unblinking. Could the ghost actually have answered? One blink, for yes?

Thinking maybe the smoke was hallucinatory, Josh tried again. "Was Ivan with you last?"

The weird luminescence extinguished entirely, plunging them into darkness. One blink?

In its place, the crystal eyes of the small stone statues began to glow around the perimeter. The glimmer faltered, then went dark, before returning to gleam steadily.

Gasps whispered around the room.

Having no idea if glowing statues meant anything or even if that counted as two blinks and she was saying Ivan wasn't there, Josh asked, "Do you remember seeing Dell that day?"

The crystal eyes actually blinked once. *How the hell. . . ?* Staggered, Josh muttered under his breath. The Lucy chant grew louder, more encouraging.

Did that one blink mean Dell *had* been in Hillvale? What else could he ask that could be answered yes or no?

"Daisy's here," Mariah whispered beneath the chant. "I feel her."

Or that's what Josh thought she said. There wasn't enough light to read Amber's expression, so he had to interpret on his own. The air almost rippled in expectation.

"Did you go back to the amphitheater after you talked to me on the phone?" he asked in desperation, hoping to at least fix where Willa might have died.

The statues blinked once. *Yes.*

The chanting escalated in excitement.

"Did you meet someone there?" Amber asked softly while Josh scrambled to arrange his brain around the supernatural.

One blink—*yes.*

"Were they driving a black Porsche?" he asked.

Nothing. Did that mean she didn't know? And that he actually believed he was talking to *Willa?*

He'd spent the better part of his life in front of an audience, with privacy in short supply. Stirred by the Lucy's strong air of awe and expectation, fearing the moment would be lost, Josh grabbed this opportunity for closure. Hoping Amber would understand, he had to say, "I miss you, babe," to the mist. "And I'm learning I never really understood you, did I?"

The crystal eyes fluttered light as if laughing, then died out.

Disappointment flooded him, but the chant continued with a note of approval, and the candles flickered back on. All the crystal wands continued to glow.

Damn, what did that mean? Could he hope Willa had accepted his sorrow and moved on? Hadn't that been the point of this ceremony? He glanced at Amber, who watched him with sympathy and understanding, thank all that was holy—

Keegan emitted what sounded like a loud Scot obscenity and caught his slumping wife. Josh leaped out of the way as a few hundred pounds of distressed giant rushed for the stairs carrying Mariah.

Someone switched the lights back on and the chant morphed into excited, anxious chatter as the women congratulated Josh for his performance and rushed to follow Keegan and Mariah.

"Overexertion, she'll be fine." Amber rubbed Josh's back as he bent over, head in hands, on her couch. "Tullah thinks the spirit of Daisy inhabited Mariah, that maybe the child is a natural medium and allowed Daisy access. Mariah is strong, but that had to be a shocking experience. And if Daisy was communicating with Willa. . . You'd have to know Daisy. She was crazy—in a good way, but very erratic."

"Willa is lying on a slab in a morgue," he said, almost angrily. "Why are we kidding ourselves with this nonsense?"

She used both hands and dug her thumbs into his spine until he yanked upright. "Because Willa *died* here and her spirit lingers. Bodies are meaningless shells that we eventually shed."

He glared at her. "Remember your body is a meaningless shell the next time you criticize it. I am not my pretty face. You are not your weight."

She wanted to laugh in relief at his quick recovery, but laughter didn't come easily after their terrifying evening. She sat beside him. "I'm aware that our bodies are mere shells that house our true essence. But I grew up playing to an audience that reacts to physical appearances. Self-consciousness is part of me. Dig back to your skinny nerd days and try to remember how that felt."

He kissed her instead. She let him, trying the kiss on for size, measuring her level of fear against their last kiss, not sure she knew what she wanted.

Josh evidently knew exactly what he wanted. He deepened the kiss until hormones overruled fear and she succumbed. Both their souls had been stripped bare enough times to know how to open themselves completely without even trying. When he cupped her breast, she shivered deep down inside and froze, but only momentarily. His kisses heated her, and the irrational panic melted. This was *Josh*, who had confronted an angry ghost he didn't believe in to keep her safe.

He ran his lips along her cheek, nibbled briefly on her ear, and simply held her breast in his palm. "I don't want to use you," he murmured in what sounded like regret. "And that's what I'd be doing right now— making the world go away. You deserve better."

"Yeah, but what if I want to settle for being used?" she asked, her voice raw.

He laughed softly and kneaded her flesh, drawing a tantalizing finger across her clothed, aroused nipple. "We might shock Zeke. This needs to be just us. We need all night and then some to learn who we are together. We're not teenagers desperate for sex."

"I hate it when you're right," she grumbled, pulling away. Her breast ached, and she wanted to strip off her shirt and say to hell with waiting any longer. "And that's your inner Romeo talking. I guess I need to seduce you with candlelight and. . ."

He covered her mouth with his hand. "If I never see another lit candle, I'll be happy. Or any more glowing crystals. Let's make it on a beach in sunshine."

She sighed and threw a glance at her still slightly glowing walking stick. "We have absolutely no idea what we did tonight."

"Yeah, I gathered that. Are your séances always this exciting? I may have to rethink one of the scenes in my film." He leaned against the sofa back, let his head drop backward, and gazed at the ceiling.

"Go home, get some sleep. And no, usually our séances are snore-inducing. Willa just had things she wanted to say, and you brilliantly gave her a means of saying them. Sort of."

He snorted. "Sort of, right. So are we deducing the Porsche contained Dell? Do we tell the cops a ghost said Dell was there? Where does that leave us?"

"With an angry woman and a maybe-man? That sort of describes Dell, doesn't it? Crazy Daisy as a spirit medium leaves a little to be desired. I have no idea how to interpret Daisy's explanation of who Willa saw last. *Ugly words for a wicked female and maybe a man* is not clarifying. I suppose we need to perform one of Hillvale's magic acts, slap around a little ectoplasm, feed the suspects some of Fee's doctored food, and persuade someone to confess." Amber rubbed her bare arms, trying to settle her nerves—and her desire. She hadn't really wanted another man since Josh. Their chemistry. . . was potent.

"Let's put on a show, like we did as Jack and Ginger?" he asked with a hint of amusement through a yawn. He stretched his long legs halfway across her small room. "Can I write the script?"

"Be my guest. I'm thinking Mariah won't be up to slapping ecto-plasm around. Keegan will probably tie her to a chair. Tarot isn't very persuasive. Maybe we can persuade Willa to perform for our suspects if we wave our sticks around. That should scare the heck out of any killers."

"You're a fine actress. With a few special effects. . ."

Amber slapped him with a sofa pillow. "Go home, Josh. You're giddy."

"I do my best work in the middle of the night." He rose from the couch and held out a hand to tug her up. "But you need your beauty sleep. Will you go to the shop tomorrow? I'd love to stand guard duty just to watch your mother cringe."

"It's Saturday. We have a wedding party coming in, and I have appointments lined up most of the day. I'm hoping Zeke won't mind staying in the house, playing games. Until my mother leaves, I'd rather keep him away from her." Amber fretted over that too. Walker had replaced her door lock with a stronger one, but she didn't trust Crystal, and Zeke was only a kid.

"You need a restraining order, give Walker a reason to lock her up. Why don't you send Zeke up to my cool new studio? Crystal won't find him there. I can download a few games, and he can blow up things until I return from the lodge. Ernest has promised a press conference that should be a real rodeo tomorrow. I'll need to blow up things after it's over." He brushed a kiss across her hair, just as if he really were her boyfriend.

If this was how it felt to have a partner, she was ready. She wrapped her arms around Josh's waist and kissed his movie-star jaw. "Your tendency to blow up things when stressed is not good for a press confer-ence. Don't say anything that you'll regret later."

"I have Ernest to remind me why I shouldn't kill Dell or throttle Crystal or jump down the throats of stupid reporters. It's all good. But I'd hide that weird stick if I were you. I keep seeing Willa winking at me." Josh kept his arm around her as he walked to the door, letting her feel as if he really needed to touch as much as she did. "It's good to have you back, kid. I need this." He kissed the corner of her mouth and slipped out the door.

Amber cupped a hand over her lips and allowed a single tear to trickle down. Tonight had left her feeling vulnerable. She needed him too, more than he'd ever know.

She knew she ought to prepare herself for the inevitable moment when he had to return to LA, but she'd never been smart about shielding herself from heartbreak—one of the many reasons she didn't leave her nest and put herself out there anymore.

But for Zeke—and Josh—she'd have to take risks again. The thought paralyzed her.

TWENTY

SATURDAY MORNING, JOSH LEFT ZEKE HAPPILY WATCHING TV IN THE STUDIO, rather than bring him in contact with the scandal-hungry slime gathering at the lodge. Ernest had opened up the living room of the suite, saving the cost of a meeting room for the conference. His project's new production head was already counting pennies.

Josh knew he was a damned good director, better than he was as an actor, and probably better than he was as a writer, since he'd never sold a script, and his books ended up in the comic section of the two stores carrying them. Directing a press conference was a snap.

"Pile alcohol bottles in the trash," Josh ordered, surveying the set-up. "Dirty glasses on the counter. And sorry, now that you've picked up and organized all my papers, you need to strew them around again. We are keeping this short by playing up my grief. Anyone who knows Willa won't buy my act, but they can sell it to the rags, so it's all good."

Ernest rolled his eyes, threw a file folder of papers on the floor, and kicked it. "Want me to smash a laptop and leave the remains in the middle of the floor?"

Josh smothered a laugh. "Would you? Pretty please?"

Ernest gave him the stink eye and kicked another file. "No. You're enjoying this too much. Willa was a mean woman, but she deserves respect, not a circus."

"Unfortunately, the press wants a circus. Once the coroner releases her, I'll give her a ceremony brimming with pomp and circumstance. I'll even wear a black suit."

"Tessa is bugging me about the funeral," Ernest acknowledged. "I think she's mostly trying to find out where her job stands. I'm telling her it's in the hands of the lawyers. I had to ask her and Brad up here for the respect part of this scene."

Grimacing, Josh sniffed his old Calvin Klein t-shirt to see if it exuded the proper aroma of despair and alcohol. "After last night, I'm thinking Willa doesn't give a damn about respect. If that was her, she's mad and wants us to find out what happened, even if she has to inhabit dirty stones to do so."

"The witches put on a good show?" Ernest asked in interest, emptying a partial bottle of wine on a paper towel and smearing it around a little to add to the rankness.

"*Lucys,*" Josh corrected. "Witches have the wrong connotation. And I'm not sure I could have duplicated those special effects even with an engineering team. Amber almost lost it, and you know what that takes. We should have brought her Ouija board."

He wished Amber was waiting for him in the other suite, but she'd always despised media farce. He hated that his presence had exposed her to the rabid coyotes, but with Crystal and Dell spewing their crap all over the press, there was no backing away now.

He hoped Amber didn't have access to the morning news. She shouldn't have to see her mother spinning tales of love triangles, kidnapping, and murder. Sensationalism sold papers, not truth or accuracy. So he'd play their lousy game.

"You put good security people on Amber's doors?" he asked Ernest, probably for the thirtieth time. "I don't want these hounds going straight down there and driving off her clients."

"Not easy at the last minute. I found a receptionist who used to carry a gun outside Steve Jobs' office in her heyday. And a burly security guard who can bench press two reporters in one hand. She should be safe."

The front desk rang, letting them know that Tessa, Willa's VP, and Brad, her favorite photographer, had arrived. Ernest sent around to the back entrance to avoid the reporters gathering in the lobby.

Red curls newly dyed and styled, Tessa rushed in to hug Josh. "Oh you poor thing! I'm so glad you called us in to help. The press is awful!"

Josh stepped back in distaste. Tessa's perfume was worse than his alcohol abuse of the suite. Once one of Willa's best friends, the two had often shared closets, so Josh sometimes had difficulty differentiating their wardrobes. "Thanks for coming."

He turned to Brad, a burly man who always looked as if he'd just climbed out of bed. But the photographer was damned good at what he did. Josh held out his hand to greet him. "I'm glad you could make it. If you have some stills from that last day, you can make a bundle today."

"Not the same as the wedding," Brad said gruffly, gazing around at the trashed suite. "Sorry for your loss. Heard you'll be getting the company. I did a lot of business with Willa. Hope you'll keep me on."

Josh didn't want to be reminded of that looming responsibility, but Tessa leaped on the opening. "You don't have to worry about a thing, Josh. Sarah and I are handling all the business calls. I'm authorized to pay the bills. You're in good hands."

Practically growling under his breath, Ernest waved the phone. "The press is getting restless. Have you read the damned script I gave you so I can let them in?"

"Read it. Memorized it. Regurgitated and threw it up." Leaving his guests to peruse the kitchen, Josh sprawled over a couch he'd deliberately set in front of a sun-filled window, ruining photo ops. On the floor, he'd set a half-empty glass of amber fluid near his hand. "If I throw a few punches, will I look grief-stricken?"

"No," Ernest said curtly. "Ready, set, action." He pushed the phone's buttons, allowing lodge security to let the rest of their visitors in.

Ernest's notes gave Josh a PR spin intended to deter the questions Amber's damned mother was stirring. As cameras filled the suite, Josh focused on the spin and not wanting to drive his fist through a few cigarette-yellowed teeth.

"Of course Willa knew Amber is Ginger," Josh said with an appropriate gesture of disgust to the first question asked. "We only just discovered Amber was living here, so Willa didn't have time to know her well. The stories Dell is spreading are just to hype his new Jack-and-Ginger production, which I intend to halt. But that's in the hands of our attorneys. You know I can't talk about it. Let's move on."

They badgered him more about Amber, but Josh picked up the colored-water glass and sipped, refusing to speak unless they asked questions he was prepared to answer truthfully.

"I've talked to Willa's lawyer, yes. I haven't talked to her father, no. I have no idea what will become of her estate if Ivan chooses to object to her will." He didn't look at Tessa, who was avidly following any reference to Willa's company. Her job was on the line, he got that. She could look a little more mournful.

He waved off another badgering question. "Lawyers are better equipped to answer legal questions than I am. I'm forming my own company to continue my film as planned. Ivan's objections and my grief shouldn't affect the lives of the people counting on this production." Absolute, total truth, except without Willa's cash, he'd have to find money elsewhere. The jackals didn't need to know that.

Brad discreetly worked the back of the room, flashing photos stored on his phone to anyone expressing interest. Crass, but effectively distracting those who didn't bring their own photographers.

Josh tossed back the rest of the water as if it really were whiskey when they began questioning him about Willa's other projects. He turned to Tessa, but she was nervously tapping her long nails on her phone while reading a text and doing nothing to help him out.

"Look, Willa was a grown woman with a full life of her own before we met," Josh insisted in growing exasperation. "I did not interfere in her company. She did not interfere with my films. She employed armies of people I never met. We had only just begun working together on my new epic fantasy. She intended to push it to the next level. We built a relationship outside our business partnership. Everything was coming up roses until this. So, sniff the gutter, if you want, but Willa's memory deserves admiration for what she accomplished, not sexist scandal-mongering."

Resisting his director's role of saying *Cut, print, thank you*, Josh flung his empty glass against the wall, got up as it noisily smashed into pieces, and staggered out, slamming his bedroom door for effect.

Video required action, and he'd given them all he had, short of throwing punches.

Not caring what happened to his startled guests, he crossed to the other side of the bedroom hoping for escape. Opening the door into the hall, he peered out to see if anyone lurked.

Harvey met him, holding a glowing walking stick. "This way. We have you covered." He hurried toward the rear exit.

What the frigging hell? More than ready to escape, Josh followed, conjuring scenarios of being kidnapped by warlocks and evil fairies or Hillvale's own Gandalf.

Harvey slipped into the forest surrounding the lodge, following a well-traveled path under the shade of towering evergreens. Torn equally between fear and fascination of his companion's glowing crystal, eager for any escape, Josh followed. Harvey had a few inches over him and was obviously accustomed to these woods. He glided over tree roots without tripping. Josh had to watch where he stomped his city shoes while he debated the need to break that stick in half. What would happen if he crushed the crystal?

"It would be nice to know what we're doing," he complained as they reached the edge of the tree line, on a ridge above the town.

"Yeah, well, the rest of us don't get scripts. We make things up as we go along."

"That's pretty much the essence of script writing. Give me goals, motivation, conflict, and we're halfway there." Josh studied Hillvale from this new perspective.

The lodge was hidden by the woods they'd just climbed through, but he could see the line of cars snaking down from the resort road into town. That would be the reporters. He couldn't hope they'd all go home. A few cars continued down the highway, leaving Hillvale behind. The rest pulled into the parking lot. One, finding no space available, snaked up the crumbling lane to the old commune farm and artists' colony above the town.

"Goals, motivation, conflict, they're all there." Harvey gestured at the town with his stick. "It's the human condition. Hillvale likes privacy, but it needs money to survive. Reporters keep the name of the town in the public eye, but not necessarily in a good way. Call us conflicted."

He gestured in the distance, where an open trolley dispelled gaily-garbed wedding guests at the amphitheater on the far side of the valley. "The wedding business puts money in our pockets and creates a happy energy. Having brides killed before the wedding does not."

"Aren't you supposed to be over there, playing for the crowd?" Josh watched the milling guests filing down the stone walkway through the roses and bushes Willa had admired. In a few weeks, that would have been him traversing those stairs.

Oddly, he didn't feel regret for the future that had crashed around him. His wedding had been more publicity stunt than a lifetime promise.

"Not everyone can afford me," Harvey replied. "I play when I want and for people I like. Otherwise, I demand a high price for my talent. If I allow my *name* to be used, my privacy violated, I expect an enormous return, monetary or in other form." Harvey pulled a baseball hat, horn-rimmed glasses, and a t-shirt out of his backpack and handed them over. "Here, play tourist."

Realizing they were heading for the commune farm where the reporter had just alighted, Josh accepted the disguise without protest. "Willa wanted to use your name?"

"Yeah. Like you, she recognized me. Most people have never *heard* of Isaac Berkovich. They just see a long-haired guitar player and itinerant busker. Willa didn't even blink when I named my price for advertising my name. It would have gone a long way toward establishing that winery my family wants up there in those hills—should we ever find water." He waved his walking stick at an area above the burned-out ground. "But playing a wedding venue would destroy my value as a concert pianist. I told her I'd play if she wanted to hold the ceremony in the Hollywood Bowl. She declined."

"But she said you were playing for us." Josh had a nasty feeling he knew where this was going, but he let Harvey take the lead. The musician had a reputation for integrity as well as brilliance, if he remembered rightly. Berkovich had been playing for the concert circuit since he was a kid—a child prodigy had to learn to be tough to survive, as Josh well knew. There had been some uproar with the pianist's management company a few years back, but Josh didn't recall the details.

"There is a difference between wanting and achieving." Harvey hoisted his backpack over his shoulder and proceeded in the direction of the commune. "Your fiancée had difficulty in distinguishing between the two. I know her kind. She would have agreed not to use my name, then told the press anyway. I was the reason she stayed at the amphitheater after you left. She'd told me to meet her there. We argued."

"Does Walker know this or are you intending to shove me down a well after telling me you pushed Willa over a cliff?" Josh strode alongside the musician as they crossed the crumbling lane and started down a freshly paved road into the town's new development.

Harvey chortled. "You're as fearless as she was. You don't think I can push you? I'm taller."

"I have more muscles and work out regularly." Josh shrugged. "And even though I've had boxing lessons and know the rules, I still fight dirty. But Amber appears to trust you, and she's psychic. I trust her. I'm going to assume you're not confessing to murder."

"You believe Amber is psychic?" Harvey asked with interest, entering a building under construction. He waved at the bare studs and concrete floor. "New museum. Every town should display their history. Ours is a little difficult."

"I can't even define *psychic* to my satisfaction." Josh gazed around, trying to envision how in hell they could display a history of weird. "I just know Amber knows things and she's usually right. What happened when you argued with Willa?"

"She threatened me with exposure. She seemed comfortable with threats. Did she do that often?"

"Yeah, that was pretty much her modus operandi, learned from her father. They call it negotiating. I call it bullying. She hated it when I didn't bargain, even in a thrift shop like Tullah's. I stupidly figure if I can afford the price and want the object, then I should pay what was asked or walk away."

"Not the path to riches," Harvey said in amusement, opening the door to a partially finished room with plasterboard walls. "Bargaining has its purpose. Threats do not. I told her to take her job and shove it. I would *not* have played at your wedding. The question becomes, who else did she threaten recently who couldn't afford to tell her to take a flying leap?"

Inside the half-finished room, Josh recognized a number of the men sitting on sawhorses and supply boxes. Two of them he'd only seen in passing—the Kennedys, owners of the resort.

Josh shook hands as Harvey introduced them. "Good to meet you. Is this where I'm run out of town on a rail?"

"No, this is where we hide when we don't want the women to know we're conspiring," the blond athletic Kennedy said—Mayor Monty.

Josh eyed the unpainted walls and sawdust-covered board floor. "Nice, maybe one step above the bunker." He turned back to Harvey. "And this is where you tell me that you left Willa alone and well after a heated argument in which she threatened to expose you to the world if you didn't play for her wedding?"

"It's where I tell you what I told Walker—Willa probably argued with every single member of her staff during the period after you left her. I didn't see her until two, so I don't know who arrived in the Porsche at one. But whoever it was must have left her wound up tight and angry. She seemed to have set up individual meetings. I could hear raised voices as I took the path out the back way. The amphitheater amplifies sound, as it's supposed to do."

"Shit, there goes our theory that Willa took the Porsche back to the lodge to pack her bags. She wouldn't have time to fit it in." Josh gazed out an unglazed window in the direction of the vortex. The flat farmland above the town had been graded and all the chaparral removed for the new development. The tops of trees could be discerned in the distance, where the hill dipped down to the vortex. "Still, if Willa wasn't killed until after three-thirty, we've established that I'm the only one without an alibi after that."

"And the Porsche driver," Walker corrected. "The photographer was still around. He spent the night here. It's possible either her vice-president or wedding planner could have turned around or parked elsewhere and walked back to the vortex before continuing down to the city. The parking lot sequence doesn't tell the whole tale. If she argued with Harvey, she could have fought with any of the locals she wanted to hire. Most of us know a lot of paths in and out of the area on foot."

"Double shit." Josh turned back to the room to study men he'd like to have as friends. "So now we have to account for everyone in town after three-thirty?"

"Everyone in town would testify they were with their friends and loved ones at the critical time, if they thought it necessary." The darker, leaner Kennedy kicked at bags of cement. "Believe me, Hillvale inhabitants shut out strangers if threatened. Monty and I have been excluded often enough because our parents made us outsiders. The Lucys accuse us of living with evil, and I'm not saying there isn't any truth to that. Bad things happen around here. The town has been keeping you in the dark because we see you as an unknown."

"And Amber? Did she know all this?" Josh tried not to sound as hurt as he felt.

"No," Keegan said firmly. "Amber has her own problems with her mother and the kid. Besides, we couldn't trust her not to tell you everything. It was hard enough for the Lucys to accept Kurt and Monty, and they grew up here."

"And what changed?" Josh gave up and took a seat on a stack of lumber.

"Last night." The antique dealer unbent his long, lanky frame from the sawhorse he'd occupied. "You leaped to our aid without fear or question. If you'd been afraid that Willa would point a finger at you, or that's how we might interpret the night's events, you wouldn't have offered us a means to talk with the entity."

"Huh." Josh considered this for all of half a second. "I work in Tinsel Town. I just went with the flow, or the special effects, whatever."

Aaron headed for the door. "Impressed the hell out of us. I tested Amber's shop after the break-in. Whoever did it didn't leave any significant impressions. I found spikes of anger and fear on the drawers they yanked open that weren't Amber's, but they're not identifiable."

Josh wasn't certain what to say to that. The other men didn't seem to find the declaration odd. "Anger," he acknowledged, wondering what that should tell him. "Sounds like her mother."

Aaron shrugged. "I have to get back to my shop. I just wanted to let you know I'm on the team for whatever is decided. Amber is one of the purest souls I've ever met, and I'm relieved that you haven't deceived her." He ambled out.

Glancing outside, Monty caught the door before it closed. "Looks like we've got a stranger roaming about. I'll give them my good ol' boy routine. Let me know what needs doing and when." He followed Aaron out.

Josh watched through the window as the mayor glad-handed the reporter he'd seen earlier. "I think I'm more officially weirded now than I was last night."

"It used to be Nulls like me and Monty against Lucys like Aaron and Harvey," Kurt Kennedy admitted. "We're still learning to work with the people we know. It will take a while before we stop questioning outsiders like you."

"It's hard to trust those you don't know, I get that." Josh jingled the coins in his pocket as he worked out the concept. "But it's like you're a closed society up here. You fear strangers and put up walls to close us out. I think history has kind of proved that insular societies not only don't work but invariably fail. The rest of the world moves on without them."

"Which is what happened after my father drove out everyone with his crooked land deals. Hillvale closed its doors and crumbled. And there are those who want to go back to the insular days, who think the rash of murders is good reason for doing so." Kurt paced around the room, checking the studs and wiring. "Superstition and paranoia go hand in hand."

"But without tourists, without new business, we can't afford schools, and the few businesses left will go broke," Keegan added. "I have a small crystal mine back in the hills. I need workers. They need houses. They have kids. They need schools. So we have to get used to dealing with newcomers."

Josh gestured helplessly. "I get that. Hillvale now welcomes immigrants. How does this solve Willa's murder?"

"That's what we're here for," the chief of police said, propping his boots up on a stack of lumber and settling in. "We want a reputation of catching anyone who thinks they can get away with murder here. Willa's secretary, Sarah, reported to the sheriff last night that Willa's phone contained a spy virus that allows it to be located even when turned off. She won't say how she found that out, but she said the phone seems to still be here in Hillvale."

TWENTY-ONE

"I can't promise you'll meet the love of your life today, but this card tells me that if you open your heart and your mind, the potential is there." Amber tapped the card the excited bridesmaid had drawn. "You have a warm heart and a good nature and you're a gift to any man smart enough to see that."

The bridesmaid was skinny and plain, even in her wedding finery. But she was glowing with happiness and exuding such joy that she would brighten any man's life. And Amber sensed the girl was aware of someone she'd just met. Amber thought it a shame that most of the men in the wedding party wouldn't visit the tarot shop. She'd love to find a match for the bridesmaid.

The wedding today was scheduled for three, so Amber had no appointments over lunch or for some hours after. She put up her cards, stretched, and returned to the front of the shop where the security Josh had miraculously produced waited.

"Are you bored out of your skulls?" she inquired of the two unlikely shopkeepers.

Behind the counter, the older lady with short-cropped spiky hair grinned toothily. "I'm having the time of my life. Those reporters now know all about my former job, my grandkids, my gambling habits. . . I kept them entertained."

The burly, bald bodyguard propped in a chair between the crystal figurines, looking like the proverbial bull, grunted what might have been amusement. "She bored them to death until they crawled out in tears of relief when she stopped talking."

"I even sold a bunch of crystals and walking sticks," the woman crowed. "That bridal party is flinging cash all over. Maybe I'll start a shop up here too. Retirement is boring."

"I am extremely grateful that you are willing to come out of retirement to help me. I don't usually need outside help, but the café across the street always does, if you're really thinking of staying. Shall we close up shop, go over there, and I'll treat you to lunch?" She didn't know how she'd repay Josh for his extraordinary gesture. She'd never had employees before and wasn't certain what to do with them, but she loved having this barrier against her mother and reporters.

"Nah, tell me what you want and I'll go over and get it." The burly guard set the front legs of the chair down. "The boss said we're to keep you out of sight, but if you want to go anywhere, we can drive you."

Amber wrinkled her nose. For Zeke's sake, she supposed she could stay out of sight until the press decided they had no story. It was not as if she was front page news anymore.

"Are you okay with fetching my nephew and dropping us at my house? He needs to stay out of sight too." As far as Amber knew, her mother was still at the lodge. That couldn't be good.

"Sure, I can do that and fetch lunch for him too." Oscar unfurled from his chair.

"Okay if I stay here?" the female guard asked. "I can eat at the desk and keep an eye on things."

While they waited for food, Amber called Josh's suite to see how he'd fared. Ernest informed her that Josh had disappeared hours ago, after the press conference, so he assumed he was at the studio apartment. Needing to see how Zeke was doing, she rang him there. Zeke answered. He hadn't seen Josh but was happy to have a ride down for lunch. Frowning, she hung up. She couldn't imagine there were too many places Josh might visit in Hillvale. Maybe, after the press conference, he'd decided to take out his frustrations on his rented bike again. He used to pick fights when he was tense. Exercise was a far better alternative.

After collecting their order and driving up to fetch Zeke, the burly guard parked his SUV in Amber's narrow driveway. "I'll eat out here, if it's all the same to you, ma'am. I've got my audiobook, and I can keep a better eye on who's around."

Carrying lunch sacks, Zeke was already halfway out of the van.

"If you need anything, you be sure to let me know," Amber said, climbing out after the boy. "I must be a really boring job."

"Each one is different, ma'am. I'm fond of the ones where I'm not likely to get my butt shot off."

Amber chuckled and followed a bouncing Zeke to the door. She hated that she had to actually lock it all the time now, but the keypad Walker had installed made it easier than hunting down keys.

Music played from the wedding further up the hill. This party hadn't hired Val or Harvey. They must have brought their own musicians.

"Aunt Amber," Zeke said worriedly, studying her tiled front porch as she punched the keypad. "Look."

She glanced down, expecting to see a large spider or snake. Instead, she saw drops of what at first appeared to be brown paint.

"I think it's blood," Zeke said somberly.

～

AFTER THE EXCEEDINGLY ENTERTAINING MEETING WITH THE POLICE CHIEF'S weird squad, Josh let himself into the lodge suite, eager to call Amber.

Instead, he almost fell over suitcases.

"We need to go back to LA *now*," Ernest shouted from the living area, where he packed up a laptop. "This isn't amusing anymore."

Josh's throat closed. He glanced around. Finding no bodies, he shut the door behind him. "What now?"

"Sarah's dead. I could be next." Ernest shakily pointed at the phone. "Call Amber. I have our bags packed. You need to make her pack too. I'm starting to believe this place *is* evil."

Sarah? What the hell?

Josh grabbed the receiver but Amber's home line was busy. He tried the shop. A gruff, unfamiliar voice answered and said Amber wasn't there. She wouldn't tell him where Amber was until Josh told her she'd be fired, and Ernest got on the line and explained who he was.

"She said she was taking her nephew up to a studio," the now-friendlier voice replied. "I'm supposed to shut up the shop, but I'm doing real good business. What would you like me to do?"

Josh rubbed his head and tried to think through the red haze of panic. "If you don't mind staying where you are, then hold down the fort. We don't want thieves returning."

He hung up and glared at the bags Ernest was collecting. "Will you tell me what the hell happened?"

"Sarah was murdered in broad daylight on *Amber's doorstep*, that's what happened! And you vanished without a trace and have no alibi again. We're getting out of here. I can call a car or you can take me back, I don't care which."

Amber's doorstep. Josh nearly sprinted for the door, but he'd learned impulse control over the years. He needed to calm Ernest and find out details before he terrified Amber with his own freak-out.

"I've been with witnesses the whole damned day," Josh told his new CEO. "I'm not going anywhere without Amber. Hire a car, if you want, but I'm taking mine over to the studio. Is that my suitcase?" He pointed at the designer bag Willa had bought for him. "I'll take that with me. As long as it wasn't Amber or Zeke who was murdered, I can handle it. What the hell was *Sarah* doing up here?" Willa's personal secretary should have had her hands full back in LA, fielding calls from all Willa's frenemies, keeping an eye on the house, and beating off reporters.

Ernest calmed down enough to look wary. "You were with witnesses?"

"The whole damned day. Did you think I murdered *Sarah*?" Josh looked at him in disgust and yanked up the handle of his rolling suitcase.

"No, but the sheriff was demanding to know where you were, and *I couldn't tell him.*" Ernest collapsed in a chair. "The body was found in Amber's backyard. Publicity will be terrible for her, but if you have witnesses. . ."

"The chief of police himself, among others, if that helps, until he got called away." Josh grimaced, realizing why Walker had left. "I better go find Amber."

"I still don't like it," Ernest grumbled. "What if the killer is after all of us? Should I call and see if Tessa and Brad made it back to LA?"

"You can check on them, if you want." Josh gave that possibility half a thought, then shook his head. "The chief just told me that Sarah reported last night that she had information about Willa's phone." He headed for the door. "If you know who bugged it, call the cops. Otherwise, everyone else should be safe, and I'd appreciate it if you stayed. But you're head of the company now. You get to choose what's best for the project."

He walked out, letting Ernest ponder his new responsibilities. Josh had forgotten Ernest ten steps down the hall as he rushed to find Amber.

A reporter was leaning against Josh's Prius. Josh shoved him off the trunk and opened it. The jackals would track him to his new place now. He'd have to hire round-the-clock bodyguards.

"Willa was a mean bitch, but she never killed anybody," the reporter said. "You can't hide."

"I'm not hiding. I'm right here and not going far. If you want to help, then keep the innocent out of this and go after the gutter dwellers—or are they not good sales material?" Josh slammed the trunk closed on the suitcase and opened the car door.

"Jack and Ginger as a murdering duo is pretty good material," the reporter called as Josh revved his engine. "Point me elsewhere."

"Find out who came up here with Crystal Abercrombie and why they're here. Work for your money." Josh pulled away, roaring down the drive, startling a couple of peacocks.

Sarah, *damn*. He'd mostly talked to the secretary on the phone and considered her another of Willa's efficient tools. Sarah had called the cops about the phone, and now she was dead. Why would she have driven all the way up to Hillvale once she'd passed on the information?

First, he needed to worry about Amber. Maybe he should take her away. Another murder would be lousy for the town and business. She shouldn't have to put up with this shit just because she knew him in a different time and place.

A sheriff's van had parked in Amber's drive. Curious neighbors hung over their fences and milled in the street. If a coroner's van had arrived, it had already left. Josh continued up the lane to the drive of the Gothic Victorian. An unfamiliar SUV was parked in front of the garage. His landlady waited in his parking space—as if she'd known he was coming.

Eager to see if Amber was upstairs and okay, Josh didn't view interference with pleasure. He climbed out and waited without speaking.

"I do not appreciate unapproved strangers on my premises," the stern, professorial lady informed him. "I understand and respect your need to protect Amber, but the bodyguard has to go."

She stalked away without further commentary.

To hell with it. Josh took the stairs to the studio two at a time. The burly bodyguard Ernest had hired sat in a chair on the sunny balcony wearing earplugs and blocking the entrance. At sight of Josh, he raised his bulk and moved the chair, gesturing him to enter.

Nice to know someone didn't suspect he was a killer.

Amber flew into his arms the moment the door opened. Grateful that she didn't question his innocence, Josh wrapped her in his arms and just hung on.

"You know I don't deserve you," he whispered into her hair. "I'm sorry I wasn't here. I'm a worthless lout with no thought of anyone but myself."

She laughed into his shoulder. "Well, if that's all you are, I'm sure I can find a place for you in my booming empire. I'm glad you're here. I'm tired of being scared."

He held her tight and rocked her until he realized Zeke was sitting in the front of the TV, studiously focusing on a video game. With a half-laugh, he set Amber down. "Okay, tell me what's been happening while I've been having the weirdest pow-wow with your neighbors."

"Did they feed you? We have a ton of leftovers." She dragged him into the kitchen and began emptying the refrigerator.

He grabbed a beer. "Explain the sheriff's van in front of your house. Can't I leave you alone for a single morning without drama?"

"Nope, I live for drama. We sit around every day, making up action scenes. You should see the knitting society theater—needles at noon," she said facetiously, emptying a carton onto a plate and sticking it into the microwave. "I don't know much. I didn't even get inside before Zeke saw the blood. We went over to Sam's. She used her walkie-talkie to reach Walker. He came over, took a look around the house, and called the sheriff. So you know more than I do. And I think I'm good with that. I really don't want to believe in evil."

"I think defining evil would be as difficult as defining innocence. There's a whole lot of gray in between black and white. But we need to know what we're up against. Apparently Willa's personal secretary died today—that's what happened on your porch."

She stared at him in disbelief and horror. Amber had a tremendously expressive face that would be luminous on camera.

Josh knew his mind was simply seeking distraction, and he continued with a sigh, "I don't suppose any of your know-everything friends could find out if anyone saw anything? Sarah had to have driven up here. Her car must be around. If there's blood on the step, the chances are good that she must have been killed on your porch."

Which made him sick to think about.

TWENTY-TWO

"WILLA'S SECRETARY?" AMBER ASKED IN HORROR. "IN HILLVALE, AT MY house?"

"Sarah was here the day Willa died. She returned to LA with Ernest, remember? I have no idea why she was on your doorstep. How could she be murdered in broad daylight and no one notice?" Josh dug a fork into the plate she set in front of him. "Sarah was a twig of a thing but not invisible."

Amber had been trained since infancy to consider food the enemy. Even when food had finally been available, she'd made herself ill eating it. So she'd found her comfort in meditation, Ouija boards, and tarot. She'd lost all interest in lunch the instant they'd spotted blood on the porch.

Josh apparently had no such problem. He dug into her food while he waited for answers. She gave his question some thought.

"With the wedding, there's been a ton of traffic and pedestrians today." She tried to think like a murderer while she forced herself to nibble at her kale salad. The salad was delicious, but she really wanted her Ouija board. "The wedding party had a big delivery truck parked on our lane, which probably blocked Sam's view from across the street. Mariah is always at her computer. I have a lot of shrubbery for privacy. It would have been reasonably easy for anyone to walk up from town unnoticed and knock on my door."

He frowned and chewed, probably picturing the lane in his vivid imagination. Amber filled in more details.

"Most of us were in town, working, since Saturday is a big business day. There may have been tourists in the lane. It's a public passage and safer for walking up to the vortex than the highway, so people park in town and cut through, even though the lane ends on Cass's property. Walker will have to interview the entire wedding party to find witnesses. And even then, they may not have seen much. My house is set back from the road behind a hedge."

He pinched the bridge of his nose and closed his eyes. "Sarah knew something. It's the only thing that makes sense. According to Walker, she told the police that she received an anonymous email leading to an app that tracked Willa's phone and that the phone was in Hillvale. The sheriff's department has an IT expert tracing the origin of the email."

"If they have the email, Walker's company can track it faster," she said, trying to be reassuring. "His company is supposed to be paid for his investigations, but he never charges Hillvale once he gets involved."

"I'll pay," Josh said, viciously tearing at a chicken leg. "I've already told him I'll pay whatever it takes to find out about Willa. I'll add Sarah to the bill. He doesn't have enough help. He had to borrow an off-duty deputy to interview your mother. I sure the hell hope he found out who came here with her. If it's Dell. . ."

"Willa warned us there was a *spy*, remember?" Amber said with excitement. "And she showed us the pervert and the Midas card. Could Sarah have been the spy? Would she do that?" Amber glanced at the bag holding her spare tarot decks. "I really don't want to have to find out if Willa is still with us."

"Neither do I. But I didn't know Sarah well enough to know if she would spy. She was certainly in a position to do so, but we know for fact that she was with Ernest and on her way back to LA when Willa died." Sipping his beer, he glanced at Zeke, now fully absorbed in his video game. "Walker has dreamed up a scheme—or his Lucy wife did. The plan was originally to draw Willa's crew back here and hope we could produce a guilty reaction from one of them."

"Let's have a show." She repeated his earlier quote from the old Judy Garland/Mickey Rooney film. "That never turned out so hot when Jack and Ginger did it. And I don't think her original crew is enough, especially now that Sarah's dead. I think we need Willa's father and maybe Crystal and Dell and who knows who else. Willa's phone would be more useful."

On that thought, she got up and called Mariah. Mariah might be able to hack a virus, right?

Before Amber could say a word, Mariah announced, "You and Zeke can't go back to your house until the sheriff clears out, and we stage a cleansing. I'm not up to another séance just yet, but maybe Cass will do this one. In the meantime, you and Josh need to get your posteriors over to Sam's place. We're having a meeting."

Amber slumped over the counter, fearing what they plotted. "Do we have to? I can't leave Zeke alone unless you can persuade Walker to arrest my mother."

"I heard Josh hired a bodyguard. Have him stay with Zeke. Didn't he tell you about our plan? We're calling it a tribute to Willa Powell and insisting her father attend. We'll help," Mariah said reassuringly.

"A tribute?" she asked cautiously.

"A show," Josh called from the counter.

They were realio trulio plotting a *show*? The thought filled Amber with horror. "The rest of you can discuss a show. I'll stay here and you can tell me about it later." Amber did her best to sound firm and decisive. "I called to find out if you know what happened to Willa's phone. Josh said they tracked it somehow."

"Spyware," Mariah replied curtly. "I haven't had time to find out if the police found the phone, but it could take months to dig anything out of it, if then. And you're essential to the show, so you need to be here, *now*, before anyone else dies."

"The town is crawling with reporters." Amber desperately tried to sound calm and reasonable, even though panic was setting in. Hillvale was supposed to be *safe*, her private cocoon. "I will not appear in public for *any* reason unless it's behind a curtain."

Josh appeared at her side, taking the receiver from her hand and speaking to Mariah. "I haven't had time to explain yet. A little case of murder has thrown me off stride. If there's room to park, we'll drive down. Apparently the lane is crawling with tourists."

Amber crushed the cardboard lunch box and trashed it. She debated walking out and asking the bodyguard to drive her somewhere safe, but where would that be? Maybe she should walk over to Cass's. A person could get lost in that weird place. Maybe even Cass wouldn't know she was there.

But she couldn't abandon Zeke.

She scraped the remains of lunch into the trash and began scrubbing the counter. She didn't eat when she was upset. She cleaned. And organized. And feathered her nest.

She needed to get back into her house so she could clean up and make things pretty. . .

She didn't know if she could ever bear to go back into her pretty house again.

She burst into tears and ran back to the bathroom.

"Need a beat here," Josh told Mariah before he hung up the phone. He followed Amber down the short hall to the minuscule bathroom. "Amber?" he asked, warily knocking on the panel.

"I'm planning retirement to Siberia. Go away." She ran the water.

"Not happening, sweetheart. That lock opens with a paper clip. Don't make me come in after you. Bring the energy here, get in my face, but don't pretend I'm Dell or Crystal." He was starting to remember the darker side of their warped adolescence. Where he would go ballistic and blow things up under stress, Amber would work her heart out, fight the good fight, and then vanish in a deluge of tears.

He'd been a kid then and helpless against the adults controlling their world. He'd grown up and learned a little about fighting back since then, he hoped.

And maybe she had too. The door popped open, and she glared at him. "I am *not* doing a show."

That wouldn't be good, but Amber wasn't dumb. She just needed more information. "I get that. But you're the person the Lucys know.

They won't listen to me. I'm supposed to write the script. Maybe you can do a reading from behind a curtain. We don't know what we're doing until we talk about it."

"You're lying. You always blink fast when you lie." She slammed the door again.

Zeke appeared, looking worried. The kid didn't need this turmoil right now.

"Your aunt isn't happy about not being able to go home." He lied some more, trying to keep from blinking. "We need to go to a boring meeting. Why don't I tell the bodyguard to take you to the suite at the lodge? We can't swim until your grandmother leaves, but the lodge has Netflix. Ernest will be there to order snacks." He hoped he wasn't lying about that. Ernest might be halfway back to LA. "As long as you stay inside, no one will see you."

Understanding the danger of his grandmother, Zeke nodded, throwing a cautious glance to the door. "Aunt Amber? Are you okay? You want me to go?"

The door popped open again, and she swooped down to hug her nephew. "Of course I don't want you to go. But I know you're bored, and I'm so sorry. Once I have my computer, we'll look up some fun things to do together."

Amber had to emerge from hiding to instruct the bodyguard about stopping at the thrift store to buy pajamas, clean clothes, and available games.

Josh grimaced, realizing it might be hours or more before Amber could return to her safe nest. His presence was destroying all the security she'd established. And he was asking her to demolish the rest. *Aw shit.* He was scum, and she'd realize that and never want to see him again.

But they couldn't let a killer go free. He'd have to play the bad guy instead of her hero.

He called and verified that Ernest had decided to stay and warned him that Zeke was on the way. "I know I can't expect you to babysit," he told his new CEO. "But until we can find an assistant we trust, I'm still counting on your help. If you can find someone to babysit, go for it. These are desperate times."

"He doesn't really need a babysitter," Ernest said. "We'll deal. We do need new PR. The conference is old news already. We have a publicity nightmare on our hands."

Josh ran his hand over his face. "And we're just getting started. I'm no Willa. I have no interest or knowledge of anything except directing. You really are in charge, unless you want to run, screaming."

"I like being paid to scream." Ernest hung up.

Amber was waving Zeke farewell when Josh set down the receiver. She wasn't fragile, he reminded himself. Emotional, yes, but she'd rescued herself once.

He didn't want her to hate him forever, but this killer had to be caught. He'd do whatever it took.

TWENTY-THREE

Amber wiped her eyes after Zeke left, then glared at Josh. "I'll listen if my friends ask. I will *not* go on stage for an audience ever again."

She'd been harboring hopes that Josh would help her find connections. She needed to support Zeke somehow. She had a professionally trained voice and had been hoping for voice-overs, not public appearances.

By refusing to cooperate with this insane idea, she was flinging away any chance of Josh helping her. She would have to abandon her security, maybe go to the city and record audiobooks for a living.

And live in the street.

Trying not to weep in fear and loss, she marched down the studio's lovely tiled stairs, ignoring the view. She could hear the wedding party wandering down to the reception, but Cass's trees hid the lane.

Josh took the stairs after her, hurrying to open the Prius door, placing a hand at her back as if she needed assistance climbing in. As if she might be precious to him?

That made her want to cry too. She'd actually started to hope that they might rebuild their relationship. Stupid, stupid her. His life rotated around money and audiences and people. What little comfort she had depended on obscurity.

Josh was silent as they maneuvered the half mile down the lane to Sam and Walker's big farmhouse. Tinted windows prevented pedestrians from recognizing them, thank all that was holy.

As was becoming the custom, Sam's tables were covered in food from Fee's café. It was early for dinner, late for lunch, but they burned energy with their discussions and snacking fought lethargy. Amber smelled the delicious scents as Sam welcomed them in the door. She was still too sick at heart to be hungry.

Her therapist had told her she was fortunate that with her ruined metabolism, she viewed food as medicine to be taken according to instructions. Amber didn't feel particularly fortunate not to enjoy the yummies everyone else scarfed down.

She shook off Josh's hand and parked herself in a padded rocking chair. She'd led such a placid life these past years that she was shocked at how draining this roller coaster of emotions could be. She just wanted to go to bed and pull the covers over her head.

She didn't think she'd ever be able to enter her cottage again knowing a woman had died there.

Saying, "Energy food," Fee handed her a bowl of cinnamon-roasted almonds that smelled like heaven. Fee walked away to deliver another plate before Amber could thank her.

Fee's ability to smell what people needed was pretty uncanny and extremely useful. Amber felt like a fraud in her shadow. What had she ever accomplished with her cards?

Maybe that was what was really sapping her strength—she felt as if all the happy years she'd spent here had been frivolous. Instead of wallowing in her pretty nest, she should have been doing something useful with her life, as Josh had. Then she'd have a real home to offer Zeke. What kind of business was reading tarot cards anyway? She couldn't really read minds.

Her mother's words cut like a knife—she was a failure.

The nuts distracted her. She nibbled a few, then stopped to inhale. She cleared her lungs and head in hopes of returning to the happy place in her heart. It was there, but it was tough to reach with all the tension building. She felt Josh inside her mind as if he were a physical presence.

She didn't turn to look at him standing at the back of the room. Like most men, he meant to use her.

She was a grown woman now. She didn't have to allow it. She had options.

Sam stood up in front of the fireplace to draw their attention. "All right, ladies, the men have an interesting presentation for us. Be kind." She turned to her husband. "Walker, do you want to do the honors?"

"No way. I'm just the informed source. Josh took our idea and ran with it. Let him explain." Wearing casual jeans and a muted blue Hawaiian-print shirt, the police chief leaned against the wall near the food table and gestured at Josh.

Next to a formidable giant like Keegan and Aaron's Scorpio intensity, Josh seemed reassuringly approachable. Except, even though he didn't have their height, he'd carried her as if she weighed nothing. Every ounce of him was restrained muscle and tension.

Carrying a bottle of water, he worked his way through the crowded room to where Sam stood in front of the fireplace. "I don't know everyone well," he told their hostess. "I'll need you and the others to work with me on this, please."

Sam perched on a high bar stool she'd dragged in from the kitchen. "Magic wands, at your service, sir."

Amber fretted at her bottom lip as Josh shoved his hands in his jeans pockets and focused on her. She wanted to squirm. But as always, his direct cobalt gaze held her pinned.

"Willa Powell and her personal secretary died here for reasons we don't understand. Since the sheriff can handle forensics but knows little about Hillvale, it seems to be up to us to find a killer by establishing motive." Josh appeared pale but determined.

"Murder motives are more complex than you see in books and film," Walker warned from the back of the room.

"I memorized your list of motivations," Josh said. "Out of the list, I'd say we're not dealing with narcotics or crime, and probably not property disputes. But knowing Willa, I'd say her death could be motivated by anything from personal vendetta to an act of rage. Money might be another motive, but none of our current suspects logically fit that pattern.

Sarah, on the other hand, was a quiet, unassuming person who wouldn't inspire hate, but who had access to much of Willa's life. Her death might fall under the motive category of someone wanting to keep a secret."

"If I may interrupt again?" Walker asked. At Josh's nod, he continued. "The sheriff just located Willa's smashed phone on the top of Amber's kitchen cabinet, along with a print photo of Willa's body as we found it in the canyon. Oddly, Sarah had photos in her purse of Josh and Amber together in the shop and at the café. She was also carrying a printed blackmail note saying she had proof that Josh had ordered Willa's death."

Amber felt the blood seep from her face. Josh looked glassy-eyed in shock.

Everyone else sat silently, waiting for Walker to continue. Swallowing fear, Amber circled a hand near her chest, reminding Josh to breathe. Nodding, he held her gaze as they both deliberately inhaled and exhaled to center themselves. No matter what their differences now, they still had their shared past to fall back on.

Walker continued. "The sheriff agrees that Sarah was killed in a manner consistent with a military-style Ka-Bar knife wielded by someone with experience in handling knives. She died instantly. That pretty much rules out Josh and Amber. A hired killer. . . is always a possibility. The really bad attempt to put the onus on Josh or Amber. . . that's right out of a fictional murder mystery."

"And Hollywood," Josh said, sounding almost relieved. "That plays into our working theories, right?"

"I prefer to keep an open mind. We're checking the photos and phone for fingerprints. I doubt that any of our Hollywood suspects have military experience with knives, but we're running background checks. If there's enough money at stake, one of them might possibly have hired a killer. That still makes them guilty. If our object is to obtain a confession, then Hillvale has a pretty good track record. I'm willing to play along." Walker reached for his pie plate, signaling he was done.

Amber tried to keep her teeth from chattering. As much as she'd like to nail Dell with murder, she was pretty certain he didn't have the guts to even *hold* a knife. But hiring a killer. . . Yeah, that was right down his rotten alley. How would they ever find proof?

"The play's the thing, wherein I'll catch the conscience of the king. . ." Josh recited. "Walker and I've discussed this. I've been scribbling a script and characters ever since I came up here. It might work into Walker's suggestion of a play, but I'll need Lucy input to explain what's possible. So this is all open for discussion. But we thought we might be able to lure the suspects up here by staging a memorial production in Willa's honor, sort of a dinner theater. Willa used to watch the Jack and Ginger show and often mentioned a fondness for the childish farces the characters occasionally put on. It's far-fetched, but it might be a draw. Your facilities aren't great, but a short memorial show followed by a buffet could give you time to meet the suspects."

"Make me greeter at the door so I can identify anyone who might smell guilty or evil," Fee suggested. "Then I can prepare food especially for them while everyone else is doing the show. I've never tried to persuade anyone to talk, but there's always a first time."

"Mariah will not be performing any ectoplasmic tricks," Keegan announced. "If Fee can't produce confessions, we need to find a better method."

Amber would have bristled at his proprietary command, only she'd come to understand that was how the Scots giant expressed his love. She supposed not all men were controlling rats. Keegan was just being protective of his dangerously intrepid wife.

"If Fee knows there's a killer in the room, I'm not promising anything," Mariah warned, holding an arm around her protruding belly. "We don't know ectoplasm causes any problems."

"And we don't want to find out," Tullah said with finality. "Let the child develop as it should. You are carrying a beautiful soul."

Teddy raised her hand. "If there's a good way for me to move among the audience, I might sense guilt, if we can produce a program that induces it. Can you do that?"

Amber wrung her hands. She'd never read the cards for anyone evil that she knew of. Her psychic gifts were pretty low key and useless. It wasn't as if she could really read minds, just. . . vibrations, maybe, but she needed her cards to translate. And it had to be a fairly intimate setting. She didn't know how she could help.

Aaron spoke up. "We talked about my sensing images left on objects.

I should probably have access to the smashed phone and the photos. But chances are good there wasn't enough intense thought on them to yield usable results. However, if we produce a show that induces guilt and the guilty person is holding, say, a wine glass, their emotion should be clearly imprinted, at the very least. If we're lucky, the guilt will produce an image. We could give each audience member a memorial glass with their name on it. After the show, I could offer to refill the glasses. There are no guarantees, but it's the best I can do."

Josh nodded. "Thank you for clarifying what's possible. I'm in over my head when it comes to what you call Lucy abilities. I noticed your Lucy sticks lit up during the séance. Is there any way of producing that outcome again? I'd like to work them into the script."

Lucy sticks. Leave it to Josh. Amber watched as everyone held up their walking staffs. The crystal in all the ones that had been at the séance still held a faint glow, as did hers. She'd thought it was an after-effect of a powerful spirit. . .

"Could Willa's spirit be inhabiting the crystals?" she asked in trepidation, remembering how the crystal ball had lit up.

"Very possible," Tullah agreed.

Oh damn. Amber shut her eyes and tried to imagine herself in another time and place, but Josh's pain and anger pushed at her too hard. He was set on closure, which might require this dreadful exhibition. She needed safety, which required staying the hell out of the public eye.

She saw no way this could end happily.

Josh could still read Amber's body language as if it were yesterday. She was shutting herself out. He totally understood.

He'd tried keeping her out of his mess, but as long as he stayed here, he'd never succeed. If he left, he'd never find Willa's killer—the one who could be targeting Amber now. He could not live with that, so he had to find a way out, even if she hated him for forcing this on her. At least she'd be alive.

He winced at the thought of Amber's beautiful spirit lighting crystal balls and doorknobs as the Lucys claimed Willa was. He had to be insane to believe this lot of weirdoes and their superstitions, but Amber believed them, and he believed in Amber. He wouldn't have survived childhood without her wisdom. She'd kept him from killing Dell when Josh had discovered the camera in the restrooms. She'd discovered where Dell hid his porn and let Josh set fire to it instead. And then she'd warned him when Josh's drunk father had tried to make deals with Dell or his toadies. She *knew* things.

So he probably should listen to her now, except Amber had one very large flaw—self-doubt. She didn't *believe* she knew things. She didn't believe she was beautiful. She didn't believe audiences loved her. She'd never known anything except criticism since birth, and she'd wrapped that doubt around her like a protective cocoon.

He hated to cut open her defensive shield and leave her exposed like a frail, wet butterfly, especially in front of her mother and Dell. Left to himself, he'd take the easy path and let the police handle everything. If he ended up in jail, so be it.

But to keep Amber safe, even if she hated him, he had to stir himself from the easy path and take the risks he'd spent a lifetime avoiding.

He had to pray that he wasn't exposing himself as a ginormous fraud, but full speed ahead had always been his problem, not self-doubt.

"As I said, I'll need your help in formulating this show to suit your various talents," he continued. "Valerie, Amber, and I are the ones with the most acting experience, so I'll have to write the script mostly for us."

He couldn't read the reaction of the tall woman in the black veil, but Walker had promised to have his wife talk with her aunt, the former actress. At least, Val didn't stomp out.

"Harvey's our musician. He says he can read the audience and fine-tune the music to suit their mood, so we'll mostly need him backstage. That leaves the rest of you for walk-on parts, if that's okay."

Amber ominously said nothing. Most of his listeners nodded and murmured among themselves. Taking a deep breath to stay focused, Josh dived in.

"We need to keep this simple. Dinner theaters are usually mystery farces. As a memorial, they're not typical, but we'll sell it as my gift to Willa. I'll donate the script rights to non-profit organizations. Since many of the audience will be theater people, they'll understand that. Lots of local theater groups are non-profit."

Amber's eyes opened. He was reaching her somehow.

"I understand Hillvale has a non-profit foundation formed to develop the museum and promote local arts, so I'll write the script to incorporate the town, in case you ever develop a theater company." There, she was squirming, but she was thinking.

"At the moment, I'm envisioning an old-fashioned Sherlock Holmes type script, except the all-knowing detective will deal with ghosts and psychics as well as the usual witnesses. I've been taking character notes since I got here, so I already have roles representing possible real-life suspects. I'm hoping Val will consider playing the part of Willa's ghost." He waited and caught a thoughtful nod from the woman in black. An actress who seldom spoke was a new experience, but he wrote fantasy. He'd adapt.

"The detective needs a sidekick who keeps a running dialogue on who is what and acts as a sounding board." Here was where the shit hit the fan. Josh braced himself. "I'd like to add a different spin and make the detective female and the sidekick male. My intention is to hit the conscience of the guilty so our psychics can find them. If the audience is to grasp that the ghost is Willa, I need them to relate to the detective's passionate search for justice, and that works better with a female in the part."

Amber's mouth fell open. She shut it abruptly, but Josh knew he'd sucked her in. This was classic Jack and Ginger, only in adult format. He'd always been Ginger's sidekick, even though he'd received star billing—simply because he was male. She was by far the stronger actor. They'd both known that. On his own, Jack would simply have been another smart-mouthed brat. Ginger had been the one who made their audience cry and shout and believe justice was served when they turned adult worlds upside-down with their mischief.

She shouldn't doubt her ability to handle this role with one hand tied behind her back.

"If anyone can instill guilt in our audience, it's Amber," he said. "A pragmatic detective doesn't inspire passion. But Amber knows how to play the role of an outraged woman seeking justice for a friend."

The Lucys began clapping enthusiastically—all except Amber.

"My mother and Dell will be in that audience, won't they?" she asked flatly over the applause.

"You're not afraid of them," Josh said, knowing it wasn't people but publicity that she feared.

"There will be photographers, if only from Willa's crew," she argued, as she always did.

"We can limit them, if you prefer, but if the point is a memorial, then the event probably should be Hollywood-worthy." He tried to gauge the level of her panic, if he should give up the whole idea.

"I choose my costume and share the directing chair." She got up and walked out, through the kitchen.

The back door slammed in the silence. Josh swallowed his anger, fear —and hope—and ran after her.

TWENTY-FOUR

THE JUNE NIGHT WAS SPECTACULAR, WITH A MILLION STARS IN A CLOUDLESS
black sky. Insects hummed in the trees, and the air was silky warm.
Amber had missed her afternoon appointments in this turmoil. She
hadn't realized it was so late.

She hugged her bare arms, feeling the flab, fighting her panic. *She'd
just agreed to put herself in front of an audience expecting to see boyish, adolescent Ginger!*

Humiliation on that scale should have a price.

Maybe she could make Josh promise to find her audio jobs if she
survived the mortifying laughter and whispers. If she had to lose the
safety of her anonymous nest, she should learn to negotiate. It wasn't as
if she had an agent.

She was shaking too badly to think straight. She wasn't poor lost
Ginger, she reminded herself. She was *Amber. . .*

She didn't feel strong, witch or otherwise.

But underneath all her fear, she knew he was right. They had to catch
the killer.

When Josh finally arrived, stood behind her, and wrapped his arms
along hers, she knew one answer anyway. She had no power over him.
She'd loved the wretch far too long to not offer anything he asked. She

was a wimp. So many things she should have done over these last lost years. . . instead of curling up and sucking her thumb.

"It's beautiful up here," he murmured, apparently studying the sky as she had been. "If we could pretend we were the only people on the planet, what would you do?"

"Perish, probably," she said with tartness. "I couldn't grow an ear of corn much less a stick of butter."

He laughed. "Okay, so I'm the romantic here, got it. Do you hate me totally?"

"Yup, always have," she agreed. "I always let people I hate walk all over me. It's compulsive."

He snorted against her ear. "Right. That's why you dumped Crystal and Dell on their bums and told adoring audiences to take a hike and created your own world. Got that."

"Since when did you start writing your own scripts?" she asked, still working on her nonexistent resistance.

"Always have. Just never get to use them. I am apparently a shit scriptwriter, but this one is so clear in my head, I could probably sit down and write it tonight. I'm a good director, you know. I may know bupkis about money, but I know how to make even a cheap production look good."

She leaned into him, taking his strong embrace for granted. Josh had always been there for her. She was the one who'd left. "I don't doubt your directing ability. I doubt your ability to rein in your enthusiasm for your script to allow me to do what I need to do. So I get to direct me. If my fat ass is about to be shown all over the internet, then it will be my choice of how it appears."

He ran his big hands down her sides to said ass and turned her around so she faced him. She couldn't read his eyes in the dark, but she'd always been able to feel Josh inside her head. She didn't need his words, which was the truly scary part of their relationship. She didn't know how much of that he understood.

"Fat is in the eye of the beholder. I happen to be very fond of your cushy ass," he said, running his hands over her posterior, lifting her against him. "And I'm in a better position than you are to know how you look from every angle. I'll show you the photos I've taken and prove it. I don't want you just for this stupid production. I want *you*."

His seductive hands sent shivers through all her soft places. It was impossible to resist when he bent to kiss her. It had been so very long since she'd been held. . . And he'd been a boy then. She'd never really known a man's embrace.

Amber slid her arms around his waist and offered her mouth. If she quit blocking him, if she opened herself up to him. . . she could *feel* the truth of his need. She knew that his desire was honest. She held Josh's *soul* in her hands.

For them, it had never been just about bodies. It was hard to climb over that painful hurdle of being used in her head, but if she let him seduce her with his kisses and his hands, her head went away and her instincts knew what to do.

She might never have a better opportunity to escape the prison she lived in.

"Promise me, you'll see Zeke safe, no matter what happens?" she demanded, her fears for her nephew outweighing all the rest.

"You really think I wouldn't?" he asked, sounding shocked. "Nothing will happen to him or *you* on my watch."

And he meant that—from his position of power and command. He didn't know what it was like to be helpless.

She needed to crawl from under her rock and learn not to be a victim.

JOSH SENSED AMBER'S SURRENDER, AND HE TOOK HER MOUTH WITH AS MUCH gratitude as passion. He might be walking off a cliff, but knowing Amber didn't hate him yet was a parachute that buoyed him. If he was very lucky, he might show her how beautiful she was and maybe she'd forgive him for destroying her security. Someday.

They didn't bother returning to the gathering but climbed in his car and drove up to the studio. The merrymaking of the wedding party carried through the clear air. It seemed a violation of universal laws to know that two women had been brutally murdered in this place where so many people came to be happy.

In the car, he kept his hand on Amber's knee, fearful the spell might break if he didn't touch her. As they traversed the stairs to the studio, she daringly caressed his ass the way he had hers, and his libido shot into rocket mode. Josh locked the door behind them and ripped her loose shirt over her gorgeous hair.

Her bra was a wonder of delicate lace and practical construction. His Amber loved femininity inside and out. She grabbed the front of his shirt as he caressed her breasts.

"Naked," he muttered against her lush lips. "I need you naked. After seeing you in black underwear, I have fantasies to fulfill."

She laughed softly and unbuttoned his shirt. "Don't we all?"

They stripped, strewing their clothes across the floor as they stumbled toward the big bed behind the blanket room divider. Josh tossed her onto the mattress. "I wanted to be your hero and do that when I was sixteen, but I had no strength," he told her, dropping down beside her.

It was dark, but he thought she might not be ready for light yet. He could feel her supple flesh just fine, and the sensuality of touch was all that mattered. She was the sexy porn star who featured in his midnight fantasies. It had been so damned long since she'd taken him to the stars. . .

"I'm a wuss, so macho displays back then wouldn't have gone over well." She ran her hands over his shoulder and chest. "I think I'm braver now."

He kissed her in all the places he'd dreamed about. "You were never, ever a wuss. You have a rock solid streak of stubborn steel for a spine," he insisted between kisses. "You just hide it beneath all your exquisite softness and fluffy façade."

"Maybe the steel has rusted from disuse," she suggested, sliding her hand lower.

He caught her hand before it went too far. "I'm on the brink of explosion already. This time needs to be about you. Let me polish your steel."

"There's that romantic again," she laughed, but she slid her hand upward again. "*Me* wants to touch, though."

"You were always a hands-on kind of person." He kissed the sweet peach of her cheek and caressed the lushness of her breasts. "Damn, I don't know how long I can hold out. Let's hope you don't need too much polish."

He leaned over and suckled at her nipple, and she cried out with such joy that he almost came undone from the music of her voice.

~

NO MATTER HOW SCARRED HER PSYCHE, HER BODY WAS READY. AND THIS WAS Josh, whose mind synched with hers so very well that Amber could get high just on his joy. He touched her with reverence and a passion that enhanced hers. She might be embarrassed by the size of her thighs as he lifted them and kissed her between her legs, but she sensed his intense desire. Just the subtle touch of lips and tongue, and he sent her over the brink into ecstasy.

He had condoms in the drawer. After that, it was all easy. They fit together like two parts of a puzzle. He shook her world. And she wept when it was over because she knew nothing could be so beautiful ever again.

"You are such a baby," he said with laughter, hauling her head to his shoulder. "It's a good thing I'm used to your tears or I'd be insulted."

She pinched the thick hide over his ribcage. "It's a good thing I know you're not laughing at me or I'd crush you."

"Thank you for understanding," he murmured against her ear, caressing her side in a manner that proved she had curves, even if they were ample. "There have been times these past years I haven't been able to tell when I was acting and when I wasn't. You make me real."

Which told her a lot about his relationship with Willa. He was a romantic. He needed love as much as he needed sex. Willa hadn't provided. That didn't mean Amber could either.

"Obviously, I spoiled you for stick-thin models. Now you know your penchant for a real woman, you can go back to LA and look past the skinny." She said it in the same way she always told him she hated him, but what she really felt was a deep, abiding sadness.

He kissed her forehead. "I deserve that. Give me time, please. I'm a stranger in a strange land right now."

She nodded. He wasn't the only one.

THEY MADE LOVE AGAIN IN THE EARLY DAWN LIGHT, BUT AMBER REFUSED TO share a shower with him afterward. *Feeling* was one thing. *Seeing* all her jiggly flesh. . . Not yet, not while she still had dreams of exercising back to muscle, at the very least. Which might mean never, she knew. Since she expected Josh to leave, she could leave him with some illusion.

She had to put on yesterday's clothes, which reminded her that her cottage had been violated, and she didn't know if she could ever go back again. Feeling stronger this morning, that made her mad instead of weepy. She might only have a few more days of her comfortable hide-out left, once Josh exposed her to the world. She wanted it back.

With no brush to untangle her hair and no pins to hold it, she held the mess back with the sparkly gold scarf she'd worn around her neck yesterday. "I need to ask the Lucys to spiritually cleanse my house," she announced when Josh stepped out of the bathroom still drying his hair and only half-dressed. "I have to go home."

Damn, but he had muscles on top of muscles these days. Washboard abs. . . Not being able to relish all that masculine glory in the light was her own fault.

"What's involved in *cleansing*?" he asked in concern. "I gather not mops and buckets? And do you need to go there now?"

She pursed her lips and thought about it. "Maybe not right now. I need Cass and Mariah, at least. We burn candles and sage and follow a ritual. I'll need a new ghostcatcher. I'd rather be able to walk back in and feel as if it's new and clean and no evil had ever touched it. But I want to have Sunday breakfast with Zeke before I open the store. Kids need traditions and structure to feel secure."

He reached for a shirt. "The café then? Or risk your mother and the lodge? I can order room service."

She didn't really want to establish a tradition with Josh in it, but she saw no way around it if she couldn't enter her cottage yet. "The lodge, I guess," she said reluctantly. "I really don't want to go out in public now that reporters know I'm here."

"More drama and a bigger draw for the play if you don't show your-self until then," he suggested. "I'll keep Oscar the Bodyguard and Nellie the Female Terrorist in your shop so you can work with clients in back. The trick will be knowing how to prevent reporters from making appointments."

"I'll only take regulars and ask for wedding guest lists. I hate losing the walk-ins, but I hate everything that's happening these days, so I'll deal. How long will it take to pull together a script?"

He kissed her until she was breathless, then led her to the door. "Coffee. Give me coffee before interrogations."

Cass's driveway abutted the highway, so Amber didn't have to see her cottage wrapped in yellow police tape. They drove through the quiet Sunday morning into town.

A few Hillvale regulars were parked at the café, but the tourists and wedding guests usually didn't leave the lodge until the shops opened. If there were reporters still around, they were probably sleeping in too.

Josh held her hand as he drove the short line of blacktop up to the Kennedy lodge. He was definitely a romantic. Cherishing the affectionate gesture, she blinked back a tear threatening to crawl down her cheek. She was wearing yesterday's clothes, no make-up, and her hair in a tangled snarl for which she had no brush, and he didn't seem to care that she was a mess.

In time, he might, she reminded herself. Hollywood directors had to attend awards shows and parties with arm candy. They were both just reacting to the newness of being together again after all these years. They'd get past it once the real world claimed them.

That thought didn't exactly make her stronger, but pragmatism quieted her nerves.

As they drove around to the rear of the lodge with the windows open, loud voices penetrated the dawn quiet. Josh started to turn the car to avoid being seen.

Amber halted him. "Wait. I recognize the melodious buzz saw of my mother's mouth. Where did she find another woman to fight with?"

They both listened but the privacy hedges around the suites prevented clarity.

"We can go in the front way," Josh suggested. "Maybe the lobby will be empty."

Oscar the Bodyguard ambled out from behind the greenery. "I get extra pay for bitch fights," he said with a grin when Josh rolled down his window. "And those are two of the meanest bitches I ever ran across. You might want to turn around and go back to town."

"Zeke is in there," Amber reminded them. "He'll come to his grandmother's defense if it comes to that." She turned to the bodyguard. "Do you know who my mother is arguing with? Can you hear what they're saying?"

He jerked his head toward the greenery. "I'm thinking the other is the lady who runs this joint. She caught your mom peeking in windows."

"Oh, for pity's sake." Amber climbed out.

"You don't have to do this," Josh said, jumping out and following. "Let them slug it out on their own."

"I'm tired of sneaking around." And furious—she just wasn't taking this *evil* any longer. Carrying her glowing walking stick, she stomped around the hedge where she could hear the voices more clearly. "I shouldn't have to hide from my own mother. And Carmel Kennedy is just plain wicked. The two of them together may blow up the town."

"You have me arrested, bitch, and I'll tell the world this two-bit dump is infested with rats and bedbugs. I know people." Crystal's high-pitched screech could penetrate walls.

"You know bloodsuckers," Carmel Kennedy said in well-modulated scorn. "Your ridiculous Hollywood leeches are no match for my connections. I could call the governor, but it will be simpler to call my lawyer. *Out,* I want you out now before I call the police chief, whom I pay, you may note."

That was a lie, Amber knew, but not any of her concern. Removing her mother from Zeke was her goal. Emerging from behind the hedge, Amber glared at the two older women facing off. "Oscar, if you'd take a photo of this, you could sell it for a fortune."

Her mother had aged badly. Despite all the lifts, her face wore lines from too much sun and too little sleep. Like Amber, Crystal was only five-three and built sturdily. No amount of starvation could carve elegance into her square frame. She'd apparently dyed and styled her graying red hair into a blond bob—or maybe it was a wig. With Crystal, it was hard to tell.

In comparison, Carmel Kennedy was all tall, model-slim elegance.

Even at this hour, she was garbed in designer exercise clothes and wearing her trademark gold jewelry. Her lion's mane of hair was pulled into a high ponytail. Surgery and Botox had pulled her jaw taut and stretched the skin over her cheekbones almost skeletally smooth.

At Amber's arrival, they both swung on her, only needing brooms to look like two aging witches.

"I am taking Zeke home with me," Crystal announced, ignoring the threat of a photo. She lived for publicity. "I have a lawyer who will have you arrested."

"What the hell is going on out here?" A male voice intruded. "Crystal, I thought we were picking up the boy and leaving."

Amber's soul shriveled at the familiar rumble. Josh instantly swung to face the intruder, fists raised.

Dell wandered past the hedge and into view. He took one look at the company and backed away. "Crystal, move it. I have meetings this afternoon." Without acknowledging anyone else, he strode off.

Amber shook in her shoes, more with rage than fear, she hoped. She wanted to run after the balding pervert and pound his face into the cement. . . But protecting Zeke came first. She tugged Josh's arm to prevent him from following Dell.

"First things first," he muttered.

Relieved that he understood, Amber shot a freezing glare at her mother. "You brought *Dell* here? To fetch Zeke? I ought to have you both arrested."

"You can't take care of Zeke. You can't even take care of yourself. Look at you!" Crystal continued without pause. "You've always been a fat, lazy slug."

"The lullaby of my childhood," Amber murmured.

Before she could say more, Josh stepped in. "That level of ignorance doesn't deserve recognition." He turned to address the now-silenced Carmel. "Good morning, Mrs. Kennedy. If Mrs. Abercrombie and her companion are a problem, I'll have my security remove her."

It was rather lovely that Josh now had the power to deflect Crystal's abuse and was willing to wield it. But recovering from the unexpected encounter, Amber didn't need his help these days.

She might be a wuss for letting Dell escape unscathed, but she could stand up to her mother.

"You will do no such thing, you murderer!" Crystal shouted. "Stay away from my daughter."

"Josh is a gazillionaire now, Mom. Want to change your mind?" Amber taunted.

With a chuckle of appreciation, he dropped his arm over her shoulders —in defiance of all the rules ever laid out for them, including their own.

"The court says Zeke is mine," Crystal cried, reverting to her original intent.

"Not if I testify in front of a judge," Amber told her. "I couldn't do it all those years ago to defend myself, but I'm not a little kid anymore, and I *will* defend Zeke."

"No judge will listen to your lies," Crystal cried.

Before her mother could continue her bullying tirade, Amber boldly did what she'd always wanted to do—she pulled off her favorite sparkly scarf and shoved it between Crystal's teeth. "Hush. Zeke doesn't need to hear his grandmother making a spectacle of herself."

Crystal grabbed for the fabric. At a nod from Josh, Oscar caught her wrists and yanked them behind her back.

"May I do the honors?" Josh whispered in her ear.

She loved that he allowed her a choice, even though she knew he was as eager to throw Crystal over a cliff as she was. Amber nodded.

"Oscar, if you will escort Amber's mother to the lobby, Mrs. Kennedy may call her manager to check her and Dell out. I'm sure there's a maid willing to pack their suitcases," he ordered politely, without need to raise his voice and terrify Zeke inside.

With her wrists caught in his big hands, Oscar frog-marched a foaming Crystal toward the front of the lodge, away from Zeke's room.

Carmel openly gaped, then swung her attention to Amber. "You and your kind are no more welcome here than that bitch you call a mother."

Being confronted with a monster from the past, then called *fat* and a witch before the day even started snapped Amber's last remaining tether. For years, she'd padded a prison to hide herself from ugly reality. No longer. Feeling like a phoenix rising from her scorched nest, Amber covered Josh's mouth with her finger. If she didn't have to hide anymore, she didn't have to pull punches either.

"The hard work of *my kind* filled this lodge last night with wedding guests. I will apologize for my mother. I will not apologize for my existence. And since Josh is paying your exorbitant rates for two suites, I think you should think twice before telling us to leave. Remember, I'm psychic. I know what you fear."

While Carmel's mouth flapped like a fish, Amber marched past and toward the rear door she knew led to Josh's rooms. Josh rushed to pull out his keycard and let her in.

Miraculously, she wasn't shaking as he opened the door for her. She didn't even bother glancing over her shoulder to see if Carmel was aiming an ax at her back.

"I think my jaw is hanging to my feet," Josh said, rapping a warning before opening the interior door. "I've seen your mother reduce you to tears. I think Carmel Kennedy might reduce *me* to tears. What in hell do you hold over her?"

"Fear. Carmel lives in a constant state of paranoia," Amber said, before she held out her arms to a pale-looking Zeke. "Never fear, *mi amigo*," she murmured as she hugged her nephew. "Aunt Amber is here."

And Aunt Amber wouldn't let a filthy monster anywhere near Zeke —or anyone else, if she could help it. No more hiding. No more shame. She had a mission again.

"Ginger used to say that, except not the Aunt Amber part." Grinning, Ernest stepped from behind the draperies and set down his phone. "I think I got all that on video. I was hoping for a knock-down, drag-out fight though."

"Did you catch anything interesting besides my mother's peeping-tom exercise?" No more curling up and sucking her thumb. Zeke needed to know he had someone strong in his life.

She had to make herself strong, exercise more than her flabby muscles.

"That should be enough. I can probably add that scene to my script," Josh mused, pouring coffee from a full carafe. "I don't think even my flights of fantasy would conjure anything that absurd. I want to add a dragon to the new project and call her Amber."

"Only if you let me do the voice-over." Amber poked through a kitchen cabinet, located the tea bags, and nuked water.

Looking relieved, Zeke bounced up and down. "Does this mean Granny will go away? Can we go back to your place now?"

If she could face down two old dragons, she should be able to face the possibility of a haunted cottage, shouldn't she?

The dragon eyes on her walking stick gleamed agreement.

TWENTY-FIVE

By Wednesday, Josh had a script. With a degree of trepidation, he handed out pages of Act One to Amber and Val. Valerie Ingersson had been a formidable diva in her younger years, preferring stage to film, so he'd never seen her performances. But from the roles she'd played and her reviews, it was obvious she was no minor talent. And Amber had edited half the *Jack and Ginger* TV scripts once she had confidence enough to confront the writers.

Josh was the one who lacked knowledge. He was a two-bit actor, and his script-writing ability had never been proven. But these characters were so clear in his head that he feared he'd totally blown fiction and gone straight into documentary—always a dead bore on stage unless accompanied by a good soundtrack and dancing.

While Amber and Val skimmed the pages, he handed more copies to the limited audience in the locked barn the town called an art gallery. Lance, the long-haired, graying artist who ran the gallery, had quietly taken a center seat. Zeke beamed at being treated as an adult and given his own copy.

Ernest had practically memorized the lines, so he just read along on the pages in his digital notebook.

The other Lucys were apparently still recovering from spending the past few days *cleansing* Amber's cottage and setting up protective barriers to keep out the inquisitive. Josh had approved of her new locked gate, but the thorny rose hedge that had almost spontaneously grown overnight was pretty strange. Stranger still was the fence of stone statues with crystal eyes. If Amber felt safe behind a magical barrier, he was fine with that. He was just glad she let him through.

"The ghost has issues," Val announced succinctly, closing the script. "I can work with that."

"She's not a cardboard cut-out," Lance agreed from his seat.

Amber lifted her expressive eyebrows at this exchange from the usually taciturn pair. Josh just took a breath of relief and watched her expectantly.

"It's pretty strong," she admitted.

"But?" He knew how her mind worked. This was just a draft, but the rest of the script would balance on the first act. He was counting on Amber to help him make it better.

"*But* you need to think like a woman. A man might look at the dead woman's luggage and just say 'She left her suitcase. Search it.' A woman, especially if she's to be a smart detective, would say something like, 'That's a Vuitton. No woman would treat a Vuitton so shabbily. Look at that lining!' And then she'd search through it admiring the quality of the clothes, noting the owner was an impossible size zero, digging into the physical to understand the personal."

"I'm not a size zero," Val said dryly.

Josh jotted notes on his laptop. "Okay. We never found Willa's suitcases, so I don't have that perspective. Good call. Can I not mention size so any actress can play the role?"

"Sure, if it doesn't affect anything later in the script. To cover all body types and ages, you don't want your female detective carting anyone bigger than a small child. And one assumes the ghost won't be lifting heavy objects. In other words, don't write anything everyone can't do," she added wryly.

"Got it. I don't see this as being very physical. We don't have fancy sets, so I'll be relying on Harvey's music for background. Be thinking about what we can use for costume. Val, I love the veil for the ghost. If I need you for any other female parts, is there something else you can wear and still be comfortable?"

This was his milieu. He was good at pulling all the parts and people together to create one whole. The enormous painted triptych of Hillvale in the background was ideal for a piece like this.

If only he could distance himself from the subject matter. . . and Amber. . . he'd be a lot more sane.

But watching Amber on that stage, reading his script and pacing just as he remembered her doing when they were young and foolish, knowing she welcomed him to her bed—but kept her distance—was taking its toll. He had no notion of how to go on with this uncertainty— or even what he hoped to achieve.

He'd spent a lifetime working hard to put bread on the table and a roof over his head. The only way he knew to accomplish that was back in the city, doing what he did best, shaking hands, pulling strings, flashing the famous smile that had paved an easy path.

With more than one goal now, he was floundering, pretending he could solve Willa's death and his own confusion with superstition and playwriting. For the first time in a long time he was walking out on a creaky limb with no net under him.

Ernest passed his phone over Josh's shoulder to show him a text message. "Tessa wants us back in town, says work is piling up. I think she just wants your body. Reply?"

Just what he needed, more guilt and another woman who wanted a piece of him. As Amber had said, he didn't like being directed, which was why he was a director, not an actor or money man.

"Our work is here," he said decisively. His gut said he had to find Willa's killer before he could move forward. "If Tessa can't handle Willa's job without us, she can bring the work here or make Ivan handle it. He'll be happy to take over." That decision made, he focused on the play. "Did you find a photographer for opening night?"

"Brad says he can't make it. I'm guessing Ivan has threatened him, and he's siding with the deeper pockets." Ernest sat back in his seat. "Or maybe Dell has enough pull to prevent Brad from taking our side. Dell is bad-mouthing you, Hillvale, and Amber."

"Tell me something I don't know," Josh muttered, returning his focus to the stage. Dell had left the lodge with Crystal in ignominious retreat. The two of them working together was old news. So far, no evidence had arisen to prove they'd broken into Amber's house. Any connection to Willa or Sarah was all in his mind.

At least the cops had found Sarah's old Chevy in the parking lot, although they hadn't found any evidence of why she'd been at Amber's door other than the blackmail note. Josh feared the sheriff was taking the photos and note at face value, but the law couldn't pin the knife on either of them and make an arrest stick.

Reading the lines for the male sidekick provided the distraction Josh needed. He called Lance up to read the other male parts. The lanky artist wasn't half bad. He and Val added a few bits that nicely fleshed out the parts of the ghost and the ghost's husband. Josh hadn't wanted to make the connection so blatant that he'd written in himself as fiancé. He had pages of notes by the time they finished a second reading.

"Brilliant, people, thank you!" he called after they read the last line. "Acts Two and Three will be shorter, more action-packed, I hope. That's where we apply the emotional screws."

"That's where Fee comes in," Amber said, taking the step down from the raised platform that had probably once been a church sanctuary.

She rocked the bohemian look of Gypsy skirts and ruffled blouses, but he really wanted her to show off the figure she'd never learned to flaunt. His mind cruised costumes while she talked.

"Put your intermission after Act One," she said as she handed back the script, "since you say that it's longest. Fee will set up a buffet. I'm not sure how she plans to get the right food to the right people, but she's been practicing. If there's any guilt in the audience, Teddy will hunt it down after that."

Josh hugged her. She leaned against him for one glorious moment before pulling away.

"Do I want to know what Fee has been practicing?" he asked, reluctantly giving her space.

"Go over to the café in the morning and find out. She needs new material. I think we're down to only two reporters hanging around, and she's reduced both to tears, so she's learning to push emotional buttons with her food. I hear that it's worse than a bar at midnight in there." Amber kissed his cheek and ambled back to collect Zeke.

"How would you know about bars at midnight?" Josh called after her.

"I read books." She laughed and headed out the side door where Oscar waited to drive her over to the pool. Now that Crystal was gone, she had returned to swimming after hours.

"I'll bring the others tomorrow," Val said, keeping the script.

"Can Fee bring her magic brownies or whatever to test on me?" Josh asked as Val turned to leave. "I'd rather avoid drunken reporters until we have something to report."

The diva waved acknowledgment and departed, with Lance on her heels. Interesting, but none of his business.

"Tessa is driving up," Ernest reported as they headed for Josh's car. "I'll be glad when you make up your mind about what to do with Willa's company. I *sooo* want to fire her."

"Mean, very mean, what did the airhead do to you?" Josh's brain was brimming with the rewrites he wanted to make and the new scene he needed to draft. He didn't have room for catfights.

"The list is too long," Ernest said airily. "Are we good for sending out press releases about your little production? Maybe once this memorial is over, we can head home."

Head home? Did he even have a home anymore? His beach house really was the toy box Willa had called it—a place for the childhood and toys he'd never had.

But he had a life and a career to conduct, and it couldn't be from here. *Shit.*

With Oscar the Bodyguard to scare off strangers and the hedge to prevent intruders, Amber had worked out a routine. Now that Crystal was gone, Zeke joined Josh and her in their after-hours swim. Oscar took Amber and Zeke back to the cottage. And when all was dark, Josh drove down to town, parked his car, and jogged up the lane to join Amber in her bed. They didn't fool anyone, and the routine didn't leave much time for conversation, but Amber still needed the anchor of her own turf.

In the morning, Josh jogged over to the studio to work, leaving his car in town so reporters didn't know about Cass's place.

"Walker called," Amber whispered as Josh climbed between the sheets some hours after their first read-through of the script. "He says the sheriff wants to close the case but all he has is thee and me. If we had gang ties, we'd be behind bars now."

"He doesn't know we have our own secret gang. You were brilliant tonight, thank you." Propped on one arm, he leaned over to cover her face in heated kisses.

"The Lucys are a gang more dangerous than the ones the sheriff knows about," she agreed, stroking his hard back. "But if this memorial doesn't work, we could go broke living behind bars and hiring lawyers."

"Now there's justice—Willa leaves me her fortune to defend myself for killing her. I suppose Ivan will take the money away, and we'll have to go to public defenders. How will that play as an ending for the script?"

She laughed and caressed his hip. She loved everything about having this man in her bed, so she hoped they weren't going to prison anytime soon. "I thought you were leaving it up to the audience to decide the guilty party. What are you calling it?"

"Haven't decided. *Justice Prevails* probably doesn't set the mood."

"*As I Lay Crying, A Time to Bill, Harpy Spirit.* . . I've been reading book titles."

"*Tomorrow is Another Day.*" He covered her with his body and began kissing his way down her throat.

She was glad Zeke's room was on the other side of the house, and that her expensive foam mattress didn't squeak.

Late nights made for late mornings. It was a little after eight before Amber stumbled from bed to shower, leaving Josh still sacked out. She was staring blankly at the open refrigerator when the phone rang. Zeke ducked past her to grab his milk. Giving up on thinking, she reached for the phone.

"Trouble with a capital T and that rhymes with C. . ." Ernest sang into her ear. "What rhymes with Ivan?"

"Not *cool*, if that's where you're going with this." Rubbing her eyes, she wandered back to the bedroom to rouse Josh, but he was already in the shower. "What's Ivan done?"

"He's here. He arrived last night with Tessa, and Dell, the persistent pervert. They know Josh isn't in the lodge. I put Tessa up in the other side of this suite and the Evil Duo in the suite across the hall. Tell Josh he needs to build his own lodge at this rate."

Amber grimaced. They really needed to put Dell behind bars. Or maybe he'd mellowed and wasn't a voyeuristic pervert anymore. Did that ever happen? Just knowing he was in cahoots with Ivan gave her cold shivers.

She could only manage one enormity at a time. "Ivan can build his own lodge and pay for his own suite. I'll warn Josh to go to the studio. Do you have any idea what they want?" She sat on the edge of the bed and tried to figure how the minds of a Hollywood exec might work. She failed.

"Josh's head, probably. I'm not sure they're buying the memorial. Have him ring me back." Ernest hung up.

Losing her appetite might help her to lose weight, but it was a very bad habit to develop. Now that she didn't dare stick her head into the café for fear of being hounded, she'd been forced to fix her own breakfast —after asking Fee for suggestions.

She added seasoning to a few eggs and beat them, listening for the sound of the shower stopping. "You should have stolen those tapes you saw at Dell's," she told her nephew. "But I suppose stolen evidence doesn't hold up in court."

Zeke wiped milk from his mouth with the back of his hand and popped up to put toast in the toaster. He was pretty good at looking after himself—thanks to Crystal's neglect.

"I know one of the guys that was there. I can have him grab a few of the disks. They're pretty easy to lift. It's just a bunch of naked kids though, no big deal." He spooned up more cereal.

Not to Zeke, who'd grown up with Speedos and nude beaches. But it was a damned big deal if those images showed up on the internet. "We'll save that option until we have no other choice. I'm just being lazy." And protecting herself.

Maybe it was time to give up passive protection and consider aggression. It would be bad enough explaining a dead body in her backyard to the guardianship judge. Explaining how she could take care of Zeke from jail wasn't happening. And then if Crystal wanted to present evidence that Amber was shacking up with a suspected murderer. . . None of them came out looking pretty.

Josh emerged, fully dressed and combing his wet hair. Her heart nearly burst with emotions she couldn't fully identify. It was just so good to see him again, to know he was happy and healthy and doing well. . . Well, almost. His visitors might turn that around.

"You'll want to hie yourself back to the studio, pronto," she told him, handing him coffee. "Tessa brought a posse. We don't need any publicity stills of us together so soon after Willa's death, or that prison cell will be two steps closer."

She set out eggs for herself and Josh, then nuked bacon for Josh and Zeke.

Josh tested the coffee, then took a gulp. "A whole posse? Not just her usual sycophants? If I had to blame anyone for murdering Sarah, it would be Tessa. They competed for Willa's attention. Does Walker have a timeline yet for Sarah's death and any suspects?" After popping a bagel in the toaster for himself, Josh straddled a kitchen chair and inhaled eggs and coffee.

"From what Samantha has told me, they can't establish a solid time of death for Sarah, so we're the only suspects," Amber told him. "In any logical world, Sarah should have arrived during the morning while I was in town and you had an entire press conference watching you. But if she arrived in the wee hours, you were at the studio alone. I was inside the cottage with no witnesses until Zeke woke up. But if they think I'd drag her into the backyard, walk across blood on my porch, and return with a bodyguard to say 'Oh, gee, look, blood'—the sheriff has seen too many crime shows."

But Willa's phone was in her kitchen, and she had no idea how it got there.

Of course, given her lack of height and cooking abilities, that phone could have been on the top shelf since she bought the place, and she wouldn't have known it. Even Viking Samantha had to climb on a chair to reach that cabinet when they'd done the smudging.

"That neither one of us owns a knife or knows how to use one or has a motive is inconsequential when there's no one else around who fits the pattern either," she added with a sigh, trying to see the sheriff's perspective.

"That phony blackmail evidence is all they have," Josh said with a shrug. "Everyone had reason to kill Willa, but Sarah was a nonentity. A killer wouldn't see her as a potential witness since she wasn't anywhere around when Willa died. I don't know why the hell she would have been near your cottage. . ." He sipped his coffee and frowned. "Yeah, I do, if the real killer planted Willa's phone in your cabinet during the burglary and Sarah had an app for tracing it. . ."

"She called the police. She had no reason to trace it herself," Amber pointed out.

"Unless there was something on the phone that she didn't want the police to see. Sarah wasn't the brightest bulb in the box. She may have thought of something after she reported it and came up for damage control. It was the middle of the night when she called the sheriff. He may have told her he'd check in the morning."

"The county doesn't have enough money for a patrol up here. The sheriff should have called Walker, but it's a territorial thing, I think." Amber finished her eggs and washed the plate.

"The mean sheriff wants to arrest the pretty girl before the hero can come to the rescue," Zeke said prosaically. "They really can't arrest you, Aunt Amber, can they?"

"No, sweetheart, they cannot. Judge and jury would laugh them out of court the minute I waddled in. No way could I haul bodies around," she reassured him, wishing she could reassure herself that everyone operated on logic. "Fee said she could use some help around the café. Did you want to pick up brownie points with her or play video games somewhere?"

"Mayor Monty said I can help at the cabin today." He jumped up. "They're putting in utilities for the trailer pads, and he wants me to watch Fee's dog. Can I?"

Amber had always loved the way the small community came

together at times of trouble. Fee's significant other kept his fingers on the pulse of the town. Monty knew the trouble swirling around them.

"May I," she corrected. "And yes, you may, as long as you pay attention to Monty. There's a lot of big equipment out there, so you have to be very careful. Put on your boots. I don't want you stepping on nails."

Zeke dashed off to find the hiking boots she'd bought for him. Like all Abercrombies, he was built sturdily. Mayor Monty was an ex-jock. They'd do well together.

"A small town is good for him, isn't it?" Josh asked thoughtfully, finishing her thought. "He can live the normal kid life we never had."

"Except there's no school here. I have to come up with a plan before the custody hearing. So let's make this memorial guilt thing happen. I need brain space for planning a future that doesn't include prison bars."

Josh leaned over and kissed her. "We'll work it out together—after I break the Evil Duo in two. But if I'm going to finish this script and toss Tessa out, I won't see you at lunch. Miss me?"

"Like a sore tooth," she agreed in their old pattern of insults, standing on her toes and kissing him back. "Don't kill Ivan, but push Dell over a cliff if you can. No one will care."

"It's that kind of talk that will put us behind bars, sweetheart," he drawled.

She almost felt a chill when he opened the front door and departed. She prayed she wouldn't be seeing him behind bars, from either side of the door.

TWENTY-SIX

"CAN'T SIGN ANY OF THIS, TESSA," JOSH SAID, FLINGING THE STACK OF documents back on the desk in the suite parlor. "The corporation hasn't been transferred to my name. I'm not on the board of directors. You've wasted your time. So, tell me why you're really here."

With wild curly red hair straight from a box, Tessa stalked up and down the room. She was sturdy where Willa had been slim, but they were of a similar height. That was the only similarity Josh could detect. Maybe the shoes—Tessa seemed to be wearing some of those red-soled designer things Willa took such pride in. Since Tessa had the run of Willa's mansion, they could have been Willa's shoes for all he knew.

But shoes didn't make a competent executive.

"I need you to tell me it's okay to sign them," she said nervously. "Willa wouldn't let me sign anything, even though the lawyer says our agreement allows it. That one contract alone is for half a million dollars. I don't want to be responsible if we can't pay it."

"And Ivan is telling you that you can't sign it, isn't he?" Josh rolled his eyes and picked up the contracts again. It was all double-speak to him.

"He's telling me I'll be personally liable if I do." Tessa flapped wet lashes and performed her best heroine-needs-hero act. "If you'll just say it's okay, sign something telling me I'm in charge, I'll take care of it. I know Willa negotiated those contracts, so they're good."

Josh rolled his eyes at the performance—there was a good reason Tessa had failed as an actress.

Ernest took the papers and scanned through them. "They're for the Chinese film project she was working on, nothing to do with yours, Josh. Ivan only works with old white guys, so he doesn't want to deal with this if he grabs Willa's company. Willa spent months working with this director and the sponsors to get an agreement. It's a pretty solid deal. She even lined up insurance against emergencies, although probably not to cover her death."

"Excellent," Josh said in satisfaction. "Sign them all, Tessa. I've put Ernest in charge. Run any others by him. The company isn't Ivan's yet, and no one has revoked your authority."

Yet. He could see Tessa wasn't suited for an executive position. Willa simply liked people she could control. But with Ernest's knowledge and Tessa's ability to sign deals, the company could function for a while longer.

Tessa scowled and snatched the papers from Ernest. Josh detected more competitiveness in action. Willa had thought competition made her staff work harder. Josh hated the stress.

"Why don't you work with Ernest from here?" Josh suggested. "Stay for Willa's memorial on Saturday. I have to go back to writing the script, so I'll head back to my office." And avoid Ivan and Dell, if he were really lucky. He was amazed they hadn't barreled through the door at first light.

"You're not staying here?" Tessa asked, a little too casually.

"The reporters are driving me insane. I found a studio with a view and a guard cat where no one can find me. And no, I'm not staying with Amber, so pass that on." Josh walked out, tired of Tessa, tired of business, tired of the scene that he'd have to return to one of these days.

Writing this script was cathartic. Half of Hollywood would have heart attacks if they recognized his characters. The other half would roll on the floor, laughing, then wait for the nuclear fallout.

Ivan and Dell would definitely not be in the latter half. If he used those red-soled shoes. . . Josh chuckled thinking about it. Tessa wasn't one of his favorite people anyway.

~

WITH FEW WEEKDAY APPOINTMENTS AND UNABLE TO TAKE WALK-INS FOR fear of reporters, Amber was reading her lady bodyguard's cards when she heard Oscar greet a customer.

She dropped the deck when she recognized Dell's voice.

"Oh crap and filthy word," she muttered, gathering the scattered cards. "Better take the position, Nellie. That's the devil out there."

"Ohhh, goodie. Can I shoot him?" The retired security guard patted her vest pocket.

"I don't think bullets can stop him." At the sound of an unfamiliar authoritative roar overpowering Oscar's rumble, Amber clenched her molars. What were the chances Willa's father might be here with Dell? Pretty darned good. "Why don't you offer to run over to the café to pick up lunch? Then tell whoever is behind the counter that I may have trouble."

"I'll tell them to deliver. I don't want to miss the fun." Nellie sashayed back to the front room, all seventy-plus years of her. Even a granny bodyguard was skinnier than her, Amber noted with a grimace.

Wondering how one went about *tossing one's weight around* as she'd read in books, she waited while Nellie took names and returned, pretending she was a secretary. "Okay if these two gentlemen visit? One Ivan Powell and Dell No-Name."

Dell never used his last name, which was some unpronounceable collection of consonants. He expected to be recognized, like Cher or Beyoncé. Amber was pretty sure even the *Dell* was short for something, but his legal papers all used the single syllable as his first name.

"Have Oscar carry some chairs back. I'll put on the tea." Deciding this was her office, and they had to follow her protocol, Amber turned on her electric kettle and picked out her favorite Darjeeling. She had a steel backbone, she reminded herself. She had friends now and no reason to be afraid.

"This isn't a social call," Dell bellowed as he pushed through her curtains.

Fourteen years had not improved the producer's looks or disposition. A burly man of under six feet, Dell had grown jowls and a bigger paunch. He still stank of expensive cologne that didn't quite hide his excessive perspiration. His graying hair had receded, but it was still stylishly cut in bristles on the sides. Suave, he was not.

"Hello, Dell. It's my lunchtime. You may stand around and watch me drink tea, if you prefer. Would you care to introduce me to your friend?" She'd always been good at socializing. Business, not so much, so she stuck with what she knew best.

"Ivan Powell." The taller man introduced himself.

No paunch on Ivan. Willa's father was as lean as his daughter had been, although in a more masculine way. The double-breasted tailored suit probably had shoulder pads, but it suited him. She was pretty certain his silver hair was the result of a good colorist, but it gave him an air of competence, authority, and wealth. Very intimidating, if she was inclined to be intimidated by someone she didn't know. She wasn't.

"Amber Abercrombie, pleased to meet you, Mr. Powell. Would you like some Darjeeling? I'm afraid I don't keep coffee here. The caffeine is too strong and interferes with my work."

"Your work? You're an actress, Amber! A two-bit one at that," Dell shouted. "Why the hell are you getting in my face now? Call off that bitch of a lawyer. We had an agreement, and you don't have anything worth my suing you for."

So far this week she'd been called a fat, lazy slug and a witch and now she was no more than a worthless, two-bit actress. It really was this side of enough, as they said in her favorite historical romances.

Years of humiliation had stiffened her steel spine. She poured tea, sat down, and shuffled her deck, forcing her visitors to either sit or rant uselessly. Silence had the unexpected benefit of leaving them off-balance. Looking uncomfortable, they finally took seats.

She studied them expectantly. "And you, Mr. Powell? Would you care to call me a few names as well?"

His eyes narrowed as he took her measure. "*You're* not the reason Josh is hiding up here. I should have known the reporters were puffing up the love triangle. I want my daughter to rest in peace. Anything you can do to help steer her company into competent hands would be greatly appreciated. I can help you pry Dell off your back."

"Now wait a minute—" Dell sputtered.

Amber waved her hand, letting the glow from the table lamp catch on her rings and bracelets. "Never mind, Dell. Mr. Powell just said I'm too fat to interest Josh, and that he'll buy us both off."

She flipped the cards and spread them. She knew how to fake a reading if needed. She had no way of knowing if Willa still lingered, but she meant to provide a good show one way or another. "Willa, what do you think of your father's offer?"

The glow in Amber's staff brightened, and a breeze rustled the tarot deck.

Well, swell, it appeared Willa was not only still here but listening. Amber wanted to cackle as the King of Coins blew off and dropped onto the Ouija board on a side table.

"Your daughter calls you Midas, doesn't she?" Amber said conversationally as she retrieved the card and the board. She felt Ivan's shock, so she knew she was on the right track.

The two gray-haired men, unfortunately, didn't believe in Willa. They looked around in suspicion, seeking the trick behind the flying card.

"You don't have to answer that," Amber told them, pulling the Ouija board in front of her. "I really am a psychic, not a fortune-teller." A psychic who had never really tried to read minds or ghosts until pushed to the limit, she realized. She'd been coasting all these years in more ways than one. "I can tell the nickname hit a sore spot. I also know you won't believe that your daughter's spirit is here with us, at least partially."

The rest of Willa was gathering outside the shop, Amber sensed. The Lucys and their crystals would be sitting on the boardwalk, leaning against posts, holding their still-glowing staffs, waiting for a signal. Nellie had moved swiftly. Good for Granny Bodyguard.

"You're too old for this juvenile crap," Dell said in disgust.

Amber chuckled. "Now I'm *old*. Thanks, Grandpa."

Ignoring her humor, he continued. "Tell your bitch lawyer to back off, and I'll tell Crystal that the kid won't fit the part. That's what you want, isn't it? To get the kid out of her hands?"

"The court will give me Zeke without your help," Amber said with a confidence she had no right to feel. But they'd pushed her patience as far as it would go. She either believed in herself, or she didn't. She placed her fingers on the planchette. "Willa, did your audit find anything on Dell?"

The planchette practically flew to YES.

Powell made a gesture of disgust. "Don't be ridiculous. You can move that thing any way you like. We came here to be reasonable, not to be treated like hysterical females."

Amber's fingers were still on the board when the tarot cards flew into a furious tornado, pelting Powell and Dell with cutting vehemence.

"Willa apparently doesn't appreciate being called an hysterical female," Amber explained, fighting back amusement—possibly of the hysterical sort. "Dell, if Willa's audit uncovered fraud, then you have motive for killing both her and Sarah. You probably ought to talk to the cops before they find the evidence."

"I did not kill anyone!" he shouted. "I was hundreds of miles away. And you can't make me believe Willa cared about anything except money with this stupid playacting."

Amber didn't have the ability to sense his guilt the way Teddy might, but she wasn't picking up any other vibrations either. Maybe Dell's brain was too addled for her to read. Maybe he really did believe Willa was only auditing him for the money and not with the goal of shutting down his porn operation, as Josh had requested.

She didn't think Dell would touch the tarot deck to let her read him better. "The police think there might be a hired killer involved. It's just a matter of time until they put the pieces together," she said, using her best acting ability to reflect complacence. "Would either of you like to place your hands on the planchette and ask Willa a question?"

They both expressed disgust and got up to leave.

Nellie, holding a stack of boxes from the café, blocked their exit. "Have a seat, gentlemen. This is some of the best food in the universe. Fee doesn't have an alcohol license, but she sent over some of Monty's health juices." Unfazed by the cards drifting around the floor, she dropped the boxes on the table.

Fee hadn't met Dell or Ivan, or Amber would worry about what the cook had added to the ingredients. Instead, she took a bracing sip of her tea and let the box Nellie gave her sit unopened.

Before the men could storm out, Amber asked, "Willa, who was the last person you saw?"

Instead of using the planchette, Willa's spirit spun the cards up and around again.

"I never should have introduced her to the cards," Amber muttered in exasperation as over half a dozen cards landed on the table. She was aware the two men had frozen while the cards flew under no visible means.

Looking at the spread Willa dumped in front of her, Amber bit back a groan. "Willa says these are the last people she remembers." She pointed at each card as she named them according to her interpretation. "Ernest, Sarah, Tessa, Brad, *Dell*, the wedding planner, and this crowded one apparently represents the people working on the wedding, like the musician, caterer, and florist. That's a lot of people, Willa," she told the circling wind. It died down, possibly in exhaustion. "Dell, you just lied about being hundreds of miles away. Do the cops know that?"

"You're making that up!" he shouted, his flabby jaws mottling.

"Hold the planchette, Dell," Amber told him, pushing the board in his direction. "Put your fingers on either side of the triangle. Let's see what happens when I ask Willa if you were there."

"Don't be ridiculous. No court in the world will listen to this!"

The cards flew off the table. The Devil card that Willa had assigned him flew out and hit Dell in his reddened nose.

"It's possible that I translate Willa's thoughts through my own," Amber admitted. "I always assumed you were the Devil card in my spread, so she's been using it for you too, I think. Put your hands on the planchette, Dell. As you say, it won't hold up in court."

"Do it," Powell rumbled. "And then let's get out of here."

"Will you back off my case?" Dell demanded, uneasily setting his pudgy fingers on the glass triangle Amber had had a craftsman design back in the days when she had money.

"Not my call," Amber said, sipping her tea. "Willa, was Dell here in Hillvale on the day you remember last?"

The planchette jerked to the YES faster than Dell could lift his hand.

Amber grabbed the fragile planchette before Dell could fling it against a wall. "As you say, it doesn't signify anything except verifying what we already know. Willa's spirit is hazy about what happened that day, hence all the cards." She gestured at the selection. "But you're free to ask her what you like. I never met Willa, but she has a strong will. I'm sure she'll try to answer."

"My daughter is dead!" Powell cried in more fury than anguish. "She's dead because of that murdering son of a bitch she wanted to marry! This little charade proves nothing."

He turned to stomp out. His unopened cardboard lunch box flew off the table, hitting him squarely on the temple. Spaghetti in marinara sauce dripped off his ear and onto the shoulder of his bespoke suit.

"Spirits don't believe they're dead," Amber said conversationally, admiring the stunned silence and Willa's handiwork. "Willa, I appreciate your help. I know you have no reason to like me, but take my word for it, these two are too dense to understand you. And yes, I know they're thinking obscenities and planning on calling their lawyers. It's okay. We won't let you down. Why don't you rest until we find more receptive minds?"

The table lamp brightened. Amber's *Lucy stick*, as Josh had called it, went dim in a ghostly signal for *Okay*. Amber nonchalantly opened her lunch. "Good meeting you, Mr. Powell. Dell, why don't you take your lunch with you? You probably ought to save every penny for your defense. Or, since I'm receiving strong impressions about your condo in the Caribbean, you'll need it for your retirement."

Powell flung the spaghetti off his shoulder before stalking out. Dell added a glare, grabbed his lunch, and followed.

Both Oscar and Nellie in the front room called cheerful farewells. Amber was quite certain they'd heard every word.

Her unused back door crashed open and a dusty, disheveled Josh fell through.

TWENTY-SEVEN

"I TRIED TO GET IN THE NORMAL WAY." BRUSHING THE DUST OFF HIS clothes, Josh accepted the untouched celery juice that Amber handed him and swigged it down. "Your witchy friends barred the door. My own damned bodyguards let them."

Looking appropriately horrified, Amber glanced out at the cliff he'd just climbed down. "There is a reason no one uses that door."

At least *someone* appreciated his heroic efforts.

"They're just rocks, easier than fighting a half-dozen Lucy sticks." In disgust, since he was already filthy, Josh took napkins from the boxes to clean up the spaghetti on the floor. He tossed cards back on the table while he was down there. "You shouldn't have to fight my battles for me. I'll go back to LA and get the buzzards off your back." It physically hurt to say that, but he meant it.

She picked up the sauce-soaked napkin from the table and flung it at his head. Not exactly the reward he'd expected.

"Don't you belittle me too! I've had enough of that crap for a lifetime. I'm an adult capable of taking care of myself. That's what my *witchy* friends were telling you. If you don't believe that, then get out."

He glared at her in irritation. "I *know* that. My day has been as bad as yours, so don't you get on my case too. But Ivan is my battle, not yours."

She dropped into her chair, still red-cheeked with anger. "That's not the way it works here. Your problem is *our* problem. We work it out together. And I had *fun*."

"Fun?" Josh stared at her in incredulity. His frilly but sensible Amber had enjoyed confronting two jackasses like Powell and Dell? "I don't recall anyone ever calling Ivan the Terrible a barrel of monkeys. He's been known to bring powerful men to their knees, quivering in remorse."

"He's a selfish asshole," she said in dismissive disdain.

Josh's eyebrows crept up. The sharp-tongued Amber peered from behind Ginger's sunny smiling self. He sat back to enjoy the rant.

"Ivan's only concern is retaining what's his and getting even with you for presumably taking Willa away," she continued. "He's a repulsive human being—but probably not a killer. Maybe we don't need a production. Just parade the culprits past Willa and let her throw spaghetti at them. Ivan broadcasted pretty clearly when frightened. I didn't even need the cards to read his mind." She retrieved a cracker from her lunch box and dipped it in her tea, still looking mulish.

She'd read *Ivan's* mind? Josh fell into a chair and poked through her box for anything crunchable. He'd had enough adrenaline for one day and needed sensibility. "Let's start over, okay? Tell me what happened."

"Nothing useful. I'll explain tonight, when everyone is together. But Willa really can't remember who she saw last. Our suspects are wide open, and yes, we can include Dell. She says he was here." She uncovered the contents of a soup bowl and tasted it.

He sipped his green drink and processed what she was telling him. "You want to bow out of the play? You think you'd be more useful in the audience with the Lucys and Willa?"

She quirked an eyebrow at him over the soup. "We have to persuade people to come up here for Willa to throw spaghetti at, figuratively, one hopes, and I'm your best bait. I'd be useless in the audience. Our suspects will be unwilling to heed Ouija boards and tarot, and I can't possibly read the projections of a few dozen people at once. It was difficult enough with the two of them. Only the spaghetti forced Ivan to think loudly enough for me to understand him."

"I'd planned on making my second act a fake fortuneteller with a crystal ball. What if I set the act up so people are called in from the audience? It's a farce. They should be willing to play along." Josh finished off the crackers Amber obviously wasn't eating.

She smiled, and it was as if a sun had emerged from behind a black cloud. "If your script can force the guilty parties to remember Willa and what they did, Fee and Teddy can narrow down the suspects to one or two. They can get word to us on stage. Fix it so one of your more innocent characters calls on the audience. It might work. Maybe."

"Not entirely certain how, but just narrowing down our focus has to be helpful. And putting the pressure on a killer in public is probably safer than letting them loose on your backdoor," he said gloomily. "Nellie and Oscar can't be with you every minute."

"We might want to keep an eye on Dell," she suggested, eating her soup. "He's in meltdown mode. It's a pity we can't put our hands on whatever Willa had on him."

"Tessa has access to all Willa's personal computer files." Josh reached for the cordless landline. "I'll have her give the passwords to Ernest and let him sift through them. He's only been inside her business computers and hasn't found anything useful. Even the name of the auditor would help."

"All that would have been in her phone, wouldn't it?" Amber asked, looking thoughtful.

"Possibly." Josh called Ernest with his request and listened to his new CEO plot heaving Tessa out a window. Once assured that access to Willa's files might be possible without window-tossing, he hung up. "But Tessa is claiming that Willa kept a cloud account that even she can't get into. I can understand why."

"An account a killer might have wanted eliminated?" Amber suggested.

"An account that might have been accessed by that phone planted in your cabinet," he agreed, back to gloom.

"But if neither Tessa nor the police can access it, then we simply need to go back to Plan A and guilt the killer into confession. Piece of cake." She snapped her fingers. "Don't you have a play to write?"

～

"MY IT TEAM COULD PROBABLY UNLOCK THE CARD IN THE PHONE," WALKER told Josh. "But the sheriff doesn't trust me to be objective. It's his case, and he's waiting for bureaucrats and overworked state facilities to unlock it for him."

"He's figuring he'll find evidence against me in there," Josh finished for him. "Understood. I know the Lucys are counting on this memorial production for results, but a court of law needs evidence. How the hell do you deal with this?"

"Well, they blew up a mountain and crushed a killer once," Walker said unhelpfully. "I try not to ask too many questions. If we ever get a Lucy up here bent on evil, we're in a world of hurt."

Josh winced and rubbed his face. "Yeah, I can see that. I'm pretty sure none of our suspects are Lucys. Willa may have threatened Harvey, but he really doesn't have anything to fear if his hiding place is exposed, no more than Amber does. I don't know how the women expect to persuade everyone Willa yelled at to show up at the memorial. There may be suspects out there we don't know about."

"We do what we can and hope for the best. Meanwhile, I have my men hunting for whoever audited Dell. My main business is corporate fraud, so that's doable. And if he's into child pornography, I want him taken out. I'll write it off as charity."

"I'll pay for that too. And Amber's lawyer is a bulldog who will hunt Dell into eternity and have a class action suit prepared before he knows what hit him, so she'll help with witnesses. If there's any chance that the court will return Zeke to his guardian, we want Dell out of the picture. It's impossible for Amber to petition the court for guardianship while this crap hangs over her head. I know she's worried."

Josh stood, wearing the stern face he seldom displayed. "And if you *ever* have any inkling that the sheriff is going for Amber, feel free to frame me. I've let her down in the past, and I won't do so again."

He seriously meant that. His life was meaningless. Ernest could hire a new director to handle the one project that depended on him. But Amber had a kid to look after, and a full life she had barely begun to live. He was the one who'd brought this crap down on her. She deserved her rainbows and sunshine.

"Amber's a lot stronger than she looks," Walker warned.

"And I want her to stay that way. You don't know what she's been through. I do."

Walker nodded. "I don't think it will come to that, but I got it."

"Thanks, and just let me know if there's anything else I can do."

Walker stood too. "It takes a strong character to accept what Amber, or any of the Lucys, can do. You don't want to be on their wrong side. Heaving spaghetti is the least of it."

Josh relaxed and grinned. "To hell with Lucys. Getting on the wrong side of Amber is my concern. Ivan and Dell practically flew out of town after she was done with them. I don't know if I'll be able to lure them back. I'm taking Amber's word for it that they aren't killers."

"They still might have hired killers, so don't get too cocky."

Josh saluted and let himself out of the police chief's barren office.

The play was practically writing itself.

TWENTY-EIGHT

"Is there a cliff I can throw Tessa off where no one will find her for a million years?" Ernest asked, slipping into his gallery seat beside Amber, looking exhausted. It was Friday evening, dress rehearsal before the memorial on Saturday. They were all a little ragged.

"Keegan has a mine in the hills. Maybe he could stash her there," Amber suggested unhelpfully as she read the final changes in Josh's script. "Could we stow Josh there too? Does he really think I can pull this off? I might as well carry a top hat and hope a rabbit falls out."

"You're sounding as negative as him. You can't be little Shirley Temple forever. Did you think he'd write you as Miss Marple?" Ernest popped a mint and typed on his notebook keyboard. "Wait until you see the costume he and Tullah have found for you."

Which was the real reason she was chewing nails, Amber acknowledged. She'd told them she'd wear a suit. Josh had insisted that Tullah had found the perfect detective dress. How big of a fool was she about to make of herself? She wasn't equipped for any more battles. Her armor had grown soft with rust.

She flung down the script and marched back to the curtained-off area they'd built for their backstage. No one had let her see the costume, which told her right there that she would hate it.

With theatrical wardrobes all over the state to call on, Josh had provided his actors everything they desired and more. Val had a stunning floor-length gray satin gown and hip-length gray veil for her ghost part. When she played the part of a grieving sister—the "sister" part barely disguising Tessa's weak character—Val wore a hat with a chin-length black veil and a short black dress that made the most of her long legs. She was practicing walking in red-soled high heels when Amber pushed past the curtains.

"I don't think the audience will even recognize that the ghost and the sister are the same actor," Amber said in admiration. "If we didn't have to be on stage at the same time, you could play me."

"I prefer the weeping, wailing parts," Val said with a curt gesture. "You may have the cold, logical, deductive part."

Wearing a beret over her short Afro, Tullah was studying her image in a mirror. "I think Ernest will cut Josh's throat after he sees me pretending to be him."

Tullah was playing the ghost's male assistant. She was tall and broad-shouldered enough to pull off the part of man, and since the assistant was gay, she could swish like a woman without being out of character. She'd let Josh order her costume, though, and that might have been a mistake. Tullah in a man's madras blazer and shiny blue slacks was a sight to behold.

"He's made Ernest six feet tall," Amber said with a grin. "That should make him happy. And you've seen Ernest. He might not wear a beret, but the madras is perfect."

"You'd better like what we found for you," Tullah told her sternly. "You can't be Suzy Sunshine. You have to be an uptight lady detective determined to bring a killer to justice."

"You'd better not have made me look like Jessica Fletcher," Amber warned. "I'm no Angela Lansbury."

"No scarves and blouses," Tullah promised. "You're too young and pretty. And your role is a *professional* detective, not an amateur."

"Over here," Teddy shouted from the dressing room. "Do I look like a Hollywood secretary?" She popped out wearing a low-cut t-shirt and mini-skirt over her full figure.

"Like every secretary I remember," Amber agreed, grinning. "These days, you probably need a tattoo or three though, maybe a nose ring."

"I can draw tattoos in ink and do jewelry without self-mutilation. Your turn." Teddy drew back the curtain. "I want to see you in something a little more upscale than flounces."

"I like flounces," Amber protested, stepping into the booth. The only dress left on the rack was a sleek, flared teal, without a flounce in sight. She hated to tell Tullah, but there was no way in heck she'd fit into that skimpy thing.

But it was a gorgeous silk wrap-around, like something out of the nineties. It just lacked shoulder pads. She wouldn't have to shimmy into the skirt the way Teddy must have into hers. Still, it had a waist, and a belt that would only emphasize what she lacked. And that top. . . Amber smoothed the fabric longingly. If she were a few sizes smaller, she'd feel like Kathleen Turner as V.I. Warshawski, only a lot shorter.

She hummed a little in appreciation that Josh had known she'd like a feminine costume. She hated to tell him that a tank top and blazer were a more appropriate choice. They'd be ugly, but they'd look professional.

Still, it wouldn't hurt to try on the silk fantasy. She'd feel ridiculous, but Lucys would never laugh at her pretensions to glamor. And Tullah and Josh would have to see to believe that the dress wouldn't work.

At least she'd worn her fat crunchers so she might have a chance of it fitting. She might be comfortable as she was, but she knew audiences. They wanted the fairy tale of beautiful people.

She stripped, then slipped the slinky silk sleeves up her arms, loving the sensation against her skin. Cotton flounces were practical, but the silk. . . was the sexy prom dress she'd always dreamed of wearing.

The skirt hooked at the waist, and the bodice had hidden buttons to keep the wrap from opening over her breasts. The slightly flared skirt draped around her legs without any other fastening. To her amazement, the waist hook went in without trouble. But the top. . . bared way more than she'd ever revealed, even in her off-the-shoulder blouses.

In this bad lighting, she could almost imagine the three-quarter sleeves hid her flabby upper arms. Although she'd need a scarf to conceal her heavy-duty bra, and even then, her cleavage would be exposed. With the belt, it almost appeared as if she had a waist. She brushed the silk swaying around her hips with longing, swished a little to make it rustle. She was half naked, for pity's sake. She couldn't go on stage like this, but oh, she loved the way it made her feel.

Arms slid around her waist, and kisses stole along her exposed neckline. "I knew you'd be gorgeous in this. I love that teal on you."

Amber closed her eyes and drank in Josh's admiration like a flower soaked up sunshine. "You might be a tad bit biased," she murmured. "No detective ever wore anything like this. And are you setting this in the 90s?"

"I am, actually, to explain the lack of cell phone coverage. So this works perfectly." He swung her around and gazed admiringly at her exposed cleavage. "Okay, scarf required unless you want to go commando under that top. I'm all for that. . ."

She smacked his arm. "I look like the Pillsbury Doughboy tarted out in a belt. I know this is a farce, but I can't go out looking like Barbie's fat fourth cousin, twice removed."

He laughed and swung her around to face the mirror. "You have breasts women pay money for." He cupped them through the silk, then ran his hands to her waist. "You're short, so you'll never be willowy, but you have a perfectly good waistline that's in dimension with your beautiful booty."

He squeezed her hips and rocked her so the skirt swayed, making her feel as if she really were desirable. Except she knew the audience was expecting straight-up-and-down Ginger, not a roly-poly bug.

"You will notice almost everyone on stage will be wearing drab colors. You will be the bright shining object of everyone's attention," he added, bringing her back to earth.

"Oh *that* makes me feel better." She pulled away and marched past him, throwing open the curtain so everyone could see her. "Peacock strutting through. Anyone got tail feathers?" She walked out into slightly better lighting.

She could swear almost the entire town was gathered to wait for her appearance. They broke into applause and hoots of appreciation. No way could she handle this much exposure.

Feeling her cheeks flame, Amber bobbed a curtsy and fled back to the dressing room, yanking the curtain between her and Josh.

"A raincoat," she cried. "I'll wear a raincoat!"

"I'll quit if you wear a raincoat," Josh shouted back.

They'd played this scene before. Back then, Jacko had always got his way. Not this time. She flung the dress through the dressing room curtains at his head. "So, quit. You always take the easy way out, don't you? Why don't you go find another Willa and just forget about us?"

"I'm not the one who walks out," he roared in outrage from the other side of the curtain. "You're the one who walked away without leaving a forwarding address. You're the one who left me for *fourteen years*, without any idea if you were alive! Get over yourself and wear the damned dress!"

She heard him storming off in a fury—rightfully, after all his hard work. Once upon a time, she would have gone after him to placate him.

She wasn't Ginger anymore.

She was Amber, the powerful witch. She glared at herself in the mirror.

Witches wore black. She hated black.

Without Josh, the whole damned play would fall apart, and they'd never find out who killed Willa and Sarah.

The silence on the other side of the curtain warned that everyone was waiting on her to fix the unfixable.

TWENTY-NINE

"Look, I've been too busy to finish this list until tonight."

The pregnant, black-braided Mariah tracked Josh to the back of the theater/gallery where he was nursing his wounds. His gut ground in knots, and he was too miserable to look at the digital notebook she waved in his face. He couldn't quit now, not after Amber had flung that accusation at him about taking the easy way out.

He'd always seen his choices as pragmatic.

"Tell me your email," Mariah demanded. "I don't want any of the other Lucys to see this or it might affect their judgment."

Josh leaned back in his chair with his feet on the bench in front of him. After the blow-up, the dress rehearsal had gone badly. Amber had returned wearing one of her caftans. No one could play to a detective in a caftan. Everyone but Amber was still reading their lines from the script. That was to be expected, but he'd hoped Val, at least, would have hers memorized. That's why he'd given her all the good ones.

Practically snarling, Josh took Mariah's notebook and typed in his contact information, then glanced at the device she was waving. "What is this?"

"A detailed background of all our potential suspects. I'm not allowed access to my bunny trails anymore, but there's so much information available online that I think I've got a pretty good picture without hacking." She pushed a button sending the list to his email.

Bunny trails. . . He'd ask another time, especially if it involved hacking. He opened his phone and tried to read the document, but it took too much scrolling. He was in a mood for smashing, not reading. "Anything pop out at you?"

"Ernest is a convicted felon, fraud and drug charges. There's a good chance he'd know how to hire a killer. That's just the tip of the iceberg. Willa kept interesting company. Even her father has a shady past."

Shit. So much for his judgment. He didn't have a head for business. He would have been better off asking Amber to read the tarot for all his employees. *Willa's* employees. He couldn't manage without Ernest, so he might as well throw in the towel now. Forget the fantasy film, find another superhero flick to direct. . .

"Bedtime reading." Josh shoved his phone back in his pocket. "I assume the cops have all this? And they know Amber and I are clean as a whistle? Although I'm not sure why whistles wouldn't be covered in bacteria." Always dissemble when in denial.

"Guilt by association?" She shrugged. "*You* could have asked Ernest to hire a killer. Amber has all of us to call on, and we're not exactly squeaky clean either. Any one of us could have shoved Willa off a cliff, although knifing Sarah might be less likely."

"In other words, not helpful," Josh said gloomily. "We'll all be laughingstocks by tomorrow evening and maybe the killer will slink back in his hole and never bother us again. Does that justify going on?"

She swatted him with the script. "I've done my part. You do yours. Amber is a *Lucy.* That means she'll do anything for anyone else before she'll do something for herself. It's a curse, if you ask me, but that's how it is. Figure it out." She waddled off.

Amber thought *she* waddled, but Mariah had it down fine, and she still looked good. Waddling was better than prancing. And Amber swayed like an amber wave of grain.

He was cracking up.

He locked up the theater after everyone left, climbed in his car, and stared blankly at the street light. Had Amber gone home? Or stuck to their routine? Did he even want to see her after she'd thrown his gift in his face?

He was steamed and stressed and had no one to punch. He needed to swim.

He didn't know whether to be relieved or not when he arrived at the pool to find Amber and Zeke already there. "How many laps?" he called as he pulled off his shirt.

"Four," Zeke called back. Amber was plowing through the water as if she had steam to blow off too.

She usually quit after four laps, but she didn't even stop to acknowledge him when Josh dived in. He easily pulled abreast of her and kept on going. He could do two laps in the time it took her to do one, so he set out to catch up.

She beat her record and was breathing hard by the time she climbed out. Josh finished up his usual laps, debated doing a few more, but he was afraid she'd run away without a word. He was angry and miserable, but he'd worked off enough to prevent blowing up, he hoped. She looked so gorgeous in her rainbow outfit that he bit his tongue and just dried off while she hid behind her cover-up.

She sat on a lounge chair and let Zeke continue splashing around. "I'm a Libra," she announced.

"So you say." He sat and dried his hair while he processed her words through his fury. "I read up on Libras after you told me that. You're a natural mediator—which I already knew. You love harmony, so everything you own matches. You've certainly got the dimples and melting smile. I've not seen you overindulge in anything—"

"Used to be overeating. Lovemaking, lately," she pointed out.

It was hard to think once reminded of their passionate hours in bed. He nodded acceptance while trying to figure out what the hell she wanted him to understand. He reached deeper into his memory banks. "You're creative. You love books. I didn't see anything about reading minds. I particularly liked the part that said you can argue both sides and finish a debate alone. You're good at that."

He studied her warily, rehashing their earlier barn-burning dispute. "Does that mean you've settled an argument? Can I ask which side you took?"

She hugged herself and watched Zeke instead of him. "I love the dress, thank you."

That didn't answer the question. "But you think I'm a lazy lout. I fail to find the connection."

"You are lazy, because you avoid stress. Stress boils your brains, hence the dress. You know I can't wear that dress on stage."

"I know no such thing," he retorted angrily. If she was ending their relationship, he might as well *boil his brains*. "I love the way you look in that pink cover-up you're wearing. When Tullah showed me that design in a dress, I knew it would be perfect."

She tugged self-consciously at the belt holding the gauzy fabric closed. "There's nothing wrong with the dress. It's me. You'd see that if you weren't treating me like Willa. If we're doing the nineties, why can't I just wear one of those blocky blazers and a blouse, something that will hide me?"

Josh grimaced and fell back against the chair. "Because they're unfeminine and *not* you. I want to show the world how beautiful you are. Things have changed since we were kids. TV and film are full of people of all sizes, shapes, and colors. I love the way you look, the way you move, the way you smile, and you smile more when you look good. You won't smile in an ugly blazer."

"My part doesn't call for smiling. You're trying to please me instead of thinking about the show. Worse, you're putting me up there to show me off, to prove a point, not because the dress fits the part. You're thumbing your nose at Ivan and Dell and the reporters and any of Willa's friends who might show up. You're saying *I've got Ginger, deal with it*. I'm not Ginger. I'll find my own costume." She stood up and gestured for Zeke to climb out.

"You worked hard on that side of the argument." Josh stayed where he was, fuming all over again. "You're wrong. You may be a mind reader, but you're not reading mine right. Start looking for the other side of the story, the one where I'm giving you a chance to be a strong woman and still be feminine."

"You're not *giving* me anything. I'll take what I want, when I want it. Go back to your studio and take another look at your script, Jacko. Write out Ginger. Write in Amber. I'll see you tomorrow." She picked up her bag and left without another look back.

Jacko was the name she'd called his character in the show. He guessed this was where she told him good-bye, as she hadn't had the chance to do when they were kids.

It was a pity Dell and Ivan had left. He *really* needed to punch something now.

THIRTY

EVEN AFTER SHE'D WORN HERSELF OUT IN THE POOL, AMBER DIDN'T SLEEP well. She and Josh had argued frequently and fervently when they were kids. She hadn't bothered arguing with anyone since. She had just packed up, moved on, and grown up. Did that make her argument last night a reversion to adolescence? Or another rung on the ladder to maturity?

Some days, she hated being a Libra.

Breakfast was quiet without Josh. He'd threatened to leave if she wore a raincoat. Would he quit if she wore a blazer? Wouldn't it be better to get him out from under her skin before he was permanently embedded?

She had all day to waffle, but tonight was the deciding point.

Zeke happily ran off to help Fee around the café. They had another group of wedding guests inundating the town, plus guests gathering for the memorial tonight. All hands needed on deck.

Oscar arrived after breakfast to drive her the short distance into town. "Café has a few reporters asking about the memorial," he reported. "Lodge is booked, so most can't get rooms. I think they're hoping for a scoop so they can go home without staying for the performance."

"Not happening," Amber said, climbing into his SUV. "Even we don't know what's going on." Especially if Josh quit.

Oscar dropped her off directly in front of her shop. "I'll be there after I park. Nellie should be inside."

A red-haired woman in what appeared to be a designer suit wandered the shop as Amber entered. Nellie gestured in her direction. "Your nine-thirty, Susan Meadows."

The woman did not emit happy wedding vibes. A jilted lover?

"Come on back, Ms. Meadows. You can choose your tarot deck while I settle in." Amber swept through her curtains and gave her office a cursory glance to be certain she'd left it neat yesterday. Willa hadn't wreaked any havoc overnight. The felt cloth covering the reading table was in its usual place. Her shelves were lined with colorful tarot decks. She lit candles as the guest entered.

"I can choose any of these decks?" Susan asked, studying the shelf that Amber indicated.

"Yes, sometimes your choice tells me a little about you, so it's up to you how you want to play this. I tell all my new customers that I am not a fortune teller. The tarot divines future possibilities based on the past and current circumstances and your personality." Amber took a seat, her curiosity aroused. This was definitely not a normal wedding guest. Susan Meadows had a lot on her mind, and weddings weren't it.

Her guest picked up a traditional Smith-Waite deck and set it on the table, taking a seat without speaking. Amber shuffled the cards while surreptitiously studying the woman across the table. Susan was probably a few years older than herself, well kept in a way that indicated a degree of money. But the expensive cosmetics couldn't quite hide the shadows under her eyes and the chipped and peeling nail polish. Susan was unraveling.

"If you'd shuffle the cards for me?" Amber handed over the deck, her inner sense on high alert. She glanced at her walking stick and caught a distinct gleam in the dragon's crystal eyes. Uh oh, something was definitely off. She waited until the deck was shuffled, then gestured at the table. "Now divide the deck into three stacks, please."

Nellie and Oscar were right outside. She could hear them talking. She just needed to be careful of what she said. Susan could be a reporter who'd managed to sneak here in disguise. Although desire for a story was definitely not the vibe she was feeling.

"Before I lay out the cards, is there a question you'd specifically like answered?" Amber tested the waters.

Susan narrowed her eyes. Amber could almost feel her suspicion. She waited, and the woman shook her dark red curls.

"No, I just wanted to see what a psychic does."

Amber pulled from the top of the stacks Susan had cut and laid three rows of three cards face-down. "The row closest to me is your past. The center row is your present. The row closest to you is your future potential." She flipped the first card in the row from the past.

The Queen of Wands—Willa. The dragon's eyes brightened.

She should just quit now, but she was on edge and growing angry. Without explaining the card, Amber flipped the next one—*the spy*. The third one—*Midas*. The occult was inexplicable. So was Willa. But the cards were clear.

Amber set her beringed fingers on either side of the layout and met her customer's eyes. "You're not Susan Meadows."

The woman scooted her chair back, looking wild-eyed, until she gained control of herself and spoke coldly. "Someone told you. Josh, I bet. Or Ernest."

"I have never seen your face in my life. They had no way of telling me who you are. I still don't know. I just know that you know Willa." Amber pointed at the queen. "And you know Ivan." She pointed at the king. "And that you spied on Willa for Ivan." She pointed at the page card.

The woman's arrogant expression crumpled, and she wiped angrily at a tear. "It's not as if I had a choice. I spied on Ivan for Willa too. They were too damned much alike."

The dragon's eyes gleamed brighter and Amber pointed at her stick. "Don't, Willa," she commanded. "Let this one speak for herself. You drove her to whatever she is."

Fake Susan stared at the glowing stick in horror. "Willa is here? She's alive?"

"She thinks she is. Characters that strong don't give up easily. Who are you and why are you here?" Amber refused to turn over the rest of the cards. She knew she should, but she was angry that this stranger had lied and polluted her space with ulterior motives.

"If you're a psychic, you should know," Fake Susan mocked, recovering a little.

"Fine." Amber flipped the first card in the present-day line. She felt the connection instantly. "Josh, as your ruler. You're afraid, because he has all the power you covet." The cards didn't say that. It was her interpretation of the images crowding into this transparent woman's mind as she spoke.

She flipped the next card. "More fear—of a lover? He holds something over you."

Fake Susan grew so white, Amber feared she'd faint. "That's not true. He loves me. He helps me."

Ruthlessly, Amber flipped the third card. The Devil. This didn't feel like Dell, but she didn't even know who this woman was. She might know Dell in a different way, but there was no denying the perversion, the dark side of this character. "Your lover kills for you?" she suggested.

"You're a fraud!" Fake Susan shouted, pushing back and standing up. "You're just trying to pin Willa's death on someone else, when everyone knows it's you. And you sit there fat and happy, scheming like a spider. I don't know how you killed Sarah, but I'm glad you did. She was a snake in the grass. And now I'm going to be what Willa was and no one can stop me."

She marched out without looking at her future. Without the person who drew the cards, Amber couldn't interpret them, but she flipped them over anyway.

The Nine of Swords—vulnerability, loss, the price of pride.

Five of Coins—desire and gratification, flattery and false promises.

The Fool—a person driven by base needs.

Well, Fake Susan certainly knew how to draw a shining future. It was probably a good thing she hadn't hung around for the interpretation. Before Amber could drop her head in her hands and massage her temples, Nellie popped through the bead curtain.

"I took her picture and texted it to Josh and Ernest. I figured one of them could identify her. I don't know how she got your appointment's name, and I'm not sure she's operating on all four cylinders."

Amber got up to heat water for her tea. "I may be a fat spider, but she's the Fool." She pointed at the card. "She's no Willa and never will be." She glanced down at the dragon head. The eyes gleamed brighter for a second, then went dark. One blink for yes?

"But is she a killer?" Nellie asked worriedly.

Amber glanced at the spread. "The potential is there, under the right circumstances. She's torn between too many people with power over her. And she doesn't have a strong character to resist temptation. I'm not sure that pointing a finger at me proves anything."

Nell's phone beeped. She checked her incoming text and turned it to show Amber. "She may be a fool, but Willa's death left her in a position of power."

Amber read the text—*Tessa*, Willa's VP.

Wow. "Ivan's spy," she said flatly. "Lovely. I wonder what she thought she'd learn stealing in here like this? Proving I'm a fraud won't accomplish much. I'd swear that woman was living in a state of terror."

"Yeah, well, I would be too if I had Ivan breathing down my neck. A woman has to have balls to stand up to a tyrant like that." Nellie returned to the front room to greet whoever had just entered.

Balls, huh. Amber had never aspired to having balls. She simply refused to be walked over ever again.

Which led her back to tonight. If she had a killer in the audience, how did she want to present herself?

This wasn't just about her making a fool of herself anymore. For the first time, she realized she could be laying her life and the lives of others on the line.

"AMBER ASKED ME HOW MUCH I'D GIVE FOR HER PRETTIEST RING," TEDDY, the jeweler, whispered to Josh backstage. She'd arrived in her t-shirt and miniskirt costume, wearing a concerned frown. "I think she's planning on leaving town after the memorial. The ring is designer quality and would make a nice deposit on a rental."

Friggin' blasphemous cauldrons of flaming shit. . . Josh caught himself before he flung his phone across the gallery.

"I hope that doesn't mean she's skipping out on tonight." Crushing down panic, pretending he wasn't Mount Vesuvius, he gulped coffee, paced, and flipped through the script. As the director, he had to stay focused and not have a heart attack. If Amber left him, he might as well go to jail for murder.

Letting the cops arrest him would be easier than directing Amber, pushing her to see herself as she was—and not as the chubby kid imprinted on her psyche. Maybe she wouldn't have to leave Hillvale if she didn't go on stage tonight.

Going to jail as the easy way out—good work, boy. Amber had a point.

He almost melted in relief as she stalked in the back door wearing a blocky pink blazer and bright orange straight skirt. A white silk shell and colorful beads completed the look—feminine and distinctive, but professional enough to work for the part. She'd been right—the cleavage had been for him. Damn, she was good.

And professional. Even after their fight, she'd showed up on time and ready. He could name half a dozen stars who would have walked.

As her sidekick, he didn't really need a costume. He was the wall her energy bounced off of. He just needed to look like his surroundings, so he wore jeans and a jacket, a wrinkled shirt with a loosened tie. She zoomed in on him the instant she entered.

Amber didn't flash her trademark smile but nodded knowingly at his outfit. "Good choice," she said in her crisp, professional voice—already in the role.

It was impossible to read her mood like this.

Ernest arrived from the front of the house, looking his usual worried self. "Ivan and Dell came back," he whispered. "I thought Brad said he couldn't do the photography, but he's out there. So are Tessa and Sarah's family. And the wedding planner. Even the money men. They're *all* here." He sounded terrified. "Including every entertainment reporter in the state."

"Along with most of Hillvale, including the chief of police, several of his men, and a few officers from the sheriff's department," Amber reminded him. "Just duck for cover if you see any sticks glow."

Amber had persuaded Zeke to stay with Mariah, telling him they might need an errand runner. Neither of them wanted him around if Dell or Crystal showed up.

Josh wanted to ask her about selling her ring, but the others were starting to crowd around, asking about the changes he'd made in the script, nervously questioning their costumes. Val sailed in wearing her gray ghost gown and veil. Harvey tuned his keyboard. It wasn't a concert quality instrument, but it produced the comic-dramatic effects the script required.

"The whole wall of the gallery is covered up with memorial wreaths and flowers," Teddy whispered as she joined the circle of players.

A farce as a memorial. It just seemed fitting somehow. Even Willa would have appreciated the irony.

They had no stage curtains other than the muslin they'd used to hide the backstage clutter. Everyone held notes. The audience couldn't expect a memorial to be memorized. As part of the cast, Josh couldn't even direct his actors to take their places if they forgot. He had definitely lost it. Willa's *money* men were out there, the ones he needed to produce his film. He'd be a laughingstock.

Being laughed at was what Amber feared—and she was still here. No backing out now.

Giving up his drug of choice, Josh set aside his coffee cup. His job began here. He addressed their announcer, the police chief's wife. "Remind them that Willa loved farces, that she started out producing dinner theater mysteries in college. Make them believe this is done in her loving memory."

Samantha had been appointed as a non-actor and a person no one in the audience could have a grievance against. She took the stage to welcome their guests and explain that they'd created the memorial to grieve for a bright light extinguished too soon.

While she spoke, Josh arranged his cast in the order he'd chosen—Val first, for the drama, Amber last, to suck them in. The reporters knew who she was by now. Her bodyguards had kept them at bay until they were slavering like big hungry cats, waiting to pounce.

And then he sent out these townspeople who trusted him, and he prayed.

The audience's silence was deafening as Val and Amber effectively set up the first act on their own. A laugh followed Tullah's first lines, playing the part of Ernest hiring the detective. Had one of Willa's staff recognized the caricature of her flamboyant assistant?

Josh slouched on stage as Amber's credulous sidekick. He could recite lines well enough and manage a little stage direction while he was at it. "Cheat left," he whispered to Amber as he passed behind her. She was trying to hide her face from the audience.

She scowled but followed his progress on stage so she was turned around. If that was tittering from the audience, Josh meant to go down and remove heads. He was so hyped, he could dance across stage, if he'd felt like dancing. He didn't.

Harvey's music took a dramatic turn and the audience shut up. The boy was good if he sensed Josh's irritation.

Murmurs arose from the crowd as each cast member appeared, representing people in Willa's life, whether the audience recognized them or not. The burly local veterinarian ambled on to portray Brad, the photographer—although the script called him Cad, the ghost's driver, who always carried a camera with him.

Val as ghost vanished into the wings to replace her long veil with a short black one and switch out her long skirt for a knee-length one. She minced on wearing her red-soled high heels, introduced as the corpse's sister. Her arrival produced a gasp and more titters. Josh prayed that meant people were recognizing the characters, not the cast. Val had been well-known once.

Amber's performance was nothing short of breath-taking. She almost had Josh weeping as she questioned the grieving sister. She brought the audience to laughter as all five-foot-three of her forced the flamboyant six-foot tall secretary to behave himself. She was astonishingly convincing at not seeing the ghost but creating a word image of her from her questioning.

The act ended with the discovery of Teddy, the ghost's secretary, dead on the detective's doorstep. A sharp gasp of recognition of the recent murder ran through the room. As his sidekick character, Josh took pretend notes while directing his company offstage, muttering his lines of doom. In place of a curtain fall, he signaled Harvey for the flourish and the little cook from the café to open the buffet.

Dropping his notebook in his jacket pocket, Josh noted Ivan and Dell suffused with fury, heading for the door.

THIRTY-ONE

Peering from behind the backstage curtain, Amber gulped as two of their suspects stormed toward the exit. If they couldn't test the main culprits, the whole production was wasted.

Josh hastily stepped past the muslin to signal Aaron. They hadn't managed fancy commemorative glasses as had been suggested, so it was cheap Prosecco in plastic their psychometrist carried as he loped after their escapees.

The Evil Duo tried to brush Aaron off, but the antique dealer wasn't a small man. He blocked the exit and must have said something concilia-tory, perhaps offering flattery. He had that kind of sophistication.

She gulped in relief as Dell stopped to swig free alcohol. Ivan grudg-ingly accepted his after Aaron made a production of writing their names on the plastic with a gold Sharpie. Then he indicated the buffet, where more bottles waited.

The escapees hesitated, deterred by the generous gesture from the sophisticated antique dealer. Amber relaxed as regal Cass sealed the deal by taking Ivan by the arm. She gestured at Dell, then imperiously conducted them toward the food. Cass didn't chatter, but she had the imposing force of the very best of society's matrons. Their suspects were in good hands.

Amber dropped the curtain and nodded thanks at Josh for the glass of wine he handed her. She couldn't talk about personal differences now. She needed to stay in character.

Her character wouldn't worry about the ass she was making of herself. The real Amber could disintegrate later.

He understood her taciturnity and stuck to his director's role. "You are magnificent. I think the reporters have already worked out who the characters represent."

"There's a journalist called Stone out there. He recognized me earlier this week but left me alone. I'll call him up with the audience participation act. I think he's ham enough to handle it." She sipped the wine and practiced breathing. This next act was all hers. She just needed Fee and Teddy to narrow down the suspects she would call on. One more hour to go.

Josh was drinking more coffee, a sign that he was stressing. She took the cup from his hand and carried it off so she could peer around the curtain on the buffet side.

The display of flowers was stunning. She wondered how many of the people who had sent them had bothered showing up. Guests were surreptitiously checking the tags.

Part of the cast was mingling with the audience, helping themselves to the food. The Kennedys, owners of the resort and half the town, stayed near Teddy and Fee. That should protect them from any irate suspects.

As focus of the rumors about love triangles and murder, Josh and Amber prudently stayed backstage, letting the others bring them tidbits of food and gossip.

"Fee says most of Willa's friends, family, and employees smell *off*," Teddy whispered, handing them plates of appetizers. "She's particularly concerned about Ivan and Dell because they're fishy, but that just means they do drugs, and Fee hates drugs. Brad and Tessa apparently smell of *skunk* and fish. I'm getting flashes of rage and guilt from all four. I think they're our main suspects. They haven't let go of their glasses, so Aaron can't look for readings yet."

"Thanks, Teddy, you've gone beyond the call of duty. You may rest on your corpse's laurels for the rest of the evening," Josh said, pacing.

"According to Mariah, three of our four suspects have been in the military—Ivan, Dell, and Brad—serving at different times. I can't see them knifing Sarah, but they may have the know-how. I don't suppose hired killers would show up, dammit."

Teddy snorted. "I'm rather glad hired killers don't show up."

"Ernest is clean?" Amber asked, still in her detective mode. Mariah had given her the same list she'd given Josh.

"Fee insists that Ernest does not smell like fish. And I sense that he's enjoying himself immensely. I'll go back out there and help Aaron gather glasses." Teddy bounced a curtsy, and still in costume, returned to her Kennedy husband in the audience.

Samantha arrived, having changed into Gypsy clothing borrowed from Amber. The skirt was far too short and the blouse had to be pinned to keep it from sliding off her tall, slender frame. She wore one of Amber's favorite shawls draped over her shoulders so the pins weren't noticeable. She'd let her platinum hair go wild and wore square rose-tinted glasses. "Walker is about to have a nervous breakdown. I'm not sure if he's worried I'll run off for a life in Hollywood or that the guilty party may think I'm a real psychic."

"I'm pretty sure they won't confuse you with me," Amber said wryly. Sam was special, and she loved her like a sister, but Sam was also the model-thin size Amber would never be.

Of course, Sam would never have curves like hers. Maybe that balanced out.

"Walker's just on edge. He hates relying on us. He's compiled huge files on everyone, but without evidence, he says everything is circumstantial. So it's up to us to produce a confession." Sam turned to Josh. "How are you holding up?"

Josh studied their slightly glowing walking sticks. "Worried."

Amber got that. She was terrified. But her detective was only allowed to be *concerned*, so she kept her character's confidence wrapped around her. She was painfully aware of Josh's frostiness. When they were kids, they'd always settled their spats because they needed each other. As adults, they could stand on their own—unless they got arrested, of course.

As the cast returned backstage, Josh sent Samantha out to take a seat at a table bearing one of the cheaper crystal balls from Amber's shop. The audience settled in their seats and chatter died with the dramatic flourish of Harvey's keyboard.

"I don't think anyone escaped," Tullah whispered, peering from behind the curtains. "Fee's food has them looking mostly mellow. If she put truth serum in the cookies, I can't tell."

No one knew precisely what Fee could do with her cooking. Neither did Fee. She could have poisoned half the audience so they'd wake up dead in the morning. Amber clutched her fingers into her palms and sought calm.

It was bad enough exposing herself to an audience after all these years, but this audience was live and might contain killers.

Apparently guessing Amber's nervousness, Josh reassuringly squeezed her arm. She told herself that was what any good director would do.

"You can do this," he reminded her. "We're here when you're ready."

Because this was where she winged it. . . Taking a deep breath, she sauntered on stage to help Sam set up the next act, the crucial one where they called on the suspects Fee and Teddy had chosen as most likely.

At her arrival on stage, the audience settled back, wined, dined, and prepared to be entertained. Lance, the gallery operator, had directed his track lights on the stage, leaving the audience with dim overheads, so Amber couldn't see everyone clearly. That was okay. They'd discussed where she should start.

"I don't believe in this mumbo-jumbo," she curtly told Sam as Psychic. "But let's see if anyone else believes you've captured a ghost in that glass. Choose someone from one of our guests."

"I'll start with a non-believer," Sam said with the wide-eyed innocence she did so well. "The gentleman in blue on the end of row four. Will you please come up?"

They'd chosen the most likely suspect to go up first, Dell. He appeared reluctant. But he didn't know Sam and had no good reason to believe she knew him.

Amber gestured at the audience. "If you want to hear our psychic prove there are ghosts, stomp your feet."

Led by Lucys, the audience stomped. Aaron arrived at Dell's elbow to escort him. Enthusiastic, the onlookers stomped louder. Caught in the thunder of a hundred pairs of feet and the nonsense about ghosts, Dell caved, although he managed to look belligerent as he climbed on the small stage.

Sam chanted and waved her hands over the ball until Val appeared in her ghost costume. Tall and solid, she was so obviously not a ghost that the audience just enjoyed her performance as the diva swept dramatically back and forth in front of the triptych mural of the town.

"Well, is your ghost here? Does she say this person killed her?" Amber asked with appropriate disdain, ignoring the spectral performance.

"That one is an old fraud," Val-as-ghost shouted, gesturing at Dell in contempt. "A pornographer who doctors his books to cheat the innocent."

Most of the audience accepted the statement as fiction and waited for a reaction. A few gasped and sat up straighter.

Sam dutifully repeated the ghost's accusation but Dell's sagging jowls had already turned purple.

"This is ludicrous," he sputtered, glaring at Amber and clenching his fingers into fists. "Did you call me up here to repeat your stupid accusations? I'll sue."

A low murmur from the audience indicated a few more understood the play had taken an interesting turn.

Josh as her sidekick arrived with his notebook. "The dead woman's auditor has evidence of fraud," he said cheerfully. "Looks like our psychic may actually have a connection with Dial-the-Dead."

Dell took a swing at Josh, who obligingly ducked as if it had been written into the script. Someone in the audience screamed, and the murmurs grew louder. Amber bit back a gasp and held onto her character's impartiality.

"I'll sue you and your lying whore!" Dell shouted, shaking his fist at her.

Already stressed and hyped, Josh straightened from his crouch with fists raised—totally out of character. Amber stuck her hand out to halt any fight so she could study the images Dell's fear and fury projected. All she saw was his pornography collection—no hint of murder.

"Fraud does not prove he is a killer," she chided her sidekick. "Madame Psychic, does your ghost call this man a killer?"

Val moaned and wept and swept back and forth across the platform.

"She's not sure, ma'am," Sam replied.

Dell stalked off, fuming. Josh gave him a surreptitious finger. Amber smacked his arm and returning to pacing as if in thought. The part of the audience who didn't know the rumors about Dell tittered, amused. The in-crowd, however. . . were people Amber would rather not acknowledge. Their murmurs were distracting.

"Then let us give a reporter the documents on fraud and pornography and let his fate be in the hands of the courts." Amber whipped out copies of the documents Walker's corporate gumshoes had pried from Willa's auditors. "Mr. Stone, perhaps you would come up and use these wisely?"

"Old news," the tanned, silver-haired TV reporter said snidely, jogging up to take the papers. "But verification goes a long way towards preventing lawsuits. Thanks. Hey, Dell," he shouted as he stepped back down. "Want an exclusive interview to tell your side of the story?"

Half the audience laughed, thinking Stone part of the cast. Others had their phones out, cursing the lack of signal as they attempted to make calls. A few were snapping photos and texting.

Dell fled. Amber checked that Aaron had swept up his abandoned wineglass. She hadn't seen any hint of Willa in Dell's thoughts. She hoped Aaron would verify her impression. He shook his head, and she sucked in air. One down, three to go.

The reporter didn't follow Dell, but settled back in his chair with a smirk. Nice to know someone was enjoying the production.

"Madame Psychic, I do not have all day," Amber said curtly. "Who else do you see in your magic crystal?"

Val as the ghost responded chillingly, "My father spied on me. He never wanted me to succeed. He thought I would fail, but I made a fool of him!"

Amber saw a lot of wise insight on Josh's part in that line, whether he knew it or not. The excited murmur of the Hollywood set said they got it too.

Sam circled her hands over the ball. "The ghost fears her father, madam. I see a silver-haired, distinguished gentleman, if the spirits would fetch him, please."

In a normal farce, the ushers or the sidekick would rush into the audience and find any man who came anywhere near the description. In this case, Tullah as the dead woman's assistant swept into the audience and took Ivan by the arm. Tullah was not small. Ivan might have been slightly taller and heavier, but flustered, he didn't resist a female African-American caricature of Ernest in madras pants and beret.

"We searched your daughter's suitcase, sir," Amber intoned in her role as impassive detective. "We know for fact that you spied on your daughter. To what purpose, may I ask?"

His spurt of rage produced a strong impression of arguing with Tessa, but nothing more, to Amber's disappointment. But then, she'd never really expected Ivan to have dirtied his hands with murder. At best, she might have hoped for an impression of hiring a hitman.

"Fathers watch over daughters," Ivan said in scorn. "Your ghost is an hysteric."

The stage lights blinked twice. That wasn't in the script. *Uh oh.*

Amber glanced worriedly to the Lucy sticks they'd placed in an umbrella rack. They blinked in tandem with the stage lights. Willa had decided to make her presence known.

Swallowing dismay, she continued with the planned action, pointing at one of the props, Josh's fancy metal suitcase. "We found evidence in your daughter's bag that you were undermining her company to prevent her from succeeding."

The stage lights and crystals flashed a victorious *Yes!*

"That's an outright lie! If anything, she was undermining mine!"

The Hollywood half of the audience practically came out of their seats at Ivan's accusation at his own daughter's memorial service. Amber turned a quelling glare on their noise, and they settled down, whispering excitedly.

"She was buying out my board, threatening to put me out to pasture. Of course, I kept an eye on her." In self-righteous fury, Ivan turned to stalk off.

Without warning, the suitcase toppled into his path.

As the fallen suitcase hit Ivan's foot, Amber saw a fearful flash of Tessa and Brad in his mind. She needed her cards to focus.

The bag slammed open, and an object tumbled out. Josh grabbed it before Ivan could recover from his astonishment at magically toppling suitcases. *None of this had been planned.*

Amber grabbed her walking stick, hoping to strangle Willa before she could cause harm.

"I'll be damned," Josh said, gaping at the object in his hand. "She must have hidden a thumb drive in the lining. How the hell. . ." That wasn't in the script either, but at least he'd refrained from saying *Willa* and totally breaking character. He amended his error by hastily correcting, "I mean, our victim must have hidden a computer *disk* in the lining."

Josh crouched to rip open the rest of the lining snaps, producing a file folder. "This isn't mine."

Had Willa *really* hidden a thumb drive in Josh's suitcase?

The audience murmurs had become a low rumble. A few people slipped out the door, presumably to find landlines. Amber scrambled for a way to bring the scene back to the script and keep people in their seats.

Ivan grabbed for the folder in Josh's hand. Someone in the audience, caught up in the action, screamed a warning. Josh dodged, flipping through the pages as he did so. Amber snatched the thumb drive from his hand, prepared to pass it on to Walker waiting at the edge of the platform.

Furious, Ivan shoved Amber to reach the thumb drive. With a cry, she felt her weak knee give out, and she toppled.

With a furious roar, Josh flung the folder at Sam's table and came out swinging.

THIRTY-TWO

UNABLE TO REACH AMBER TO STOP HER FALL, ALREADY RIPE FOR BATTLE, Josh reverted to his angry youth. He plowed his fist into Ivan's liposuctioned midsection, releasing his stress and fury on the man who'd hurt Amber and tried to ruin his own daughter. His blow produced only an unsatisfying *oomph*.

Several women cheered. Others screamed. Men shouted in shock. Josh didn't care if this shredded his reputation.

He'd stored a lot of rage against this tyrant, and he wasn't done. His second blow caught Willa's father beneath his glass jaw, and the taller man toppled backward over the suitcase. It felt damned good avenging the women Ivan had mistreated.

The audience erupted in chaos.

Ignoring the spectators and his stinging knuckles, Josh held out his hand to help Amber to her feet. Instead of accepting his offer, she plopped down like a lead weight on Ivan's middle to prevent him from sitting up. Josh wasn't psychic but even he could feel her steam.

"Bloody despotic bastard," she muttered under her breath.

Josh ached to call off this farce before she got hurt, but trouper that she was, she dived right back into her role of detective. With self-importance, she held up the thumb drive and papers to the impassive cop crossing the platform. "Chief Walker, if you would escort the gentleman out of the room with our victims' evidence, I'll continue my murder investigation."

Which meant, Josh thought, that she couldn't pin murder on Ivan, *damn*. He nursed his fist and watched for any signal that the old goat might be their suspect. Nothing. The audience was now at low roar, but not a single light blinked. Crap. Without knowing what was on the thumb drive or in the file, they'd have to continue as planned.

Amber stood up so Walker and one of his men could lead Ivan away. Public assault would barely dent Ivan's reputation. He had too much money and power.

This time, when Josh offered his hand, Amber took it, using him and her stick for balance.

"Madame Psychic, does your ghost say her father is a killer?" Amber asked, returning to the script.

Val railed and cursed and said nothing of the sort. Shakespeare would have loved her.

Punching hadn't settled Josh's inner turmoil. He was on edge, forcing himself not to pace, as Amber went through the routine of calling the next suspect. They'd planned on bringing in Ernest, if only for the laugh factor—but she unexpectedly called for Tessa.

The audience quieted expectantly. Everyone now seemed to understand that the farce wasn't entirely about fictional characters, even though it memorialized Willa's love of irony and brutal humor.

Tessa was practically belligerent as she marched up, unaccompanied. "You've got nothing on me," Willa's VP declared before anyone spoke a line. "You won't trick me with your phony winds."

Interesting. They hadn't used any fans to create wind. Did Tessa have prior experience with Willa's spectral presence? Josh shot Amber a glance, and her lips tilted upward. *Shit*. Tessa had been bothering Amber too.

By now, the audience was practically on the edges of their seats, occasionally stomping their feet and whistling as Amber engaged them with gestures and expressions. She'd taken to encouraging them with finger waggles, lightening the mood.

Josh felt less easy when Amber held her walking stick and pretended to limp toward Tessa. He hoped it was pretense and that she really hadn't hurt herself.

When Val removed her stick from the umbrella stand and handed one to Sam, Josh sensed trouble. He glanced to Walker, who'd stayed behind after a plainclothes detective led Ivan away. Walker frowned—not reassuring.

"You inherited the lady's company, did you not?" Amber intoned. "And you spied on her for her father?"

"I was her best friend," Tessa shouted, apparently captivated by the power of having center stage. Or maybe Fee *had* put truth serum in the food. "She counted on me to keep an eye on her father. And then she hooked up with this bastard. . ." Forgetting the play's characters, she pointed at Josh. "And she started doing weird things like auditing friends of her father and refusing to finance people she'd helped before. She even fired an old friend and threatened to donate his salary to charity. I just tried to hold it all together until she recovered her senses. And then she fired *me*."

Josh thought his head might spin off his neck at this backward perspective of Willa's actions. Willa had been cleaning house because of *him*? She'd *fired* Tessa, when? Which friend? And *threatened* but *hadn't* given the salary to charity—

Because she was dead?

But processing this flood of information wasn't happening while he watched Lucy sticks glow brighter. If that meant Willa was here. . . Pretending to take notes, Josh eased between Amber and the glass ball on the table.

"Tessa, shut up," a male voice cried from the audience.

Excitement and fear rippled through the audience as Brad shoved from his seat and stalked toward the front. Shit, now he needed to stand between Amber and Willa and Brad—Josh wanted his own damned Lucy stick.

Amber abruptly pointed her stick at Tessa. "*You* planted the deceased's phone in my kitchen. *You* had the opportunity to push her off that cliff. And believing you inherited the company, *you* had the motive to kill her." She shouted the last dramatically.

The reporters who'd left looking for a phone had returned and were now frantically texting. Others headed for the door, only to be warned land lines were in scarce supply—the entire town was here, clinging to their seats.

Except for Brad, who stormed the stage—wielding a deadly-looking knife.

Josh didn't have time to wonder if Amber was reading minds or Willa was whispering in her ear. He was closest to the weapon. Before the photographer could rush the stage, Josh side-kicked Brad's knee. In the same movement, he grabbed the knife-wielding arm. In a perfect world, he'd have the leverage to flip the larger man to the floor.

The world being imperfect, Brad didn't stumble as planned. He hacked with his knife instead of going down.

As Josh located the pressure point in Brad's elbow, finally bringing him to his knees, piercing pain slashed through his side.

THIRTY-THREE

Chaos. Blood. Agony.

Flashing, angry impressions of a knife, a porch, a falling body.

Humiliation and satisfaction and a scarf around a woman's throat. . .

DIFFERENT, PLEASURABLE IMAGES OF A SUN GODDESS IN SILK AND LACE. . .

The latter joy-filled vision distracted from the horrors of Brad's angry mind. Amber recognized herself as Josh saw her, but his agony overrode the pleasure.

The roar of the audience faded beneath these more immediate sensations.

Head exploding with confusing scenes and emotions, she clung to the image of herself as goddess to keep from screaming at the sight of Josh bleeding and in pain. She grabbed the shawl from Sam's shoulders and dropped down beside him, pressing the cloth to his side to staunch the blood. She clenched her molars, but that didn't keep tears from leaking as he flashed his crooked grin and attempted to help her hold the makeshift bandage.

He saw her as a goddess! Tears coursed down her cheeks.

Brad's mind intruded, clouded with rage and projecting a devastating video of violent acts. Amber squeezed her eyes closed in hopes of shutting out the horror—or halting the tears.

Men rushed to hold Brad down. Vaguely, she recognized the red-haired woman screaming curses and trying to beat her way through the crowd. She now understood that the woman who had called herself Susan was really Tessa, and that Brad was her lover. Amber glanced over to see Val and Sam rushing to restrain Willa's hysterical VP.

Finally squeezing the violence out of her head, reassured that no one else would be attacking them, Amber held onto Josh and tried to make sense of it all.

But Josh was all she could think of. "Willa is here," she warned him. "Don't you dare die and join her or I'll come after you myself. You'll get no rest ever again."

He managed a chuckle. "Not dying, promise. Hurts like hell, though. Tell Willa to perform for the audience and distract them."

"Not funny. You tell her." But Amber glanced around at the blinking Lucy sticks. Even the stage lights were flickering again. The suitcase skittered across the stage, aiming for Brad. One of the policemen kicked it back, and Willa created an angry tornado that would have sent papers flying if Sam hadn't grabbed everything on the table. Amber hadn't been lying. Willa was definitely here and in a state of fury.

"Walker, don't take Brad away," she shouted as the police chief wrestled the photographer into cuffs. "Someone bring me my stick, please."

"What are you doing?" Josh asked anxiously, trying to prop up on an elbow.

"No clue," she replied as the town's wiry nurse practitioner broke through the mob. "Let's just see what happens. Brenda is a healer, so let her do what she does best." She leaned over and kissed him.

Then taking the stick Sam handed her and using it as a crutch, Amber pushed to her feet and let the local nurse take her place. The stick practically vibrated in her hand, but there were so many agitated people projecting so many thoughts. . .

Walker watched her with his flat eyes narrowed. He motioned men to step back as Amber approached. She'd seen flashes of Brad wielding that knife on a woman, yanking a scarf—the one around Willa's neck? She focused on the knife on the floor as she poked Brad with her staff. "You killed Sarah with that same knife," she said with conviction. "She told

Tessa she knew where the phone was and wanted to reach Willa's cloud account before the police did. There was information in there on you, wasn't there? Information that caused her to fire you. I'm betting you helped Dell with his pornographic film."

Brad glared and said nothing, but his terror provided the mental image she needed.

"He took pleasure in killing Sarah," Amber told Walker. "He enjoys killing. He's done it before. If I remember correctly, he was here with Tessa for Josh's news conference the day Sarah died."

In the background, Tessa screamed, and the telltale wind picked up.

Aaron arrived carrying a plastic wine glass with Brad's name on it. "Amber is right. He was thinking of killing Tessa because he fears she's losing it."

The stage lights rattled and went out. Amber hoped someone had switched them off in fear they'd fall. The rest of the gallery remained illuminated from the normal overheads.

Amber swung on Tessa. A uniformed sheriff's deputy held her now, waiting for orders. He looked a little wild-eyed at the weird wind and situation, but he didn't flinch when Amber approached.

The other Lucys gathered around, sticks glowing. Teddy, the empath, murmured, "She *is* losing it. She's terrified, and she's feeling guilty as hell."

"Brad's the lover in your cards, isn't he?" Amber asked conversationally, tapping Tessa on the chest with her stick. She received a violent impression of Brad shoving Tessa against a wall and Tessa's sexual response. She liked being molested. Sickened by her own memories, Amber had to slam shut the door on that image or she'd dissolve into a quivering ball of hysterics.

She glanced at Josh for reassurance. He looked pale as Brenda worked on him, but he gave her a thumbs up that she had this. She was a dragon goddess.

"Brad helped me," Tessa protested. "He was the only person who ever helped me."

The wind howled and Tessa's red hair stood on end.

"Willa didn't help you?" Amber asked conversationally, equilibrium restored as all around her descended into chaos.

"Willa fired me!" Tessa shouted. "After everything I've done for her, spying on her father, having Brad take those photos of Ivan with Dell and his sluts, giving her everything she wanted, she fired me!"

"Tessa, shut up!" Brad roared, wrestling with the men holding him.

With Brenda's healing touch, Josh was on his feet already. Amber anxiously bit her tongue, recognizing the look on his face as he realized Brad had to be Willa's killer. Before anyone could act, Josh swung his fist at Brad's midsection. The photographer groaned and slumped in Walker's arms. Looking stoic, the chief yanked him straight and hauled him out of Josh's reach.

A brief look of agony crossed Josh's handsome features, but just like a character in one of his superhero films, he shook off the pain and nodded at Amber. "Bring the energy, kid. You're on a roll."

Turn on the emotion, got it. Taking a deep breath, trying not to feel his pain, Amber swung back to Willa's former VP. "On the eve of her wedding, Willa fired you?" she shouted, ramping up her anger, intensifying Tessa's fear. "She'd spent most of that day firing people, hadn't she? Including Brad? Did she threaten to send his salary to charity after learning from the auditor that he worked with Dell? And why would she up and fire you for no good reason? Is that how Willa ended up at the bottom of a cliff?"

And there the image was, full force, Tessa furiously shoving Willa off one of the boulders overhanging the vortex. The fall wasn't steep or long, but it was rocky. Tess's rage was almost a physical blow. Amber stumbled backward, letting her stick catch her.

The cheap glass ball on the table flew, smashing Tessa on the side of the head.

Tessa screamed as blood trickled down her temple—just as it must have trickled from Willa as she lay unconscious and abandoned on the rocks.

The deputy continued to hold Tessa while an angry gale whirled around her.

"You sent Brad back to help her, didn't you?" Amber demanded, guessing wildly, still seeing the image from the photographer's mind of yanking a scarf around a woman's neck.

Tessa whimpered. "She was alive. I couldn't lift her. He was the only one still around to ask for help. He told me she was dead."

"And so she was, after he strangled her," Josh said coldly.

Tessa screamed as the wind whipped her hair and clothes.

They had a confession. The farce was no longer a farce.

And the wild fury whipping through the gallery, flinging the memorial wreaths, had the feel of grief and devastation. . . and acceptance. Willa knew she was dead.

Unless she was sent ahead soon, she could easily become a violent poltergeist.

The Lucys touched their glowing sticks together and chanted, slowly corralling Willa's energy. The wind spun and dipped as if it had lost direction. While Tessa wept and Brad ranted, the chant grew louder. Lights flashed, the wind whooshed, and abruptly, the stage fell eerily quiet.

Amber almost collapsed in exhaustion until Josh caught her, still holding his side with the makeshift bandage. "Let the cops do their schtick, babe. Let's blow this place."

She almost smiled at the classic Jack line. "Abercrombies don't run, Jacko. Let's just go home."

THIRTY-FOUR

AMBER STILL DIDN'T HAVE A TV, BUT HER ON-LINE NEWSPAPER GAVE HER insight into the public outburst of outrage over Dell and Ivan's arrests on more charges than she could count. So far, no allegations of molestation had come forward, so maybe she'd been the only lucky one. She'd been a girl after all, not worth a lot.

The stash of porn films, however, had furious mothers, victims, and the public up in arms. Class action lawsuits were being filed. Several of Crystal's clients were involved, and she'd been named as an accomplice. Amber could certainly testify to that. The files stolen from Ivan and stored on Willa's thumb drive and phone had been a treasure trove of information. Crystal and Dell would never work in the industry again, and jail time loomed.

The phone rang. She'd been ignoring the press calls for days, but recognizing the number, Amber actually picked it up.

"Your mother ceded guardianship to you," Amber's lawyer, said in satisfaction. "With prosecutors breathing down her neck, she's most likely headed out of town. The rumors are that she helped Dell find some of those kids he filmed. I don't think the court will argue that you're Zeke's best hope."

Amber let relief roll over her. Her nephew was in his room, on a computer Mariah had loaned him, blowing up space battleships. He was safe. That was her most important goal. Now, she could work on the rest.

"Thank you. Is there any chance you can rescue my residuals to pay your fees? You've earned every penny, but it will take me a while to find work and repay you." She scrolled through the emails on her own computer as she spoke. She had options. She'd been flooded with requests for television appearances, some of them even paying gigs. The publicity from Willa's death provided most of the impetus, she suspected, not her talent.

"The auditor did his job," Alicia said. "The prosecutors have impounded Dell's accounts. I have them going after your mother's funds. I'll let you know if what I retrieve doesn't cover my bill. I'm raking in a lot of new cases because of this publicity, so don't feel guilty about the delay. You just work on giving that kid a good home, and next time, invite me to the show."

Amber laughed as Alicia hung up. There were good people in the world if one could find them. Generally, though, it was only bad people who made the news.

She twisted her favorite ring around her finger. Did she sell it or take up one of these gigs to earn the deposit for a house down the mountain where Zeke could go to school? How much did she really hate being sucked back into that life?

The phone rang again, and she checked it anxiously. Josh had been hustled off to the hospital, then to make statements at the sheriff's office and then to hold press conferences. Now that the coroner had released Willa's body, he had a funeral to plan, since Ivan's involvement with Dell had left her father incommunicado.

She hadn't heard from Josh in thirty-six hours, except in wild text messages, usually incomplete, when he grabbed a minute for himself.

Caller ID showed an unknown number. She ignored it and checked her text messages again, reading through Josh's to reassure herself that he was okay.

Don't go. . .

They're all insane. . .

Help, they think I'm Frankenstein. . .

She smiled at that last one, another line from Jack and Ginger, when

Jack had to have stitches. She even understood the *Don't go*. He was afraid she'd leave like last time, before he had a chance to talk, but he couldn't find a way to say it in text messages.

Her cell beeped with another message from Josh.

ANSWER YOUR PHONE!

The landline rang again with the same unknown number. This time, she picked it up.

"I'm covered up in lawyers," Josh cried from the receiver. "Ernest dragged me to LA and I have Willa's lawyers and Ivan's lawyers and I need you! Don't go. Make Cass save my studio. I'm coming back, I promise."

"Want me to send a rescue squad?" she asked, hiding her fears with amusement.

"Please, please. Come off your mountain, charge up your phone, and I'll direct you. I'll not be responsible for my actions if I don't get out of here soon."

"I can't drive. You'll have to hire a car," she pointed out, laughing.

"I can hire a car," he shouted. "I have Willa's fortune and can hire ten cars! What do I do with all this?"

"Save the world?" she suggested, not wanting to think about how Willa's inheritance would boggle his numbers-hating creative mind.

"Yes, exactly. I'll save myself. Don't go. Stay right there. I'll hire an army and be right with you. In a few hours more or less. They're coming to take me away. . ." The connection broke.

She smiled through her tears and texted him a dragon image.

JOSH LAUGHED AT THE DRAGON IMAGE. HE TOSSED THE LAST STACK OF documents back on the lawyer's desk. "I'm dying here. I need sleep. I need food. I need a woman who understands me. Ernest, hire anyone you need to help you, but let me go now."

"There's still the funeral," Ernest protested. "And the press conference where we explain that on the eve of her wedding, Willa chose to clean house and reveal her father, Dell, and their cohorts for what they are."

"I'll call the funeral home, order a heroine's service. But I will not stand up in front of the media and tell them Willa was a saint. My telling her about Dell put a gun in her hand. She used that audit as the first step in getting rid of traitors and to take over her father's corporation. I don't want to be around to explain that to news hounds. I'll return for the funeral out of respect, but then I think I'll become a hermit." Josh pushed out of his chair.

Willa's—now his—lawyer stood with him. "You just became a very rich man, Mr. Gabriel. Let me take you out for a drink to celebrate, at least."

Josh clenched his side, the only excuse these power brokers grasped. "I'll pass out. Another time. I'm taking painkillers and going to bed. Ernest?" He lifted his eyebrows at his new CEO, who was now wearing a well-tailored but garishly green suit.

Ernest held up his top-of-the-line cell phone, a product of his newly exorbitant salary. "A limo is waiting. It has wi-fi. If you leave cell range, text whatever you need."

His new executive intelligently realized Josh had no intention of returning to Willa's mansion—ever. "More like, you'll hound me all the way up the mountain. I'll buy the mountain so they can't put up cell towers," Josh said without resentment.

He knew he was in no shape to drive himself. Loss of blood, lack of sleep, and stress had him woozy and weary. He nearly fell into the back of the waiting limo. Giving the driver instructions, he sprawled on the seat and worked his way through his call list.

His new personal secretary assured him she'd spoken with Sarah's family and arranged her funeral. Josh hadn't really known Sarah, and her parents didn't know him. He owed them nothing after he'd learned the contents of Willa's phone, but the parents were innocent, and their grief needed to be recognized. And he thought maybe Sarah had cared enough about Willa to immediately notify the police of the tracker app—before realizing the danger the phone represented to herself and Tessa.

The secret files Willa had kept on her phone—and thumb drive—did not reflect well on Willa or anyone with whom she worked. Willa had learned, not only that Tessa and Brad were spying on her, but that Tessa was embezzling from the firm, and that Sarah was implicated. Presumably, Sarah had hoped to delete anything incriminating before turning it over to the sheriff—but Brad had preferred to take no chances that she'd protect him. He'd been the one to plant the phone and photos.

The police had searched Sarah's computers and traced the tracker signal app back to Ivan, who admitted installing the spyware in his daughter's phone.

All the irony would make a terrible spy novel. Remembering some of Willa's tactics, Josh suspected she used information to blackmail her employees into doing anything she wanted. And in the end, it was her father's spying that had broken the case.

Plus Amber's immense and scary talent. She'd forced Willa's ghost to reveal the contents of his suitcase lining!

After all the backstabbing and poisonous behavior of Willa's world, Josh felt nothing but relief for the escape his personal goddess offered. He prayed Amber would forgive him for being so crass as to settle for Willa's wealth and fame.

The police had the thumb drive and the file Willa had left in Josh's suitcase. That must have happened before she'd left the lodge that day, because it was Tessa who had driven up to pack Willa's things and drive her car to the parking lot. Willa had apparently wanted her friend out of the way while she fired Brad.

Brad had confessed to heaving Willa's suitcases in a dumpster down the mountain before turning her sporty red car over to a chop shop for fast cash. Tessa having the keys had made his task easier. He'd simply driven Willa's car to the vortex, loaded her body in it after he killed her, and driven off, leaving everyone to think it had been Willa leaving town.

Brad had also destroyed Willa's camera with her photo journal of everyone she'd spoken to that day, including him and Tessa, but she'd apparently uploaded the images to her cloud account when she'd gone to the antique store and used Aaron's wi-fi. Along with the fake blackmail photos that Brad had planted on Sarah—ones of Willa's body that he'd taken himself—the cops had enough evidence to lock him away forever.

Josh's head hurt. He didn't even want to begin unraveling the nasty nest of lies and deceit. His imagination simply didn't work with that level of paranoia, and fraud was beyond his capacity.

He had a film to direct. . . and a woman he wanted more than all the wealth in the world. Focusing on the positive was what he needed, if he could just figure out why in hell Amber might want a mess like him—or if she would be better off without him.

She'd been living in peace and harmony for years. He'd showed up and shattered her life.

She talked to dead people and read minds. His Amber was one hell of a scary woman. But she'd offered him the only peace he'd ever known.

He had a few hours to figure this out, right?

He fell asleep before they escaped LA traffic.

BY THE TIME THE LIMO ROLLED UP HER LANE, AMBER HAD SORTED HER options. No one was offering her voice-overs yet. Connections were her goal, not publicity, so she'd sorted accordingly. Her performance the other night was already all over YouTube. Who needed more publicity than that? If there was laughter, it wasn't at her specifically, so she could bear it. No one was comparing her to her old shots of Ginger when they had ghostly emanations to cackle over. And there was still lots of meaty scandal to chew through, none of it on her. She could live with that.

The limo pulling up in the lane, however. . . brought mixed joy and terror. Zeke had run down to help the grocer with some shelf rearranging. With any luck, he hadn't seen the car. So if that was Josh out there. . .

They might have all of ten minutes privacy, tops.

The uniformed chauffeur opened the rear door and a dress-suited Josh stepped out. She suspected this was as formal as it got for him. He looked as if he'd slept in the suit for a week. He had bed hair standing up on one end and falling in his eyes. His coat was unbuttoned to reveal his half unknotted tie and a wrinkled shirt falling out of his equally wrinkled trousers. He didn't appear to have shaved in a week.

He looked gorgeous. His cobalt eyes crinkled at the corners when she stepped out on the porch. His lips crooked in his lopsided grin. And he just stood there, beaming stupidly, as if all he wanted to do was look at her.

Which warmed her inside and out and made her flush. If she recalled the mental image he'd projected when he'd been shot—she'd die of embarrassment knowing he was stripping her naked like that. "Do you intend to come in? I think your driver will have to park in town. My driveway isn't that big."

He signaled his driver, who touched his cap and returned to the car. Then Josh ambled up the walk, not showing any sign that he could have died two nights ago.

"You didn't go," he said, holding the cocky grin.

"Of course I didn't go. This is where I want to be." She led him inside, where the phone was ringing, again. She was tempted to ignore it, but caller ID showed Mariah, so she answered.

"We'll take care of Zeke," Mariah said without preamble. "Make the rich bastard take you to a nice dinner at Delphine's. Take the night off. We've got your back." She hung up without Amber having to say a word.

She stared stupidly at the receiver a second longer before putting it down.

Josh wasn't smiling anymore. "Something wrong? Where's Zeke?"

"For a change, everything is fine," she said in wonder. "Zeke has been adopted by the town. You don't look as if you've come from Willa's funeral. Come in and tell me what's happening."

He captured her waist and kissed her.

She hadn't realized how much she'd feared he was here to tell her good-bye until she collapsed against him and sucked up every ounce of passion he offered and returned as good as she got.

He steered her toward the bedroom. She didn't resist.

They had so much to talk about. . . but they needed clear heads for that.

Amber winced when Josh did as she tugged off his shirt, revealing a proper bandage strapped around his ribs. He didn't let a little pain stop him from yanking off her blouse.

"You'll go to dinner with me tonight and wear that teal dress, won't you?" he asked as he tumbled her into the bed. "I'll take pictures so Teddy can make a necklace to go with it."

She laughed and kissed his stubbled jaw and neck. "I'll wear the dress. I don't need a necklace. I have tons." Her bedroom wall was layered with them.

"Pearls and diamonds," he insisted, "Not beads. I don't want you selling your rings. Those rings are important."

She gasped as he kissed her in all those places he'd learned these past weeks. She'd like to tell him she would never sell anything he gave her, but her mind had quit working. She no longer cared that she was naked in broad daylight as long as he kept on doing what he was doing.

～

HOURS LATER, WHILE AMBER SHOWERED, JOSH CALLED DELPHINES TO BE certain they could get a table. Whoever answered assured him he could have a table anytime he liked, as long as he was bringing Amber. He chuckled and gave them their ETA, then turned to admire Amber as she strolled out drying herself without a speck of self-consciousness.

She was a lush Venus, and he had to force his prick to behave. Loss of blood and the last hours made that easier.

"Can Dinah fit us in, or do I need to see what I can rummage up?"

"You're Hillvale's superstar. As long as I bring you, they said they'd fit us in anytime. I like this town. Unlike in Hollywood, it doesn't matter if my latest flick bombed. We're celebrities as long as we do our part, right?" He dragged on the trousers Amber had pressed for him while he was showering.

"Your matinee star status does not guarantee you a preferred seat, right. I think in Dinah's case, she just needs to like you more than whatever poor tourist is waiting for an opening." She shimmied into what she called her fat crusher.

"You know you don't have to wear that elastic for me, don't you?" He couldn't get enough of watching her, so he unabashedly studied her gyrations as he buttoned his newly pressed shirt.

"I wear them for me, so don't let your head swell. Start telling me everything. Is your film on track again? When do you have to go back?"

He watched as she tucked her perfect, non-plastic breasts into armor. "You ask me that after what we just did? Why would I ever leave? Are you planning on throwing me out? You realize I haven't had sex that spectacular since we were kids?"

She studied him with a puzzled frown. "I haven't had sex at all since we were kids, but I live in Hillvale where available men are scarce. What in heck have you been doing?"

"Dating the wrong women, apparently. That's not the discussion here, although I'm getting pretty chuffed thinking you're all mine, so let's quell that egotistical rot and move on. Did you just want me for your boy toy?"

She blushed and reached for her wrap-around dress, avoiding his question. "Chuffed? What Brit have you been hanging out with?"

"Amber Abercrombie, if you won't have this discussion, we're going to end up back in that bed until you make up your mind," he threatened. "Don't make me starve while you argue every side of this case. I want you. I *think* you want me. Tell me you won't mind if I move to Hillvale—unless, for some warped reason, you want to return to LA." He made a show of unbuttoning buttons he'd just fastened.

She sighed and sat down on the messy bed. "Of course I don't mind if you move to Hillvale. I'd love it. And arrogant asshole that you are, you know I want you. I just have no idea what you'd *do* here. I have to leave for a place that has a school. I was thinking of renting an apartment in Baskerville, down the mountain. I need to learn to drive so I can drive back up here on weekends. I'd have to hire someone to work the shop during the week."

Josh mentally cheered as she called him an asshole and said she wanted him—that was his blunt Amber, the strong one he remembered. But he frowned at the thought of her leaving the cozy nest she'd created. Amber could feather any nest she landed in, that wasn't the problem. "You belong *here*."

"Zeke belongs in school. I'll still be able to come back on weekends and in summer." She stood again and finished fastening her silk dress. "You'll be in LA or wherever, directing your films. It's not as if you'll have much time here."

Josh gnashed his teeth in frustration as he knotted his tie. "LA isn't in another country. It's not even in a different state. I have one film to direct and enough money to subsidize small countries after I'm done. I *hate* the city. I want a ranch or a winery. I want a studio like Cass's where I can write. It doesn't matter anymore if I don't make any money at it, I want to *write*. And after I have written, I want you to tell me where I got it wrong."

She flung a pillow at him, then studied her wall of beads. "Aries, leaves petty details to others. You're supposed to be the romantic between the two of us."

Wham, that's what he was doing wrong! He was flinging around money and wants and needs as if providing security would make them both happy. Amber had thrown away security for the insane risk of surviving on her psychic talent. She didn't care about riches the way he had.

He'd spent these last years slowly building his reputation and his career on the off chance that someday his success might be enough to chuck Hollywood and let him write and sell books and scripts. He'd been suckered into thinking that money would buy him happiness, stupid fool. He had more money now than he knew what to do with, and he'd be miserable if he didn't have Amber.

"Light bulb moment," he declared, wrapping his arms around Amber's waist and tugging her away from the beads. "Let's start over." He swung her around to face him and just looking at her beautiful turquoise eyes and slight frown cheered him immensely.

"I love you," he said with all the fervency welling up in him, finally understanding and accepting his need to be here with this woman. "I've loved you since you kicked my shin and made me behave. I love you for believing in me even when I gave you no reason to do so. I love you for your ability to handle any crisis and mediate any argument, even ones between the two sides of that brilliant brain of yours. I'm not entirely certain I love the spooky side of you that raises ghosts, but I definitely respect it, and I know that part of you belongs here in Hillvale. Is there any chance that you will ever find it in your heart to love someone as slow to catch on as I am?"

She pulled his head down to kiss him, and he accepted any encouragement she offered. He kissed her back, knowing Amber needed time to think before she could answer, praying she wouldn't tell him to take a flying leap off the nearest cliff.

THE RUSH OF JOSH'S EMOTIONS ALMOST OVERWHELMED AMBER WITH THE images they conjured—hers as well as his. She remembered that first kiss when she'd kicked his shin because that's what she'd been told to do, not because she wanted him to stop. She remembered the time he'd sneaked her the tangerine she'd been told she couldn't have and how delicious the stolen fruit tasted when they'd licked each other's fingers.

But these moments like this, when he kissed her as if she were the only woman in the universe. . . She felt his desire and his crying need for what she offered. Not just physical desire, but the desire of two souls who belonged together.

She placed her hands on his chest, feeling the bandaged result of his protecting her from a crazed killer almost twice his size. This was one argument they didn't need to have. "I've always loved you, numbskull. How could I not? You just look at me with those big blue eyes and crook that smile and I'm at your feet. And that was not good for my mental or emotional health when we were young. It wouldn't have been good for either of us. We both had to learn to stand on our own."

Josh wouldn't let her push away but held her close, kissing her hair. "You took the risk I wouldn't take. You got out of there. Your courage makes me love you even more. If I take more risks now, will you be okay with that? I haven't had much time to think, but I don't want Willa's millions. I don't want any more stress in my life and all that money comes with way too many ties attached."

She leaned her head against his shoulder. "You can set it on fire for all I care. But I am Zeke's guardian now. I need to plan for his future as well as mine. Unless you're planning on building a school to get rid of that money, I have. . ."

Forgetting his stitched side, he lifted her up and down in excitement. "I can *do* that! Maybe not a whole school, but a small one, for the local kids, until we have enough for the state to fund a public one?"

She stepped back and gaped in amazement, as much at his ability to lift her up and down as his declaration. And then the possibilities slowly dawned on her. . . "You'll stay here, *with us*? Write your books in Cass's studio, until she throws you out? We'll be—"

Josh swung her around. "A family," he crowed. "We'll be a family. We'll raise our own Jack and Ginger. I can have friends like your weird friends and not Tinsel Town sycophants after whatever they think I can give them. It will be really weird, but I'm ready."

"You do not even begin to know how weird it will be," she said breathlessly, breaking away from his exuberant dance. But Josh was smiling so hugely, she thought maybe with his creative mind, he did understand, just a little bit. And that's when the magnitude of all he offered hit her.

"Me, you really love *me*, not Ginger or the psycho psychic, but the fat woman who goes swimming in her underwear!" She couldn't contain her astonishment.

"I particularly love the psychic psycho in her underwear," he whispered, advancing on her. "And I hope you're not too hungry because I want to see how hard it is to pry off that underwear."

Shrieking, Amber raced for the front room. "Food first, and then you can cut my underwear off me!"

THIRTY-FIVE

AMBER WATCHED IN ADMIRATION AS JOSH, DRESSED IN A BLACK SUIT AND wearing a cobalt blue tie, shook hands and accepted the condolences of well-wishers attending Willa's funeral.

Wearing a boring navy suit out of respect for the occasion, she lingered in the back of the room, in the company of people she knew. Ernest was particularly good at steering the curious away. He'd even toned down his usual color-blind outfit to a reasonably somber gray tuxedo coat with a pink cummerbund.

"Miss Abercrombie is only here to pay her respects," he told a TV anchor sidling in their direction. "Contact Gabriel Productions if you need an interview."

"I suppose I should hire a secretary of some sort," Amber fretted. "You're too important to play the assistant any longer."

Ernest shrugged. "Just use Josh's people, unless you want to get back in the business. I'm hiring Mariah to run background checks on anyone I employ so we'll run a tight ship. Unlike Willa, I'm hiring people we can trust, not ones we can blackmail."

"Like yourself?" she asked, because she knew Ernest needed to say this.

She was trusting her prescience a little more these days.

He shot her a narrow-eyed look, then shrugged. "It's not easy being poor and gay in this town. I got into drugs and took a wrong turn. Willa may have hired me because she thought she could hold my conviction over my head, but I proved useful even though I refused to do anything that would put me back in jail. If there's anything worse than being poor and gay in this town, it's being poor and gay in prison."

"Good thing, since Josh now has a whole spooky town of psychics and empaths to tell him if there's trouble," Amber complacently replied. "If you have any problems, you just drag the culprit to Hillvale, and we'll take care of it."

Ernest chuckled. "Then take my advice and don't be a stranger to Josh's business. He may throw away all Willa's money, if he likes, but his talent will make more. If he uses you for voice-overs, others will come calling. You'll need a secretary and a manager."

She watched the beautiful people milling in the theatrical dome of the funeral home. She gathered from the hand-shaking and whispering that this was mostly a peculiar cocktail party for meeting, greeting, and gossiping.

"I enjoy acting," she acknowledged. "I am not temperamentally suited to do what it takes to move up the ladder. I'll accept any decent offers that float my way and set the money aside for Zeke's education, but I will not actively pursue it. Zeke and I will be happier in Hillvale. So will Josh, I think, but he also needs an outlet for his creativity."

"That's why we now have Gabriel Productions. Josh is in the process of selling Willa's company back to her father. I want nothing to do with Ivan anymore," he said with a shudder. "We'd already removed Josh's project from the line-up and started our own list of sponsors. I'll run the business. He can produce his scripts and sell his damned books, if that's what he wants to do. And if he insists on looking into wineries, he has a lawyer prepared to set up a division of the corporation for that."

Amber admired Josh's smile as he sought her out across the crowded room. He hadn't forgotten her back here. He was just paving a path for her in the way he knew best. She would return the favor by offering the safety of her home.

"You're a good man, Charlie Brown," she told Ernest as Josh pushed his way back to her. "You handle the circus. I'll handle our clown."

Ernest snickered and sidled off to talk to his latest favorite reporter about Willa's confrontation with Dell before her death. Stone thought he had a national story in Dell's child pornography ring and no longer needed Amber's input, thank all that was holy.

Putting an end to Dell's depredations may have been Willa's only good deed in life, but it was a significant one. Amber hoped that had sent Willa's spirit to a good place.

Josh caught Amber's arm and steered her toward the exit. "The marble urn at the cemetery isn't ready yet. She'll be interred quietly, without this spectacle. Our day is done here. I have better plans for you."

"Dinner overlooking the beach and sunset?" she suggested.

"From my toy box, yes. I haven't decided to sell it yet. I need you to tell me if it's a place you might want to hang out occasionally." He led her to the waiting limo.

"We had limos growing up," she reminded him. "We had suites overlooking LA. I don't need any of this."

"I know. You need Hillvale and friends. But you're talented and talent needs an outlet. You may be happy starring in local productions and raising money for the town, but every once in a while, you might want a mini-vacation. Or a place to stay the night if we come into town on business. And if you don't, it's okay. But I have a surprise for you, so we may as well make this a night."

As the car rolled through the streets, he scooped her onto his lap and covered her in kisses, so Amber didn't really care about the fate of his toy box. Zeke might enjoy visiting LA. Maybe Val would come out of her shell and decide to do theater again. They all had choices now that Josh planned to pour his new wealth into Hillvale.

The future lay before them in glittering promises and excitement.

Once the limo deposited them at Josh's beach house, she could see it was little more than a cottage of wooden shingles and nearly-flat pebble roof. Josh led her through the small, tropical yard, unlocked the front door, and gestured her in. He flipped on bright overhead lights that illuminated the front room, otherwise shadowed by overgrown birds of paradise covering the window.

The framed photographs crowding the walls distracted her from the tropical jungle outside the door. The effect should be creepy—but it wasn't. Josh had talent.

They were photos of her—dancing as Ginger, laughing at the television camera, smeared with ice cream. And then there were the more recent ones, all the fat photos she'd dreaded seeing on TV news, the ones she'd feared would make a laughingstock of her. She gaped, then holding her breath, studied the effect.

There she was in her usual Gypsy dress, looking up and laughing, with her hair catching the glint of sun from her window—just like the one of her as a dancing Ginger. The child could have been any child, sturdy and happy and thoughtless. The adult—the adult had the shadowed eyes of knowledge and the lush lips of a woman who knew what she wanted. The size difference was irrelevant—here was the goddess Josh saw when he looked at her.

He'd taken a shot of her stepping out of the pool, with her sopping wet sunset-pink suit clinging to every curve.

That was her as the detective in the bulky pink blazer, looking stern and judgmental.

The one of her in the teal silk, laughing, sitting at a table adorned with linen and crystal brought her to tears.

She was beautiful. She really was beautiful.

Josh held her from behind, pressing his chin into her hair. "I don't lie, kid. And I'm not blind. See for yourself. This is who I see when I look at you—so much beauty, so much character, and the smile. . . That smile would smite armies. I want to see that goddess in creamy white and rose, approaching me down Hillvale's rocky aisle. I want to see her outshining the sun while holding my baby in her arms. Tell me you share my vision."

Amber could hardly swallow, much less speak. She turned in his arms and hugged him close, resting her head against his shoulder. "No wonder you're a great director," she finally choked out. "You make even the worst of us look good. And if that was your idea of a proposal, then the answer is yes. Only an idiot would let you go, and I'm no idiot."

Josh laughed and covered her face in joyous kisses. Then catching her hand, he led her to the back of the house. "Then come enjoy the sunset over the Pacific with me and we'll plan our escape from reality."

Amber took off her concealing suit jacket, revealing her flabby bare arms in the silk shell for all the world to see as she took her place on Josh's battered porch. Maybe tomorrow she'd buy another bathing suit and swim in the surf.

Josh popped a bottle of champagne and they settled in to enjoy the happiness they'd been denied too long.

CHARACTER LIST

Hillvale residents:

Aaron Townsend—owner of antique store; practices psychometry

Amber Abercrombie—tarot reader, former actress

Brenda—retired nurse practitioner

Carmel Kennedy—mother of Kurt and Monty; emotional vampire

Cassandra—family once owned all of Hillvale; Sam's great-aunt on paternal side

Chen Ling Walker—Hillvale's new police chief and owner of corporate investigative agency

Dinah—cook and owner of café

Fiona Malcolm McDonald—café cook; engaged to Monty Kennedy

Harvey—itinerant musician, friend of Monty's, related to Menendez family

Keegan Ives—mineralogist

Kurtis Dominic Kennedy—architect; part owner and manager of Redwood Resort

Lance Brooks—Carmel's brother; artist who lives at resort;

Mariah (Zoe Ascension de Cervantes) computer engineer; creates ghost-catchers

Montgomery (Monty) Kennedy—Hillvale's mayor, part-owner of Redwood Resort

Orval Bledsetter—retired vet

Pasquale—Italian grocer

Samantha Moon—environmental scientist

Theodosia (Teddy) Devine-Baker—empathic jeweler, married to Kurt Kennedy

Tullah—owner of thrift store; psychic medium

Valerie Ingersson (Valdis)—goddess of death, former actress

Wan Hai—feng shui expert

Amber Affair characters:

Josh Gabriel (aka Jackson)—Hollywood director; Amber's former boyfriend

Zeke Abercrombie—Amber's nephew, son of her late sister, Amethyst

Crystal Abercrombie—Amber's mother, Zeke's grandmother

Willa Powell—daughter of Ivan; Josh's fiancée

Ivan Powell—Willa's father; Hollywood producer

Ernest—Willa's assistant

Sarah—Willa's live-in secretary

Brad Jones—Willa's hired cameraman

Alicia—Amber's lawyer

Oscar—bodyguard

Nell—security guard

Stone—reporter

ACKNOWLEDGMENTS

This is the page where writers admit they cannot write books in a bubble. I've survived in this business for going on forty years because of all the wonderful, talented people who helped me along the way. It would take a book to name them all.

Rather than pretend I'm an Oscar winner thanking my husband and numerous editors and agents for believing in me, I'll just say thank you to the people who made this book possible—and fun—and that includes you, the reader.

As always, I am tremendously grateful for all the talented members of Book View Café Publishing Co-op. Without your support, I wouldn't have the stamina to do everything necessary to produce a book.

In particular, I'd like to thank Julianne Lee for teaching me "director speak" so Josh doesn't sound like a total space cadet. And Mindy Klasky, editor par none, who keeps my flights of fancy and laziness under control, and Phyllis Irene Radford who forces me to really look at my characters. Then there's Kim Killion, graphic artist extraordinaire, without whom there would be no books because only she understands when I tell her the cover needs "people with magic crystals."

There are so many more, always ready to answer my stupid questions—you know who you are. Hugs and kisses!

CRYSTAL MAGIC SERIES

An exciting new series from the author of Unexpected Magic and Tales of Love and Mystery

Sapphire Nights
Book 1 of the Crystal Magic Series

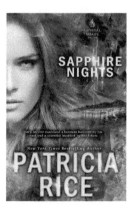

A lawman haunted by his past . . . a scientist haunted by her future.

Samantha Moon arrives in Hillvale bereft of friends and family, money and memory. All she has to her name is a stray cat . . . but that's apparently enough for the people of Hillvale to take her in. Except for L.A.

investigator Walker, who sees how Sam's arrival disturbs the deceptive peace of the small California town.

Topaz Dreams
Book 2 of the Crystal Magic Series

An empathic woman searching for safety. . . An architect yearning for dreams. . . And the haunted house that endangers them both

Teddy Devine-Baker arrives in her childhood home of Hillvale with a box of crystals and enough trouble to fill her VW van. With Teddy's life in pieces, her parents' old house is her last refuge, but Kurt Kennedy—the aloof architect whose sword-wielding heroics once tickled her childish fancies—claims it belongs to him.

Crystal Vision
Book 3 of the Crystal Magic Series

He is Earth, she is Air, together they catch Fire....

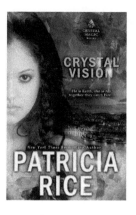

Mariah lives off the grid by waitressing, weaving ghostcatchers to send Hillvale's ghosts across the veil, and keeping clear of electronics that haunt her—until the day her friend and mentor, Crazy Daisy, is murdered, and Mariah goes on the hunt for a killer.

Her prime suspect is geologist Keegan Ives. Following clues left by Daisy and Hillvale's past, Keegan and Mariah are caught in a whirlwind of crystals, power, and cyber-fraud. If they survive, will their world be changed for better—or worse?

Wedding Gems
A Crystal Magic Collection
Book 4 of the Crystal Magic Series

Succumb to temptation and follow the call to Hillvale - population 325 - a cozy little mountain town filled with love, mystery, and ghosts...

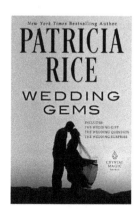

Award-winning author Patricia Rice presents three romantic novellas from her celebrated Crystal Magic series—together for the first time in one collection.

The Wedding Gift

Having overcome the obstacles of their past, Samantha Moon and Chen Ling Walker are ready to walk down Hillvale's eccentric version of a wedding aisle. Can they also conquer the complications of the present —a mysterious doll that won't stay in one place and the dubious assistance of a feng shui master who moves in with them?

The Wedding Question

While juggling the demands of their busy lives, Theodosia Devine-Baker and Kurt Kennedy find that love and living together require just as much work. Halloween always brings out Hillvale's spooks, but when Teddy declares a ceramic dragon is sending smoke signals, Kurt wonders if it's time for him to flee the eccentric community to look for a more normal life.

The Wedding Surprise

With Christmas excitement raising Hillvale's spirits—both literal and figurative—Keegan Ives and Mariah are setting out on new careers and a new relationship. As the town's future draws them in different directions, can their love survive an unanticipated bundle of joy?

Azure Secrets
Book 5 of the Crystal Magic Series

A chef who brews magic challenges a mayor with secrets

After a childhood of being tossed from foster homes for claiming she can detect liars by their scent, Fiona Malcolm McDonald does her best to conceal her secret these days. But when she sniffs a wrongdoer and drives him off with jalapeño cheesecake, she loses still another cooking job and is homeless again. She places her last hope on her mentor in Hillvale, a town as weird as she is.

ABOUT THE AUTHOR

With several million books in print and *New York Times* and *USA Today's* bestseller lists under her belt, former CPA Patricia Rice is one of romance's hottest authors. Her emotionally-charged contemporary and historical romances have won numerous awards, including the *RT Book Reviews* Reviewers Choice and Career Achievement Awards. Her books have been honored as Romance Writers of America RITA® finalists in the historical, regency and contemporary categories.

A firm believer in happily-ever-after, Patricia Rice is married to her high school sweetheart and has two children. A native of Kentucky and New York, a past resident of North Carolina and Missouri, she currently resides in Southern California, and now does accounting only for herself.

ALSO BY PATRICIA RICE

The World of Magic:

The Unexpected Magic Series

MAGIC IN THE STARS

WHISPER OF MAGIC

THEORY OF MAGIC

AURA OF MAGIC

CHEMISTRY OF MAGIC

NO PERFECT MAGIC

The Magical Malcolms Series

MERELY MAGIC

MUST BE MAGIC

THE TROUBLE WITH MAGIC

THIS MAGIC MOMENT

MUCH ADO ABOUT MAGIC

MAGIC MAN

The California Malcolms Series

THE LURE OF SONG AND MAGIC

TROUBLE WITH AIR AND MAGIC

THE RISK OF LOVE AND MAGIC

Crystal Magic

SAPPHIRE NIGHTS

TOPAZ DREAMS

CRYSTAL VISION

WEDDING GEMS

(THE WEDDING GIFT

THE WEDDING QUESTION

THE WEDDING SURPRISE)

AZURE SECRETS

AMBER AFFAIRS

Historical Romance:

American Dream Series

MOON DREAMS

REBEL DREAMS

The Rebellious Sons

WICKED WYCKERLY

DEVILISH MONTAGUE

NOTORIOUS ATHERTON

FORMIDABLE LORD QUENTIN

The Regency Nobles Series

THE GENUINE ARTICLE

THE MARQUESS

ENGLISH HEIRESS

IRISH DUCHESS

Regency Love and Laughter Series

CROSSED IN LOVE

MAD MARIA'S DAUGHTER

ARTFUL DECEPTIONS

ALL A WOMAN WANTS

Rogues & Desperadoes Series

LORD ROGUE

MOONLIGHT AND MEMORIES

SHELTER FROM THE STORM

WAYWARD ANGEL

DENIM AND LACE

CHEYENNES LADY

Too Hard to Handle

TEXAS LILY

TEXAS ROSE

TEXAS TIGER

TEXAS MOON

Mystic Isle Series

MYSTIC ISLE

MYSTIC GUARDIAN

MYSTIC RIDER

MYSTIC WARRIOR

Mysteries:

Family Genius Series

EVIL GENIUS

UNDERCOVER GENIUS

CYBER GENIUS

TWIN GENIUS

TWISTED GENIUS

Tales of Love and Mystery

BLUE CLOUDS

GARDEN OF DREAMS

NOBODY'S ANGEL

VOLCANO

CALIFORNIA GIRL

ABOUT BOOK VIEW CAFÉ

Book View Café Publishing Cooperative (BVC) is an author-owned cooperative of over fifty professional writers, publishing in a variety of genres including fantasy, romance, mystery, and science fiction. Since its debut in 2008, BVC has gained a reputation for producing high-quality ebooks. BVC's ebooks are DRM-free and are distributed around the world. The cooperative is now bringing that same quality to its print editions.

BVC authors include New York Times and USA Today bestsellers as well as winners and nominees of many prestigious awards, including:

Agatha Award
Campbell Award
Hugo Award
Lambda Award
Locus Award
Nebula Award
Nicholl Fellowship
PEN/Malamud Award
Philip K. Dick Award
RITA Award

World Fantasy Award
Writers of the Future Award

CPSIA information can be obtained
at www.ICGtesting.com
Printed in the USA
LVHW040921220419
615060LV00016B/265

9 781611 387858